CLAWS OF
DEATH
OF

BOOKS BY ANGELINA J. STEFFORT

THE WINGS OF INK SERIES
Wings of Ink
Heart of Night
Claws of Death

THE QUARTER MAGE SERIES
The Quarter Mage
The Hour Mage
The Never Mage
The Ever Mage

THE SHATTERED KINGDOM SERIES
Shattered Kingdom
Wicked Crown
Shadow Rule
Lost Towers
Secret Court
Dark Refuge
Reborn Throne

THE TWO WORLDS SERIES
Blood of Two Worlds
Heir of Oblivion
Knight of Redemption
Rule of Dominion

THE BREATH OF FATE SERIES
Torn
Unraveled
Unforgiven
Tethered

THE WINGS SERIES
White
Black
Gray
Spark
Fire
Ashes
Crash

CLAWS OF DEATH

ANGELINA J. STEFFORT

CLAWS OF DEATH

THIS BOOK IS PART OF THE

First published 2024

Copyright © by Angelina J. Steffort 2024

Ebook: ISBN 9783903357907
Print: ISBN 9783903357877

Cover by Fantastical Ink.

PAPER RAY MEDIA

"Never confuse a single defeat with a final defeat."
—F. Scott Fitzgerald

CHEREA

The Trembling Deep

Aceleau

Jezuin

Brolli

The Hollow
Mountains

CEZUX

Mouth
of the
Gods

Claws of the Gods

Bay of
Hope

Cliffs of Ansoli

Ansoli

Fort Perenis

Seeing Forest

Plithian Plains

Horn of
Eroth

Meer

Quiet Sea

T A V R A S

Gulf of
Tears

Dunai

SOUTHERN CONTINENT

ONE

MYRON

The air reeks of betrayal and anguish as I wake from what should have been my final slumber. I wish I wouldn't remember what happened, but I do. Every little detail is sharp and clear in my mind like the morning dew on the branches above me. A gray sky peeks through the cover of leaves, promising the end of night. My limbs protest as I roll to my side in an attempt at getting to my feet, and iron coats my tongue as I bite back a groan.

"Myron." Royad's voice is like the sun hiding behind the towering clouds. "By Shaelak, you're awake."

1

I am, but I don't get a word out. In my mind, I am clinging to the view of Ayna's dirt-streaked face above mine as she
begged me not to give up.

Don't you dare say goodbye.

That crease of fury on her forehead.

We're getting out of here.

And terror as she realized there was no way out for either
of us as she dragged me one step after the other until my legs
failed me and the drug fully kicked in.

Stay awake. Do you hear me? Fucking. Stay. Awake.

I tried. Gods, I tried.

It's too late.

Ephegos found us, and I failed my mate.

"Can you hear me?" My cousin is leaning over me, his
tan features unusually pale.

I nod and blink away the memories.

"Ayna?" It's worth a try, but no one responds when I
whisper her name.

Royad's hand wraps around my shoulder, guiding me
into a sitting position until my back rests against the smooth
bark of a tree. Four pairs of eyes are staring at me as I scan
the small clearing for any sign of my mate ... and find none.

"Welcome back." Astorian dips his chin at me while his
hand clasps Princess Cliophera's where they sit side by side a
few feet away by a dead fire.

Clio gives me a tight smile that promises nothing good.

I don't ask what's wrong because instinctively, I already
know. I don't need to glance to my right to identify the
fourth person as Herinor.

Ayna isn't here.

But my cousin is, and so are the Askarean general and his mate. And the male who saved Royad. "Thank you."

Herinor's eyes reflect a pale green in the morning light as he presses his mouth into a tight line, shaking his head at me. "Don't thank me before you hear the full story." His features set into a grim mask, and I see the male who once guarded Ayna for me in what I used to call my palace—before he betrayed me to help Ephegos's cause.

"Here—" Royad offers me a canteen of water. Where he got it, I don't care. It's not spiked with the horrible drug that took me out in the dungeon and took away all capabilities of defending my mate. I chug down a third of its contents and wipe my mouth with the back of my hand, closing my eyes for a moment as the coolness of the water seeps into me. "You've been out for two days."

That might be a new record. I don't know what was in the syringe that landed in my arm instead of in Ayna's, but I'd gladly take the blow all over again if it means she gets to fight for her freedom.

"Two days?" I barely sound like myself, throat clogged with anticipation of the worst. My hand flicks to my shoulder where the mark connecting Ayna and me is tingling so lightly it could pass for a mild irritation of my skin. I know better, though. That mild nuisance means she's alive.

"Next time you pass out, choose to do so when we have horses. I'd hate to carry you again." Clio elbows Astorian, who's giving me a grimace of a smile. They are both in the same clothes I last saw them wearing, their faces an array of clean skin and dirt like they tried to wash away the grime of the dungeon and their escape. It's a small relief there's no blood.

"They took turns," the princess corrects, her gaze darting between Astorian, Royad, and Herinor. It's only then that I notice the fourth male is missing.

"Silas?"

Royad's gaze darts behind the tree I'm leaning onto, throat bobbing as he shakes his head. I whirl around and spot the bronze face of the male a few feet away. A blanket is draped over his chest, covering the hundreds of cuts Ephegos and Katrijanov left on his torso. His skin is ashen, hair matted against the sides of his face, and his jaw is slack, no trace of the sarcastic warrior Crow who likes to make my life miserable.

"Is he…" I don't dare finish my thought. If he's dead, we lost another Crow. Another one of my people.

Royad wipes a hand across his face, fingers tracing the scar running from his temple to the corner of his mouth.

Instantly, I can breathe more easily. Not dead. "No. But he's been unconscious all this time."

"We took turns carrying him, too," Herinor informs me, and I am about to thank him again when he adds, "I left Ayna behind at the palace, Your Majesty."

Fury like nothing I've ever known floods me, and it doesn't matter that my body is sluggish and my magic locked down from the drug when I launch myself at Herinor with murder on my mind.

TWO

AYNA

My skirts sway with the music as I turn in Erina's arm, led to spin by his iron hand. I'm sick of the strings and cembalo, sick of the sophisticated demeanor the Tavrasian king puts on display, the bland smile he keeps pinned on his lips as he stares me down with glacial eyes.

How many days have I been dancing? Since the moment I recovered enough of my strength to remain on my feet or sit through an official dinner, I've been forced to play the king's accessory. I've danced at his bidding, have curtseyed and smiled, have even worn his ring to appease him and the eager courtiers who've been pining over our engagement.

At least, the wedding has been pushed back a month due to my *unexpected illness*, as Erina called the condition my temporary escape and his drug put me in. All my wounds are healed, courtesy of Ephegos, who never fails to smirk when he studies me with those too-warm brown eyes from the corner of the sepia and gold throne room whenever Erina puts me on display like tonight.

My legs are tired, as is my mind. I have barely eaten, and what little I get down comes up again with the next dose of the drug Ephegos injects me with every few hours. Running didn't buy me freedom, but it freed the males the King of Tavras held captive in his dungeon. At least, that's what I keep telling myself, or I'll go insane from fear for their lives. Clio and her mate are out, as is Herinor. An image of Myron's limp form draped over the Crow's arms comes back to me, and terror sets in, threatening to devour me whole if it wasn't for the inked mark on my shoulder through which I can feel my mate like a lifeline.

They made it out. All but Kaira.

I plaster a smile to my features as I spin across the polished floors, out of Erina's rigid arms and back in, led by his firm grasp, for if I don't, Kaira will suffer. Erina made that very clear the first day after they returned me to my chambers, demonstrating it with a cut along the part-Flame's arm, which he left bleeding. The pleas in her eyes as I was forced to stand by and watch are something that will haunt my sleep for a long, long time.

Kaira didn't escape. How she ended up in captivity when she was supposed to have run with the others, I haven't had a chance to learn. Every time I get to see her, Ephegos or one of the guards he now commands in Katrijanov's stead are present, and I won't give away a single word about the fairies who escaped under their scrutiny. Too much is at risk. If what Ephegos said is true and Erina found a way to replicate the magic-arresting weapon faster, it's a matter of time until he'll be ready to invade the fairylands. Kaira and my lives are secondary to what might happen to Eherea if Erina wages war on the fairylands. Askarea will only be the beginning.

I send a prayer to Shaelak that the others made it across the border and have warned the Fairy King.

"You seem distracted, dove." Erina's lips twitch in that cruel way he only ever shows when I cringe at his voice. "Is anything the matter?"

The words I have for him aren't pretty—and they sure as the darkness behind Eroth's Veil will earn me more pain. And if he abstains from torturing me, Kaira will suffer in my stead; he's made that pretty clear.

"Nothing." I twirl under his arm, walking in time with the music the way I learned when I was a child. It's a traditional Tavrasian dance, the music too light for my mood, and the sickening proximity to my dancing partner no longer avoidable once he hauls me back in. I swallow the anger, the disdain, and inhale a calming breath. I can do this. I *have* to do this, keep Erina occupied, keep Ephegos's attention bound so he won't spend time developing new methods of defeating the immortal creatures I now call my family. Every hour I buy them brings them closer to preventing a surprise attack on the fairylands. Any day I stall increases the chances they'll survive.

As for me... I am far from giving up. I'm fighting my own war right here, even though my weapons aren't steel and magic. Those have been taken from me alongside the hopes of escaping the pending wedding. But I can use the time to figure out a way of freeing Kaira. Maybe once I've spoken my vows, he'll let her go.

I'm fully aware it's a futile thought. There is no way Erina will let his leverage escape. What he doesn't know is the menace of a Crow he thought was loyal to Ephegos has a soft spot for the part-Flame, and if Herinor decides to come for her, I doubt there is a thing that can stop him—except for Ephegos. The bargain he made with the traitor Crow is the one thing that prevented him from getting me out of the palace.

"I could swear you are plotting my demise behind those gray eyes of yours," Erina whispers, finally drawing me back to his chest, too close for me not to notice his woodsy scent.

I blow out a breath through my nose, ridding it of the unwelcome sensation. "Perhaps I am." I'm tired of playing the pliant bride, and perhaps it's stupid of me to let my temper slip even in the slightest, but Erina has seen the lengths I'm willing to go to save the ones I love—he's counting on it—so for once, I speak my mind. Yet, that won't free me of him. I can't give up the role he's forced me into: the lost heir of Tavras.

It's in the courtiers' eyes when they follow me across the dance floor, in the whispers filling the air when Erina leads me through the palace halls. It's in every bow and curtsey.

I'm not merely Erina's bride; I'm a princess in my own right. Despite the fact that the Jelnedyn line has eviscerated my own bloodline by watering down the Milevishja name so thoroughly it no longer carries weight, the people of Tavras remember now that there is a face to attach it to. A royal Milevishja. One who's trapped to secure Erina's own throne.

My gaze slides to the side of the room where Ephegos is conversing with a woman in brass and moss-green robes. She looks old enough to be his mother even when Ephegos is older than any other creature in this room. Sheets of fire-red hair frame her features, piercing dark eyes sparkling as she laughs at something the Crow says. She is unearthly beautiful the way only fairies are, but her hidden ears prevent me from confirming she is one of them.

"Whatever it is you're planning, remember you're not the only one with an agenda." Of course, he finds a way to phrase his threat diplomatically; he's a king after all.

I don't bother asking what that agenda is. Instead, I push away from his chest to step around him in a small circle the way the dance demands. At least, it grants me some air to breathe that isn't laced with his suffocating scent.

The velvet and satin skirts of my bead-encrusted dress sway with the motion, heavy and pompous like the throne room that could have been mine had I been born in a different time. A part of me wonders what it would be like to sit on the throne carved from dark wood atop the dais at the end of the room. The golden, onion-shaped ornamentations finishing the backrest glint in the candle light illuminating the room, and for a moment, I can see myself sitting there, a knife in my hands dripping crimson stains of Erina's blood.

The satisfaction the image gives me should disgust me, but with everything Erina has done, I can't bring myself to chastise myself for it. Perhaps it's the spark of coiling darkness that comes with the Crow slumbering deep inside of me. Perhaps it's an instinct deriving from the mating bond rooted even deeper.

"We have a public appearance coming up," Erina informs me the moment I face him again, his lips twitching in that same cruel smirk that makes me want to punch it off his features. Bonus points if he loses a few teeth in the process. "Time to show off my beautiful betrothed to all the nobility of Tavras."

"All the nobility of Tavras?" It's a hassle to keep my hands relaxed in his unrelenting grasp when they so desperately want to ball into fists. My gaze darts around the throne room packed with nobles and courtiers. "You mean there is more?" I'm convinced by now each last lord and lady in Tavras has gotten a peek at me.

"Well, of course. What you've seen so far is only my loyal court here at Meer." He moves me through the center of the dance floor without regard for the other dancers scrambling out of our path, and I have a hard time suppressing the urge to apologize to a lady in a sepia silk gown who stumbles as she rushes out of her king's path. Erina's guards flank us the moment we leave the parquet, their weapons gleaming at their hips as they escort us to the dais at the front of the room, where Erina seats himself on his throne while I am left to stand at his side like an accessory he can't be bothered to stow away.

With a slow gesture of his bejeweled hand, he summons Ephegos, who swiftly marches up to the foot of the dais, bowing low before approaching the king. His gaze is warm brown embers when it meets mine, and gooseflesh raises on my skin at the familiarity of that look—the same one he gave me before I blacked out in the dungeon the day I almost escaped.

"Is everything prepared for tomorrow?" Erina prompts the Crow, following his movements as he climbs the stairs to stand on Erina's other side.

"Everything is ready. The audience is set to start at noon and will take until late afternoon, judging by the number of responses we received.

"An audience?"

They both face me, Erina with amusement, Ephegos with more ice in those brown eyes than the color seems to allow.

"The nobles of Tavras have come to Meer from all over the realm to see their future queen in the flesh." Erina extends a hand, running a finger down my bare forearm where the eggshell silken sleeves of my dress don't cover my skin.

While I'm still trying to figure out how he can be certain none of those nobles will turn on him the moment they realize the Milevishja heir is real, I don't know. Perhaps it's the fact that none of the courtiers in attendance have dared question the rightfulness of his rule, even when I'm right here, proof that not all Milevishja blood was spilled by Erina's ancestors. The rightful Queen of Tavras.

The title doesn't sound right, even when it's merely a silent thought. *This* Milevishja is a pirate, born to roam the seas. And if I do belong on a throne, it's one that no longer exists: that of the Crows.

"See it as a test run for the wedding, dove." Erina's smirk drives a shiver of disgust down my spine. "I will need you to be on your best behavior. My people need to recognize you for the beautiful creature you are, and that's hardly achieved with that frown on your lovely face."

"Be glad it's only a frown," I utter under my breath, gaze on the gracefully dancing crowd as I ignore the scrape of his fingernail along the side of my palm before he weaves his fingers through mine.

"You will do well to remember you are here at your king's mercy, Wolayna," Ephegos reminds me—not that I need a reminder with the leverage they have over me. If only I could get near Kaira so we could communicate through our mind connection. It's the one advantage we have—and even *that* we don't get to use.

"I know." I give him a sweet smile that sours my stomach. "One wrong word, one wrong step, and I'll bemoan the consequences."

Erina's gaze bounces between Ephegos and me as he follows our conversation with mild amusement. "Perhaps it's time you admit your defeat, Ayna." He adjusts the golden band on his brow, a modest version of a crown, just enough of a reminder of who he is and what he represents, of the power he holds in this realm.

Oh, the things fairy males will do to save their mates... His words come back to me, and it dawns on me that between all the dancing and smiling and forcing myself to play my role so Kaira won't get hurt, I forgot there is a real danger that Myron won't head for Askarea to warn King Recienne. He might as well turn around the moment he wakes and realizes I'm not there—and head right back to Meer.

To save me.

And that's exactly what Erina and Ephegos are hoping for because they know exactly that, while I'd do a lot to keep Kaira out of harm's way, there is nothing I won't do to keep my mate safe.

ANGELINA J. STEFFORT

THREE

AYNA

E arly fall and city dust lace my view as I glance out the open balcony doors of the throne room, a bland smile firmly in place to please the countless nobles stepping up to the dais upon which Erina presides on his throne while I stand beside him in my emerald silk gown. The bodice is too tight for my liking, and the sleeves tug in the wrong places, making it hard to bend my elbows as I lace my fingers in front of my stomach. One after the other, the lords and ladies bow, curtsey, eager eyes scanning my figure, my features, the long braid draped around the crown of my head, the pearls resting on my collarbones. My bad hand weighs like lead where a broad golden bracelet covers the tattooed chain identifying me as a Fort Perenis prisoner, and the engagement ring Erina insists I wear everywhere only adds to the sense of being shackled.

"It's an honor, Your Majesty." The woman in front of the dais rises at her king's command, her sparkling blue eyes finding me as soon as Erina turns to study me with fake adoration the way he has all morning. "Lady Milevishja, I'm honored to stand in the presence of one of the old blood-lines." There is a cold quality to her tone that doesn't match her warm brown skin tone and the soft waves of her grizzled hair, and I almost cringe as I meet her gaze.

"A true Milevishja in this palace after so many years," Erina muses. "And what a lucky man I am to have found her."

"That she agreed to marry you is more like it," someone mutters behind the throne. I don't need to turn around to identify the voice as that of the older guard who accompanied me from my room to the audience after breakfast; my Crow senses might have been dulled by the drug, but they surpass any human ones anyway.

Lips twitching at the signs of sarcasm, I'm tempted to turn and give him a sign of appreciation, but the woman in front of the dais rises from her curtsey, smoothing over her sweeping, gold-embroidered, chocolate satin skirts, and something flickers in her eyes that makes me wonder if she heard him, too.

With a quick glance, I confirm her ears are rounded. Clearly human, unless she is of a diluted fairy bloodline like Kaira…

"Lady Andraya," I use the name Ephegos supplies from my other side the way he has all morning, a threatening presence running this audience in a black-and-blue uniform that makes him even more dangerous than his brass or sepia attire used to. He's head of Erina's armies now. However he convinced the King of Tavras to allow a Crow to lead his military forces, I don't even want to know.

"Lady Andraya is from the southern coast of Tavras, overseeing the ports along the Gulf of Tears," Ephegos informs us while I debate sitting down on the chair next to Erina's throne. A restlessness has risen within me that surpasses the constant drug-induced exhaustion, and it's become difficult to keep still, so I opt for remaining on my feet, quietly tapping my toes on the polished floor beneath my skirts where no one can witness.

"It must be wonderful to live by the coast," I say in that same bland tone I've been using with all the nobles who've come to gawk at the Milevishja woman they believe belongs by their king's side.

"There is nothing more breathtaking than the inky turquoise of the waters in the early morning when the sea traffic is still quiet and the town fast asleep." Lady Andraya's lips part in a genuine grin letting a hint of mischief slip onto her heart-shaped face that I hadn't expected from the middle-aged woman. "I've heard you yourself know one or the other thing about the beauty of the oceans."

Beside me, Erina clears his throat, his hand finding mine and clasping it so hard I rethink my response twice.

"I've always been an admirer of the waters surrounding our realm, but I haven't been able to travel far enough to the south to see the Gulf of Tears for myself." I put on my best intrigued face while keeping a hint of innocence that will not give away how far I've travelled otherwise. "Is it true you can see all the way to the Southern Continent from the cape?"

My father used to do trade with the Southern Continent, but I never got much out of him about what treasures could be found there. However, I don't tell her that. It's obvious she knows something about my past; I don't need to give her anything else, or she might make the connection of which Milevishja I exactly am—the pirate child of a traitor merchant who tried to assassinate his way back to a throne that might, in a different life, have belonged to him. The daughter of a mother who offered up my hand in marriage to please the King of Tavras.

The air reeks of betrayal more and more with every minute I ponder that, no matter if my father hadn't committed treason and my mother hadn't taken me away from the city, I'd have ended up here anyway, right beside Erina. And in a different life—a life where I wasn't a Crow Queen—I might have been content in this exact place, at Erina's side.

I might have never known what a monster he truly is, might not have seen past his handsome mask and his courtly manners. I've seen the true him, though, and there is no going back. I've seen the vile measures he is resorting to in order to establish more power, to gain more lands, more wealth. The *friends* he's made to make it happen.

A sideways glance at Ephegos makes my blood chill.

"You need to take her on a tour along the coast, Your Majesty," Lady Andraya urges Erina with a conspiratorial expression taking over her features that makes me wonder how well the two of them know each other.

Erina doesn't give away any sign of familiarity. All he does is give a noncommittal nod before he waves her off, eyes already on the next noble waiting in line behind her.

"I'd love to," I tell her as she curtseys once more before walking to the side door where the guards usher the guests out into the courtyard. Where they go from there, I can't tell; my view is on the gardens and on the seemingly endless line of elaborately dressed lords and ladies waiting to bow to their king—and stare at the Milevishja heir.

"You're not going anywhere near the ocean," Erina murmurs as he tugs me closer, grasp tightening painfully around my fingers.

I want to tear my hand away, want to run down the stairs past the unassuming nobility of Tavras, and disappear to my room, but Ephegos has already taken a cautionary step closer, taking a stance at my side, and while he doesn't need to touch me to lock me in place, it's the symbolism of the gesture that is more reminder than anything that I am a prisoner here, not the admired fiancée of the Tavrasian king the crowd believes me to be.

Biting back the retort on my tongue, I lean closer to Erina, brushing my free hand over his unmovable fingers in a pretense-affectionate touch that sure gets his attention. In a flick of surprise, his eyes meet mine as I put on a smile I know will get me his full focus. "I want to see Kaira." It's a murmur, and for an outsider, it might appear like I am uttering words of undying love to my husband-to-be, but it's a bold demand, for it won't matter where Erina believes I should or shouldn't be going if I manage to speak to my sister through our mind connection and we make a plan to get out of here. I just need to get close enough to her to make it work.

"You aren't in a position to demand anything from me," Erina responds with an equally deceptive smile, and I think I hear women fawning over the gesture as he brings his free hand to my cheek, stroking a thumb along the side of my face.

I hate him. More than I hate Ephegos. He could just let me go, make a contract with me that I will abstain from ever aspiring for my throne, and we'd both have what we want. I'd even leave Eherea so he can be sure I will not interfere with his plans. But Erina needs me for his power trip, and there is nothing I can do—except to rid him of his leverage and get out of here before Myron can do something stupid such as coming to my rescue. He won't survive it this time.

"Please?" It costs me all I have not to spit at him as I plead to see the one person I call an ally in this Shaelakforsaken palace, but I plead anyway. "I promise to sit tight and smile prettily for the rest of the audience if I can see her for a few minutes afterward." Desperation has clearly gotten the best of me if I resort to measures such as this, but what other options do I have? What cards can I play when the drug has emptied my sleeves of all tricks and plans?

I lean down even further, not failing to tuck my elbows a bit tighter to my sides to push my breasts higher in the already tight corset, and Guardians bless him, Erina isn't immune to the sight. It's enough to sidetrack him long enough that, when I repeat my plea, he dips his chin, reassembling his regal expression as his gaze lifts from my décolletage back to my face. "For a few minutes." His gaze veers past my shoulder to Ephegos, who will clearly be the person escorting me to wherever they are holding Kaira. "And if she tries anything, cut the woman's fingers off."

I feel myself blanch but hold it together as panic creeps through my veins like little bugs leaving poisonous trails.

"Understood?" Erina's eyes lock on mine, his fingers lingering on my cheek, sliding down the side of my neck, along my shoulder until he clasps my other hand firmly in his.

I nod.

"Now, sit down and smile, Ayna. I have a court to please." He releases me, already summoning the next noble to the foot of the dais with an idle wave of his hand.

Ephegos stands behind my chair as I half sit, half drop into it, catching my breath, and his hiss of warning is enough for me to assemble my best befuddled-female face.

Sit through another hundred or so nobles, smile at them, give them pleasant phrases, and make googly eyes at their king. I can do that if it means I'll see Kaira. I might not have a physical knife to ram into Erina's back, but a metaphorical one is waiting in the form of the mind connection Kaira and I share—and I'm ready to use it in whatever way I need to in order to get my sister out of here.

FOUR

AYNA

E phegos isn't gentle when he ushers me down the familiar stairs to the dungeons. Quite the opposite. By the time I make it to the humid half-light of the place of horror, his claws have pierced into my biceps so often I wonder if he is guiding me down by my arm merely to have a chance to hurt me.

"It's been a while since we've had the chance to speak alone." The Crow shoves me a few steps ahead of him, his sword at my back, just in case the extra dose of the drug he gave me before dragging me down here isn't working.

It is. I'm unstable on my feet, and the nausea is back in full force.

"I could go another while without it," I comment under my breath, only half intending him to hear.

"Oh, but it's always so pleasant to see you suffer, dear Ayna." He means it, I can tell by the delight in his tone as he allows the tip of his sword to slice the skin beside my spine where my dress shows the welded scar I carry from my time at Fort Perenis.

As I cringe away, he holds me back with his claws. He doesn't show them often, probably still denying he's a Crow rather than a Flame, the traitor, but there is nothing he can do to hide it when his animalistic nature breaks through. Right now is one of those moments when the predator shines just beneath the surface, and Ephegos's features shift ever so slightly as he loses a hint of control.

"If you're still pissed Myron got away, you should choose your words better when making bargains with traitors." It's a low blow, but if he can relish my pain, I can relish upsetting him. It's one of the few pleasures I have left, the reminder that Myron got away. That all of them got away—except for Kaira and me.

No one has informed me yet how Kaira ended up in captivity, but I'm determined to find a way out before I ask her. It doesn't really matter how she ended up here as long as we get out.

"He's a stubborn bastard." I don't imagine the hint of embarrassment in Ephegos's tone. It's a slight shift but enough to give away that he realizes he was the one to leave backdoors open in the deal with Herinor.

"*That* we can agree on." No one is more surprised than I am that I'd nod at something coming out of Ephegos's mouth. I use the moment to catch him off guard. "What exactly *is* your bargain with him?" Not that I expect him to answer.

"That's between Herinor and me and none of your business, Ayna. Behave and I might not cut off Kaira's fingers." He steers me past a corner I recognize—the one where the guards once surprised us on our prison break. I almost feel Myron's presence, his magic as he silently eviscerated them to clear our path. Then I remember that I'm the prisoner now, and Ephegos won't lift a finger to help me.

"Why her?" Perhaps it's a bold question, but if I want to find a way to get her out, I'll need to gather information. The more Ephegos gives away about his thought processes, the more likely I'll be able to outsmart him later. At least that's what I hope. She is a part-Flame after all, a member of the Flame tribe, even if merely a minor one. "Why would you capture one of your allies?" I should have asked this question a long time ago when Kaira was put into Ephegos's service at this palace.

The smirk Ephegos flashes makes me wish I'd never met the Crow. "Does it matter?"

It does, but I don't tell him that. Instead, I give him a mock grin as he comes to walk by my side, claws locked so tightly around my biceps my arm has gone numb, and sword casually at his side. At least, that dulls the throbbing pain enough to let me think straight.

I haven't had a chance to speak to the Crow alone since my attempted escape almost two weeks ago, and now that I'm alone with him, I wonder if I should use the opportunity to push for information he might never reveal in front of the King of Tavras.

"It matters if you want to step into the Flame Matrone's footsteps one day. Isn't she grooming you to be the next leader of their kind?" Holding my breath, I wait for his claws to rip out a chunk of my flesh, but all he does is stare me down with those too-warm brown eyes. So I push harder. "Or should I say *your* kind. You seem to be on the side of the Fire Faires more these days than on the side of your own kind."

If the hiss gurgling from Ephegos's throat is anything to go by, he is one wrong word away from tearing out my throat. Good Erina needs said throat to remain intact so he can make me his wife and use me to breed little baby monarchs. Hiding the shudder of disgust behind an even wider grin, I drag my feet to a slower pace, forcing Ephegos to take more of my weight as he marches me through the narrow corridor into the area where cells line the dusty rooms.

"It's none of your concern what I do and why."

True. It isn't. "As long as it doesn't put me into a forced marriage and hurt everyone I care about, it isn't." I hold his gaze, my entire body trembling from fear of what he'll do if I push him too far. If he'll snap my neck if I shatter his control.

"I've said it once, Ayna, and I'll say it again so you remember: It's nothing personal. If Myron didn't love you, I would have never dragged you into this. I'm not a monster after all."

My opinion differs. A lot. "Nothing personal?" I grit my teeth against the shivers that come with the exhaustion of staying on my feet so long after a whole day of audiences in the throne room. Even my undrugged self would have been ready to drop into a bed and sleep for a full day. But this version of myself is ready to collapse on the spot and never get up again. Only, I don't have an option. It was me who wanted to see Kaira. Me, who demanded it. So I'll have to see it through. "Sure feels personal being strapped to a torture table." The memory alone is enough to make me flinch at the phantom pain where the leather straps once cut into my wrists.

Ephegos's laugh is as unexpected as it is cruel. "It certainly is personal with Myron, and you're his mate."

That says it all.

"Kaira isn't my mate, though. If you consider the Flames your new family, why not her? Why lock her up and use her against me?" If only it were that easy to get the Crow to spill all his secrets.

"She's a tool in a longer game, Ayna. You are too young to understand the makings of immortal war, but you'll understand in time. You're no longer human after all."

"Not entirely," I agree, even when I can't access the magic slumbering deep inside of me or even think of shifting into my Crow form. The first female Crow in millennia.

"Give it a few hundred years and you'll be cut out to play this game yourself. You'll learn that friendships and alliances are fleeting. Only bargains guarantee loyalty. Those, and power."

I don't want to know what his life has been like to make him into such a monster. With all the hardship induced through a curse he had no part in deserving, with being driven from his homelands and then locked in a tiny forest for ages—

A twinge of pity flickers through my body, but then I remember Myron remained good through it all. Myron and Royad.

Ephegos tugs me around the next corner, his footfalls silent on the dirty floor while my own feet alert the entire dungeon.

"You think too much, Ayna. We all would have been better off if only you were nothing more than a pretty face."

Before I can demand to know what he means by that, he points ahead at the end of the corridor between cells at the thin shape in rags huddled on a palette of straw under the high-up window.

"Kaira—" I whisper.

The Flame stirs with a groan, and the sight of her haughty features, half-starved, bloodied, and dirty, makes my knees buckle.

Ephegos drags me on until I get my legs under me again, but it's an effort driven by the need to avoid the pain of his claws bearing my entire weight at my arm, not because I feel sudden strength.

Because I don't. Strength leaves me completely when Kaira's dark eyes find mine across the torch-lit distance, stumbling toward the bars separating her from freedom.

"*Ayna!*" Kaira is smart enough to use our mental connection to express the relief of seeing me alive—and all the panic as her gaze slides to Ephegos.

"I won't ask if they are treating you all right, because it's obvious they aren't." I make the accusation clear with a sideways glance at Ephegos while in my mind I say, *"We need a plan to get you out."*

"You mean both of us," Kaira corrects with a frown that makes the crusted blood on her forehead flake. Aloud she says, "They have been feeding me enough to remain on my feet, which is more than I expected of those bastards." She doesn't hold back with the hatred in her stare as she directs it at Ephegos once more.

I'm surprised the Crow doesn't punish her for her boldness. Then, I should be used to Ephegos not being predictable in any way. Had he been, I'd have seen his betrayal coming. What I do know is he probably doesn't see Kaira's imprisonment as *personal* either.

"Let her out so I can speak to her like a person." It's a reckless demand to make, but I make it anyway, just to see if there are any magical locks on the door that I am not aware of or if brute strength will do the job of breaking her out when the time comes. Guardians, let that time be soon.

Ephegos shakes his head. "Nice try, Ayna." But he steps back, releasing my arm from his grasp.

I nearly groan as the numbness makes way for an assault of pain.

"Any ideas?" Kaira prompts as she stays well away from the iron fence separating us. When she notices my observation, she clarifies, *"those bars will drain your magic, no drug injections needed."*

"I remember." I do. If only I had part of my Crow reflexes and strength available to shove Ephegos into the barrier, I'd level the playing field and rob him of his magical advantage,

but I'm barely strong enough to keep upright. Damn those drugs. Damn this entire palace and Erina's unholy alliance with a megalomaniac Crow traitor.

Kaira's lips split into a distorted grin as she follows my train of thoughts. *"I've tried."*

"No success?"

"Obviously, or I'd already be out of here." Her tone has more humor than I could ever muster in a situation like this.

It's almost too easy, too familiar, slipping back into our silent conversation. As if no time has passed at all and nothing changed when, in reality, everything has.

"At least, leave us alone for a few minutes." Forcing the desperation out of my tone is a challenge in itself.

Ephegos raises a brow. "Not that it will make any difference when I can hear you whisper from the end of the corridor."

All right... No privacy then.

"Let him believe he's privy to everything we say. It will fool him into a false sense of security." Of course, Kaira is right. We'll need to give him a conversation to listen in on though, or he'll know we're up to something.

"Easy..." Kaira tugs on the dirty fabric of her servant uniform—apparently, they haven't bothered giving her fresh clothes since they locked her down here. The need to hurt Ephegos for what he's done only increases when I spot the scar on her forearm where Erina sliced into her flesh. If it weren't for the Crow traitor, my sister wouldn't be behind bars. The irony is that, would I tell him who Kaira truly is to me—blood, a half-sibling just like Sariell was to him—he

might understand. Since understanding won't change any of his reasoning though, I keep my mouth shut, waiting for Kaira to work her magic.

"The guards make sure I get enough to eat. They give me fresh water every day. I even had an opportunity to bathe," she rambles, giving Ephegos an inconspicuous conversation to listen in on while we both do our best to think up a plan to get her out.

"And you didn't take it, given the state of your dress?" My comment makes Ephegos laugh, and for a heartbeat, I see the friend I believed him to be. The male who'd laugh and joke with Myron and Royad. The laugh gets stuck in my throat as I meet his gaze, and I find more of the cruelty I have learned him capable of lingering there.

"Since no one will grant me an audience with the King of Tavras, why bother cleaning up? Surely, not for the barbarians that are the guards." Kaira's eyes spark, and I remember what she did with Julj, the guard at the side gate of the palace, to get us in and out on our rescue mission.

Any of the guards susceptible to your charms? It's the only thing I can think of since neither of us is in the physical state to fight our way out.

Kaira's grimy braid slides over her shoulder as she shakes her head.

"The King of Tavras doesn't care to be bothered with a halfling like you," Ephegos comments. "As a matter of fact, he couldn't care less what happens to you, Kaira. He's only keeping you around until Ayna's mate decides it's time to get her out."

"Which he won't." My retort has less bite than I was going for with all the foolish hope meddling with my emotions at every mention of Myron, and my shoulder tingles right above where Ephegos's claws severed my skin. If he can feel my pain through our bond, he might not be as wise about a rescue attempt and simply turn around from wherever Herinor took him and run back to seal all our fates.

"You still haven't grasped the severity of a fae mating bond, have you, Ayna?" Ephegos seems genuinely curious as he leans closer to study my face.

Ignoring the prickling sensation of discomfort, I turn my back to him and focus fully on Kaira.

"*Not the way Julj was. They have more experienced soldiers down here. Julj was a young, hormone-driven fool.*"

I can't argue with that. Allowing Kaira to charm him got him killed after all. He wasn't even smart enough to figure out she was using him.

"*Any potential allies among the palace staff upstairs?*" she asks in return. "*How about your new handmaiden?*"

An image of the various women fleeting in and out of my rooms to help me dress when it's time for Erina to parade me in front of his court floats into my mind. "*I never see them long enough to gain their pity. They are all convinced I'm the luckiest woman in Tavras.*"

Another person comes to mind—

Lady Andraya brought up my past in a cryptic way that makes me believe she knows more than she let on. That doesn't make her an ally though, just a woman who might sit on information the King doesn't want her to have. Leverage, but nothing I can use against him.

"*Perhaps there are people who are aware I'm not here out of my own free will,*" I say into Kaira's mind, "*but there is no way for me to speak with them privately. Erina makes sure I'm never alone with anyone longer than a few minutes. He switches out servants and guards so I can't build relationships. I don't know who I could trust, even if I had time to speak truthfully.*"

"Oh, I do think he'll come," Ephegos continues our audible conversation while I do my best to block out what that thought does to the chambers of my chest and the warmth spreading from the inked lines on my shoulder. "And when he does, I'll no longer have need of the Flame halfling."

Kaira shudders, and this time, I catch a glimpse of thought she didn't intend to send my way. It's a whisper of terror, but I see it anyway.

"*Whatever we do, we'll need to do it soon. The moment Myron shows up, I'm dead.*" She means it.

"You saw her. Now it's time to return to your chambers, Princess," Ephegos interrupts before I can respond.

"I'm not a princess." Not even half true. Technically, I am. And not-so-technically, I am more than a princess. I'm Queen of Crows—*his* queen. Naturally, Ephegos doesn't acknowledge my title and role for the Crow Fae.

Before I can tell him I don't care, time's up, his claws lock around my arm again, the only sign he'll ever show of his Crow self, and he drags me away from the cell.

"*I'll return soon. I'll find a way so he lets me visit you again.*" Perhaps then we can figure out something—anything—that will help us get out. "*I promise.*"

But Kaira shakes her head. "*Don't come back.*" Before I can object, she adds, "*Find a way for Erina to summon me to your chambers. We're more likely to escape if I'm already out of the dungeons.*"

She's right.

"Be brave, Ayna," she calls after me in her audible voice while, in her mind, she tells me, "*I don't want to die in here, Ayna. And I don't want you to suffer for the rest of your days. We'll find a way.*"

I wish I had her faith.

"Enough." Ephegos shoves me past the corner, and Kaira's presence fades from my mind.

At least, now I know the length of a hallway is enough distance to sever that connection. The momentary sense of achievement fades fast the second I realize I'm alone in my head again. Alone with Ephegos and a palace of ignorant people who won't lift a finger to help me.

FIVE

MYRON

A new scar is forming on Herinor's skin right where I split it at the edge of his jaw. The male was smart enough not to fight back after he told me it's his fault Ayna is still in Meer rather than with us—with *me*. He took my punches with grace, never complaining when I landed a few good hits born from the force of my fury. Had my magic kicked in then, I'd have happily killed him for his failure, but with my powers bound by the drug, all I managed was to add to the landscape of white lines on his features.

That was days ago. Herinor has done nothing to heal himself—as if accepting the pain gives him some sort of redemption. He hasn't spoken to me either. Perhaps that's for the best. I'd only lash out again, and this time, any blow would be deadly. My powers are back almost in full force, and the battle injuries from the dungeon have nearly healed entirely.

Yet, I'm not enough to save my mate from the prison Erina and Ephegos put her in. Astorian spent hours talking me out of blindly running to my own demise, convincing me to think things through instead. Erina has the substance to bind magic. A weapon that evens out the advantage we have over the human soldiers. Combined with the drowsiness and nausea that comes with the ingestion of the drug, even our physical superiority won't matter.

We need a plan, and a good one.

I shift on the rock I've been using as a seat, eyes on the small fire crackling in the gentle wind sweeping across the grassy plains. How I've allowed the fairy general to talk me into taking even a step away from Meer is beyond me. Perhaps it's the reassuring knowledge that I'm not the only one who lost something.

Herinor saved me, but the part-Flame he has a soft spot for disappeared while he got me out.

My gaze cuts through the smoke, finding Herinor studying me while he rubs his fingers across the uninjured side of his face. Princess Cliophera sits next to him, legs crossed at the ankles, and stares out into the darkness of the open land.

After centuries of being confined to a forest, the lack of shelter deeply unsettles me. *Anything* deeply unsettles me these days. Especially when it isn't a plan to get Ayna out of Erina's hands.

"We'll get her back," Royad placates my rising temper, his hand resting firmly on my shoulder as he watches me study the others.

It's as much a promise as anyone could give who has no power over the outcome of this drama.

"Sooner rather than later," I add to clarify I won't be sitting around one day longer, no matter how we're all fighting to regain our powers. Even Cliophera is still recovering, despite having a majority of her ice-summoning ability under control once more.

"Can't you just step through the world with that magic of yours and summon an army?" Silas prompts, joining the conversation from his spot by a boulder where he has made himself at home on the grass, turning over the meek weapon in his hand. If I didn't know the Crow can turn any piece of metal into a deadly weapon, I'd believe he's concerned the short blade won't be enough to disembowel Erina's guards and pin Ephegos's traitor ass to the ground.

"That would be convenient," Astorian answers for his mate, arm wrapping around her shoulder more tightly as if he's worried she might slip away if he lets go for as much as a heartbeat. "But neither of us is in a state to site-hop after what we've gone through." The absence of his usual smug and teasing tone tells me all I need to know about how drained they both still are.

"Don't you think I'd have already site-hopped straight for my brother and warned him if I could?" Clio adds with familiar bite. At least, her anger is no longer directed at me since her mate is once more free.

37

Mine isn't, though.

"So, if we can't go back to Meer without reinforcements, we'll march north until we make it to the Seeing Forest." I'm more surprised than anyone by Herinor's determination. Perhaps it is because Ayna isn't the only female left behind.

"That's the plan." Royad shoves a hand through his hair, lifting his face to the purple sky. "If we're lucky, not all of the Crows we left behind have been detected and killed off by the Flame hunters."

My stomach turns as I'm torn yet again between what's best for my people and what is best for their queen. I'd let them all die if it means she lives.

"I never want to set foot in that Shaelakforsaken forest again," Silas grunts, slumping his back against the rock and stretching his legs, crossing them at the ankles. His injuries are healing well. A few more days and the cuts on his skin will have fully disappeared while his magic returns bit by bit.

"Neither do I," I admit. "But I will go to the ends of the world to get the Crow Queen back. And if you want a place in this court, so will you."

I'm not proud of my tone, of the threats I issue at the rugged male who's become my friend, but I mean it all the same.

"This is about more than a female," Clio reminds me with a sharp look, and gods bless her, she's right. "If we don't warn Recienne before Erina mobilizes his armies, the fairy-lands will not be prepared."

And with the magic dulling substance, the humans would be a real danger to Askarea.

"I won't care about what happens with your lands if my mate doesn't survive."

Much to my surprise, neither Clio nor Astorian burns me with a glare. Instead, their eyes fill with pity, one pair liquid jade, the other warm auburn. They both know what it means to fear for their mate's life and won't judge me for it.

"We'll head north at first light." Royad leaps in before I can say something I will regret.

Not that we need light to move, but we all need rest. So, we lie down around the meek fire and close our eyes. All but Herinor, who offers to take the first watch while the rest of us recover from what is partly his fault.

Before taking up his post, Herinor crouches beside me, lowering his voice to a whisper. "Kaira and I might not be mated, but I second the sentiment, My King. I don't care what will become of any of us if I don't get her back."

"She was supposed to go with Cliophera, Silas, and Astorian when Ayna and I went back to get Royad. What made her return to the dungeon?"

The guilt in Herinor's eyes is a stark mirror of my own feelings when I think of Ayna stuck at the palace.

"I don't know." Rising to his feet, he prowls to the large boulder a few feet beyond Silas's and sits down, gaze on the horizon, a fearless warrior keeping watch over a group of travelers. But the slump of his shoulders tells me that, internally, he's beating himself up for Kaira's fate.

I don't remember falling asleep, but when the sun wakes me with unrelenting brightness, I know I must have dozed off long enough for the moon to fade in its searing presence. When I roll into a sitting position, Silas and Astorian are already gnawing on last night's leftovers while Royad and Herinor are still fast asleep. Despite my gratitude for the extra moments of rest my cousin is getting, I am equally infuriated that no one cared to wake me at first light.

A sweep across our makeshift camp tells me Clio took the final watch of the night. Her relatively short frame—short for a fairy—thrones on the same boulder Herinor occupied last night, but her gaze is on me, measuring and weighing.

"I would have kicked your Crow ass out of its slumber a long time ago had Tori not insisted I let you sleep." Lips quirking in what could be a smirk or vast disapproval, she hops off her vantage point and saunters over. The linen pants and tunic she's been wearing since the escape from the palace are crusted with dirt and blood the way all of our clothes are, a reminder of what we've gone through together. "And judging by your expression, you feel very much the same about Royad, or you'd have long blasted him out of his dreams."

"Nightmares," I correct with a sober face. When Clio merely blinks without understanding, I add, "If Astorian has shared even half a word about what we all endured in the dungeon, you'll know that none of us will have anything other than nightmares until Erina and Ephegos are defeated."

Her face falls, gaze flicking to the fairy general, who's gone still, a slice of meat halfway to his mouth. Even Silas has lost his usual sarcastic comments. I could swear the Crow's hands are shaking.

Clio's prompt apology comes as a surprise, but I wave it off. "Don't worry, Princess of Askarea. I know you've endured similar and worse at the hands of my own people. I won't judge you for not treating me as if nothing ever happened. The scars on my body are enough of a reminder."

From the corner of my eyes, I watch Silas press his hands to his thighs to steady them. Astorian's chest heaves in a long, forced breath before he picks up his conversation with the Crow.

Princess Cliophera, however, pulls her lips into a small smile, a humble one instead of the wide, taunting grins of hers I'm used to, and the gesture is enough of a peace offering for me to return it with a smile of my own.

"For all the terror of your captivity, Tori is lucky to have shared it with a Crow like you." There is nothing but sincerity in her expression as she inclines her head before joining Astorian and Silas by the fire.

The fairy general scoots aside, making room for her to sit on the patch of dry grass, and hands her a piece of meat, but his gaze finds mine across the dying flames. He dips his chin in silent agreement, and so do I, lucky to have found such an unlikely ally in the fairy male. Releasing the tightness in my chest, I follow Clio's lead and huddle by the fire until Royad and Herinor wake minutes later, their yawns wide, but my cousin's features are no longer exhausted, and I'll take that as a win.

We eat in silence, each of us fighting our own demons as we stare into the embers, until the remains of breakfast have been devoured and there is nothing left to do other than to pack up and leave.

Everything inside of me screams as I turn away from the direction I want to go, but I won't do Ayna any favors by barging in the palace doors and getting myself captured all over again. With a sigh, I trace the outline of the bird tattoo on my shoulder and relish the warmth spreading through my arm and down my back from where it responds with a tingle.

The thought that Ayna can feel my touch brings me comfort as I set out after Astorian and Clio, a grim-faced Royad at my side. Herinor and Silas bring up the rear, and I'm not entirely certain how I feel about having the two of them behind me. Silas will stop any attempts Herinor may make, but despite saving me and saving Royad, turning his back on Ephegos and walking away... He left Ayna behind, and I don't know if I can forgive that.

SIX

AYNA

L ife at Erina's palace has become an endless sequence of dreading the next dose of the magic-nullifying drug. Had the substance at least made me delirious, I could have lived with it, but all it does is create endless hours of nausea and weakness.

The only good thing is that Ephegos has decided I'm no longer worth his time. He sends guards to inject me rather than bothering to do it himself. Then, when he was the one to dig the needle into my arm, at least, I knew where he was and what he was up to. These days, I have no indication of what the traitor Crow is doing, if he's plotting new terrors, or if he's simply waiting for his plans to come to fruition.

It's been three weeks since my escape and recapture, and all I can show as progress is that I've learned that begging isn't beneath me. Every day, Erina parades me in front of his court, and every day, I plead with the guard who escorts me to the reception rooms and formal banquets to check on Kaira for me when the king won't allow me to see her. I'm not foolish enough to believe any of them will hear me. Their sepia palace guard uniforms tell all about where their loyalties lie. As for the blue-and-black uniforms of the military Ephegos now leads, they appear all too often in the pompous palace, shiny weapons on their belts and stern expressions on their faces as they scan the courtiers walking the hallways.

Today is no different. An older guard is escorting me to lunch with the King of Tavras, his lined face set in a stone-like mask and his hard blue eyes on the path ahead. It's the third time he's taking me. In the beginning, Erina tried to never have the same person accompany me, but it seems he's run out of trustworthy men to haul me from room to room, so I'm starting to recognize the faces showing up at my door with orders to make sure I follow the king's summons.

"What's on the agenda today?" I frown at him, fighting to keep a dignified posture despite the weight of the drug lingering in my veins like lead. All I want is to lie down and curl up in a ball until it passes. One of the maids forced me to drink some water earlier so I wouldn't faint, and as I notice the cluster of people by the throne room door, I wish I hadn't and would lose consciousness instead of another moment under the scrutiny of Erina's loyal followers.

The guard faces me, gray brows rising high on his forehead as if he can't believe I spoke to him. "Lunch and a harp concert."

I bubble a laugh that sounds like I swallowed dried moss, and his features turn into a grimace.

"Harps?"

The man nods, placing one hand on the pommel of his sword while he guides me along with his other hand. "Hurry, Lady Wolayna. Your future husband doesn't take kindly to being left to wait."

As we continue down the hallway, I spot Lady Andraya's grizzled hair among the onlookers. Her dark eyes find mine across the room, and she inclines her head the way she did the last time I saw her.

"She's a wild one, that lady," the guard comments as he notes the direction of my gaze.

"Wild?" Another laugh—one of surprise—readies itself in my throat, but I bite it back for the benefit of keeping the casually neutral expression I've adopted as part of my being put on public display.

The man clears his throat. "A lady who oversees an entire port city? She's powerful for sure. Did you know she used to live in Meer before she married?"

Lady Andraya and I have exchanged a few words over the past few days whenever she came to pay her respect to the king, but all I've learned so far is she speaks more boldly to the king than any other guest I've witnessed.

"Powerful," I agree. "But wild?"

I'm not sure I imagine the blush on his cheeks as he turns to face the throne room door once more. At least, his grasp is gentle as he pulls me over the threshold, keeping up appearances that I'm here out of my own free will. Erina made it very clear to me that, if I as much as indicate that I'm a prisoner here, he'd make sure Kaira suffered.

So, I keep my silence, bound by invisible chains on my magic and my will.

"My name is Pouly, by the way." The man doesn't look at me as he introduces himself. "I will escort you again tomorrow." It's the last thing he says before releasing me into the throne room where the crowd of nobles curtseys and bows at the appearance of their future queen.

I don't even have time to react; Erina is awaiting me on his throne, and the presence of dozens of armed men surrounding the room is enough to keep me in line. I stride up to the dais where Erina had a little table set for the two of us beside his throne.

"My lovely Ayna." With a single gaze, he drinks in the low, gold-embroidered neckline of my sepia dress before he meets my eyes. "I was beginning to think you wouldn't join me today."

"I'd never dare," I whisper as he stands from his throne to meet me at the top stair as I climb up the dais.

"Because you know what I'll do if you misbehave." The glint of malice in his eyes is swallowed up by the practiced expression of regality, and I suppress a shudder at how easily he can hide his true nature. It's a shift as severe as that of Myron between his fae form and bird form, but Erina is merely human, and that makes things so much worse.

I place my hand in his open palm and allow him to escort me to the table where I sit on a golden brocade chair and face the sepia and gold napkin draped across the gold-coated plate. Erina takes the seat across from me and waves a hand, gesturing for his guests to sit down at the tables scattered throughout the room. I catch a glimpse of Pouly standing against a nearby wall a few feet from the table where Lady Andraya is sneering at the revealing dress of a young woman.

In the far corner, two harps are set up with two chairs waiting for musicians to occupy them. I drown out the murmuring crowd by focusing on the open windows overlooking the gardens. Fall is creeping into this part of Tavras slower than farther up north, but the first signs are obvious. Not long and greens will turn to yellows and reds, then to browns like the death Erina is ready to bring upon the fairylands.

As if summoned by my thought, Erina brushes a finger along my forearm. "After the wedding, we can take strolls outside. But for now, I'd rather not give you another opportunity to sneak away." The smile on his face makes me sick to my stomach.

Help me, I want to cry out. *Anyone. Get me out of here. Get* Kaira *out first.*

My words dry up at the image of my sister bleeding yet again because of me.

"We'll take a nice little walk with your Flame friend, Ayna." He only adds it to clarify she'd be there to carve open should I dare try anything.

"Will she attend our wedding?" I give him a bitter smile. "You know, the way you had planned to have King Myron attend."

"Don't speak his name in these halls, woman. There is a new King of Crows." A clear warning, but not enough to

47

make me believe what both Erina and Ephegos have been hoping: that Myron might be dead after all.

I feel him, though. In my tattoo, he's ever-present like a soothing touch, like a tender stroke along my skin.

"Ephegos will never rule over the Crows. If anything, he'll betray you the way he betrayed his own people. There is nothing in that male's heart other than selfish hunger for power, and if you believe for one moment he won't walk right over you the second he no longer has use for you, you believe wrong."

It's the most I've ever said to Erina and probably the most honest, so it's no surprise he's staring at me with those dark brown eyes that want to peel my skin away and shove every thought back into my skull.

"Well spoken, my lovely fiancée." He leans in so his lips are at my ear, and I fight the urge to retch all over his pressed uniform. "Don't think I don't have an ace or two up my sleeve."

No one hears our exchange—the distance to the other tables makes sure of it—but I can't help wondering if one of the other nobles notices my discomfort at the king's closeness—not that I shy away from him. I know better than to do that, but the tension doesn't leave my body until Erina leans back in his chair and picks up his fork when a servant places a plate of fish and greens in front of him.

"Eat, Ayna. Who knows when's the next time you'll get a proper meal." The way he says it informs me he has plans.

I do exactly as he says, eating the meal set in front of me with more enthusiasm than I feel. Any bit of strength I can gain will help me the moment I get out of here. If

Kaira stays down in the dungeon any longer, she'll lose even more weight and muscles, and it will be on me to drag her out of the palace. Because we *will* escape. I won't accept another outcome.

By the time we reach dessert, two women in sepia and turquoise dresses have started playing the abandoned harps, the music a blend of traditional Tavrasian songs and something more melancholic that I can't place. I'd ask Erina, but he bends closer as he notices where my attention lies and explains, "The music of Dunai, the heart of the Southern Continent."

It's only then that I notice the two women have darker features than Tavrasian folks from even the most southern parts of the realm.

"*Guests* from our southern neighbors," Erina adds with a smirk, and I realize they might be *guests* as much as I am. I don't dare ask.

The way their fingers glide across the strings of their instruments is dizzying and exhilarating all at once, and for a moment, I wonder if this music holds magic of its own, a power that can't be dulled by a drug made from Flame blood.

One of the players notices my stare, her black eyes snapping up without her fingers failing to continue the intricate melody. She inclines her head before turning to do the same with Erina.

I don't know how long I listen to the music, escaping, if only in my thoughts, for a little while. In my mind, I conjure Myron's face, his ocean blue eyes, his sharp features, silky black hair, the cords of muscles lining his arms and chest.

The scent reminds me of wind and forest and freedom. As if in response, my shoulder tingles, and I can almost feel his touch on my skin. Heat flushes through my veins, and where weakness and fatigue reigned a moment ago, a sense of new strength fills me.

"Lady Wolayna." The music has swept me away so thoroughly I barely notice Lady Andraya's voice as she addresses me from the foot of the dais. "My apologies for disturbing you during this outstanding performance." She curtsies briefly as I turn my focus on her. Today, the lady is dressed in a gown of bold azure and her neck loaded with thick golden necklaces and bracelets.

My gaze falls on my own wrist where a wide golden band hides my Fort Perenis tattoo.

"What is it you'd like to speak to my future wife about?" Erina inquires with less patience than any monarch should hold for his subjects.

Lady Andraya merely shakes her head. "I came to say goodbye. I'm needed back at home before the month ends, so I regret to inform you I won't be able to attend your wedding."

The strange thing about the situation is she is speaking only to me, even when her king is right next to me, demanding answers.

"What a shame I won't see you in your wedding gown. I'm certain you'll look even lovelier on your wedding day." Her words are polite, cordial, but the expression in her eyes... Something about it is off, as if she is truly asking a question rather than paying me compliments.

"I can't wait." If only I could speak the truth. The way she keeps waiting, keeps her full attention on me while the rest of the room is captivated by the harp players, tells me there is more to it than a simple goodbye.

"It will be good to finally call her my wife," Erina involves himself yet again in the conversation.

Graceful like a queen herself, Lady Andraya inclines her head at him and smiles. "I can imagine it will be a relief to finally call this lovely creature your own."

Again, I don't know if it's only me, but I hear more meanings in her words than just what she says.

I can't ask her for help in front of Erina. I can't ask her for help at all, not even in a dark corner. If Erina ever finds out, he'll make Kaira pay for my mistake. However, I can give her an indication that something is amiss. Just a tiny sign. Even if it won't make a difference.

"I would have loved to see the ocean again before my wedding day," I say as casually as I can manage.

Lady Andraya casts her gaze to the empty plate in front of me then to Erina, who is waiting on pins and needles for her response. He can't hurt me here in the throne room in front of everyone, but he can hurt me later, have others hurt me for any word misspoken.

"I see." It's all the woman says before curtseying deeply to Erina. "Good luck, Your Majesty. You picked a beautiful wife. I hope you'll be able to keep her."

Before Erina can come up with a response, Lady Andraya strides away, crossing the room and vanishing out the door. I wait for Erina to call for the guards to stop her, to throw her in the dungeon, but all he does is stare—at me.

"The ocean?" His smile has slipped, and the wineglass in his hand seems forgotten.

I swallow the panic at what he might read into my silent cry for help. "I miss the waves and the endless blue on the horizon." The shrug I muster is more to hide my shaking than because I feel it.

Erina dips his chin. "After the wedding, I'll take you as a reward for being a good bride."

I don't believe a single word.

SEVEN

AYNA

About three hours later, I'm no longer able to stand on my own feet. My dress weighs like it is soaked with water, my limbs shaky, and a pulsing pain hammers in my head. Thank the Guardians, Erina ordered me back to my chambers where I'm sitting on the chair by the window and focusing on Kaira in hopes of picking up anything from her end.

Naturally, I don't expect anything to happen. Both our powers have been subdued, and I'm too far away from her to hear a whisper of her thoughts. I'm about to doze off in my chair when the door opens again. Jerking upright, I ball my hands into fists, an instinct from my time as a pirate that

I won't get rid of easily—good thing people usually don't surprise me in my sleep.

"Lady Wolayna?" It's the guard who took me to the throne room earlier, his forehead creased and jaw tight as if he's actually worried I'll strike him.

"Pouly," I remember his name.

The man inclines his head. "You have been summoned."

Stifling a groan, I push back to my feet, swaying for a moment before I manage a slow step. My head, however, I keep high, no matter what awaits me this time.

Pouly watches me with more nervousness than I care for.

"Is something the matter?" I try to keep my voice steady—without success.

In response, he slowly shakes his head. "This is a time-sensitive matter, so I'd appreciate it if you hurried."

Doing the best I can to get back to my manipulative, controlling, and torturing fiancé, I want to retort, but hold my tongue, doing my best to walk toward him in a straight line instead. "I'm exhausted, Pouly. Perhaps there is a way you could send a servant ahead to deliver a message to Erina that I'll be late."

His gray brows raise. "The king has nothing to do with this. And there is truly no room for delay."

Something about the way he meets me halfway across the room and slides an arm under my elbow to keep me steady is wrong. It's a familiar gesture yet distanced enough to make it clear he's a guard and I'm his charge.

"Hurry, Princess," he murmurs as he helps me to the door, and I realize two things at once: First, he addressed me by the formal title I should hold in these lands, and second, he really isn't taking me to Erina.

Instead of the wide ornate hallway and curved marble staircase to the throne room, Pouly takes me to a side corridor I've used before—the day Kaira, Clio, and I escaped from this palace.

"Where are you taking me?" What should sound like a protest comes out as a whisk of air.

"Not far, Princess Wolayna. We'll be meeting the others soon."

"What others?" I stumble over an uneven step as he takes me down another level of wooden staircase into another, even narrower corridor.

"Focus on walking. Questions will be answered in time." He adjusts his grasp, sliding one arm around my waist while he opens a door with the other.

Darkness greets us alongside the humid odor of the dungeon.

Not the dungeon. Not the dungeon. Fear floods my veins, pushing back all reason, and my heart launches into a wild gallop. The last time I was brought into the dungeon without my request, I was strapped to a table next to Myron. The image of his blood-smeared body still haunts my sleep.

Digging in my heels, I fling my arm out, grabbing for anything I can use as an anchor so he can't drag me any farther. What if, this time, they have Kaira on a table and I'm forced to watch her bleed again? What if—

My hand finds iron bars and closes in reflex, clinging desperately to the metal. It's my bad hand, though, and even at my full strength, my stiff wrist won't allow me to hold on strong enough to outmatch Pouly, who utters a curse about how this should have been easy.

Whatever he means by that, I don't care. I claw at him with both my hands as he detaches me from the bar and pulls me deeper into the dungeon.

"For the Guardians' sake, Princess. Get yourself together. I'm trying to help you."

At his words, my body sags until I am nothing more than a sack of potatoes, and my chest tightens with both hope and fear that he's lying.

Before I can protest some more, or demand to know what is going on, we round a corner, and the shimmer of orange torchlight illuminates the space in front of us. There, Kaira sits huddled against the dirty brick wall, her face so dark with grime I barely recognize her, but her eyes find mine, and all panic ebbs away.

"You're late," a familiar voice greets from the corner of the room, making my head snap to the side to spot a woman in leather pants and a dark blouse. Her grizzled hair is what I recognize first; then, the slash of white that is her smile against the brown of her skin.

"Lady Andraya." Pouly beats me to it, bowing his head as he delivers me to sit beside Kaira. "She's in a bad state. I might need to carry her the rest of the way if we want to keep our schedule."

I sag against the wall, Kaira's arm snatching me up the same moment her voice enters my mind. "*Thank all the gods those Crows pray to that you weren't discovered on your way here.*"

Tears shine in her eyes as she adjusts her position to face me. "*We're getting out of here, Ayna. Andraya and Pouly are helping us.*"

A million questions involving who they are, why they care, and why they would help in the first place, cross my mind, but Lady Andraya crouches before me, bracing, scrutinizing my face, the boneless sack I've become, and nods once at Pouly. "Carry her then. We have only a narrow time window before the guards get back from their rounds."

Pouly apologizes as he scoops me up and unceremoniously throws me across his shoulder. "We'll be out of here soon enough, and then you can try your own feet again," he explains. "But for now, please don't fight. We're trying to help you."

Kaira's encouraging nod convinces me this is not a trick and we're actually being broken out of this prison. "*We'll be all right.*"

I don't fully believe Kaira as we make our way down a narrow hallway, Lady Andraya leading with a torch in hand and Kaira right behind us, her hand gripping mine whenever the path allows it. The humid air smells less of decay by the second, something I notice only as I allow myself to breathe through the uncomfortable jostling on the guard's shoulder.

"I thought you were Erina's guard," I whisper, anxious not to make noise that would draw anyone's attention.

"I am."

My stomach tightens with the sort of nausea coming with betrayal I'm all too familiar with by now, but I swallow it down at a soothing squeeze of Kaira's hand.

"*You'll learn everything once we're out,*" she speaks into my mind. "*They got me out of my cell; they'll get both of us out of this shit hole.*"

It doesn't ease the fears of being discovered, of being returned to Erina's or Ephegos's feet, or of the pain that follows any disobedience, but if my sister trusts them, I'll trust them. She's gotten me out of here before.

I don't know how long we've been walking by the time the corridor ends in another wall and Pouly sets me to my feet. Immediately, Kaira's arm falls around me, steadying me even when she's unstable on her own legs.

"Here is the key." Pouly extracts a small, dark piece of metal from his pocket, fiddling with it in what looks like a crack in the wall but, in reality, seems to be some sort of keyhole. Because, a moment later, the wall swings back, silent like a ghost, revealing a tunnel wide enough to fit an armed guard.

"This is an emergency exit for the royalty residing in this palace." He gestures at the slab of rock that moves effortlessly at a touch. I only realize it is stone attached to a wooden door, like a door hidden in a bookshelf, when Lady Andraya ducks into the darkness first, making the light from her torch dance along the opening. "It was built in by the early Milevishja kings to get their court to safety in case of a siege. I'm not certain the current king knows it exists."

"Let's hope he doesn't." Kaira slides into the tunnel after Lady Andraya, letting go of me as Pouly lifts me over his shoulder once more. "This is brilliant. How far out does it take us?"

"I would be surprised if he did. And these tunnels are long forgotten by the current royals of Tavras. All the way to the city walls." Pouly's voice is muffled as he follows the two women's lead, careful not to hit my head on the rough stone wall as he turns to shut the door behind us.

We all heave a deep breath.

"Let's get out of here." Lady Andraya waves us on, setting a pace I would never have been able to make by myself. "I have a carriage waiting."

I don't ask for details, don't even want to know as long as we make it out of here. Everything else can wait.

Stale air wafts past with every step, telling stories of ancient kings I might not even know the names of—kings whose blood runs in my veins—while three sets of footsteps tell a new story. That of our escape.

After what feels like an eternity, the tunnel makes a turn left, gradually climbing until it ends in a set of stairs, which in turn ends in wooden double doors tilted above our heads.

"This is it." I could swear I hear a victorious smile in Lady Andraya's voice as she lifts her hand to knock on the wood, which looks ready to crumble, and I hold my breath as the doors swing open, collapsing halfway, and debris and earth rain down on us.

Pouly staggers back, grabbing Kaira by the arm at the last moment and dragging her away from the avalanche while Lady Andraya presses against the wall, narrowly escaping the heap of soil attempting to bury us. Dust climbs into my nose, making breathing a difficult endeavor, and I cough, eyes watering as I blink against pink and purple light streaming in through the wide hole where the door had blocked our path.

"Let us help you out, Lady Andraya," a voice says, and I only realize Pouly had his sword drawn when he sheathes it, obviously trusting the man who's bending over the opening, holding out a hand for the lady who's brushing the dirt off her blouse.

Lady Andraya climbs out with the man's help; then they pull Kaira up together, assisting her with her slow steps across the unstable heap covering the withered stairs. At last, Pouly drags me off his shoulder, handing me into two pairs of hands ready to lift me out of the tunnel. By the time I'm laid down on the grass beside where Kaira is panting for air, Pouly has climbed out after us, and two men in dark, inconspicuous brown clothing cover the entrance with shrubs and dried grass.

"You can rest in the carriage," Lady Andraya comments, helping me to my feet and guiding me to the cabin of what looks like a carriage merchants use to transport goods of low value. I barely take notice of the hedges growing beside the tunnel or the tall walls rising behind it. Lady Andraya is adamant enough to stuff me into the cabin within heartbeats, Kaira following suit before the lady climbs in after us while Pouly takes the reigns. She knocks on the roof with a fist, and the vehicle sets in motion with a soft sway.

We made it. We're actually out of the palace.

"All right," Lady Andraya says with a smile as mischievous as a little girl stealing candy. "It's time to hear the full truth, Princess Wolayna."

EIGHT

AYNA

The full truth, it turns out, has to wait until the carriage rattles us into the shelter of a nearby forest. Kaira won't turn her focus from the window, scanning the scattered houses and ramshackle stables beyond Meer's city walls for potential danger, while Pouly steers the carriage along the tight paths. I flinch every time we slow down, at every turn we take, every winding curve of the path, my heart nearly stopping at the thought that someone might have discovered us.

The carriage slows at the edge of the forest, navigating a route off the main road and into the denser greenery where we can slow down and take a breath.

"The towers above the tunnel are unmanned for that brief period of time when the guards change," Pouly reassures me when the carriage stops and he hops into the cabin, making me look away from the opening door. "If they'd spotted us, they'd already be on our asses by now."

He cuts a nervous glance at Lady Andraya, who grins in return. "Don't mind me and my noble ears. We have enough foul-mouthed *asses* in our own ranks."

The smirk on Pouly's face allows me a glimpse of the man he would be under circumstances less dire and dangerous than this rescue mission he seems to have taken upon himself. "Well, I'll assume those don't look half as good in a uniform as mine."

A hysterical sound bubbles up my throat, and both Pouly and Andraya give me their full attention.

"Ever since the demise of the Milevishja bloodline, there have been rumors that one of them survived. Rumors whispered only behind closed doors for fear a Jelnedyn could hear them and go after the supposed heir." Lady Andraya's gaze meets mine as she pauses, waiting for a reaction or for a verdict, I can't tell.

In my chest, my heart races at the mere thought of someone knowing about my father—potentially about me—and never saying a damn word.

"*Keep your calm, Ayna,*" Kaira warns, her mental tone as weak as her posture as she rests her head against the back of her seat.

I force patience into my veins until Pouly places a gentle hand on my forearm, his dirt-streaked fingers familiar after him carrying me through the tunnels beneath the palace.

"A group of loyalists has been biding their time until the day a sign of the true heir emerged," Pouly continues, and a shudder rakes through me at the meaning of his words.

"A sign?" Just to clarify.

Andraya nods. "A sign that it is time to step out of the shadows and fight for the rightful king or queen."

"Queen," Kaira throws in as she gives me a pained smile. With everything else going on, it's easy to lose track of the countless cuts and bruises marring her person. How she can stay so calm and collected with Pouly's and Andraya's revelations is beyond me.

"While you were sleeping in silk sheets, Pouly and I had time to plot an escape," my sister supplies, grimacing at me. "But that's beside the point."

"You're safe with us, *Queen* Wolayna," Pouly reassures me, and my heart makes a heavy thud at the claim they put to my name.

Queen. Not of Crows but of Tavras.

Stars dance in my vision, and before I can demand to know how they pulled off preparing the rescue mission, I black out.

Stars illuminate the night as I wake to the absolute stillness of the carriage. I can't tell how long I've been out, only that it must have been several hours. Across from me, Kaira's head rests in Andraya's lap like a child, and the lady's hand strokes back the woman's hair in a soothing motion that has nothing to do with the fierce noble whom I'd met at court.

"She's been through a lot," Andraya whispers when she notices I'm awake. "Erina and that Crow bastard were ready to break her. Had I not pulled her out of her cell, today might have been the day she would finally fall apart."

"Why did you free her?" It should be a simple question, but the way the lady's forehead creases tells me it isn't.

"Anyone whose presence in Erina's dungeon gives him such leverage over my queen needs to be saved." Her hand stills on Kaira's forehead, gaze drifting to the darkness outside the window. "When Pouly and I managed to sneak down to the dungeon this morning, she told us everything about how the two of you ended up in captivity."

"She knew? About the rebellion?" My head hurts from more than just the aftereffects of the drug.

"Not before we met. But I'm convinced she's all in, now that she knows."

"Where are we?" Bracing one hand on the wall of the carriage, I sit straight, scanning the darkness outside. My stomach is upset just like it was after my first escape from Erina's palace. Only this time, I don't vomit right away. The drug is slowly leaving my system.

Beside me, Pouly is watching the outlines of the trees, his human eyes probably struggling to make out individual branches in the semi-darkness. My own eyes, however, see colors and shapes in the forest that make even this part of Eherea appear magical. Twigs weave into each other, reaching through moonlight like fingers through a cobweb. We must have stopped only recently, for the landscape looks nothing like the outskirts of Meer that were still visible when we entered the forest.

"North. You look better," Lady Andraya notes, carefully reaching under the bench with her free hand to extract a bundle of gray cloth. "Here, eat some of this."

When I don't react, Pouly grabs it and unfolds the cloth, revealing a loaf of rye bread. "It's as fresh as our plan allows."

The glance he gives me makes me tilt my head to examine the round loaf. "You still need to tell me all about that plan." I take the chunk Pouly tears off and nibble for a moment before I need to stop and wait for my stomach to settle.

"I was about to when you passed out." Pouly's grin is buoyant, but his posture is tense, as if he's expecting an ambush any moment.

"I'm awake now." I force down another bite of bread. If I want to get back to strength, I need food. And water.

As if reading my mind, Lady Andraya pulls a canteen from the same spot she'd been hiding the bread and hands it to me. "We've had people stock up the carriage with water and dried provisions since Erina sent out that pamphlet announcing he'd marry the Milevishja princess." She points under the bench where two boxes are sitting half-hidden behind her legs. "Just in case we'd get a chance to break you out sooner."

"Just in case," I murmur, mind grappling for things to make sense.

The water definitely helps, cooling my throat and my head as the weakness gradually fades.

"The rebels are always ready to aid a Milevishja royal, my princess," Pouly explains, but all it does is raise more questions.

"Rebels?" A glance at Lady Andraya in her pants and the roguish grin on her face informs me they mean it.

"I've been part of the rebels since long before you can remember, Wolayna." The lady gestures at me with more warmth in her eyes than her expression should allow. "When your mother packed up her bags and left Meer with you after your father's death, I should have known. I should have known that a Milevishja executed meant he posed a danger to the Jelnedyn throne." Her throat bobs and her brow creases as she studies me in the half-light the moon and stars provide. I could swear the sun is nipping at the darkness, for from the corner of my eye, I can make out an orange hue that doesn't belong in the night.

"He was murdered." It is Pouly whose voice shakes with anger.

"He was executed for treason," I correct, but the words don't feel right anymore. I know the truth now, that my father had sent an assassin to kill Erina and his family. He wanted to claim his birthright and got caught.

Lady Andraya and Pouly share a glance that makes my stomach churn.

"I learned only recently why he was *executed*," Pouly admits, "or I'd have called for aid the moment you set foot over the threshold of the palace."

I'm not sure what touches me more—that he has committed himself to a cause that aids my bloodline or that he's outraged on my behalf. If there was any shred of doubt they mean me no harm, it's wiped out now.

"How long have you been in Erina's service?" It's the first question I can think of because I can't remember the man from my first captivity in Meer.

Pouly folds the cloth over the bread and sets it down between us on the black leather of the bench. "I used to be stationed in the south"—his eyes meet Lady Andraya's once more in an unreadable gaze, and the woman shakes her head—"but I asked to be transferred to the palace." He clears his throat. "And before you ask how I gained the king's trust so fast that he allowed me to escort his prisoner bride through the palace, our group has ways of advancing people up the ranks."

Drawn by the lack of decoration on his shoulders, my eyes wander to his uniform. "You aren't high up in the chain of command," I assess what I remember from my childhood spent between Tavrasian nobility and military, and from what I observed during my captivity.

"That's on purpose. I needed to remain inconspicuous. A reliable puppet to execute the king's orders." His features twist as if remembering what those commands entailed. "Since I hold no responsibility in the chain of command, it will be a day or two until they notice I'm gone. That's why we waited until yesterday to get you out."

When I open my mouth to ask what he means, he continues, "It had to be on my day off so I wouldn't be missed right away. This ensures us a head start."

"Your group must have a lot of influence in order to place people in the right spot to rescue someone so fast," I note, eyes still on Pouly's uniform, trying to process the reach of the rebellion—and that there is a rebellion at all.

Lady Andraya shrugs. "Enough. We have people all over Tavras, from the southern ports to the borders of Askarea. For generations, we've been building a small, reliable network. Especially in trade where lots of information travel alongside goods."

"It helps that our cause is supported by plenty of wealth and Erina's court works on coin and power." Pouly gives me a meaningful look.

"But why not just kill the Jelnedyn king then?" Kaira has a point there.

Lady Andraya merely shakes her head at her. "That would have been rash. Assassinating the king without a Milevishja heir to take over the throne would have alerted the Jelnedyn line to our existence. If an assassin got captured and spoke under torture, there is no guarantee they'd keep our secret. We'd be discovered and eliminated one by one while the next Jelnedyn sat on the throne. No, thank you." Emphatically shaking her head once more, she pins me with a gaze full of hope and pride. "For so long, we've been waiting for word of a real Milevishja heir to reach us. And here we are." She gestures at me like at a treasure, eyes lighting up with reverence. "The last Milevishja princess. Queen of Tavras."

"And a fugitive," Kaira adds, sitting up with a wince.

My heart swells at the sight of her grin. "You could have warned me someone was coming for me," I scold her lightly, forgetting the twisting and turning knot that is my stomach, if only for a moment.

"Now where would be the fun in that?" Her voice is a croak, her hand clutching her side where fresh blood stains her garments. But the smile is genuine, and it means everything.

"Let me take a look at that." Lady Andraya notices the wet spot the same moment I do and motions for Kaira to lift her shirt, which she does to expose a sickening array of dark blotches on her stomach and ribs where she must have been beaten, and in the midst of them, a stab wound.

"It's nothing," she murmurs, but the way she's gritting her teeth only reinforces the image of how she's been brutalized. Pouly reaches under his bench, pulling out a box with medical supplies, and pours something on a piece of cloth.

"This will make sure it doesn't get infected," he says as he presses the cloth to her wound without warning.

I gasp alongside Kaira as a flash of her thoughts flares in my mind. *Fucking Eroth's Veil, that hurts.*

Lady Andraya clasps her hand as she's fighting tears.

"Only for a little while, but it will save your life." Pouly seems to know what he's talking about for he exposes his forearm to show us a jagged ten-inch scar that looks nothing like it's been stitched and properly bandaged at any time. "Got that in a fight with a Tavrasian soldier years back when they tried to ferret out our rebel group. They got too close to the truth, so we chose to confront them."

I hold my breath. "If Erina knows about the rebels, tying me to him by force makes even more sense. This way, he doesn't need to worry about anyone dethroning him."

Lady Andraya nods. "The rebels would have a Milevishja queen the way we've always hoped for, and he wouldn't lose his power in the process."

Pouly gives her that same unreadable glance, but this time, she nods. "It's the other reason why we waited to get you out of the palace."

"We needed to be certain you weren't there out of your free will," Lady Andraya takes over. "It's why I tried to talk to you as much as Erina would allow during the banquets."

I remember each time the lady had assessed me in the throne room. Each look and the subtext I thought I'd imagined. But she *had* been trying to gauge if I was truly willing to marry Erina.

What had I said? *I would have loved to see the ocean again before my wedding day.*

And Lady Andraya had understood.

"And once we knew, we made haste," Pouly concluded the story. "The rest is logistic details that don't need to concern you anymore. We won't return to Meer before we can put together an army that will win you back your throne."

A heavy silence falls over the carriage, Kaira clutching the cloth to her wound with a less pained and more concerned expression on her face, Andraya measuring me with those dark eyes, and Pouly sitting back on the bench, shoulders relaxed as if he's just shed a weight.

"Thank you." It's all I can bring myself to say, and it doesn't even remotely begin to express my gratitude and the debt I owe them for saving my life—and my sanity.

"The horses have rested enough." Pouly gently pats me on the forearm before opening the door and sliding out into the night to resume his spot on the driver's bench. "Time to leave this place behind us."

NINE

AYNA

B y the time we make it out of the forest, it's late morning, and when we stop for longer than to tend to our needs or water the horses by a stream and a few hours of rest here and there so they can recover, it's another five days later. I stretch my arms above my head, grateful for the absence of the persistent nausea that has defined the carriage ride, and glance at Pouly, who's engaged in a discussion with Andraya. My sensitive ears allow me to hear the entirety of the conversation about supplies, pending weather changes, and the need to lift fresh clothes for each of us so we don't get detected through our smell two miles against the wind.

Tuning them out, I join Kaira, who's staring out into the flat grasslands stretching in front of us.

"The Plithian Plains." I don't know what makes me say it aloud. Perhaps it's the need to hear it so I believe we truly made it out of Erina's palace.

Kaira nods, rubbing her side where her wound has been bandaged. Her bruises have developed various shades of purple, yellow, and green, depending on how far back the individual assault reached. *"Now we need to find the others."*

The fact that she speaks in her mind makes me wonder if she doesn't want Pouly and Andraya to hear her, so I form my response in my head, too, projecting the thought at her. *"What do you think their plan is?"* I gesture at the two rebels who saved us.

"Whatever it is, it involves you on the throne of Tavras with an ugly crown on your head." The smile on Kaira's face is as much comfort as it is a mockery of her usually fierce nature. *"And before you ask, no, I've not suddenly grown soft just because someone stuck a knife between my ribs. I can still kick ass and laugh about it."*

"As if there has ever been any doubt." We share a sisterly look that allows me to appreciate we're both alive, free, even if not in the way I'd hoped to be. *"We need to run again, don't we?"* I don't believe I'd be able to if it came to it, so I pray to the Guardians that our saviors will support my wish to find Myron and the rest of my family.

Kaira shrugs, but the exhaustion in her eyes tells a story of everything but the nonchalance she tries so hard to keep up. *"Only if they don't agree that involving your mate and the high fae of Askarea is a good idea."*

When we briefly shared about Erina's plan to conquer the fairy lands and how Ephegos seems to be pulling the strings, the genuine shock in both Pouly and Andraya's eyes verified they'd been as clueless as the rest of the kingdom. This is worse than we'd thought. Who knows how long it will take to convince enough people of the truth to fight by our side? And the rebels? They might be loyal to my blood-line, but are they willing to stand with fairies? Creatures of their nightmares? And it's not like we have magic at our disposal right now to fight our way out should they disagree and decide not to want to let us go.

Swallowing all doubts and concerns, I focus on the one thing that kept me going through all those terrible days in Erina's palace. But I'm not the only one who had someone out there who kept her fighting, so I pull myself together and respond to Kaira's thought, *"Don't you have a fae brute you'd like to see again, too?"*

A hint of pink tints Kaira's cheeks, and she brushes her hair back in a surprisingly awkward gesture, giving her the look of a nervous girl rather than a tormented woman. I take that as a yes.

"Well, then it's time we find out if the rebels are with us or against." Ignoring the assault of autumn smells floating on the steady breeze, I turn on my heels and head toward Andraya and Pouly, who've resorted to tending to the horses.

Much to my surprise, they don't debate when I tell them I need to find Myron. Instead, they bow their heads like I've given an order instead of a request and pull out a map of northern Tavras, where travel routes are marked in interrupted lines.

Another hour and we're back in the carriage, heading along the side roads where we don't need to fear running into patrols or merchants.

"If we keep going at that speed, we'll need to swap out the horses soon," Andraya notes with a frown, her gaze on the proud animals grazing in the meadows we're passing by.

"You mean steal them?" Kaira wants to know, a mischievous grin on her lips.

Andraya smirks, the facade of the lady shed entirely over the past days of traveling together, leaving behind a woman of practicalities and pragmatism. "Let's say *borrow*. We'll leave our own horses as a token until we can return what we take."

Not that I believe we'd ever get the opportunity to return to the exact same farm to do so. Besides, I'd done my fair share of stealing as a pirate, so what are a few horses?

Eventually, we end up taking four horses from the last farm we pass by before nightfall and disappear into a small forest lining the side of the road.

I use the silence of twilight to trace the tattoo on my shoulder and think of Myron—where he is, if he's all right, if Herinor managed to convince him not to run blindly back to Meer and get himself into trouble.

For days, I haven't felt anything from him, not even one small tingle. Perhaps that's because I've been so focused on our escape and then on ridding my system of the magic-suppressing drug. Now that my mind is on him and only on him, I can feel him in the inked lines along my skin, can sense him like a presence hovering at the back of my mind.

"I'll find you, Myron," I promise, allowing the wind to sweep up my words and carry them into the crowns of the trees, above them, in hopes they'll reach Myron. It's a foolish thought, but it allows me to not grab a horse and ride off then and there. There are miles and miles and miles spreading in each direction, and he could be anywhere. The likelihood that we'll find him is as tiny as the needles the evergreens around us refuse to shed.

We don't spend the night resting but take turns driving the carriage to put as much space between us and Meer as we can. It's only when the caw of a bird that doesn't belong in the night sounds from the trees ahead that I allow myself a flicker of hope.

Only a flicker.

But it's squandered by a thud of something heavy hitting the carriage roof, and all my senses go on high alert.

"Down," Kaira hisses, already covering me with one arm as she draws the knife Pouly handed her the moment she could stand on her own feet. A rush of power that I've failed to summon for so many weeks comes to life inside of me, and for the first time since Ephegos recaptured me in the dungeon, my magic makes itself known.

Andraya hands me one of her daggers while aiming the one she keeps at the roof as if expecting a blade to slice through any moment.

For a heartbeat, silence rules, the tension palpable, and the carriage is too small for the power stirring in my veins. Up and up it rises until I have no room for it in my body, and it spills through my veins.

"Watch out!" My shout dies in a flash of bright silver as power breaks from my skin. Kaira ducks under the bench while Andraya presses into the corner, as far from me as the cabin would allow.

It hurts… Guardians does it hurt. Like fire and iron and ice all at once. Like death and rebirth and the moon squeezing through my blood vessels.

In the distance, I can make out voices. Screams perhaps. The carriage doors burst open, wood splintering under the force of my power, and, for a moment, I finally hear Kaira curse in all colors of Eherean violence.

Then darkness brushes up against me, soft and gentle in a swirl of feathers. For a breath, I wonder if I'm finally turning into a bird again; then his scent fills my nose, and an abyss of emotions swallows me up.

"Stand back," someone shouts in the background. I know the voice, but I don't care what they want or why they're here. All I care about is the weight of Myron's arms falling around my shoulders, pulling me up against his chest, the uncontrollable need to eradicate every last tiny space between us. The touch of his lips against my forehead as he cradles me to him.

"I found you," he whispers, and the sound of his voice tunes out the entire universe. "I found you."

His breath is cool against my skin, his grasp on me firm—or maybe it's me clinging to him in relief and desperation.

"Don't let go." Tears suffocate my words, but Myron understands anyway.

"Never." On my neck, his fingers tangle with my hair, securing my face more tightly to him. "Never again."

In this moment, the world might have come to an end, and I wouldn't have cared. As long as he was here.

"Breathe, Ayna." Another kiss to my forehead and another, until I believe this is real and I'm not fantasizing about the day we'll be reunited. "Calm your magic, or it will destroy both of us."

It's only then that I notice the strain in his tone, the anguish that has nothing to do with our separation.

Myron loosens his grasp just enough for me to take in the torn expression on his beautiful face, the angry red blotches marring his skin around where my fingers lie against his chest, and it hits me like a cannonball.

I'm hurting him. Somehow, my magic is attacking without my permission, harming the male I'd die to see unharmed.

He doesn't shy away from my touch though, his expression soft despite his obvious pain. "It's all right, Ayna. It's all right. Take a slow breath." He inhales, holding the breath before he releases it. "Exhale. You're safe, Ayna. I'm here. We're together."

I can't even begin to understand what's happening when, like a lullaby, his voice strokes my magic to sleep, and slowly, the marks my hands burnt into his skin disappear, leaving nothing but smooth skin behind.

"Myron." It's nothing more than a breath, for I have nothing left when the outburst of my power has drained all my reserves. But it's enough to summon Myron's mouth to mine in a hard, desperate kiss that speaks of the fear and terror of the past weeks, of when I believed I'd lost him in the dungeon, the moment Herinor picked him up and carried him away to safety—and left me behind.

We both live or we both die. I won't leave without you. I'd been prepared to escape the dungeon with him or die at his side, but I'd not been ready to see him ripped away from me all over again. And I'm not now.

Never again will I allow for anything to separate us.

As I swear that to myself, the angry power in my veins fades, and all that's left is Myron's taste on my tongue and the feel of his body against mine as we kneel in the wreckage that once was the carriage.

TEN

AYNA

"You two are disgusting." Astorian is grinning at me from a few feet away, his tousled hair full of leaves and tiny twigs.

With a groan that runs through my entire body, Myron tears away from me, his gaze following mine and a frown twisting his features.

"What are you doing here, Tori?" he prompts, one hand remaining in my hair and the other one on the small of my back.

"Just making sure you don't get yourself caught again," the fairy male replies, a smirk on his lips and an arm braced on the trunk of a fat oak.

I take this moment to force some sense back into me and detach myself from Myron to assess the damage my magic has done.

A lot.

The carriage wheels are the only pieces intact; the horses have fled into a thicket of firs where they stand with wild eyes and steaming breath. But what's worse is the three motionless bodies at Astorian's feet.

Stifling a gasp, I scramble to my feet and bolt for what I expect to be my sister's corpse.

"Don't sweat it, Ayna," Astorian comments as I drop to my knees beside Kaira's hips. "They are alive. It will take them about a quarter-hour to recover."

Kaira's relaxed features are scattered with tiny cuts from where pieces of the splintering carriage must have hit her. A glance at Andraya informs me she suffered the same fate. Pouly seems to be the only one who got out of the way in time.

"Those three weren't abducting you, were they?" He pushes away from the tree, prowling to stand behind me where Myron is already hovering like a shadow. I don't need to look to sense his presence. My tattoo tells a story of his closeness that makes my skin tingle and the hair stand on the back of my neck.

"No." I shake my head in emphasis before the two males can make any different assumptions. "They actually rescued Kaira and me."

Myron's leg brushes my shoulder as he inches closer like he can't bear even this smallest of distances, and I allow myself to lean into him. My head is still spinning from the outburst of my magic, and my hands are shaky from the shock of finding Myron and Astorian rather than Erina's guards ambushing us. I don't dare ask about the others yet. If Myron and Astorian are here, chances are Royad, Silas, Herinor, and Clio are safe, too.

"Then it's time to wake them, I guess." Astorian steps forward, placing his hand on Andraya's arm, and I taste the magic in the air as he sends a burst of power into the lady whose eyes flutter open promptly.

He's making a move to do the same to Pouly, when a large bird plunges from the treetops, body shifting into the form of a huge male. I don't need to look twice to recognize Herinor, but I do need to stare to make sure I'm not imagining the way he crashes to his knees across from me by Kaira's shoulder, face torn in anguish at the sight of her motionless body.

"If she's dead, I swear to Shaelak, I don't care who you are or who you're mated to. I will kill you." He grinds out the words like steel over gravel, and ice slides down my spine at the authenticity of his threat.

But before Myron can tear his head off, I grab Herinor's hand and place it above Kaira's heart. "Feel that?"

For a brief moment, his features go slack. Then he closes his eyes, listening to the slow thuds of Kaira's heart.

It is only then I realize how much of the night I can hear: the whisper of leaves in the wind, the rustling of bird wings, the heavy breaths Herinor is trying to calm, and heartbeats. Kaira's, Pouly's, and Andraya's human ones, but

ANGELINA J. STEFFORT

three strong, violent ones belonging to the magical creatures around me. Then there are the swift, hard beats hammering in my own chest, telling a story of my own survival.

"Shall I do the honors, or do you want to…"

"I'll do it," Herinor cuts Astorian off before he can infuse Kaira with his magic and wake her up.

Myron's hand finds mine as he crouches beside me, brushing a kiss to my temple, and I can't stop a sigh from escaping at the simple touch. I'd been fearing never finding him in the vastness of the Eherean realms. Instead, I can relish his presence and the knowledge he's alive.

"What, by the Guardians, is going on?" Andraya asks as she scrambles away from the males surrounding us while Pouly's first reaction is to draw his sword and point it at Astorian, who stands closest to him.

"Don't embarrass yourself, human guard," he admonishes with a grin that would send lesser men running. "I'm as invested in the Crow Queen's safety as you are."

That earns him a pair of raised brows from Andraya and a grunt from Herinor, whose eyes never leave Kaira's face as he waits for her to wake.

"You mean the Queen of Tavras," Andraya corrects, Pouly supporting her statement with a nod.

Astorian, however, bursts out in laughter.

"What's so funny?" I rise, trusting Herinor to wake up my sister, now that I've seen Astorian do the same for Andraya and Pouly. Like a shadow, Myron straightens with me, a menacing form at my shoulder, but doesn't interfere as I wait for the fairy general to explain himself.

"You've made quite an upgrade to your life since those creatures retrieved you from prison, haven't you?" He points his thumb at Myron, who tenses to strike yet remains where he is as if waiting for me to land the first blow. "From traitor pirate to queen of two realms in the span of mere months..."

"Shut up, Tori," Myron eventually snaps when I don't respond, overwhelmed by the conundrum that should have been plain before my eyes yet I haven't been spending a real thought on.

I'm Queen of Crows and the true Tavrasian heir. One kingdom is right here, my feet touching its soil, and a group of rebels on standby to fight for me, while the other one consists of one king and about twenty more Crows, who no longer have lands to call their own.

Then there is the problem of me having become more than only their queen. Even if my bird form doesn't come to me at will yet, I'm a Crow shifter just as they are.

Kaira's groan as she rolls to her side under Herinor's touch saves me from more questions that would force me to voice any of my thoughts. Before she can notice him, he flinches away, leaping to his feet and standing back to make room for Andraya and me.

"Thank the Guardians," Andraya abandons the discussion to reach under Kaira's shoulder and support her as she scrambles to her feet.

Herinor, however, has retreated a step, glowering at the trees rather than expressing a shred of the passion leading him to threaten my life. The relief is clear in his posture, though, and I am almost certain the moisture beneath his left eye isn't sweat.

"What happened?" Kaira prompts, gaze finding mine in the midst of drama.

To my surprise, it's Herinor who takes it upon himself to inform her. "Myron took off out of the blue, so Tori and I followed to make sure he wouldn't get himself trapped and captured again. I don't know what Tori found when he arrived, but when I made it here, Tori was just healing you from whatever disaster hit your carriage."

"My magic hit the carriage," I correct him. "And I'm not a disaster… Or, only on occasion."

That summons a grin to the male's scar-flecked face, and his eyes dance with hope as he studies Kaira, smoothing out her tattered clothes and flipping back her dirty braid.

"Shouldn't we take this conversation elsewhere?" Kaira suggests, scanning the forest around us as if expecting guards to hop out of the trees any moment. "The blast of light might have alerted people."

"You mean the three farmers miles away?" Myron prompts, arm winding around my waist and pulling me an inch closer into his warmth. "Because those will need hours to reach the next outpost and alert Tavrasian soldiers."

Kaira bestows on him the most exasperated frown I've ever seen. "I mean the Flames," she explains. "We're near the borderlands, and Jeseida has hunters and spies…"

Herinor nods his agreement. "Jeseida has visited Erina's court before. I don't know what exactly she's up to, but it can't be good if she's working with the Tavrasian King."

Kaira's gaze falls to Myron, pondering. "Doesn't being mated to Ayna technically make *you* the King of Tavras?"

Myron flinches—actually flinches—at her statement but eventually shrugs. "Being married to me made my mate the Crow Queen, but it's up to her if she'll grant me the same right should she ever take up her crown."

"Which she will," Andraya interjects, the sternness of her expression as unfamiliar as the disheveled state of her appearance. Her gaze meets mine, dark eyes full of hope and a hint of concern. "Right, Wolayna? You will claim your throne."

I don't have an answer to that, so I say nothing. Instead, I wrap my arm around myself, refusing to allow the pressure of their expectations to weigh on me more than they already do. "What will happen is written in the stars, and who am I to challenge them?"

While the rest of them merely stare at me, Myron leans down, his breath a rush of heat on my cheek, and whispers, "You changed *my* fate, my queen. You can do anything."

I want to turn my head and capture his mouth in a dizzying kiss, but Kaira and Herinor are right. We aren't safe here. My outburst of power created a beacon anyone could have spotted. It's only smart to leave behind the remains of the carriage and run—or fly in Myron's and Herinor's case.

So we do. Postponing any further discussion of who shall have a crown and of which territory, we abandon the site of destruction. Pouly and Andraya set free the horses, who immediately bolt for their home stables—at least, no one will come looking for them. Then, Astorian takes their hands, a surprisingly bland smile on his features, and disappears with them without a warning.

"I'll never get used to seeing them do that," I note, eyes on the spot from where Astorian just pulled my two travel companions through time and space.

"It's creepy," Kaira agrees, brushing dirt and leaves off her sleeve. I notice she's moving without a wince of pain, and the bruises and cuts have vanished from her face, leaving behind only traces of blood.

A glance at Herinor confirms he is studying that same proof of violence which is older than the assault of my own magic, and the fury contained in his gaze is something I never want to get in the path of.

"Shall we, then?" Kaira turns to Myron, and when he doesn't respond—"I don't assume the fairy brute will be returning for us magical creatures, will he?"

"Perhaps not the *brute*," Clio's voice claims, making us jump as the female pops up behind us.

The moment I turn, she sweeps me into a rib-crushing hug. "I didn't believe Tori when he said—" She broke off with a sob. "Guardians, Ayna. You're alive."

An entire mountain collapses in my chest at the sight of the Fairy Princess.

"I told you she's alive." Not a hint of doubt resonates in Myron's words as he stands there, watching Clio squeeze the breath from me. "But she won't be for much longer if you suffocate her with one of your terrifying displays of affection."

As if realizing that, despite my reluctance to let go of her, I am indeed struggling for air, Clio releases me, sweeping Kaira into a similar embrace while I pant for air.

ANGELINA J. STEFFORT

ELEVEN

MYRON

The cool forest air turns into smoke-laced humidity the moment Clio sets us down on the rocky ground of the cave, hand firmly grasping mine until we no longer sway in the fire-lit space that could host a pack of wolves or—in our case—an unlikely group of humans, Askarean fairies, and Crows. How I hate this mode of travelling. I hated it when Astorian tested his strength by taking Royad and me on a short site-hop, and it's not gotten any better since. Apparently, I'm not the only one because Kaira is hurling up her dinner at the mouth of the cave, Herinor watching from a few feet away as if he's not quite certain he should offer his assistance.

Then, what would he assist her with?

"Ayna!" Royad is the first to notice the Crow Queen, who's still clinging to Clio's other hand. He gets up from his place behind the crackling fire, almost stumbling over his own feet as he rushes toward us across the dim space that has been our home for the past days.

"Good to see you awake and breathing," she greets him with a bright smile, and my heart nearly bursts at the sight of their cordial exchange, arms falling around each other in an embrace full of trust and relief.

It's such a heart-warming sight I don't even think of answering to the hint of jealousy rising in the pit of my stomach. I stand it all of a heartbeat before I am right behind Ayna, staring Royad down as he meets my gaze.

Reluctantly, he withdraws from her, but not without an eye-roll telling me he knows exactly what's riding me and he'll tease me about it later.

I can live with that. What I can't live with is another moment of not touching Ayna.

So, I take her hand in mine, savoring the warmth of her skin and the fact that I will be able to sleep for the first time in weeks, knowing my mate is safe and Ephegos and Erina cannot reach us in our little hideout. At least, for now.

"I must say, you gave us all quite a scare," Tori notes when he steps into the cave, guiding Kaira back inside by her elbow while the Flame clutches her stomach, softly cursing the effects of site-hopping. "When Herinor returned with Myron draped over his arms after the dungeon debacle, we didn't know if we'd ever see you again."

"Thank you, Tori," I mutter at him, voice dripping with sarcasm. But he isn't wrong. Despite knowing Ayna was alive, I didn't allow myself to believe I'd see her again, let alone so soon.

"You must be exhausted," Silas says, dark eyes gleaming in the glow of flames as he bows his head an inch at his queen before gesturing at the boulders we use as seats by the fire. "Come, sit with us. Tell us everything over a cup of stew."

"Stew you cooked and which tastes like an eel kissed the butt of a hog," Clio notes with a pointed look at the copper pot hanging above the fire.

She brought back a few basic utensils for survival after she and Tori regained their ability to site-hop and took off to warn King Recienne of Erina's plans. Much to my surprise, they hadn't stayed at Aceleau, leaving us Crows to our fate, but returned with blankets, pots, a stack of bundles filled with dried fruit and meat, clothes, and weapons.

It's mere coincidence they were both there when I felt the call of Ayna's magic in the mark on my shoulder. And thank the Guardians they care about my mate enough to have rushed right after me when I took off with an unintelligible sound followed by Ayna's name.

"I don't care what the stew tastes like as long as I don't smell like that." Ayna shoots Silas a grin, and the male bows again, so atypical for the harsh warrior I've gotten to know.

Her gaze bounces to Clio, who gestures past Tori and Kaira at the dense bushes. "Andraya and Pouly went to the pond to wash up." She reaches into the bundle filled with clothes to extract a long tunic big enough to fit any of the males in this cave. "This should work until your clothes are washed and dry."

"Thank you." Ayna is just reaching for the fabric as the woman and man return from their brief bath, Andraya's wet hair bound back in a dripping bun and her pants and shirt five sizes too big, but she wears them with pride while the man keeps tugging on the hem of his borrowed tunic as if he hasn't worn anything like it in all his life.

"Andraya and Pouly," I use the names Clio provided, and their eyes snap to me, slight distress tearing on their features as they stop in front of us. Royad steps to Ayna's shoulder while Silas stands at mine, the two Crows framing us like guards.

"King Myron." Andraya curtsies with her head held high, and I get the impression she is used to navigating court rooms more than adventurous flights through nightly forests. But the look in her eyes—I've seen that before in my own people when they were unhappy with my father's rule, or mine. She's a rebel through and through, as is the man who hasn't left her side, gaze flicking from wall to Crow, from Crow to fairy, and from fairy back to wall, scanning every inch of the cave for danger.

"Thank you for saving her." I give the two humans a long look, willing them to understand just how deep my gratitude runs. Ayna hasn't told us much before Clio site-hopped us here, but what she's shared is enough to know I should be bowing to them, not the other way around.

Andraya raises a brow. "We didn't save her for you. We did it for Tavras."

I incline my head anyway. "It doesn't matter why you saved her. She's here because of you, and I won't forget that." Motioning for them to sit by the fire and have something to eat, I guide Ayna toward the pond. "We'll talk about everything," I say over my shoulder to Andraya and Pouly, but it's also a warning for the others to not push me right now.

I've been barely holding myself together since I found Ayna in the midst of splintered wood, flaming silver like a star, and if I don't get some time alone with her before the rest of the world crashes down upon us, I'll knock out the pillars from under the skies myself, Shaelak be damned.

But Ayna isn't ready to walk away from her saviors. Before we exit the cave, she stops by Kaira, nodding at her as if in one of their silent conversations, and embraces the Flame. "Find out all you can, and share everything that happened. You don't need me or Myron to discuss these past cruel weeks."

Spoken like a queen, and much to my surprise, Kaira inclines her head. A half-sister to my mate. Family.

Ayna's hand curls around mine as she nods at Royad, Herinor, and Silas, then at Tori, and they all bow—Silas, Herinor, and Royad low, at their waist, and Tori a mere inch, but they all acknowledge her for what she is, and my heart sings with pride.

When she starts walking again, I am convinced the past weeks didn't break Ayna. If anything, they let a silent strength thrive inside of her that will become the death of our enemies.

And I will grin as she feasts on their blood.

TWELVE

AYNA

"*Be careful out there,*" Kaira warns me as Myron leads the way into the thicket along the outer wall of the rocks housing the cave.

"*I always am,*" I reassure her, smiling to myself about how many times I've bemoaned that I had no one who cared if I lived or died. That was then—at Fort Perenis. Now, I have a family. A sister, a mate, friends—"*You make sure not to antagonize Herinor too much while I'm gone. He's a sensitive little bird.*"

Her chuckle sounds in my mind as I imagine Herinor as a small, fragile crow. "*He's a bloodthirsty monster who'll eat the hearts of his enemies—and his friends if we're not careful.*"

When I don't respond, she adds, "*You know what he is, know his past. You experienced his ruthlessness first-hand.*"

"*But I also experienced his determination to do things right this time around,*" I remind her. He left me behind in the dungeon, but he saved Myron. He did what he could without outright breaking the deal he made with Ephegos. And he's still alive, so there must be some wiggle room.

I don't tell her all of that. If she isn't already aware, she'll probably pick it from my mind anyway.

She doesn't comment, or I'm out of reach for our mental communication.

"Just a little farther," Myron says, his gaze on the shades of dark emerald that is the forest surrounding us.

A little bit ahead, I can make out the gurgling of water twining with the lament of a nightbird. Nocturnal animals scurry through the undergrowth at our approach, and the wind carries the scent of fall and magic.

"How far north are we?" I glance at the patches of sky, the hints of pink kissing wispy clouds.

Dawn is about to break, and I'll need to face reality soon enough, but for now, I relish the blanket of fading night.

A moment later, Myron turns right, gently pulling me along until we stand at the edge of what is more a tiny lake than a pond. Steam rises from the surface, stirred into rippling waves by the cool breeze. Dense greenery blocks the scenery from view on three sides while, on one side, it collides with the slanted rock we've been following.

"The water is warmer than the air," Myron comments when he notices my shiver.

It's not because of the crisp temperature or the wind, though; his proximity radiates enough heat to warm us both. Now that we're alone, I'm acutely aware of his naked torso, the muscles flexing in his arm as he lets go of my hand to step closer to the pond. Suddenly, breathing becomes a challenge.

He's beautiful, from the raven waves on his head to his booted feet. My gaze follows the length of his spine, lined with cords of strength, to the expanse of his shoulders where, on one side, a frame of night-stark ink outlines the shape of a crow mid-flight. The intricate swirls expand to his bicep and curl up his neck, disappearing into his hair.

His shoulders rise and fall in a slow rhythm as he stares out at the water—and I stare at him, spellbound like I'm seeing him for the first time. Then he drops the bundle of fabric in his hand and shucks his boots, reaching for the waistband of his simple cotton pants at the same time. I hold my breath, ready to be caught staring as he exposes his backside fully. But Myron doesn't look at me as he strips out of his clothes and wades into the water until every last inch of his powerful legs has been swallowed up, and my gaze lands on his ass once more. When that disappears beneath the surface, too, I realize my dry mouth, my tied tongue, my shaky hands.

He turns around, running wet fingers through his hair in an attempt to tame the black mass. The hard grooves and edges of his chest and abdomen ripple with every move, drawing my eyes to glide along what's visible of his body. But it's the wicked grin on his lips that holds them captive as he gestures at my travel-worn, magic-assaulted dress.

"Take your time, Ayna."

My heart is a violent drum in my chest, my body a mess of shivers—and not the bad kind. Because this is my mate staring at me with depthless ocean eyes, inviting me to join him in the water.

We don't have time. Erina is probably already searching for me, and Ephegos's wrath will find us wherever we go, but for now, I don't care. I tune out every last bit of the world that doesn't belong in this moment where Myron's full focus is on me, and his lips part, sucking in a sharp breath as I raise my hand to the neckline of my dress and peel it off my right shoulder first, then shove it down over my left, until the already damaged fabric tears on the side and the whole thing comes sliding down my torso. It catches on my hips, and I wonder if I should let it linger, enjoy Myron's hungry gaze roving my chest, watching my nipples peak as if he'd just touched them with those capable hands of his.

The heat pooling between my legs advises me otherwise, though, and a moment later, I step out of the dress, dropping it in a bunched heap on the ground.

Myron's eyes burn with longing, his fingers absently stroking the surface of the water as if he's imagining touching me, and I'll give it to him, I can almost feel his phantom hands on me.

I don't think I've ever watched Myron as intensely as I'm watching him now: the way his eyes darken when they meet mine, the power in each gentle motion, the sheen of moisture he leaves behind on his lower lip as his tongue sweeps over it.

I'm exhausted, drained from using my magic, hungry from days of travel and weeks of not eating properly, but in this moment, I'm alive. I'm awake. And my entire body lights up under Myron's gaze.

"You are the most beautiful creature I've ever seen." His hands still, and so does the breeze caressing my skin. Like a bubble of safety, his magic wraps around us, gently brushing up against my arm, my waist.

My lids shutter at the overwhelming intensity of this single sensation, and I wonder if I'll combust when he puts his hands on me instead.

"Even with the dirt and grime of travel?" Stepping into the water, I give him a grin, and Guardians save me, he was right.

The water is perfect, a few degrees warmer than the air, almost like a hot spring. I can't hold back a groan as I wade deeper into the pond, allowing Myron's magic to guide me until I'm a few steps from him and the water reaches the edge of my ribs.

"Even covered in blood, you'd be a sight to behold." He moves closer, but his hands remain at his sides, just visible beneath the surface, not reluctant to touch me but idle, wait-ing for me to make the first move. The water reaches just below his hip bones now, barely covering his arousal.

Closing my eyes so I won't succumb to the tempta-tion just yet, I sink into the warm depths, rinsing off all traces of my captivity until my skin tingles and my lungs protest. When I come up, strands of hair cover my breasts, and the cool air raises goosebumps on my skin. The heat in my core is still there, though, and the longer we stand face to face, Myron a mere arm's length away, the harder the beating of my heart, the stronger the sensation in my shoulder right where the crow mark connects us, calling, calling, calling, until I can't stop myself and I close the distance separating us.

Nothing has ever felt so good as crashing against him like a wave, our bodies sliding around each other as he wraps his arms around my waist, lifting me while I lock my legs around his hips. He lowers himself into the water so we're covered up to the shoulders, and Guardians, his hands—

His hands slide down to grab my ass, lifting me into position so his cock is poised right at my entrance while his mouth roams my neck, my breasts, licking droplets of water off my skin.

"Gods, how I've missed you." With a groan, he sheathes himself inside of me, and I scream out with pleasure as he slams into me. I hold onto his neck with one arm, finding his mouth with mine, while the other hand wanders the planes of his chest, slides to his back, his neck, to knot in his hair.

Slowly, he pulls out again, allowing the water to come between us for a heartbeat, two.

"Please," I whisper between kisses.

"Please what, my queen?" He's breathless, tense, every last muscle in his body coiled tight as he withholds what we both need.

"Please fuck me into oblivion." The words are out before I can think, and I have the briefest of recollections of him using that exact same phrase once, on our wedding night. Only, then he'd asked me to pretend while today... Today, there is no pretending. There's only the raw force that is our need for each other.

His wicked tongue slides into my mouth, claiming me in a deep, desperate kiss, and he grabs my hips, walking us toward the wall of rocks at our side.

"Repeat that for me." He presses me up against the stone, one hand protecting my head while the other one holds onto my hip, and he pushes into me an inch, then another, teasing while I clench around whatever of him I can get. The blue of his eyes has turned near black, pupils blown out with desire, and his grasp on my flesh has turned near painful.

"Fuck me, Myron."

Like a leash, his self-control snaps, and he thrusts into me, hard and fast, setting my core aflame with pleasure and greed for more of him, always more.

I'll never get enough of this male, of the way his body fuses with mine in mind-blowing perfection. Every thrust drives me closer to a cliff, every slide of his tongue against mine claims my senses. I barely feel the rock biting into my back as I use it as leverage to take him even deeper, and Guardians, I don't care who hears me when I moan with every new thrust. Myron moves his hand from my hip to my swollen breasts, squeezing and stroking with expert fingers. When I think I can't take any more and I need to come then and there, he pinches my nipple ever so slightly, and the world explodes in a kaleidoscope of stars. Myron doesn't stop, though. And I don't want him to. His hand cradles my head, thumb caressing my neck, and he stops kissing me, eyes drinking in my face as I fall from one climax to the edge of the next.

His other hand slides between us while he slows his thrusts, drawing circles around my clit until all I can feel is the glorious desperation of wanting more of him.

I can't think anymore, can't even remember my name, shivers of pleasure rolling up and down my spine with each time he brushes up against me. He's the ocean, and I'm a ship tossed over his waves. He's the wind, and I'm the sail, catching onto him as together we gain speed.

"Come for me, Ayna," he whispers, and it's all there in those few words—all the feelings spoken and unspoken that might ruin us both forever.

My entire body is strung tight, chasing the bliss of the moment, and Myron is right there with me as I fall over the edge a second time. He's shaking, quivering inside me as he finds his release, and he buries his head against my neck, inhaling me like that's the only way he can breathe.

The last throes of my own release keep me locked to him until our hearts slow and the bubble of bliss slowly lifts from our steaming skin.

"What will we do?" I ask as he lowers me to my feet, one hand cradling my cheek as if he can't get himself to let go just yet.

Myron leans in for a slow, deep kiss, both his hands framing my face., then brushes his lips to my forehead. "It doesn't matter what we do, Ayna, as long as we do it together."

THIRTEEN

AYNA

The cave isn't a comfortable space to sleep in, but I get used to it fast. It doesn't matter where along the roughly hewn walls I lie down each night as long as it is next to Myron. We've spent the past few days catching our group up on the details of our separated journeys, the danger of Erina's new weapon, the feud between Myron and Ephegos, and Andraya and Pouly have given more details about the Tavrasian rebels.

Since the great slaughter of the Milevishja line by Erina's ancestors, the rebels have built up a network of spies and mercenaries willing to put the true Milevishja heir back on the throne. Naturally, this includes lots of secrecy. Secrecy of a sort that didn't allow for anyone to find me before my mother took me away to the edge of Tavras where I finally disappeared onto a ship and sailed away.

A glance at Myron, Silas, and Royad chatting by the fire tells me it might have been for the best they didn't, or I'd never have met the Crow King.

As if in response to my thought, my tattoo tingles, and on the other side of the fire, Myron reaches for his own shoulder, a smile on his lips.

"*Honestly, your head will explode if you keep thinking all the time,*" Kaira notes from where she's nibbling on a piece of bread. "*Mine will for sure.*" She raises a brow, which doesn't go unnoticed by Herinor, who's sitting a bit away from the other Crows, quietly talking to Astorian.

Clio left for Aceleau again, keeping her brother in the fairy capital up to date on everything that happens in this little cave. Andraya and Pouly are resting at the back of the space, curled up side by side, arms tucked under their heads. The two rebels insisted on taking the final watch of the night, and I didn't have it in me to refuse them despite the fairies, and even I, all being better equipped to detect disturbances than they are.

"We should go to Aceleau together," Royad notes loud enough for everyone with fairy senses to pick up, so my Crow hearing does, and I can't help but frown at my friend.

"You know we won't stand a chance against them if we don't get support, even if we find a few survivors in the Seeing Forest," Myron backs his cousin's approach. "If Erina truly found a way to produce the magic-nullifying drug faster, he has a weapon that will work against armies."

Myron shared their original plan to search for Crow survivors in the Seeing Forest first, but with Erina making such progress with his weapon, we have no time to lose.

"It's bad enough they extract the foundation for the drug from Flame blood," Kaira throws in, a shudder raking through her body. The fact that none of her injuries are visible any longer doesn't mean she didn't suffer and it didn't leave a mark.

"Fucking bastards." Herinor launches to his feet, pacing behind the fire like a caged animal. "I knew there was a deeper meaning to those meetings with Jeseida—"

"What meetings with Jeseida?" Both Myron and Royad whirl on him, menace in their eyes as they wait for Herinor to deliver a reason to kill him.

They don't fully trust him yet, despite his aid in freeing Myron and the others, and right they are. The male's allegiance is still bound to Ephegos by bargain, and if he isn't careful, he'll end up hurting us or killing himself defying Ephegos's orders.

Herinor stops, folding his thick arms over his chest. "The ones Ephegos took with the Flame Matrone near the end of my time at the palace in Meer?" He phrases it like a question. "You never asked if Ephegos had met with her, and I'm rather fond of my life, so it didn't occur to me to volunteer the information unless necessary."

Myron leaps at him so fast I barely see him move, arms shifting into wings and fingers into claws as he grabs Herinor by the throat and pins him against the cave wall. Neither Royad nor Silas interfere as Myron squeezes Herinor's windpipe so tight I believe he might crush it.

"We need to know everything if we want a chance to stay a step ahead of Erina. Do you understand me? *Everything.*" The last word comes out as a growl, deadly and full of command.

"Could you kill him later, Myron?" Astorian slinks toward them, ignoring how Kaira has shrunk against me in clear fear for the Crow fighting for air yet not lifting a finger to defend himself. "He's telling the truth."

"Because he cannot lie," Myron amends, glaring at the fairy general over his shoulder as he releases Herinor's throat, the male slumping against the wall, panting. "He's telling the truth because he's a Neredynian fae, and we cannot lie."

"Old news." Astorian holds out his hand to the Crow warrior, who promptly takes it, allowing himself to be pulled up. "Now, tell us everything, Herinor, or I swear to Eroth and his vengeful children, I will pick up right where my crowned Crow friend over there left off." I've seen Astorian smirk and grin and dole out mock threats these past few days, have heard stories from Clio of how he likes to do the same with her brother, but this is something entirely different. This is a real threat, one that makes my hair stand at the back of my neck. His lips are a thin line, eyes hard as the stone he can bend with his power, and the hold he has on Herinor's forearm is anything but comforting.

"*He'll kill him,*" Kaira whispers into my mind. "*He'll rip his head off.*"

"*Don't be so dramatic.*" I try to make it sound lighthearted, but my voice—even the one I use to speak into my sister's head—is too shaky. "*Herinor isn't stupid. He won't let it come to that. If he dies, it's because he breaches the bargain he made with Ephegos."*

"Like that makes it any better." Kaira hops to her feet, shoving up her sleeves and brushing back her braid. "Apparently, male communication issues are the same in any species." With a few strides, she's on the other side of the fire where Silas and Royad stand at Myron's flank as if to protect him from the part-Flame with little more than a spark of power. "Oh, get over yourselves." She shimmies between Silas and the wall, making her way to Herinor whose eyes grow bigger with each of her hasty steps.

Without regard for retaliation, she shoves against Astorian's shoulder, motioning for him to get out of the way as she grabs Herinor by the collar of his shirt.

Much to my surprise, Astorian yields, and Herinor doesn't move, nostrils flaring as Kaira raises to her toes and whispers, "What do you know about the production of the drug?"

While Herinor blinks, struggling to form words, in her mind, Kaira opens a channel I've experienced before—the night she kept the guards at the palace gate occupied so we could sneak in.

What I see isn't what I expected, though. Instead of all the wonders of how a fairy drug is made, a violent toss of emotions engulfs me. It's a push and pull of doubt and attraction, repulsion and desire. I'm a nutshell in the ocean that are Kaira's emotions until she manages to form a clear thought.

He smells like the flowers you lay down at the grave of a loved one.

The thought is so random—and startling—that I only realize she wasn't speaking to me but merely thinking.

"I don't know if that's a scent I'd be attracted to, but whatever works for you, sister." Barely able to hide my smugness at filtering into her thoughts, I get up and follow her around the fire, stopping a foot away from Myron, who struggles not to hop in front of me to block Herinor's path in case he should decide to attack me.

I almost laugh. He wasn't there to protect me in Meer, and he doesn't need to protect me now. I have my powers back and can protect myself.

My tattoo tingles as if in answer, and warmth streams down my spine like a stroke of Myron's fingers.

Kaira, however, stands ramrod still, whether from embarrassment that I heard that intimate thought or because she's fighting not to jump Herinor—or stab him—I don't care. I fold my arms over my chest and study the Crow warrior and the Flame as they stare each other down.

Just when I think the cave is going to crumble under the tension, flashes of thoughts fill my mind. The sense of Kaira's hand so close to Herinor's throat, the warmth of her fingers as they brush the skin right beneath his collarbone. Her scent… Salt and herbs and embers. I'm only beginning to realize I'm no longer in Kaira's mind but in Herinor's, and the channel she made is one extending into his thoughts, allowing me to read them as she does when the images shift, and I'm in a torchlit room.

Everlasting fire illuminates the space where I've been ordered by Ephegos to wait. It would make a good torture chamber. The table's already there, as is a rack of tools I could use to break my enemies. Instead of exploring the assortment of hammers and pliers and knives, I sit on the single chair at the side of the room, wondering if Myron has realized I abandoned him.

When Ephegos offered to become part of the rebellion, it was an easy choice. Myron hasn't done shit to break the curse in years. Marrying one pitiful female after the other doesn't count. Even if this year's bride seems to have more spirit than any other before. I wonder if she's ever realized the monster she married will be the death of her like he was of all the other brides before her...

The scenery changes, ripping me out of the familiar torture chamber where Herinor first cut me to alert Myron through the mate mark. The breath I suck in nearly chokes me as I'm thrown into another memory of Herinor's. This time, he isn't alone. A female with brown skin and chestnut hair fidgets where Ephegos is extracting blood from the vein in her forearm while Jeseida swirls a clear fluid in a glass vial.

"Just a few drops. That should be enough for a first test." The Flame Matrone smiles at Ephegos like a proud mother, and he seems to stand taller under her approval. Honestly, the familiarity between the two of them is sickening. I never would have joined him had Myron shown a flicker of promise. But he's given up on our people while Ephegos is forging a future for us.

"Ready?" Ephegos withdraws the needle and holds it over the vial, letting two thick drops of Flame blood drip into it. Crimson streaks spread like a spiderweb before the Matrone stirs it with a flick of her hand. Fire sizzles in her palm, engulfing the potion with heat and magic. I've seen her do that before when they tried Crow blood. But our blood doesn't work.

"What's so special about Flame blood that it blocks fairy powers?" Astorian asks out of the blue, drawing all eyes to him, including mine.

"You read minds, too?" I blurt out, earning a dip of Astorian's chin and a horrified gasp from Pouly and Andraya who have woken from the tumult.

Astorian reads minds. Of course, he does. He's the one Clio referred to all those weeks ago… *I know someone who does. It's an annoying power. If I ever see him again, I'll ask him to help you learn to control it.*

"Funny enough, I'm not surprised to have another mind-reader in the group," Myron says with death in his voice, and Astorian has the good sense to yield a step as Myron turns toward him.

"Nothing to worry about, Crow King." The fairy general shrugs with less of an apology in his tone than I would have expected when dropping news of such impact. "You have impeccable shields. All of you." He gestures at the Crow males, who all stand rigid like they are fighting not to rip Astorian's throat out. "Even the Flame and the Crow Queen are quite adept at it," he amends, giving me an intrigued glance that makes Myron growl a warning. "Your mind is a fortress. How you manage to lock me out is a mystery."

"We'll share everything we learned as soon as we're done here. But can we focus on the important stuff first?" Kaira interrupts, whirling back on Herinor, who flinches under her stare.

"*I don't know what makes it so special, but there's something about the ancient Flame blood that seems to counteract all other magic. Perhaps it's the gods' way of justice,"* Herinor answers Astorian's question in his mind, and I'm surprised nobody objects when we fall back into our silent interaction. I don't miss the taste of disappointment in Herinor's tone, though. He didn't know either.

Astorian inclines his head at the Crow and settles back on the boulder where he was sitting before everything started, and Myron, Royad, and Silas relax just enough to take the palpable tension out of the air as the male relays every last one of Herinor's thoughts to them.

Herinor, however, is back in the torture chamber, but this time, he's not a spectator. He's strung to the table, hands balled into fists and leather bindings cutting into his muscles as he strains against them. And I'm back in Herinor's head.

"I said I'd do it. You don't need to tie me up," I plead with Ephegos, *who injects the drug into my arm like I'm nothing more than an experiment. Perhaps I am.*

He knew my loyalty would be fickle since I have always believed in Myron's way. But after millennia of being trapped, I've become impatient. And so has Ephegos.

The pain as the needle pricks my skin is nothing compared to the agony when the drug rushes my blood. By Hel and Shaelak, and even Shygon and his cursed dragons, this is torture. If Ephegos manages to make this into a scalable weapon, I don't want to be on our enemies' side. Then the drug kicks in for real, and all strength leaves my body, limbs slacking as my magic is drained from me. I can't move—can barely breathe. My tongue slides back in my mouth, and I gurgle against my own spittle, fighting for air.

"*It's killing him,*" *Jeseida notes, jotting down a few numbers and letters on a piece of paper.* "*Maybe this is all a fool's attempt after all.*"

"*It's not.*" *Ephegos sounds convinced. Convinced enough to grab my head and turn it sideways so I don't suffocate. He does nothing though to make the pain stop. Doesn't try to heal me or relieve the agony chasing my blood in any other way. Gods, he could have simply knocked me out, saving me the torture.*

But he wants to know every last detail of what happens, watching me for hours, days, as the drug slowly recedes from my system.

I don't pass out. I'm too strong for that. Don't even sleep, the effects of the drug not allowing me to nod off from exhaustion.

"*We need to adjust the dosage, experiment to get rid of the side effects. It will be difficult to interrogate people if they are paralyzed,*" *Jeseida points out, earning a raised brow from Ephegos, who seems to delight in my suffering.*

"*Let's see if it's permanent first.*" *He stalks around the table, picking up a small, bone-hilted knife and setting it to my bare bicep.* "*Perhaps he's just pretending.*"

He rams the blade into my flesh without warning, and I barely manage a breath. A breath that should have been a scream, but my tongue isn't cooperating, and my limbs don't lash out at the Crow, no matter how I will them to.

I have no clue how long I'm down in the chamber by the time I can finally move my fingers, then my whole hands, my arms, and legs. My wound is still bleeding, my healing powers nullified by the drug as much as the rest of my magic. Ephegos leans over my shaking body and whispers, "*Go, get some rest. We'll start the next experiment tomorrow.*"

FOURTEEN

MYRON

Every time I glance at Tori, my mind boggles. It's no different now that I'm blocking his sword in the makeshift training ring we arranged to keep in shape. Fury emboldens my strikes, even knowing what the fairy general is capable of. Maybe that particular skill of his makes it all the easier for me to attack without relenting.

With any other opponent, I'd always hold back at least a little bit, not ready to see them bleed—Royad, Silas, and even Herinor. After all the stories he's shared about his time with Ephegos, how he'd been used over and over again to test the early versions of the drug. How he'd lost his ability to move and speak while Ephegos and Jeseida kept injecting him with new potions, prodding him with sharp tools to see how far they could push him.

And he'd traded his loyalty. To a traitor who made him a slave of pain.

My blade batters down on Tori's with such force the general staggers back.

"Good. Let it out, Myron. Holding it in will only harm you on the battlefield." Signature smirk in place, he balances his stance and readies to defend again.

Bastard. He should have told me about his mind reading. We could have used it as a weapon. I lower my shield to hurl that thought right at him alongside another strike of my blade.

Astorian takes it in stride. "It's a magical ability," he pants. "It's not like I could use it since we were all drugged."

"You used it before, I'm sure." I am. From the very beginning, Tori was reading me way too well, trusting me almost too easily. "Is my shield really that good?"

Tori tilts his head, pacing the length of the hedges behind which Silas is sparring with Pouly and Andraya. The two humans are surprisingly adept with weapons. Especially the southern Tavrasian lady who prides herself in leading a rebellion.

"It's perfect now."

"But it wasn't before?" I won't be satisfied until I know how much of my mind he's seen.

"You were still recovering from returning from the dead," he admits. "There *were* holes I could sneak through."

I run through the many conversations I've had with Tori, all the times he might have triggered more thoughts with his questions than I'd been willing to answer … then decide it doesn't matter.

"You should have told me anyway." I don't know why I'm disappointed or why I think he would have revealed such a weapon to an enemy. "At least, since we got out of the dungeon and didn't kill each other over any disagreement."

Tori flashes a smile. "Am I hearing the sweet sounds of friendship, King Myron?" His tone is mocking, but something tells me he's not.

"I wouldn't feel betrayed if I hadn't come to trust you, Astorian."

Instead of readying for a new strike, I place the point of my sword in front of me, closing my eyes and soaking up the autumn sun. The leaves rustle their melody, and in the distance, the pond lashes soft waves against its shore. Ayna's voice weaves into the background like a silver thread leading right to my heart.

"We were captured together, suffered together, almost died together." I don't need to go into details to recover all those memories that run like scars through our selves. "We are about to fight a war together, for fuck's sake."

Tori sheaths his own sword and marches up to me. "It doesn't matter. I've always kept it a secret. Only my closest circle knows. Clio, her brother, and his mate. And now you do, too."

"And Royad, Silas, Herinor—whom we still don't know how to fully trust—Ayna, Kaira, and the humans." I give him a pointed glare. "It's becoming a long list, Tori."

"Too long," he agrees. "But I'd really hate to kill any of our allies off. At least, for now." The joking tone is back, but he means what he says. He'd do it—end someone for knowing such a secret. I might do the same thing were it my ability.

"We can't afford to lose any of them." Not to mention that I'd personally see to making his own end long and painful if he as much as considered hurting Ayna.

"I know. We'll need all the forces we can get, human or magical, to win this war." The way he speaks about war when we haven't seen any armies makes me acutely aware that this isn't just Tori, the smirking male, but Astorian Remanier Alves DeLoor, the Fairy King's general and chief strategist. Nothing he does is without purpose, nothing he says, no matter how well packaged in laughs and teases, a wasted word. This male might be the smartest, most loyal one I've ever met—apart from Royad, of course. I should feel honored to call him a friend.

"I am honored to call you mine," Tori responds to my thoughts, and I realize I forgot to pull up my shield after lashing out at him. "It's all right," he adds. "It's nice to know you still consider me a friend after all the deception."

Pulling up my shield, I march a few paces closer to him, studying the dirt on his features, the sweat from the strain of an even-matched fight. I've been deceived too many times, burned by Ephegos then Herinor. I should know better than to trust anyone, yet Astorian is the one creature I want to forgive. With every horrible encounter in our past, the wars raging between our people for centuries and centuries, the way his king kept me trapped in a forest… It doesn't matter. He's proven loyal, not only to his own king but to his mate, to his word, and to all creatures of magic by being willing to fight Erina and Ephegos in their endeavor to take Askarea.

"I might try to stab you in your sleep in retaliation," I quip, earning a broad grin from the male. His hair is bound back, strands of auburn dancing in the breeze, and his eyes sparkle.

"I would expect nothing less, *my friend.*"

When we return to the cave, Kaira and Ayna are deep in conversation with Andraya and Pouly. Royad, Herinor, and Silas returned before us and are cleaning their weapons near the rebels. The sight of them huddled around the fire brings a foreign sense of family to my stomach.

Odd as it may seem to call so many different species a family, that's what they've become, each of them unique in the role they played in reuniting me with my mate. I owe them all, even if Royad will never hear it, Silas is too cynical to believe it, and Herinor… I don't owe him anything with his most recent show of side-handed loyalty. But Kaira, Pouly, and Andraya—them, I owe.

When she notices us, Ayna's head whips around, and she meets my gaze for a few short heartbeats, a smile spreading on her lips, and warmth originating in the mate mark runs through my entire body. No matter how much I appreciate my patched-together family, I'd rather have a moment alone with Ayna so I can thoroughly show her how much I've missed her since she slipped out of my arms this morning.

Tori rolls his eyes and stalks right over to the Flame and my Crow Queen, engaging them in conversation about mind reading. With everything he kept hiding from me, he's now doing his best to help the two of them with their abilities.

Of course, Ayna is still skeptical that she can read minds, too. She believes it's a projection from Kaira's mind to hers only, but mind readers come in different tastes and variations. Some can read only, some can project, some can do both, and some aren't even aware of what they're doing.

Perhaps her ability isn't one of picking words from people's minds, but she can sure as Hel's realm detect all the moods I'm going through. That, however, Silas has explained, is a mate thing with Crows. He's old enough to remember what a mated Crow is.

Though, all of this doesn't change that we can't stay in this hideout forever. Erina surely has noticed his intended queen's absence by now. I bet my non-existent kingdom on it he's already scouring his entire realm for her. We're close to the Askarean border, but not out of Tavras yet, which makes this place more vulnerable to discovery.

Wiping the sweat from training off my brow, I settle next to the group, back against the cave wall, and allow Royad to pick my sword from my hand to clean it.

"We need to make a decision." Trying not to flinch as all eyes turn to me like I just announced the end of the world, I bring up the topic we've all been dancing around. "Erina and

Ephegos both won't rest until they find her, and the gods know what they'll do next."

Ayna's throat bobs as I meet her gaze. She knows I'm right. They all do, but we haven't made a choice about how to proceed.

"Clio alerting King Recienne was the first step, but will he be ready to fight?" My eyes wander to Tori, who's straightened into the posture of the general, features tight as if calculating all possible moves and their outcome. "Will he help us?"

"He won't doubt you, and that's not just because you strange creatures can't lie." On instinct, my magic races out to pin the female with copper hair who just popped up out of thin air to the spot where she stands. Ice crackles in the air, sneaking along the invisible thread binding her. Instantly, Tori is by her side, hand raised in reflex to protect his mate when Cliophera doesn't need anyone's help. Royad and Silas are on their feet, blades raised and magic at the ready.

But Clio merely rolls her eyes, continuing where she left off. "It's because *I* told him the whole story, and he believes his *sister*. So, get your shit together, Crow King, and reel your power back in before you hurt yourself."

Before I can snap a harsh comment at her, Ayna is darting toward the female, shoving Tori aside as she throws her arms around the princess. A laugh bubbles from her throat, and Clio smirks at me over Ayna's shoulder the way she used to when she showed up at the Crow Palace in the Seeing Forest to disrupt my assemblies. "Unfortunately, Ayna seems to be the only one who remembers how to welcome me back."

She untangles from the embrace, winding an arm around Ayna's shoulder and grabbing Tori's hand with the other, pouting at the male. "I thought at least you'd remember."

The shocked expression on Astorian's face reminds me he never truly told me much about his relationship with Clio. I know she's his mate; they both know about it and seem ready to destroy the world for each other. But I have never seen them kiss.

I don't know if I let the thought slip through my shield or if I actively throw it at Tori the way I did during sparring, but the male flashes me a glance full of torment and hope, of hesitation and a lifetime of determination that tells me he heard it anyway.

"*What the fuck are you waiting for?*" I say in my mind, and I could swear the grin is back on his mouth as he crashes it down on Clio's like a starved male.

Clio's surprised gasp is smothered by Tori's snicker as he pulls away then leans in to whisper something into Clio's ear.

Ayna clears her throat, forgotten by both fairies, making them jump.

"Good, now that we have your attention, shall we continue?" Clio drawls, meeting everyone's eyes as if we can't hear her heart race in her chest. "Recienne wants you to visit his court. All of you."

FIFTEEN

AYNA

We're packed and ready by the end of the day, but Clio and Astorian don't take us to Aceleau until the next morning. Herinor and Silas grab the bundles with the cooking utensils while Pouly and Andraya each pick up a bag of clothes. Clio and Tori take turns site-hopping us out of the cave, leaving Myron and me for last.

In the circle of rocks at the center of the cave, the fire has burned down, the scent of smoke fading as Myron stirs the air with his magic.

"We'll be fine," Myron whispers, pressing a kiss to my forehead.

My arms latch around his waist on instinct, the rush of his presence so new, yet familiar, and I rest my cheek against his shoulder. "I hate when people say that. It makes me anticipate the worst possible outcome."

The chuckle rumbling through his chest is halfhearted. "What would be the worst possible outcome?"

Instead of the hundreds of horrifying scenarios involving him captured, tortured, mangled, or dead while I need to live on, I kiss the sliver of skin showing beneath the loosely tied collar of his shirt. The shiver running through his body eases my fear, turning it into something warmer, more docile. With a deep inhale, I allow his scent to fill my heightened senses and focus on the way my shoulder tingles under the feathers of the inked bird.

"We'll be fine," he repeats. "As long as we're together."

I have no objections. All I want is him—day and night, alone for myself. I'm greedy and needy and entirely out of control when it comes to this male, but the look in his eyes when I enter a room and he finds me, the way he seems to light up and gravitate toward me, it's enough to know he feels the same.

"As long as we're together," I echo.

Myron seals what sounded a lot like a promise with a fervent kiss, tongue colliding with mine in a dance I should have gotten used to by now yet can't seem to ever get enough of. His hands roam my back, wandering up to curl into my hair, almost undoing my braid as he kisses me deeper. Heat pools in my core like it's been waiting just for a touch of him to be released, and I lower my hands to his waist, ready to slide my fingers over the front of his pants where hard arousal strains against my stomach.

"Save it for later, younglings," Tori calls from the cave mouth. "The King of Askarea awaits your presence at court."

Myron groans his frustration while I untangle from him with more reluctance than a mere kiss warrants.

It's never a *mere* kiss with him. It's the universe and the stars that populate the night skies. It's silk and velvet and hot, molten ore. It's diamond and steel and anything and everything that could destroy me, yet never will, because his strength will only break my enemies.

Ignoring Myron's growl of warning, Astorian saunters over, holding out both hands in invitation while his handsome face features a bored expression. "Ready?"

Smooth, glimmering rock is the first thing I see as we hit solid ground after being torn through the folds of the world. My stomach churns, and my head spins, making dots of light dance in my vision like little suns. At a sound of nausea escaping my throat, Astorian elegantly drops my hand and steps aside.

Myron is there in an instant, his arm around my waist, even when I seem to be more stable on my feet than him.

"I just need a moment to breathe," I say to no one in particular.

Then, I don't have any idea who else is witnessing my moment of weakness. Scents of flowers and foreign spices mingle with the familiar ones of Myron and Astorian. Footsteps echo in the distance, approaching faster than my ability to stand upright, and just when I think I need to expel my breakfast at Myron's feet, Clio's laugh joins Myron's words of comfort and Astorian's ones of mocking.

"Guardians, Ayna, one would think you'd have gotten used to all the magic features our lifestyle provides," she chimes, voice unnaturally loud as it bounces between walls of too-colorful rock. "You look like you need a hug." Unceremoniously, she pulls me into her arms and squeezes until my breath gets lodged in my throat, and I cough.

"Too much?" She lets go only to pull Myron into her arms next. "You look like you need one just as much."

Myron's half-growl, half-hiss of surprise draws a laugh from Astorian, who has sauntered to the tall doorway a few strides ahead from where he watches the Crow King's struggle not to attack Clio out of instinct.

At least, I'm distracted from my nausea long enough to take in the enormous entrance hall of what has to be the Fairy Palace in Aceleau.

"Welcome to my home." Releasing Myron, Clio joins Astorian with a few swaggering paces, her long, copper dress flowing around her legs like molten ore. It matches Astorian's ability to liquefy rock, the image so vivid that, when he slides his hand around her waist, I wonder if he could solidify her into a statue of metal and stone at will. Not that he ever would. Nothing the male has done has ever made me believe he'd harm a shiny hair on her head.

As if reading my thoughts, he tilts his own head, fixing me with his auburn gaze. "Interesting idea, but not practically possible." A smirk graces his features as he turns to Clio and kisses the question of what he's talking about off her lips.

"Where are the others?" It takes me a moment to realize Myron and I are the only ones from our group of misfits in this room.

"They are in the throne room." Astorian gestures toward the room behind him, and I glimpse a large space lined with glimmering walls and columns. Unlike at Erina's court, this palace seems to be only sparsely populated. The absence of guards along the tall hallways tells me Recienne isn't afraid of attackers or that prisoners might sneak out of his palace, and the lack of courtiers gives the place a refreshing aura of peace after so many weeks of being put on display whenever I wasn't locked up in my room.

The air tastes of something floral I've never smelled, and the faint scent of magic lingers like the dew on a late summer morning. It's a unique blend I would find delightful were my stomach not tight with worry over what's awaiting us on the other side of the threshold.

"Come on in." His voice carries in like midnight velvet on a phantom wind, and my hair stands on my neck.

This is the voice of centuries of enmity wrapped in deadly charm. The Fairy King.

Myron's hand wraps around mine as if ready to pull me out of harm's way should this be a trap, but he follows as Clio and Astorian lead the way into the sun-flooded space.

I don't know what I expected, but not the simple stone throne on a dais at the far end of the room. Beams of light dance along the glimmering columns, multiplying into millions of stars. To the left, grand balcony doors stand wide open, allowing a view of the gardens beyond the palace. I have a faint memory of stepping into Erina's throne room for the first time, the balcony there, and the summer gardens below the windows.

This, however, is different. Hedges frame walkways lined with spreads of wildflowers and vines. Gravel paths curve in seemingly random patterns toward a stone fountain at the center of the garden, and I could swear I see deer stalking near the edge of the park where it melts into wild brambles.

Someone nudges me forward, my feet reluctantly moving toward the dais while my eyes seem spellbound by the tamed wilderness beyond the balcony.

"Everything will be fine," Myron whispers, the thumb of one hand brushing the bottom of my ribs while his other hand hangs casually by his side, within reach of his sword. The tension coiling through his body is infectious, commanding my limbs to ready themselves to fight or run or both. In my veins, my power rises, ready to be drawn upon if necessary. I battle it back into a low simmer. No matter how painful the history between Myron's and Recienne's people, we haven't come here for old grudges or revenge. We are here for an alliance that could save all of Eherea.

Tearing my gaze away from the greenery, I force myself to take in the male on the throne—the male who caused Myron so much pain.

I don't realize how much resentment I hold for the Fairy King until I meet his golden gaze when we stop a few feet from the dais and he pulls his full mouth into a quirked line.

"Welcome to Aceleau, Wolayna." On his forehead, dark strands of hair shift like on a breeze, shimmering with colors reflected from the walls in all hues of the rainbow. For a brief moment, I wonder if my human eyes would have noticed; then I decide it doesn't matter. I'm this half-Crow creature now, and I'll take whatever my senses give me. "And Myron…"

Recienne pauses, leaning his chin into his hand, elbow braced on the armrest of his throne. His cream shirt wrinkles under his black velvet jacket, gold buttons shimmering like little suns. But it's not the attire that makes him so spellbinding. It's his eyes.

Solid gold set in a beautiful, tan face.

"Fairy King." Myron is shaking as he forces his head to incline at the monarch who trapped him in a forest for centuries, and waves of hatred roll off of him like the waters of the Quiet Sea break against the Cliffs of Ansoli.

On his throne, King Recienne of Askarea seems to not have a care in the world. "You brought your bride."

His eyes move back to me, sliding down my form like snakes over marble, and I could swear his smirk turns into one of delight.

Trying not to seethe at him, I take Myron's hand, holding on, both to keep him from snapping and doing something he'll regret and to keep myself from screaming my rage at the monarch who kept my mate from finding his freedom.

"*I hate him,*" I chant in my head. "*I hate him. I hate him. I hate him.*" Because I do.

It's only then that I notice the others by the wall across from the balcony where Kaira is nodding her agreement while, in her head, she calls the Fairy King all sorts of names even I am reluctant to repeat, pirate and all.

"I bring my *wife* everywhere," Myron growls, tension coiling even tighter if that's possible. Why he doesn't call me his mate in front of the Fairy King must remain a mystery. Perhaps he doesn't want to give King Recienne more leverage than absolutely necessary. Their history surely suggests any kernel of power he hands the fairy male is a bad idea.

"Even to the battlefield?" Recienne's question hangs in the air, sucking the calm out of even Astorian and Clio who, until now, have kept a serene confidence in this meeting.

On the side of the room, Royad and Silas have their hands on their blades, ready to draw them at the slightest misstep of the king on his carved throne, while Herinor's fingers flash with a bright sort of power reminding me of what I failed to contain in the carriage.

Myron seems the only one capable of putting on an unreadable face, no matter how ready to kill he is. "*Is* this a battlefield, Recienne?" Omitting his title might have rattled Erina or any other monarch in Eherea, but not the Fairy King who managed to contain a whole people in a forest. Recienne is dangerous and calculating. A master of pulling strings on his enemies. No matter how I've come to like Astorian and Clio, I don't trust this male.

"*Neither do I,*" Kaira agrees in her mind, showing me a flicker of fire as if wanting me to know she's ready to burn him at any misstep, no matter how tiny.

Recienne's chuckle is sunshine laced with darkness. "This, I've been told by my general and the sister who's run off to rescue him, is not a gathering of enmity but one to forge unlikely bonds."

I can't figure out whether that's real humor in his voice or a facade he's spent centuries building. All I see is a beautiful deadliness inferior only to Myron's. A shudder rakes along my spine as the Crow King adjusts his stance and his arm brushes my shoulder where the tattoo tingles with anticipation of an eruption of his power.

His voice rumbles through me as if he's speaking from within me, our connection stronger than ever in the face of this potential explosion. "Unlikely indeed."

SIXTEEN

AYNA

S urprisingly, it's the Fairy King's general stepping in to save Myron from himself and remind both kings of the purpose of this meeting. "Keep it together, Myron. You no longer hunt for brides nor demand for any. The bargain is moot. Recienne is no longer your enemy." He turns to Recienne as if to prove a point. "And you, your Majesty, should remember Myron is not his father."

Cold calculation infuses every word as Astorian fills his role as Askarean courtier and strategist while Clio scans the Crows, the Flame, and the rebels by the wall like a guard ready to step in should our entourage decide now is the time to let one of their blades fly.

"You're right. King Myron is not Carius, and this audience isn't about the past." Recienne's words surprise me. I wouldn't have taken the Fairy King for someone who agrees with anyone—unless it suits him.

His face changes to smooth, beautiful, yet unreadable, all colors of the rainbow dancing over him as he stands from his throne, gesturing to the door we came through. "Take them to the guest quarters. I'm sure they'd like to freshen up before we discuss the situation over a glass of wine and a proper meal."

Eyes skipping over Myron and me to study Royad, Silas, and Herinor, the Fairy King strolls down the stairs toward the side of the room. "Whatever you think, your blades won't be of any use should you decide to attack. You'll need to use your magic, and that won't be of much use either, now that I know your names."

He disappears before he reaches the inconspicuous side door near the group, and we all stare wide-eyed at the spot that hosted the Fairy King a moment ago.

"What does he mean by that?" Andraya demands, a bit shaky on her feet in the wake of who they call the most powerful fairy in all of Askarea.

Astorian smooths back his auburn hair, glancing at Clio as if for help. The mask of the general has fallen away, a hint of concern leaking through instead. "He means name control."

"Name what?" Pouly blurts while a million thoughts are rolling from Kaira's mind to mine.

"Askarean high fae can execute control over a person through their name. It's one of the things lower fairies fear most. But

CLAWS OF DEATH

we're not lower fairies, are we? Herinor is a Crow, whatever that means for controlling him through his name. I have no idea if Crows can be controlled at all. They aren't Eherean creatures after all, so different rules might apply to them. Or they might be strong enough to block it. But Ayna... She's not a Crow. Not really. She can shift and all, but what does that make her? And I'm only part-Flame. I've never needed to shield against name control, but it's possible I'm no better off than Andraya and Pouly. At least I'd have felt it if a fairy had tried to control me through my name. Clio and Tori seem to be of the kind who don't resort to such terrible measures. At least, not with us."

She's definitely not intentionally projecting her thoughts, which means I'm reading them as they leak from her mind. What that means, I don't have the capacity to analyze right now since Clio is gesturing for us to follow her back to the hallway, and we march after her like a band of misfits in a cage of jewels.

"Name control," Clio repeats. "Fairies pulling on creatures' strings like on puppets. It's one of the most powerful forms of magic, and I wouldn't wish it upon anyone." She waits for us to start moving, ready to herd us out the door. "Now, let's get you all freshened up before we dive back into discussions that don't do well on an empty stomach."

We leave the throne room, following Clio down a long corridor, up a set of polished, sparkling stairs, and past carved columns that remind me of Myron's residence in the seeing forest. Gods, I miss the times when my only worry was whether or not my questions made the Crow King bleed.

As if summoned by my thought, Myron's gaze snaps to mine, his arm winding around my waist as we trudge af-

135

ter the Fairy Princess with more noise than an army of fairies would ever make. There is no point trying to be stealthy when the King of Askarea already knows we're here.

"Down there. Last door on the left." Clio gestures at the set of doors lining the hallway we turn into at the top of the stairs. The air tastes of hay and butter croissants, both smells of summer that seem to roam this part of the fairy realm later than even the Plithian Plains.

Andraya and Pouly obediently head in the direction Clio indicates while Silas and Royad make no move to leave our sides, both ready for battle even when they trust Cliophera DePauvre. We're in enemy territory of a different sort. While in the wilds of the forests, the Crows' history with the fairies has long stopped conjuring feelings of animosity and distrust, being here in the fairy palace makes my hair stand on the Crows' behalf. If someone had trapped me in a forest for centuries, I don't know if I'd ever speak to them again with anything other than my blade.

"*We need allies,*" Kaira reminds me through our mental connection as she stops a step behind us alongside Herinor. "*Twenty Crows and a part-Flame aren't enough to take on a traitor Crow, the king of Tavras, and his army.*"

It goes unsaid that we need to be smart about trusting the rebels. Even with Andraya and Pouly so fiercely on our side, they have different motives from ours. The rebels want to see a Milevishja on the throne while I…

I simply want Ephegos and Erina to pay for what they did to us. If I'll ever take up the Tavrasian throne remains a whisper between stars.

"There is enough space in there for all of you," Clio informs us. "Fresh clothes will be provided. I'll have something sent up for you." Clio studies Myron, then me, a frown on her face, and shoves her hands into her pockets. "The Queen of Askarea is roughly the same size as you, Ayna." Her gaze grazes my comparatively tall frame— "Roughly"—and a smile tugs on her lips. "I'll see you in an hour. Don't go exploring on your own. Recienne doesn't take kindly to busybodies, and we all know that's what you all are."

Her grin does little to appease the fear gathering in my stomach. She's still our friend, isn't she? We haven't just walked into a trap.

It's what I tell myself as I follow Silas into the luxurious suite the fairies provided for us, silently wondering if Astorian didn't join us for a reason. Is he already discussing strategies with his king? Did I trust the wrong person again?

I remember it doesn't matter whom I trust because, eventually, it doesn't matter if they consider themselves our friends as long as they consider themselves our allies.

"Ayna," Clio calls as I step over the threshold.

Myron stops with me, shoving his shoulder between Clio and me in what seems to be a subconscious gesture rather than a proactive attempt at protection. With a hand touching his bicep, I push him aside, clearing my view on the Fairy Princess.

Her eyes sparkle all shades of jade as she throws me a look that might have inspired fear, had I not seen it a hundred times on her during our time at the Crow Palace.

"Clio?" Forcing myself not to fidget under the stare of all of our party, I hold her gaze, willing calm into Myron's veins so he won't make a mistake.

"After your king and mine figure out how to not kill each other in an alliance, you and I will work on your magic." Her words are as surprising as they are shocking.

It's no secret there is enough tension filling the halls to slice open anyone's throat, but Clio jumps in, addressing, for the first time since I got my powers back, the subject of actually helping me.

My shoulders sag with relief, and for a heartbeat, I could swear Myron smiles, but when I turn toward him, his expression is as sour as when we left Recienne's throne room.

I don't respond before disappearing into the room, but in my heart, I know she's the right person to help me unlock the depths of my powers—even when my magic seems to be that of Crows now rather than the fickle water-wielding Vala gifted me. I still need to rediscover that liquid spark inside of me.

The Crows and Kaira follow me into the suite where Andraya and Pouly are standing by a set of silver brocade sofas and armchairs reminding me of metal rather than comfortable furniture. The main room is big enough for us all to scatter while, along the fir green and cream walls, a few sets of dark wooden doors lead to individual bedrooms.

"You need to control your temper, or we'll lose the willingness of the only fairy out there who can actually make a difference in this war." Royad has his opinion ready, dishing it to Myron in front of everyone.

Andraya sucks in a breath as if readying herself for a blow of magic to rush the room while Pouly grabs for his sword like the guard he is.

"I didn't see you playing the diplomat," Silas points out at the Crow King's cousin without batting an eyelash. "And frankly, he doesn't deserve diplomacy after everything he did to us."

"None of them do," Herinor interjects, "yet here we stand in the royal residence of the very king who decided we weren't worthy of our own freedom."

He isn't wrong. Then, we all agreed there is no way around this visit and that we trust Astorian and Clio enough to facilitate discussions. The friendship I've found with Clio and Kaira isn't the same as the cool respect the Crows hold for her, but when I watch them interact with Astorian, it's clear the males share a bond just as strong, knit together through their time in the dungeon. Herinor seems to be the only outsider in the group.

"And everything we did to him." Myron stalks to the chair closest to the wide, silver-curtain-framed window and drops into it, eyes on the greenery behind the window. It's a familiar sight even when we're one level up from the throne room. "Never forget what my father did to earn Recienne's hatred, yet he is ready to talk alliances." He props his head up in his hand, elbow braced on the armrest. A phantom wind moves loose strands of his hair, making them dance across his creased forehead. "Don't forget that Clio was once held captive by Carius the Cruel. Yet, she forgave us. Tori forgave us."

I don't need to meet his gaze to read that he'd never forgive a people who took me away from him.

By the time the clothes pop up on the coffee table we've all gathered around, the discussion has ebbed, and we've all retreated into our own thoughts. Even Kaira hasn't spoken to me through our minds, and I've been focused on every tiny shift in Myron's mood.

After the Crows all added their opinions to the pile, Pouly and Andraya seemed ready to bolt from the raw amount of power filling the room. Kaira kept watching in silence, only nodding on occasion and avoiding Herinor's burning stare whenever she agreed with Royad or Silas.

In the end, it doesn't matter what any of us think if Myron can't hold his temper together. I have hopes, though. He wants Erina and Ephegos defeated as much as I do, so he won't risk an alliance, no matter the hatred and history between the Crows and the King of Askarea.

Herinor is already digging through the stacks of fabrics for something remotely like armor, grunting his disapproval when he comes up empty-handed. Pouly has opted for a pair of black pants and a deep purple linen shirt entirely too big for his human frame, but it's better than the fairy-sized black tunics loosely covering Royad's and Silas's muscled torsos when they reappear in the main room after washing up in the spacious bathing chamber.

Royad's eyes sparkle like sapphires in the sunset light, and Silas stares at Myron with onyx and impatience as he studies my still-unchanged attire.

"Isn't it time for you to get ready?" He clears his throat. "Your Majesty."

Myron crooks a brow at him. "You don't really want to start calling me *Your Majesty* now, do you, Silas?" He stands from where we are sitting side by side on the settee by the cream and fir wall then holds out his hand for me. "I was waiting for my queen to be ready to join me."

All he does is wink at me as my heart launches into a tailspin, my tattoo tingling and heating as if he's touching it. "Ready?"

Bobbing my head, I let him guide me to my feet and follow him to the bathing chamber, grabbing the only bundle of female clothes left while Andraya and Kaira are changing in two of the adjacent bedrooms.

I'm not remotely ready to step in front of the Fairy King once more, but losing my dirty clothes sounds like an appealing idea. Especially with Myron there to help me out of them.

The bathing chamber is large enough to host all of our travel party, but when Myron shuts the door behind us, leaning against the wall beside it, it's like we're alone in this palace, this realm, this world. His ocean eyes gobble up the sight of me in my faded tunic and pants, my braided hair, the heap of fabric in my hands, and he leans a shoulder against the marble-tiled wall beside the door, folding his arms across his chest.

"I have no intention of letting you put on those clothes once I've peeled you out of these." Like a gust of ocean wind, his gaze grazes the front of my tunic where the fabric pulls in at my waist. Heat rises in my belly, spreading like a spring tide, and I take a deep breath, breasts turning heavy under his stare. It's been a few days since we last took a moment together to simply enjoy each other's presence, and his former enemy's bathing room is definitely not the place my mind should ponder all the various ways he could bend me over the bathtub edge and take me, or how his weight would feel on top of me if he pinned me against the fir and cream patterns adorning the tiles beneath our feet. I'm not even looking at the chair in the corner, wide enough for him to sit and accommodate my knees if I straddle him—

"Whatever you're thinking, I want it all." Myron pushes away from the wall to follow me to the center of the room, sunlight reflecting in the mirror to our sides and painting lines of gold and fire on his features.

Myron's fingers brush mine as he takes the clothes from my hands, his gaze never leaving mine, and drops them on the floor in a heap of midnight blue and silver.

"We should get ready." My voice trembles as I try to convince myself I can ignore the desire flickering to life inside of me.

Myron cocks his head, fingers tracing the neckline of my tunic, leaving a trail of goosebumps on my skin. "*You* should get ready, Ayna."

"For what?"

I don't get another warning as he grabs my hips and shoves me toward the chair, thumbs hooking into the waistband of my pants and tugging to my calves as he sits me down. I suppress a yelp as my bare ass lands on the green velvet cushion, and Myron lifts my arms above my head, pinning them to the high, carved backrest while his mouth crashes down on mine.

"Don't move," he orders me as he lets go of my wrists, and I hold still, eager for more of his kisses.

The next time his lips touch my skin it's not my mouth, though. With expert fingers, Myron tugs my shirt over my head, dropping it beside the chair as his breath flashes over my breast. I moan my approval as his tongue flicks my nipple then circles around it, teasing.

A part of me remembers that we will be summoned to meet with Recienne again soon, but I no longer care when Myron kneels down in front of me, hands roaming my sides, down my hips, to the inside of my thighs. Each touch leaves a trail of fire, each breath coming harder than the last. My heart beats out of my chest, heat pooling in my core as Myron pushes my knees wide and his gaze snags on my center.

A wicked smirk curls his lips, and before I can remind him there are six people next door who could overhear us if he makes me scream, Myron lowers his head between my legs and licks straight through my core.

My hands snap to his hair, fingers digging into the black waves like I'm a drowning woman and he's my anchor, and his chuckle dances along my wet flesh like an overture to the pressure of his tongue following a heartbeat later.

This time, I squeal, thighs shaking in his grasp and pleasure coiling tight inside my belly.

"You're fucking beautiful, Ayna," he hums, lips brushing my folds in idle kisses. "And you taste like a Shaelak-given miracle."

I want to touch him, want him inside of me when I come. But when I tug on his shoulders, urging him to fill me with his hard length, he shakes his head.

"Fuck me, Myron."

My plea drives a shudder through his body, but Myron merely lets go of one knee to guide a finger to my entrance. It's not what I wanted, but I don't complain when he adds a second finger and slides them in, pumping slow and hard in time with my quivering muscles while he keeps licking and sucking.

The room brightens in a streak of silver light a moment before I splinter with ecstasy, and a part of me wonders if that was him or me or if we are being attacked, but Myron's relentless tongue pushes me farther over the edge until I forget I exist at all, and his touch is the only thing I live for.

SEVENTEEN

AYNA

When Clio picks us up half an hour later, my body is still tingling with lingering pleasure, and the cocky grin on Myron's face makes me wonder if this is the same brooding male I met all those months ago. It's a good look on him, though, seeing him with something other than worry or anger defining his features.

I loop my arm through his, savoring the closeness while simultaneously wondering when I'll get to return the favor and sit him down in that exact same chair to—

"*Don't want to hear it,*" Kaira interrupts my thought before I can get to the interesting part of how exactly I want to—

"*Really, don't want to hear it, Ayna,*" she repeats, flashing me a glance that is as unreadable as the ones she's been shooting Herinor since he put on those fancy fairy clothes Recienne's court provided.

"*I wasn't aware I was leaking thoughts,*" I respond in my mind, wondering when exactly the training Astorian has been giving us will kick in. He hasn't taught us much apart from how to cut off mental intrusion by forming a shield around the mind the way we would around our bodies, but I never learned how to physically shield, unlike Kaira, who seems to have a naturally built-in wall when it comes to her thoughts.

Perhaps training with Clio will help me master both sorts of protection.

"*You were practically screaming your romantic plans at me,*" she retorts, and part of me is glad Astorian isn't around to witness what my head can't stop thinking about. Myron's cock in my—"*For fuck's sake, Ayna. Stop it.*"

An involuntary giggle escapes my mouth, earning me confused glances from the Crow males and our human companions.

"*Just because you haven't had fun with the Crow warrior of your choice doesn't mean my thoughts about my* mate *need to be chaste.*"

That gives her pause for a moment, but a hint of something shimmers through our connection that gives me an idea of how little chastity her own mind knows when it comes to Herinor. She slams down her shield so fast I don't get to see if those are memories or daydreams, and almost bumps into the male walking in front of us.

Herinor stops in his tracks, hand on the hilt of his sword, spinning around so fast he ends up at a foot's distance from the Flame, and I try not to chuckle at both of their surprised faces as Herinor realizes no one is attacking him, and Kaira scrambles to get out of his proximity.

"*Still haven't made up your mind if you want him?*" I tease, keeping my face straight after all, but Kaira steps around the Crow, joining Clio at the front of the group, asking questions about the glimmering stone the palace is made of instead of deigning to respond to me.

I turn my attention back to Herinor just in time to catch him exchanging a glance of exasperation with Silas, who is shaking his head at him.

Whatever is going on between Kaira and him, they better figure it out.

"Recienne is waiting for us in the dining hall," Clio informs us, leading the way past the throne room to a set of carved, wooden double doors framed by a pair of fairies in black leathers. Whether they are palace guards, military, or the king's personal guards, I can't tell. "I spent the time you took to get ready to remind him of why we're all here and that old grievances have no place in this gathering." Her gaze lands on Royad, moving from Crow to Crow until it ends up on Myron as we stop right by the door. "We are no longer enemies. You all would do well to remember, too."

She's my friend. Of course, she isn't *my* enemy, but I can see the tightness in the Crows' shoulders as they nod one by one, Myron the last of the group to add his agreement.

"We have a past that makes alliances difficult, yet I've come to call you my friend." Astorian appears from the side corridor, clothed in black finery that makes him appear every bit the courtier even with his warrior's body. There's the look again—the same one they exchanged when we saved the male from his cell in Erina's dungeon.

Find one, find both, Myron said to Astorian then. This time, the conversation is wordless as Myron nods at him like they've been to Eroth's Veil and back together.

Astorian returns the nod, a faint smile on his lips. "Just remember that when you speak with Recienne tonight."

Without another explanation, he opens the door with one hand, taking Clio's with the other, and together they lead the way into a marble-tiled room with a long oak table large enough to host twenty or more guests. The skirts and long, wide sleeves of Clio's jade chiffon dress billow like on a phantom wind as the two fairies make their way down to the head of the table where King Recienne is lounging in the largest chair, surveying the room.

His gold eyes scan our party with a flicker of amusement, snagging on the two humans and lingering there for a while as he takes in Andraya's older features.

"Please, sit." With a wide gesture of his arm, he invites us to join him, and a part of me recognizes the danger he poses, even when so expertly hidden behind a nonchalant veneer. This is the king who kept the Crows in check, won a war against them, locked them up in a forest—

I stop myself right there at a stern glance from Astorian. Whether he heard my thoughts or not, he sees right through me.

"How about Myron and you take the chairs next to the King," he suggests, motioning for us to join them at the head of the table where he and Clio are sitting down to Recienne's right, leaving the two chairs to the Fairy King's left free for us.

The reluctance in Myron's steps is obvious as I slide my hand into his, guiding him to our intended seats. Right by the end of the table, I stop, dipping my head an inch to demonstrate I have manners, then reach for the backrest of the chair closest to King Recienne to play buffer between the two kings in case they can't behave themselves.

Before I can touch the hardwood, Myron's hands are there, pulling the chair out for me, and I slide into it, guided by his invisible power caressing my back and circling around my waist. A shiver spiderwalks up my spine at the gentle sweep of magic, and I want to lean into him. It's the most encouragement I'll get from him that he's on board with the situation and will do his best.

Not like I'm expecting anything different from the king who was ready to sacrifice himself and his own happiness for his people. He'll do anything to stop Ephegos and Erina, even if it means forming alliances with a king who used to be his captor.

Once Myron is seated next to me, Royad and Silas sit down on Myron's other side. Clio waves Andraya and Pouly over to sit on their side, across from the two Crows, leaving Herinor and Kaira the only ones standing.

Silas is quick to offer the Flame the chair next to him, and I could swear a growl is building in Herinor's throat when Kaira follows the invitation.

However, Herinor remains on his feet the same way he did in Erina's palace. The deja vu drives a shiver down my spine.

"Aren't you going to sit?" King Recienne inquires, folding his hands in front of him on the edge of the table, his gaze on Herinor.

The latter shakes his head. "I'm not a noble. I'm a soldier." As if that is any explanation, he stands behind Myron and me, hand on the hilt of his sword.

Recienne raises a brow while Astorian cocks his head and Clio rolls her eyes, but none of them object. The Fairy King merely raises a hand, flicking his fingers, and the doors swing shut on an invisible touch.

When I glance around, I notice there are no fairy guards stationed in this room. Whether that's a good sign or a bad one remains to be seen. All I know is that Herinor will have our backs—at least Myron's since his bargain with Ephegos is still in place and he can't help me or he'll pay with his own life.

Absolute silence falls, the humans not breathing and the Crows remaining unnaturally still as Recienne glances around the table, taking in his guests with those unreadable eyes, and my heart is ready to beat out of my chest.

Myron's hand is on mine, fingertips turning into talons as he seems to be fighting his instinct to shift in the presence of an old enemy.

Only, he isn't. King Recienne of Askarea is the brother of the fairy we saved. The friend of the general who suffered alongside the Crows in Erina's dungeon. And these males are too proud or too scarred by their past to even look at each other like they could be stronger together.

Words build in my throat, but I can't get myself to speak them. Even Kaira doesn't comment on the many ways I want to call both kings cowards as they keep staring at each other like in a competition. Astorian's warning glance at Myron has as little impact on the silence as Clio's for her brother.

So, I pull together every last ounce of courage I have left after my last experience in a palace and address the Fairy King directly. "Your palace is even more impressive than I expected, Your Majesty. I particularly enjoy the choice of rocks for the walls. I mean, who else has a glimmering palace."

Beside me, Myron has gone even more rigid, and Herinor takes a step closer toward his king, letting me believe he's ready to throw himself in front of Myron should King Recienne smite me with his power and some of it might slip past and hit the Crow.

The Fairy King merely stares at me, but the corners of his lips lift in a hint of a smile.

"They're from the quarry in the Hollow Mountains in the very south of Askarea, where the fairylands meet Tavras and Cezux." His voice is as smooth as the first time he spoke, but there is more warmth in it, like he's pleasantly surprised yet reluctant to show it.

"It's beautiful," Andraya chimes in, picking up on what I'm doing.

So is Kaira, who adds what Clio already shared with her in the hallway. "The Hollow Mountains have natural caves full of stalagmites; at least Princess Cliophera explained so to me. What I'd do to see those caves one day."

"Stop calling me *princess*, and you might." Clio snarks in the Flame's direction, earning a raised brow from her brother.

151

"Is that how you make friends, Cliophera? Because if it is, I should try being less polite, and this palace might fill up with more unlikely allies in this pending war you've been talking about."

I'm not certain if he's serious, but the way Astorian is grinning tells me he's not, only full of wit and humor that he prefers remaining undetected.

But the knot in my stomach eases, and I can breathe again as I realize this is not going to end up with any of us in a fairy dungeon.

Clio rolls her eyes, snapping her gaze to her brother. "This war I've been talking about will be knocking on our doors sooner than we care for if we don't do something about it." For a moment, I think he's going to scold her for speaking to him like that, but his smile is genuine now, and the way it changes his face is a shock. He's handsome—was handsome before—but this is the radiating beauty of a male who has it all. Confidence and power shine in every gesture, along with a well of unconditional love that reminds me of the bond Kaira and I share even when that of my sister and me is only starting to bloom.

His gaze snaps to mine as if he senses my scrutiny, eyes narrowing for a heartbeat. "I can see why my sister is so convinced that we need you at our side."

"You mean the Crows," I correct, and part of me wants to bite my tongue while the other part remembers I'm a queen in my own right—of two kingdoms. One without a crown.

Recienne shakes his head. "You, Wolayna. If you manage to keep a bunch of grumpy Crows under control, you are someone I want to call an ally."

Before any of the Crow males can object, he flashes them a placating smile. "No offense. But had I had this woman around a hundred years ago, I might have sent her in as a weapon instead of attempting to blow up your entire kingdom."

Myron's growl reverberates through the room, convincing me he's ready to leap across the table and attack, so I grab his hand harder, putting on my sweetest smile.

"Well, I'm not a weapon, and my grandmother, who was around a hundred years ago, is no one you would have wanted to mess with, so we better leave the past in the past, agreeing that we're all glad to be here, alive, and no more females need to be sacrificed to save the Crows."

Recienne's throat bobs.

"I don't know where you've been living, but these Crows saved your sister, Your Majesty," I roll on without any sense of self-preservation because, in my heart, I know Clio and Astorian would have never brought us here had they feared their king intended to harm us. "These Crows were cursed and tormented and robbed of all their chances to free themselves from a horrible fate because of the imprisonment you placed upon them." I don't even stop for breath, ignoring the horrified gazes Andraya and Pouly are giving me and the head-shake of warning from Kaira. "Myron's father was the one you had the quarrel with, not Myron. He merely tried to save his people. And—knowingly or not—you did your best to keep him from ever succeeding. So, be grateful that he didn't brush off your general and leave him behind in the dungeon. Be grateful for his willingness to forgive and cooperate to help that same male find his mate and bring her home." My hands are shaking, but I can't stop myself despite the knowledge that this will cost me—will potentially cost all of us. "Fucking be a male about it and say thank you so we can all move on."

Someone takes a breath to interrupt me—or to respond—I don't care. I'm not done.

"And you." I whirl on Myron, clutching his claw hard to reassure myself he's not yet readying himself to attack King Recienne or me for the way I'm pushing this meeting down the drain. "You can't blame this king for protecting his kingdom from a people who have only brought misery to its females. You can't blame him for not knowing about the curse when none of you were able to speak of it. He was doing the best he could to keep his people safe, and you were doing your best to save yours."

Myron is staring at me like he's never seen me before, and somewhere at the back of my mind, I know I should have long stopped speaking, that this might have been too much and one of the two kings will tear me to ribbons before or after they rip each other apart.

But whatever Myron is about to say or do is swallowed by the Fairy King's laugh filling the momentary silence.

He laughs and laughs, not a hysterical sound, but one of true amusement, an infectious one that makes me want to smile even when I'm so upset I might fall apart at the seams, destroying the lovely blue and silver satin dress I'm wearing.

"Spoken like a true queen, Wolayna," Recienne eventually says when Myron tenses to leap at him and Herinor draws his sword an inch, ready to back him up.

EIGHTEEN

MYRON

I t takes more than a few deep breaths to will calm into my veins. If I wasn't seeing Recienne laugh with my own eyes right now, I'd believe this is a ruse, but the Fairy King is amused by my mate's fury. He's laughing like he finds endearing how she's straining to get us on the same page.

Admittedly, diplomacy has never been her strong suit, but she has a point. She's right in all but one regard: I wasn't trying to save my people. Not after a while. I'd given up on them. The only ones I was willing to save were Ayna and Royad. And when it came to it, Ayna was the only one I gave my life for.

I don't say any of that, though. My particular weaknesses are nothing to be laid out in front of a king who is gloating at our misfortune.

"Spoken like a true queen, Wolayna," Recienne says with too much dignity even when what he does resembles a laughing fit.

I'm not certain I hate the Fairy King, but the behavior certainly does nothing to make him the least bit likable.

Instead of the hundreds of ways my freshly returned Crow power might destroy the fairy, I think of the way Ayna's thighs quivered in my grasp as I made her come... and come, not even an hour ago. Her taste is still on my tongue.

Ayna's hand tightens around mine like a vise, and I realize her Crow strength is still something she needs to get used to. I don't flinch, though. The situation is dangerous enough without my interference. My queen can handle herself and, according to Recienne, me.

He's not wrong.

I'll let Ayna handle me in any way she wants.

"Because she *is* a queen," Clio jumps to Ayna's aid, surprising me yet again. This female is more loyal than I'd thought any fairy capable of. Then, Tori has also already proven a convincing ally when we were searching for our mates. A friend...

I can't think of what that means, or I'll be right back to Ephegos and his betrayal. *He* was my friend. Before he partnered up with Jeseida and became a Flame at heart. I can't help but glance at Kaira, who's chosen to turn against her people just as Ephegos has chosen to turn his back on his. The irony doesn't escape me.

"A queen of two kingdoms," Tori adds, ready to support his mate—or speaking out of conviction. "Tavras and the Crow Kingdom."

"There is no Crow Kingdom left," I murmur.

Of course, everyone in the room catches it. Even the humans. Andraya and Pouly stare at me like they are wondering if I'm planning to make Tavras my new home, given their queen is my mate. What a mess.

"That's something we still need to figure out," Royad throws in, always the supportive one in our little group, while Silas frowns at no one in particular. I wish I could just shift and fly away with Ayna, leave the worries of this world behind. Across the ocean, Neredyn lies with its vastness. I've listened to the older Crows over the years, and all their stories are the same. The beauty of the lands, the lush forests and wild waters surrounding the kingdom, the palace, high like a tower and perfect to host us in our bird form and our fae form alike—

An ache in my chest makes itself known even when I've never laid eyes on what used to be our home.

Tori cocks his head at me. "There better be. You made a promise."

As if called by the ancient fae magic ruling my body, the promise returns to my mind, taunting me with its need for fulfillment. *If you work with me to find them both, I'll take my people and leave Eherea.*

"I haven't forgotten." It's all I can say without bringing those lines of worry to Ayna's forehead.

At least, the course of direction has ended Recienne's amusement. His full attention is on me now as if waiting for me to spill my secrets.

When I don't respond, his gaze wanders to Astorian, who shrugs. "It was a promise made under duress, and we might still need the Crows in this war. I'd hate to see a capable, powerful ally leave in times of need."

"Leave?" Ayna whispers, making my stomach turn into a tight knot. I *can't* leave her. And I can't take her from her homeland, especially since she's the rightful queen of Tavras. But technically, the promise includes her. She's become one of us. A Crow. And mine. That makes her *my Crow.*

I merely shake my head. Astorian is doing what I've known him for all my life: political manipulation, turning things in his own court's favor. Only, this time, he knows that I'll benefit as much from it as they will.

I need to be here to fight Ephegos when he attacks, need to see Erina bleed for his crimes against my mate and the people she calls friends. Need to see them both suffer for what he did to me and mine. I can't leave.

Before anyone can dig deeper, Recienne clears his throat, and we all sit back.

"First, Wolayna is right. I do owe you my thanks, Crow King. You were willing to sacrifice your freedom to save two of my court."

No one is more surprised than I am by his words, and even knowing that Eherean fairies can lie, I feel the sincerity in them. And Shaelak bless my mate for her boldness. She cut right through the drama, calling two kings out.

Because she was right about me, too. I know Recienne measured me by the standards of my father. Carius the Cruel is who he feared and hated, and I've never done a thing to make him think any better of me. Clio relayed my efforts to him, but never the why. She only knew that I was willing to give up the deal I'd struck with Recienne before to get her support in saving Ayna.

I'm not too proud to admit that it's a struggle to receive such words of thanks, knowing my people hurt his kingdom for centuries. But it's a start, so I incline my head in acknowledgment and force out those three little words I should have spoken a long time ago. "I am sorry."

The room is silent as a tomb as we hold our breaths to see if the male whom I'm used to viewing as my dungeon master accepts my apology. Ayna's fingers tighten around mine near-painfully, and I find myself squeezing hers back.

Eventually, Recienne dips his chin. "You helped bring my sister and my general home, yet I need to see your sincerity for myself before I fully trust you." He flicks his finger, making Ayna and the humans jump as a colorful feast in copper pans, silver platters, and ceramic dishes appears in front of us, covering the table between us. "Let's eat first, though. Alliances are best discussed with a full belly. Shuts down our natural hunting instinct."

I'm not certain I imagine the glint of seriousness in his eyes, even when he's otherwise broadly smiling at me, but I wouldn't put it past the Fairy King to murder me in my sleep. The Crows have been a thorn in his kingdom for long, long centuries after all. Calling Tori my friend won't change what my father did to these lands, what he took from these people.

"We wouldn't want that instinct to come to life," Herinor notes flatly, and this time, I don't imagine it when Tori cuts the Crow warrior a warning glance that would shut even me up. I've got to give it to him; Herinor merely shrugs and saunters to the empty spot next to Kaira, plopping down in a chair after all, now that it's been established we will all attempt to be civilized.

"What's for dinner?" Shaelak bless her, Kaira disperses the tension with a question and a grumbling stomach, drawing the attention of the entire party as she bluntly reaches for the domed, silver lid on the platter closest to her and lifts it to set free the aroma of herbs and fruits I haven't tasted in my life.

"Fruit pie. That's for dessert." Clio snatches the lid with her magic, floating it back onto the dish while, with her free hand, she picks up the cover on a large bowl at the center of the meal. "Try this for starters."

I don't know what I was expecting, but certainly not the informal procedure of each of the Askarean fairies helping themself to the various dishes presented along the table, using both cutlery and their powers to get them onto their plates.

"Try the lentils," Astorian nudges Recienne with his elbow, pointing at the small bowl right in front of him. "The kitchen fairies tried something new."

Through the mate mark, I can sense Ayna being as flabbergasted as I am at the sight of the casual meal while the rest of us are hesitant to touch the foods. Well, not all of us. Kaira has her plate filled with various greens and meats, gaze following every bite Clio takes as if in reference to what is edible and what isn't.

It's only when Ayna clears her throat that Recienne stops his fork halfway to his mouth, eyeing us as if he hadn't noticed our reluctance. "If you're hungry, you'll need to help yourselves. I'm not going to spoon-feed you." His gaze is on me, and this time, a hint of humor accompanies the harshness of his tone.

I'm not certain what to make of him yet. Similar to Astorian, I've faced Recienne of Askarea on a battlefield, have negotiated terms with him, and dealt with his powerful magic. I've never had a meal with him, let alone a conversation that didn't involve demands, threats, or even bloodshed.

So, I put on my blandest expression, forcing my talons to retract and my claws to turn back into fingers and let go of Ayna's hand. "When the curse hit, I was too young to feed myself, and my mother was killed by Vala's punishment. Spoon feeding is how I survived my early months." I wait for the words to sink in and, when they do, immediately regret them as Ayna gently squeezes my hand as if in comfort. I wasn't going for a hit there. This was meant for the Fairy King, to shame him out of his enigmatic cockiness. Keeping my face blank, I amend, "I prefer forks now."

My effort isn't in vain. Recienne's lips quirk, and he dips his chin as if to say, "touché", and Ayna's head turns, gaze palpable on my face as she tries to read what I have planned.

Nothing. I have planned nothing. Nothing other than making sure none of my party comes to harm in this palace.

NINETEEN

AYNA

The food is fantastic. Rich flavors. Hearty breads and light sauces, meats and vegetables, cheeses and fruits in various forms. What they all have in common: They are seasonal and spiced in a way that allows for the ingredients to shine rather than bury them the way Erina's court seems to like their meals. Perhaps, I never learned to appreciate the food I was served there because I was constantly nauseous from the drug and I knew I'd expel each meal quite timely and re-experience it in the inverted path.

After the initial face-off between the two kings in our midst, I've made my way through three helpings of meats

163

and vegetables, slices of bread, and am now staring at a piece of the fruit pie Kaira discovered earlier.

The fairies and Crows haven't tried to kill each other, which was to be expected when it comes to Clio and Tori, but not the Fairy King himself. He is scary as fuck, mostly because he hides his viciousness behind a veneer of polite smiles and the occasional laugh. Myron is behaving himself, no longer sniffing every bite before putting it in his mouth. I understand his concern, though. We were all drugged for too many weeks, and the drug was delivered through our meals. I would be just as careful if it wasn't for Clio and Tori, who are shoveling food into their mouths like they aren't princess and general.

"Here—" I'm about to lower my fork into it when Clio sends a flash of her ice magic into my dessert. "The fruit filling tastes best frozen."

She is right. It's so delicious I close my eyes as the filling slowly melts on my tongue, bringing forward notes of blackberry and apple. There is pear in the mix, too, and cinnamon. My Crow senses delight in the experience so much I don't notice Clio froze Myron's pie as well—and he didn't pull up the fickle shield he's managed since his escape from prison to block what he could have mistaken for an attack. I'd have felt his power flowing. I always do.

"You never offer to freeze mine," Tori complains, much to King Recienne's amusement, who smirks at his general. "That's because you don't deserve frozen filling."

"You still mad at me for losing your sister?" Tori flashes his teeth, and I could swear a hint of bloodlust shimmers in his auburn eyes.

"*I*'m mad at you for a lot of things," Clio interrupts the conversation before the Fairy King can respond. "Especially for not kicking Recienne's ass and leaving it up to Ayna."

My heart skips a beat as I wonder if this is the moment where everything goes sideways. Myron is so tense once more I can feel his magic push against my tattoo as if trying to escape there if he won't allow it to leave his body otherwise.

But Recienne just laughs. There is no hint of discomfort in the gesture, no fear, nor aggression. He is genuinely amused, and this seems to be normal for their dinner conversations. What I should think about it, I'm not certain. All I know is that I'm relieved we've gotten through dinner without escalating anything.

And it's been such an amazing meal. Only, time is running out, and I can't wait any longer to discuss an alliance. If Recienne won't help, we're on our own. There are Crows in the Seeing Forest who have no idea what is coming for them. We need to warn them and prepare for whatever is coming for us.

It takes all my courage to speak up again, but this is for my people. Both of them. "Thank you for your hospitality, Your Majesty."

Recienne inclines his head. "It was a pleasure having another human holding magic at my table."

The comment makes me curious enough to want to ask about the *other* human. If he means his queen. But the alliance is more important. If things go well, I might have time to meet her after all.

Steeling my spine, I take another bite of pie. Chew. Swallow. "Erina has improved the process to produce the magic-nullifying drug. If he manages to equip a human army with it, he'll be unstoppable."

The air in the room changes so fast I nearly choke on it, but Myron and Astorian are right there with me, throwing in their knowledge as we recapitulate what we've learned about Erina's plans and Ephegos's involvement.

"The Flames will fight at their side," Kaira adds. "Jeseida, their Matrone, is still bitter about the loss of her lands in the Seeing Forest, and with Ephegos as an adopted son of sorts, she's probably already dreaming of a Flame kingdom."

Recienne listens to all of it, studying Royad and Silas as they add details about the effect of the drug, the cruelty of the Tavrasian king, then listens to Herinor as he lays open as much as he can about what he knows about Ephegos's involvement without losing his life over it. Herinor in particular captures the Fairy King's attention like no other in the room. Be it the no-nonsense attitude or the way he claims to be a warrior even when he's obviously good enough to be a king's confidant.

"Tell me, Herinor… Where do you believe Erina will strike first?"

Herinor doesn't flinch under Recienne's scrutiny, merely shakes his head, golden-blond strands dancing around his face. He's shaven, making the scars on his features stand out even more. What he's done to earn them, I yet need to learn.

"I have no idea what the human king will do. And I'm unable to say what Ephegos will do."

Astorian frowns at him, as do Clio and Kaira. I'm not disappointed, though. I've been on the receiving end of Herinor's restrictions before, so I know not to expect his aid. But this is fresh for them. He's helped them all before. Helped them so he didn't need to help me. Speaking of Ephegos's plans directly, however, seems to be beyond his ability, and I really don't want him to die. He's valuable even in his unpredictable ability to assist. Plus, Kaira likes him.

"Hey, I heard that," Kaira complains in my mind, and I can't help but smile.

"Good. Perhaps it's time you acknowledged it and did something about it." I don't add that Herinor might be more inclined to put his life on the line with every word he speaks if he believes Kaira will reward him for it, but the expression on Kaira's face tells me she heard me anyway.

"Assuming I'm willing to work with you, what can you contribute?" Recienne's tone is all business as he turns to Myron, disregarding Herinor like he's no longer part of the conversation.

For a heart-stilling moment, Myron and Royad exchange a glance, making Andraya and Pouly shift in their chairs as they wait for the magical beings to put their strength on the table.

"If the Flames haven't gotten them, there are eighteen more Crows hiding in the Seeing Forest.

"Eighteen…" The Fairy King muses. "Eighteen Crows against a human army."

"An army who can level the playing field in a heartbeat if they hit us with their weapon," Royad supplies, and I'm surprised by the impatience in his tone. He's disliking the Fairy King's demeanor as much as Myron and Silas—even when Silas hasn't said a word, I can tell. His posture is tense, his expression that of a male ready to stab someone if we don't get to the point soon.

I'm right with him.

"Eighteen Crows at full, ungodly power," I cut in. "They might be worth fifty of yours." I shouldn't be provoking a king who has a history of locking up my Crow in a forest, but if we don't make progress soon, Erina and Ephegos might stand at our doorstep by the time we make a decision whether working together is worth it.

"She might be right." No one is more surprised than I am when Recienne agrees with me—to a degree, but it's not an objection to my statement.

Of course, Tori catches right on. "If we have eighteen Crows, each worth fifty of our own soldiers—"

Recienne holds up a hand. "Let's test that theory first." His gaze swings from Astorian to me, to Myron. "And if you're right, we'll come up with a better plan than open war."

TWENTY

MYRON

Dust and streaks of dried blood speak of violence and merciless battles in the arena built from inconspicuous gray stone behind the palace. A few rows of wooden benches stacked along the sides like an auditorium inform me whatever slaughter occurs here usually has an audience. I'm not certain whether this is a place of sparring or torture, but knowing the Fairy King, it's probably both.

From the center of the space, Tori grins at me, teeth flashing unnaturally white in the pale morning sun. "Don't worry, Myron. I'll leave him in one piece."

169

With his free hand, he's pointing at Silas, who is armed with a single broadsword matching the dull training weapon Tori holds in his other hand.

Silas adjusts his stance on the packed earth and gravel ground. "Don't hold back, fairy." The glance the Crow cuts Tori is nothing short of feral. Silas is a cold-hearted bastard when it comes to swordplay, and even Recienne has deigned to leave his palace to watch his general test the strength of one of my best soldiers. Of course, Royad was first to offer to face Recienne's idea of a challenge, but Silas is right: He's the only one in our Crow group who knows what it means to work with his full powers while also not being restricted by the foolish bargain Herinor made with Ephegos.

"I'd much appreciate it if neither of you ends up in pieces," Recienne throws in with that handsome smirk on his features that makes me wonder if he rules by charming his court rather than threatening them the way I'd assumed firm in place.

Beside me, Ayna shifts her weight, bracing her forearms on the wooden fence enclosing the training area. The leathers Clio provided for her fit like a second skin, and I barely manage to keep my fingers away from the seam following her waist or my thoughts from what it would feel like to stand behind her, my hips lined up with the curve of her ass.

Royad clears his throat, elbowing me to bring my attention back to the two males in the arena just in time to watch Tori land the first blow. Silas catches the brutal strike with ease, swirling under Tori's arm like a whirlwind. I've seen him make this move before while sparring with Crows, but with the fairy opponent, it's an entirely different thing. Where I used to see a feathered monster—a monster just like the rest of us—now I see grace and skill. I see a true asset and a friend who'd go to the ends of this world to protect his species.

Tori stumbles a step but catches himself fast enough to parry Silas's swing. If I'm honest, I haven't seen one of my Crows fight a fairy since the last war, and the sight brings forth memories of a time when every drop of fairy blood was a win to us.

Today, drawing blood isn't the goal. All we need is to know how fast we tire in comparison to the fairies. How much stronger our blows are and how much quicker our blades.

So far, it looks like an even match. Nothing Silas does gives the impression Tori isn't up to the task, and the fairy general is dishing out his fair share of attacks that make me wonder if we were wrong after all and Crows aren't any better than the average Askarean fairy. They certainly outmatched us twice during our time in the Seeing Forest. Then, that was before the curse was broken and our full strength was restored.

"Stop playing around and try like a big boy." Silas doesn't feature as much as a grin as he taunts Tori, blade lifted to catch whatever the fairy male throws his way.

By the time Kaira groans her complaints that this leads *nowhere*, Recienne's brows are furrowed, his arms folded over his chest, frowning at the display of what seems to be an evenly matched fight.

Clio is standing beside her brother, hair braided back and leathers of a warrior in place. She's fiddling with her shortsword, ready to leap into the arena, while Herinor and Royad both stand ramrod straight, observing their kin face the fairy who'd once filled their nightmares.

"He seemed less threatening in the dungeon," Ayna notes, gaze following the fighting pair.

I'm not certain she means Tori or Silas, but I agree. She's never seen any of us in full-on battle mode since the curse was broken. In the dungeon, when we fought Ephegos and Katrijanov, I was still recovering from the drug, and my powers were not fully unleashed. What she'd make of me if she saw the darkness of my vast magic, I'm not sure she'd ever look at me the same way.

"They haven't used their powers," Clio responds. "No way Silas will land a blow once Tori unleashes his powers on him."

Recienne nods and shouts for them to stop holding back, which is all Silas needs to hear to send a flash of silver power at the fairy general. Tori anticipated his bold move, though, watching the light dissipate along the shield he conjured while he vanishes into thin air with a cocky grin, only to reappear behind Silas and land a hit on the Crow's shoulder.

Ready to protect Silas, I prepare to haul my own power into the arena when Silas's body lights up with the same silver glow as his magic, and Tori is blasted aside. The male lands on his ass, cursing colorfully and rubbing his backside as he scrambles to his legs.

"What the fuck was that?" Clio reaches them first, sword pointed at Silas's throat while she assesses Tori's state. Of course, Tori brushes off her assistance, pride or frustration getting in the way as Silas shoots him a broad grin.

"That, my dear fairy friend, was a taste of my power. And if you still doubt I'm worth fifty of your soldiers, you better start dragging those up here so I can rip them to pieces one by one." He glares at Tori then at the Fairy King. "And if you doubt I mean it, you better not bet your general's or your sister's life on it. I'd hate to be the one to start a new war. Especially when we're already in the middle of one with Tavras and the fucking Flames."

Herinor claps his hands while Clio checks if her mate is still intact. "You better keep your opinions to yourself," she shoots at him, and I have to agree. Herinor is already a liability. He doesn't need to make enemies of the Fairy King and his court when we've already made it this far. No matter how strong we are, we'll need them to defeat Erina and his drug-wielding army, and those Flames and traitor Crows who've abandoned me to serve the piece of dirt that Ephegos is.

I'm about to voice exactly that when one of the fairy guards detaches from his post by the entrance of the arena, carrying a note a messenger handed him a moment ago, and approaches Recienne with hasty steps.

Before the male can make it halfway to his king, Recienne flicks his fingers, floating the piece of parchment from the guard's hand and unfolding it, reading with a thick line forming between his brows.

"What is it?" Tori demands, his defeat already forgotten. Silas sheathes his sword, following the general to the side of the arena where he leans next to me against the fence, shrugging as if he hadn't just blasted one of the most powerful fairies we know into the sand. My father used to say that, with our Crow powers intact, the Askarean fairies could have never trapped us and defeated us. Silas is surprisingly quiet about proving Carius the Cruel right, whether it is because he, for once, knows to hold his tongue or because he doesn't want to draw more attention when, in reality, all eyes are already on him.

Recienne's silence is as unnerving as it is to not know whether Silas's display of power just bought us a new enemy, but when he does speak, all worries are forgotten. All but—

"We've been attacked."

My arm is around Ayna in an instant, power rising to the surface, readying to strike, while she reaches for her dagger on instinct. It will take her some time to draw upon her Crow magic first.

"How many?" Tori's all-business tone drives ice into my veins, as does Recienne's quick orders to add guards to the wall surrounding the palace.

"They slayed three. The rest got away." The Fairy King exchanges a quick glance with his sister, who seems to be ready to march into battle.

"At least we caught them before they could do actual damage this time." Tori jerks his chin in a general southern direction, dust forgotten as he absently rubs it. He has a bruise on his cheek, and another one peeks through the gap in the collar of his shirt, exposing the edge of a collarbone that's already purpling. Silas got him hard enough to leave a mark.

Tucking the information away for later, I demand, "Who attacked?"

That lands Recienne's attention on me, his golden eyes near glowing with fury. "The Flames have taken it upon themselves to burn down my kingdom."

The throne room is no more welcoming than it was the first time we entered. This time, however, we're no longer there to negotiate an alliance. It's clear both sides need one.

"We have soldiers patrolling the borderlands in the south," Tori explains while Recienne whispers something to Clio that is too low to hear. "Ever since the curse on your people has been broken and the Flames attacked together with that rogue Crow, we've been keeping an eye on the situation." He exchanges a brief glance with his king at the word *rogue*, but apart from that, Recienne the Second doesn't seem to be paying much attention to his general's attempts at explaining the situation.

"What do you mean, *keeping an eye on the situation?*" I prompt, wondering how many more surprises I can take. "Has this happened before?"

"The attacks have been going on for a few weeks. I was actually on patrol myself the day I caught you sneaking out of the Seeing Forest." Tori's lowered brows tell me everything I need to know about how little he appreciates my questioning.

Thankfully, Ayna doesn't care what the general appreciates because she winds out of my arm, bracing her feet apart as she glares up at him. "How many have you lost? You said the Flames are burning down your kingdom. How often have they attacked? Where? What do they want?"

Before Tori can respond, Recienne abandons his secret conversation with Clio, stepping in to answer Ayna's questions. "We've lost too many. And before you even think of questioning whether or not I care for my people, every life lost is one too many, even those of our enemies."

I'm so stunned by his response I almost miss that he isn't answering her other questions. He's purposely avoiding to give specifics.

So, he doesn't trust us yet. Fair enough. I don't trust him either, but at least, now I know we could easily fight our way out if he ever decides to hold us captive.

Instead of rubbing that in his face, I step to Ayna's side, putting all pride and smugness behind me. This is about more than our ancient grudge. This is about the future of Eherea.

"How can we help?"

TWENTY-ONE

AYNA

Every life ... even that of our enemies. I can't stop staring at the beautiful Fairy King whose wrath once bound the Crows to a forest. In this moment, he seems almost ... human. Like the mask of the king has slipped, revealing the brother Clio loves so much—and the male who surely would go to the ends of this world for his people. The ice in his gaze is gone, and the amused arrogance wiped off his features.

Every life.

"How can we help?" Myron's voice is low, composed, his arm brushing my shoulder as he joins me like a second half of a front we pit against the male who was once his enemy.

In this moment, not a hint of hatred or distrust lingers, even with Silas's victory over Astorian. It's like someone opened a gate and we're filing through it one by one until we come out on the other side united. Even Herinor and Royad have joined us as we wait for King Recienne to tell us more.

"Help…" he muses, gaze flicking from one Crow to the other until it lands on me once more, liquid gold and burning embers. "I almost lost my sister and my mate to the Crows, Queen Wolayna. But no matter how deep my resentment for their species runs, I can see their king has a valiant heart, or he wouldn't have sacrificed everything for a human woman." There's more to his words than I can read, like he's asking for absolution rather than judging his newest ally. Before I can figure it out, he turns back to Myron. "The Flames have been setting traps for my fairies like for common game. So far, fifteen of my soldiers have gone missing without a trace. Go to the Seeing Forest. Warn the remaining Crows, and make sure you don't get caught. Send them to Aceleau for training. I'll make sure they work with my own armies by the time you get back from your quest."

"What quest?" Royad beats me to it.

The smile on Recienne's lips is nothing like the smug smirk he seems to be wearing like a second skin. It's cold and a clear warning to everyone who doubts his power in this realm.

"Find and free my soldiers, and I'll accept you as a true ally, Crow King," he growls at Myron, not sparing any of us a glance. "Find them; return them—alive."

The ruthlessness of his order tells me everything I need to know about Recienne of Askarea: he will stop at nothing to protect his own. Every life might count, but he'll gladly sacrifice them if it means his own people will be saved.

And after what I've experienced with my new family, I understand him. I'll stop at nothing to save *my* own. My new family, my new people. I might technically be Queen of Tavras, but I hold no power there. So, I'll save the feathered people I have left.

"Deal." Myron doesn't even flinch as I take the decision from him. I'm the Crow Queen after all, and if the Flames are burning down parts of Askarea, I'm certain it has something to do with their hunt for the leftover Crows who haven't sworn allegiance to Ephegos. Recienne's soldiers might have simply gotten in the crossfire.

Beside me, Silas squares his shoulders, and Herinor cracks his knuckles on Myron's other side. Royad seems to be the only one not fully convinced.

"Why send us? Why not your own men? I know first-hand how skilled they are?" Royad's referral to the Crow Wars erases Recienne's smile.

"Because I've sacrificed too much to keep my lands clean of the conflicts your people have been inflicting. The Flames are searching for Crows, we know that much. I'll grant your feathered friends refuge until you return my men. Then we'll know if your superior strength is worth anything in this war."

I know then he hasn't just come up with this idea. It's what he meant when he said we'd come up with a better plan than open war. He was testing us, our strength, our magic, our wits. Now he's sending us on a mission in exchange for protecting what few of our people are left.

He knew his people were being taken, and now he's using this mission to test our loyalty.

"Your queen already agreed, Royad." Myron shakes his head at his cousin before pinning Recienne with a look. "Where do you think they're holding them?"

My eyes find Clio's, hurt constricting my chest. If she knew what Recienne's plan was all along…

"*She didn't,*" Kaira interrupts in my mind before I can finish the thought. "*She didn't know. Neither did Tori. At least, not about their king's plans.*"

It's a weak consolation but better than the full force of betrayal building up in my chest. "*How do you know?*"

I'd almost forgotten my sister, but as she steps out of the shadows nearby, she's more confident than I've ever seen. "We should start looking at the Matrone's residence," she says out loud. "That's where they brought you first, and that's where they experimented on the Flames and … Herinor." The male's name comes out rough and reluctant as if she's sworn never to speak it, but it's out, and Herinor's gaze snaps to the Flame's, a million words dancing in his light green eyes.

Herinor clears his throat, but before he can speak, Silas claps his hands. "The residence of doom it is." And Herinor's words cease before they can spill.

"We leave tonight." Quick like a snake, Myron's hand curls around mine, pulling me along as he turns and marches back toward the main palace.

About an hour later, we're packing provisions in our room, each of us stuffing a bundle of foods into the packs Clio and Tori provided for our mission. We were given fighting leathers in the latest Askarean fashion in addition to weapons of preference. I'm now wearing two daggers strapped to my hips while Myron is wearing a sword strapped to his spine. Herinor's belt is stuffed with knives of various sizes, and a long sword dangles by his hip. Royad's bow peeks over his shoulder, and his quiver doesn't only hold arrows but a long, elegant blade, which he didn't stop fussing about like it's a treasure. Silas is wearing a hatchet and a sword, and Kaira's wearing a bow over her shoulder and a sword at her hip.

Myron hasn't spoken much since we returned to our room, a dark cloud of worry following him wherever he goes. He reminds me more of the brooding king I first met than of the passionate male who elicited all sorts of moans from my lips not even a full day ago.

As if sensing my stare, Myron turns his head, hair shifting to shield his features as he leans over his pack, stuffing in a spare shirt.

From their vantage point by the window, Pouly and Andraya are observing our busy preparations, Andraya's brow rising every time I meet her gaze. "You're still set on going without us?"

They weren't pleased when we told them we're headed on a mission, but it's a stretch to take even me with my unreliable powers. Bringing two humans to a Flame lair would be irresponsible to no end.

"We'll need someone to rally the rebels," I tell her instead of repeating my reasons.

"Erina won't be searching for you," Pouly supports my claim. "He thinks you left Meer through its main gates. You're the perfect person to put pieces into place to gather the rebel army."

"He'll be searching for you, though," the lady says to Pouly, and the concern on her features is real. "We can't risk you being discovered." She means it, but the way they are looking at each other makes me wonder if it's for fear of blowing their mission or fear for *him*.

"Someone needs to make sure you don't bite random people's heads off on your path through Tavras." The guard is grinning, more handsome than a man his age should be capable of.

Deciding it's none of my business if Andraya makes Pouly glow like a youngling, I hand them the final pack. "Tori promised to take you to the Tavrasian border. You'll know your path from there."

Andraya nods. She's told us of the small farm belonging to the rebels in the Plithian Plains near the border. Royad offers a bundle of bread and dried meat, dropping it into the bag I hold open. "This will last you a few days. Make sure to find a safe place to stay the night. And when you see rebels, tell them—"

"Tell them their queen is calling for their aid," Kaira finishes for me, throwing her arms around the woman first, then around an awkwardly hugging Pouly.

"Their queen isn't calling for anything," I correct. "Tell them to prepare to defend their home from a tyrant worse than the most recent Jelnedyn king." They don't need to know I haven't decided yet if I want to rule a kingdom that has caused me nothing but pain.

"I'll tell them to be ready when their queen calls," Andraya says with a curtsey, something she hasn't done since she left Erina's throne room and something I'd never demand of her—queen or no. "Plus, don't worry about me. I've been sneaking secret messages around Tavras since long before you were born. I know what I'm doing." She leans in, weaving her arms around my shoulders and pulling me into a tight embrace. "I helped get you out of Erina's gilded cell after all." When she lets go, she's smiling, but the dread of our escape is clear in her eyes. "Be safe, Wolayna."

Much to my surprise, she doesn't complain again when Tori knocks on the door a few minutes later, holding out both hands to site-hop Andraya and Pouly back to Tavras.

I don't know when I'll see them again, only where to send a message when the time comes to go to war.

How I wish it'll never come to that.

As they vanish into thin air, Clio stands in Tori's place, a wry smile on her lips and a snowflake at the tip of her fingers. "We haven't had the chance to train your powers." Her regret about the fact hits me right in the chest, leaving little space for all the retorts about the last time we trained together welling up.

"We haven't." And I still can't shift into a bird at will. I have no idea if I can shift at all, but I don't say that. I simply hug her, ignoring the hard leather pressing against my skin. I'm not used to wearing a full uniform like that, but I'll take it if it means the Flames can't fry me as easily.

When I detach from my friend's embrace, Myron is behind me, placing a hand on my shoulder in silent support. "The next time you see her, she'll kick your ass up and down the arena," he says to Clio, and it's only a half-joke. Because I know, like I know the path of the sun in the sky, that Myron will not let me walk into enemy territory unprepared. He'll teach me himself until I can fight like a creature kissed by both Vala's and Shaelak's blessing.

The tension in my body eases a bit, and I lean into his touch, lips tipping up at the sides. "It's a promise."

I only hope that my promises haven't become binding like the Crows'.

TWENTY-TWO

AYNA

The mood is everything but cheerful when Clio takes us to the border of the Seeing Forest in batches of two, and I would have asked why the former mysterious greenery stinks like a cold bonfire had I not been prepared to expect the aftermath of flames. Where once ferns and thickets dominated the path, soot-stained skeletons of trees are the only ones witnessing our arrival. Flakes of ash hover in the air like on a phantom wind, taunting whoever dares search for greenery and butterflies. From our little gathering by the stream separating fairy territory from former Crow lands, I can make out the outline of the palace ruins behind wafts of lingering smoke.

"This is a grave." Nobody is more surprised than me when Herinor combs through the few surviving bushes with his sword, a somber expression on his face.

"Anyone specific you're looking for?" Clio quips, flashing ice crystals at her fingertips, prepared to douse heat with her freezing power.

Herinor shrugs, but the way his mouth pulls into a tight line tells me he is, in fact, wary of this place.

"It's not like there are any female Crows left to await you for a rendezvous," Silas notes, painting a grin onto Herinor's face, but the male cringes as he notices Kaira's stare.

"Even if there were female Crows, I wouldn't be interested." He's quick to respond. So quick that I almost miss the pinkish tint on his neck.

"He's not lying," Myron narrates, slightly amused but mostly alarmed by the otherworldly silence falling over a forest that once brimmed with life.

"Because he *can't* lie." Kaira's right, and we all know it. "The question is: why?"

"Why we can't lie?" Herinor grumbles. "Because Shaelak willed it so."

"Must be a cruel god." I'm about to agree with Kaira when Myron jumps in. "I'm not certain what's more cruel, lying to people who deserve better, or the brutal honesty we're forced to speak."

I shoot him a damning look. "It's not like you haven't been twisting words." It's true. The curse was one thing, but they all have been meddling with phrasings to make things sound different from what they actually mean. "The only actual lie I've ever heard you tell is that your people remained within your borders. And that was before the curse was broken." I vividly remember the day when Myron spoke for his people to the copper-haired Fairy Princess we now call our friend. "The Crows had long undone the wards and were coming and going as they pleased."

Clio arches a brow, taking a few steps into the ashes that once were a carpet of moss and ferns.

It's rare that I catch Myron wordless, but this is one of those moments. He rakes his hand through his hair, searching for a response that won't damn him, a truth he can speak without giving away everything, whatever he's hiding.

"He's a diplomatic bastard, that's what he is." Silas plays with his hatchet, balancing it in his hand like he's assessing the weight.

"Now *that's* a lie," Herinor counters. "He's not a bastard. Just stinking feathered nobility."

"Same thing." Silas cuts the male a glance that speaks of all the things he'll do to him if he won't shut up, but it's too late. I've realized that lies are in the eyes of the beholder.

"Which borders were you talking about?" It's a simple question. One I expect a simple, un-twisted answer to.

Myron, Shaelak bless him, isn't set on playing the two males' game. He merely gives me a small smirk that says it all. "The borders of the Crow Kingdom." When I don't immediately understand, he adds, "But the Crow Kingdom technically no longer exists."

"You *had* a kingdom in the Seeing Forest," Clio objects. "Those borders—"

"Weren't the borders of my kingdom. Without a true place to set roots with my people, I defined my realm to be wherever my Crows are." Myron's teeth gleam white in the afternoon sun as he flashes a grin at the Fairy Princess. "The sky's the limit."

"Not even that," Royad chimes in. "The sky's our domain."

It's almost comical how Clio's mouth opens and closes without words coming out until eventually—"Someone should teach you some sense of honor, Crow King."

But there's humor in her voice, and I could swear she's impressed by his inventiveness, almost as if his callous bending of the truth earned her respect. "Tell me the forest isn't burned."

Before Myron can attempt this lie, Royad leaps to his aid. "The forest isn't burned."

Clio rolls her eyes. "Tell me *this* forest isn't burned."

For a moment, I believe Myron can actually say it. Then he closes his mouth, grunting with frustration.

"At least, you're not bleeding," Royad tells him, and I don't imagine the relief in his tone. Their blood-stained lips when they spoke about the curse is a terror still haunting me in my sleep.

"And I can't say it." Myron draws his sword, gaze flicking over the site of destruction. All the while, he hasn't withdrawn his senses from his former home. I can tell by the way his nostrils flare, his chest heaves when he scents the heavy stench of burned wood and flesh drafting through the ruins of the forest.

"This forest isn't burned," Silas says with the most bored expression I've seen since the beginning of the conversation. "There, I said it."

My jaw is dropping, but Herinor comes to my aid, explaining before I question everything I've learned about Crow Fae so far. "You mean *this particular part of this forest* isn't burned," he specifies, pointing at the patch of green Silas is standing on. "If you have to be a fucking bastard about this, at least be an *honest* fucking bastard."

Kaira's chuckle bubbles through the mist like rain falling onto a water-deprived meadow, the sound so startling it makes Herinor cringe all over again. This time, I don't miss the blush creeping all the way to his nose.

"You're all fucking bastards," Clio clarifies, turning on her heels and marching ahead into the no-longer-depths of a mostly vanished forest.

We follow without question, even when I really want to know if she'll escort us the whole way to the Flame residence. Recienne might have sent us in alone to prove our good intentions for this alliance, but Clio seems to be dead-set on keeping us company anyway.

Whirls of ashes dance around scorched tree trunks in magical bleakness, guiding my attention to the myriads of pathways that could once have led to my freedom. Our footsteps are the only sound, though. Not one bird flutters in the sky; not one rodent scurries between the occasional pillar of steam rising from the ground.

The path is wide enough for three of us to walk next to each other, but Myron grabs my hand, pulling me to a halt at the back of the group while the others march on at a slow and steady pace. They could shift and fly. Clio could site-hop. Apparently, screening the wasteland for any sign of life is more important than speed, so they stick to walking lest they miss a footprint, a broken twig, a fiber of fabric, a feather, or anything that would hint at where to find our target. We're on a mission after all.

Brushing a thumb across the back of my palm, Myron turns toward me, ocean-blue eyes capturing mine with ease. I don't want to stare at him like a complete fool, but when it comes to this male, apparently I have no sense of shame. Because I'm shamelessly ogling his beautiful features, the way his leathers stretch over the expanse of his shoulders—

"I've never lied to you," he interrupts my train of thought before I can catch fire the way the forest did not too long ago.

"Because you can't lie," I repeat Kaira's earlier point.

With a swift tug on my hand, I'm chest to chest with the Crow King, the pommel of his sword pressing against my spine where his sword hand is resting on the small of my back. Midnight lashes frame the endless waters of his gaze, and I'm tempted to lose myself in there. "Because I'd never lie to you, even if I could. You're my mate, my queen, the beginning and end of my world. If I have no kingdom in this realm, you'll be my kingdom instead." My breath catches as he lowers his face a few inches, his scent of earth and moss and the salt of the coastal brine climbing into my nose, making my entire being listen. "If there's nothing left for me in this world but you, I'll have all I need. I'll thank the gods and be a happy male."

I no longer know where the others are. I thought I heard them a few paces ahead, but the world has gone silent behind Myron's shield; the wind has ebbed, the taste of the destruction the wildfire left around us swept away by Myron's breath on my tongue as he leans in so close I can feel the warmth of his lips in the slightest of touches.

"You're *mine*, Ayna."

His words race through me like a string of fire itself, only to be soothed by the brush of his tongue against mine as I inhale his kiss.

"And I'm *yours.*" He kisses me deep and slow, my skin tingling from where his mouth molds over mine to where he's securing my hand against his heart. "Together, Ayna... *Together,* we're eternal."

I'm about to wrap myself around his body when Royad's shout of warning shoves me right out of the dreamy state Myron seems to be so perfect at sending me into with nothing more than a glance, a touch, a single kiss.

Cursing the gods, the Guardians, and all other beings who might have an impact on this realm with their godly acts, I detach from Myron, who has already raised his sword, a shield of silver power shimmering around us like a wall of solid, gleaming air.

"If I asked you to hide, would you at least consider it?" His frown is proof of how well he's been holding back his protective side, allowing me to decide whether I want to face whatever gruesomeness is awaiting us where the others disappeared behind a cluster of dead trees.

"Consider, yes. Actually hide—" Shaking my head so wildly my hair threatens to pull free from my braid, I inform Myron there is no way in this world I'll stand by and watch him risk his life while I remain tucked away somewhere supposedly safe.

I get it, though. The impulse to protect him is a relentless hum in my chest, ready to push me over the limits just to see him spared from harm. It's enough to jerk me into motion.

Myron follows me toward the others, his footsteps so much quieter than mine as we sneak up on the copse of dead trees they disappeared behind. In my veins, a thrum of power rises, welling like a wild ocean as fear grips me tighter with every pace. Shadows are moving by the trees, but I can't make out what they are. I count the absence of winged fairies as a plus. At least, it isn't Ephegos's traitor crows.

At least that's what I hope. No matter how well we fight, we're a small group, and Ephegos has the traitors and Erina's soldiers at his disposal. Not to speak of the magic-sedating weapon. If he found us, we're fucked.

The sizzle of Myron's shield grazes my hand as I reach forward with my blade to shove aside a branch. The charred thing crumbles at my touch, dropping to the ground in a pile of black ashes.

It's then that I spot them a few paces behind the trees, slender silver blades sheathed at their hips and hands raised in front of their chests, palms outward as if in defense. It's not the desire for peace that drives them to perform that gesture, though. Sparks of orange flame rain down from their fingers, searching their way across the scorched ground right to the side where Kaira and the Crows are standing.

Flattening myself against the trunk of a dead tree, I pull Myron with me, out of sight from the Flames. If we're lucky, they haven't noticed us, and we can sneak up on them from the other side.

Our luck won't go as far.

Just when Myron's weight leans into me behind the tree, back against my chest so we both fit into the slender hideout, someone screams, and all hell breaks loose.

TWENTY-THREE

AYNA

A gust of heat sears my throat, making my lungs spasm as a wall of fire hits our tree. Kaira's scream is replaced with my dry one a second before Myron's magic blasts the tree behind us apart. Burning splinters of wood fly through the air like in an explosion of lightning and fire, and part of me understands what happened in the Crow palace all those months ago, how they thought something went wrong with the combination of Flame magic and Crow power. It *is* the combination that tore Myron's home to rubble.

"Don't fight, and you'll keep your lives." One of the Flames steps out of the perfectly straight line they're forming, his leather armor fitted and his hair cascading down over his shoulders like flames of their own.

"Arebar—" The sound of Kaira's voice brings instant relief. The name she's speaking, however, brings terror.

Arebar crosses half the distance between the line of Fire Fairies and my friends, his gaze directed at Kaira. "It's been a while, child."

"*Child,*" Kaira repeats in her mind with contempt. Out loud, she shouts, "You never called me a child when we slept together." The bite in her tone tells me she's ready to spear the male with the arrow nocked on her bow. Herinor's shoulder has shoved slightly in front of her, his expression giving away that he will join right in the moment Kaira unleashes her wrath on Arebar. She controls her anger, hands only mildly shaking as she stays her arrow. "I wish I were still a child. Innocent ignorance is a great state of mind."

She sounds confident, even when I can sense her trembling through our connection. Royad and Silas have their blades drawn, Silas's hatchet loose in his grasp as if he hasn't decided if he'll throw it at the fire-haired male or hold it in his grasp while spilling blood. Clio is the only one I can't find between the ruins of trees, and I have to admit, the panic coming with her absence has everything to do with the close friendship that has grown between us. She's an experienced fighter, wielding powerful magic, and can take care of herself. She probably site-hopped right out of danger, leaving us to fight the Flames, confident we could handle them after Silas's display of strength in Recienne's arena. Still, there's a part of me that won't stop worrying.

"You weren't the most experienced back then, so perhaps I should have." Arebar's features remain serious as he mocks my sister, making me consider the merits of simultaneously stabbing him and ripping him to shreds with my Crow magic. If only I had control over it, I might have done the latter already.

As I measure the distance to the Flames, I'm not the only one to notice the ground around us is steaming, even with little to nothing left to burn. The twenty Flames are aware of it too, judging by the way they are holding their wall of fire close to them once more when it barely finds purchase in the space between us. If they've come to burn us alive, the forest won't be made into a trap the way they might have managed the last time they attacked here. The thought is a meek consolation, considering that my friends *can* burn. Only the silvery shimmer of a shield around them makes my heart a bit lighter.

"You've always been too weak to fight at our side, Kaira," Arebar spits. "Too weak, too little of a Flame. Worthless."

I'm about to throw a retort at Arebar, but Herinor beats me to it. "You fucking prick can't possibly know the meaning of the word *worth*."

Why his eloquence surprises me is beyond me. He's proven to be a better conversational partner than a friend. At least, for me, where any allowance of support may cost him everything.

Arebar's laugh echoes through the dead land like a flame of ice. "So, you're the poor lad she's stringing along these days?" He shakes his head. "Pity. You should have found a female of your own species rather than fall for a Flame weakling like her." He puts a finger to his lips, a grin forming. "Oh, I forgot… You don't *have* females."

The fact that he knows Herinor is a Crow might have something to do with the feathers sprouting on the male's neck as he seems to struggle to control his temper.

"It's none of your business, Arebar." Kaira is keeping a level head even when Arebar seems to be on a personal mission to destroy her. I wouldn't be surprised if that's the reason the Flame Matrone chose him to hunt us down.

"But it is when a Crow takes one of our females. Again."

"I'm not *taking* anything." Herinor's voice is trembling, but he can't possibly be lying. Whatever is going on between the two of them, he hasn't forced anything.

Arebar merely hurls a fresh assault of fire at my friends, making me hurtle toward them. To do what, I don't know. Fight them with my daggers? Or my uncontrollable magic? Neither seems so great an option. I might as well blow them up with a strike of my Crow power that gets out of hand.

A minor part of me wonders if I've become delusional, believing I might be stronger than any of them. Herinor and Silas are ancient warriors who know how to handle their power, and Royad and Myron have made impressive progress since the curse first broke. It's only me and my unpredictable magic that's blessing and curse in equal parts.

The first wave of fire bounces off what I assume to be Herinor's shield just as I arrive at Kaira's side, Myron one step behind me. Herinor sends a strike of silver power toward the Flame, and we all watch with horror as it is consumed by the ball of fire Arebar sends out to meet it. The smirk on his face tells me Arebar isn't finished. Calling his small army to action, he summons the simmering wall of fire they have been maintaining at their fingertips, sending it across the scorched space.

Royad is in front of me in an instant, protecting both his cousin and me with a thin shield and his body as the heat-wave splinters Herinor's layer of power. Silver magic sprays at the Flames, and the curse ripping from Kaira's throat isn't the only one, but I don't have time to turn and check who got hurt, her or the grumpy traitor male she has a soft spot for. The Flames are marching on us, and they are fast.

Hiding sounds like a great idea right about now, but it's too late. I've made my choice to stand with my family. The first Flames' blades are met by Royad's arrows when they are fifteen paces away, flashes of silver power curling around the missiles which hit hard, even against swords. Sparks of Crow power weave through the air while the Flames are rebuilding their fiery shield. Myron's broad form slips past me, joining Royad at the front, Silas completing the trio as he steps to Myron's other side, patting away smoldering pieces of leather from his armor.

"Those fuckers got me." His tone tells me everything I need to know about how much he hates the Flames—and that they're in serious trouble.

"They got Kaira, too," Herinor grumbles, making my head jerk to the side to assess her state. The stench of freshly singed flesh assaults my nose, and I understand the fury in the male's gaze. He's ready to stab every last Flame soldier through the eye for what they just did, and I cannot blame him.

Kaira swats away the flecks of ash from her lower arm, hiding a wince as she throws back her braid. "I'm a Flame; I can handle a small burn," she complains, breaking free from Herinor's gentle hold on her upper arm where her armor is dangling from her shoulder. It's only then that I notice the angry red blotches and painful blisters on her exposed skin. "It's nothing," she insists, shaking her head at everyone who's about to disagree. "Focus on the battle."

So we do.

The next wave of fire hasn't hit, allowing us a moment to breathe while we meet the Flames' swords with our own weapons in a clash of metal and silver power. Screams of pain tear the air where the Crows' magic hits its mark. In the tangle of limbs and metal, Royad, Myron, and Silas are engaging the enemy in front of me while I stab at the ones breaking through their line of defense. I wonder if, in a one-on-one fight, any Flame could survive them. But we're outnumbered here, despite our resolve to tear them limb from limb.

Herinor and Kaira are raining down their fury on the Flames to my right, meeting each blow with one of their own. Kaira stabs and strikes like a true warrior, but her injuries are catching up to her, and where she was able to push back a Flame before, she now staggers away when her opponent releases her from a deflected hit.

My Crow strength is fueling my own attacks, my blade biting into Flame skin and bone as I hack my way toward Kaira.

It's not enough, though. No matter how hard we strike, the Flames are slowly pushing us back. If they release another wall of fire, I'm not sure the Crows' shields will be able to withstand it. Let alone the feeble layer of magic I've managed that doesn't even remotely resemble a shield.

Strike and parry. It's all I can do, suppressing curses when my bad hand gets tired and sluggish. They are twenty. Twenty flames against four grown Crow males, one part-Flame, and one no-longer-human creature without proper control over her magic. We should be able to hold our ground.

Should.

Myron and Royad spin to the side, angling their swords to spear a Flame pushing to get through the gap between them with his sword aiming directly at my chest. Blood sprays as they pierce through leather and flesh, and the Flame's scream dies in a gurgle as they draw out their blades, already on the next opponent.

"Thank me later," Myron says with a wink, but his voice is shaky.

That Flame would have gotten me in the heart had they not taken him down. A heart which is racing in my chest as I'm processing what just happened.

My hands are shaking, but my legs are stable, ready to stand their ground as the next Flame makes it past the three males. I don't wait to see his face, merely strike before he can get any ideas. Within a heartbeat, my steel tastes Fire Fairy blood. I don't care whom I hit and which part of their body, as long as I draw the life out of them.

Big mistake.

The Flame I got is fashioning a gash across their upper arm, but it's mostly his armor I destroyed. The grip on his sword hasn't loosened; there is no crimson trail running down his arm, and he isn't swaying on his feet. What he's doing is grinning widely at me, perfect teeth exposed and deep brown eyes alive with the fire he's summoned to his other hand.

"Give up, Princess." Arebar pins me with his gaze. How he spilled past the others, I can't fathom with my heart pounding in my throat and my magic straining to break free. I can't let it. The others are too close; if I lose control, I'll kill them.

"Not a chance." Grasping my daggers harder, I take a measured step back to bring some space between me and the fight behind the Flame leader.

Thank the Guardians, Arebar bites, following me a step, grin broadening as if he knows he's got me.

"There's nowhere you can run. Nowhere you can hide."

He's right. He's not going to use his sword to slowly batter me down when he has that vast fire at his disposal. He doesn't even need to come near me to destroy me, and the forest no longer allows for any refuge, not even a quick hideout. If I don't manage to shield, Arebar's fire will eat me alive.

The thought hasn't fully formed when the damned Flame releases his power, sending it straight at the center of my chest. The blast finds purchase on my leathers so fast I can't think or even scream as panic delivers me back into its clutches. I can't think of Myron or Royad or Silas, not of Kaira or even Herinor, as my power rips free of my skin, exploding like a silver star.

My body goes numb; my ears are ringing, vision blurring as I fight to stay on my feet.

I need to fight. Need to protect Myron. Need to—

I need to, but my limbs won't respond as they start burning from the release of power. Every last fiber of my being is so fucking hot. Like Arebar set me on fire after all and I'm being roasted alive.

"Ayna!" Someone shouts my name. I can barely hear them though over my own screams.

I'm on fire.

An orange glow surrounds me like a sphere, little flames dancing along my skin, my vision, as I stumble, fighting my way toward I don't know what. The Silver Stream isn't far back.

I won't make it another three steps before my armor is burned through, and Vala's water magic isn't more than a whisper at the back of my mind. I won't make it—

"Suffocate the fire," someone barks. Through the mate mark, I can feel his panic like another assault of heat, but I welcome the sensation, focusing on only that part of my body while I attempt to compartmentalize the rest of myself.

Something hits my side, and I topple over, groaning with pain as a weight covers my entire body, hands running over my limbs and head, my face and throat as if to smother the remaining flames.

"You'll be fine," the voice from before tells me, and I recognize it as Myron's satin timbre, but the actual words, I don't believe.

In the background, the noise of battle continues to rage, and I wonder if Myron abandoning the fight means all our doom. Before I can come to a conclusion, the pain of searing heat is replaced by the bite of frost and snow.

"What the fuck do you think you're doing?" Clio's disapproving tone might have been meant for Myron, but something tells me she's talking to me.

Myron's weight rolls off me, leaving me fighting for breath. My heart battles the ice creeping through my veins while I'm no longer sure I feel the rest of my body. One thought won't leave my head, though, and it's more soothing than the situation should allow for: Myron is alive. I didn't kill them all with my outburst of magic.

TWENTY-FOUR

MYRON

"You're an asshole extraordinaire," Clio hisses at me. I've had all sorts of accusations and curses hurled at me by the Fairy Princess over the past weeks and disregarded them all.

This time, I'm not immune. This time, I missed my duty to protect Ayna and was nearly too late when the monster of a Flame set her on fire with his cursed magic. Gods, I can barely look at my mate with the blistering burn marks mocking my failure.

I'm not saying anything to Clio because there is nothing I *can* say. No excuse.

"Want me to heal her, or will you do the honors?"

"Of course, I will heal her." What a question. "Your ice might have saved her life, but I'll heal her myself." Because I won't trust anyone to be as gentle and thorough as I'll be with her. "Now move out of my way."

Clio shrugs, throwing her magic into the battle behind us. Royad and Silas are working together with Herinor and Kaira to lure the Flames into their blades before they can set off another blast of fire. Thankfully, Herinor's shield is holding most of the strikes now that his guilt about Kaira's injury is fueling his fury.

Silas is doing a great job at sending sparks of silver power at the remaining Flames, weakening them and distracting them from pulling up an endless stream of fire. It's the best they can do two fighters short, but they are getting Clio, and the fairy immediately sends her ice magic into a loop of sizzling flames one of the Fire Fairies has drawn up right before Royad's face.

My heart continues beating, only because I trust Clio; much as she despises me, I trust her.

Kneeling down by Ayna's shoulder, I place my hand on the side of her neck where trickles of blood have replaced the blisters. Fucking Flames.

If this was an ambush, Recienne better not have anything to do with it.

It *does* strike me as a bit suspicious that the Fairy Princess disappeared just when the attack happened.

The view of Ayna's red and blistered skin surfacing from where her leathers are falling apart in places is almost too much to bear. She could have been dead.

She *will* be if I'm not promptly healing her.

So, I send my healing power into her body, willing calm into my veins and a steady leash on my magic so I won't accidentally hurt her.

The rock on my chest slowly lifts as the blood ceases trickling down her neck and the burn marks slowly fade from angry crimson to pale pink.

"I'm sorry, Ayna." Bending over her face, I brush a kiss to her forehead. "I'm so sorry."

She doesn't wake, doesn't groan and spit her blame at me. Whether it's the injuries or the insane blast of power she set free to eviscerate Arebar, I don't know. All I know is that my chest is aching, and my head is dizzy. The tattoo on my shoulder is cold as ice where it was scalding a minute ago. Like someone has frozen our connection.

"Wake up, my queen." Stroking my fingers down the side of her face, I lift her into my lap, wrapping my arms around her to provide some warmth where Clio's power has driven all of it from her form. Ayna's steady heartbeat suggests she's far from dead, but my fear is real as I wait for her to stir in my embrace while the last of the fight dies down behind us.

Worth fifty fairies… I'm no longer sure any of us Crows is worth even three fairies.

"What happened?" Royad is the first to find us as soon as the last Flame has been slayed. His sword still drips with blood, the same as Silas's hatchet as he stands next to my cousin, rubbing his shoulder where a gash is already healing.

"Myron's little mate almost blew us all up," Herinor comments from a few paces away, wiping blood off his cheek with the back of his hand while his gaze darts over to Kaira, who's sitting on the ground beside him, leaning against the leftovers of a fallen tree trunk. Where before skeletons of a forest greeted us, nothing but dust and lumps of scorched wood is left within a hundred feet radius, and most of it isn't the Flames' fault.

Ayna's power caused that, her untrained Crow magic going rogue to protect her.

My body is still shaking from the force of her attack, and I'm grateful none of us passed out, while the Flames seemed to be less resilient against the vast energy erupting in Ayna's release of power.

"Myron's *queen*," I correct, tone laced with violence, "saved her life and probably all of ours." I don't want to think about what could have happened without her magic breaking free. It certainly put a few Flames on their asses after it tore through Arebar. "It's not her fault she hasn't been properly trained." *It's mine*, I silently add. "Besides, how did they find us so fast?"

Glancing over my shoulder, I search the wasteland for Clio, finding her wiping her sword on the leathers of a Flame corpse. "Where did you disappear to?"

Clio shrugs. "I could ask you the same thing."

I'm not embarrassed for secretly kissing my wife behind the trees like a young male, but I was there to defend the others once Royad warned us. "I asked first."

I've got to give it to Clio; she doesn't as much as flinch when not only I but three other Crow males stare her down. "I went to take out the backup."

Silas barks a laugh. "You're kidding." When she doesn't respond, he turns to Royad and me. "She's kidding, right?"

This time, anger simmers in Clio's jade eyes. "While you were busy sucking your mate's tongue, I went ahead to scout the area. It's easier with my site-hopping and less dangerous than when any of you shift into your bird form and risk your feathers."

That catches me by surprise so hard my chest constricts.

"Now, get over yourself, and stand up. We've got somewhere to be. Ayna will wake up soon enough."

When she said *somewhere to be*, Clio did have a place in mind. Night has crept into the rubble of my former palace by the time we arrive there, Ayna safely in my arms and the others fully recovered from her assault of magic. We'll sleep in the shelter of the broken walls and set out south in the morning to track down any remaining Crows before we hunt for Jeseida's murderous Flames.

With what I've seen of what destruction has haunted my former kingdom, I'm reluctant to believe any of my people are left lest hope springs to life, paving yet another path to the pain of my own failure as a king.

"You can lay her down here." Royad clears the area behind a fallen pillar in the remains of my old throne room at the center of the battlefield, making space for me to place Ayna's sleeping form on the hard stone.

Nodding my thanks at him, I kneel with Ayna in my arms, gently sliding her onto the piece of blackened stone.

When I turn around to ask if any of the other's packs survived the encounter with the Flames, Clio is holding out a blanket, lips pursed and brows knitted in the resemblance of a wordless apology. "I'll take the first shift while you rest."

Herinor prowls up behind her, inclining his head. "I'll keep you company." His gaze, however, is on Kaira, who's curling up against a boulder of cracked marble.

We all look a little worse for wear, but I get Herinor's attitude. I won't rest either before my female awakens.

Kaira rolls her eyes. "Your stubborn ass needs a break, too."

"I'd rather be a stubborn ass than leave your sleep unguarded." Herinor's words are sweeter than he makes them sound, and a pinkish tint only true fae eyes can spot in the dark rises in his cheeks.

"I didn't know you were such a romantic, big bear," Silas cuts from the side, stretching out his legs and resting his head against a piece of wall that's still intact.

The laugh Herinor responds with sounds forced enough to make me believe he's trying too hard. "Don't get me wrong. It's not because I care so much about the female. It's because I worry she might slit my throat if I dare close my eyes next to her."

That costs me a chuckle. I see the twisting of his words untangle even as he is forming them. It's not because he cares about the female—even though he does. But he *is* genuinely concerned she hates him enough to slit his throat. Even with the secret glances Kaira has been stealing at him, he hasn't realized there is more going on.

It's almost comical to see a seasoned warrior like him grappling for straws to protect his heart.

"Well, you'll just need to risk it because *I'm* keeping first watch with Clio." I don't care if he's tossing all night next to Kaira. His king has spoken.

It takes a while for everyone to settle down and doze off, their slow, deep breaths and soft snores as familiar as my own heartbeat. It comes with spending weeks in captivity with the same people. You get to know them inside out. Literally at times. Trying not to remember the images of blood and gore from our imprisonment in Erina's dungeon, I focus on Ayna instead, but those pictures are permanently etched into my memory. As will be the pale, cold features that are my mate's as she lingers in what could be a coma—or hibernation.

Clio has taken up post on a high segment of a broken wall, scanning the surroundings with her fairy vision. With a sigh, I make my way toward her, climbing the set of rocks behind which Ayna sleeps, but it's a far hike up to the wall. One I assume I won't be able to make without site-hopping abilities. Unless I use my bird form, of course.

I pull on the curtain of feathers separating my fae self from my crow self, watching it turn into smoke on a wisp of wind. My entire body turns lighter, arms elongating ever so slightly as black feathers eat up my limbs and torso, shaping the hard lines of my body into those of an aerodynamic creature. I used to despise this form, despite the freedom it brings with it, but with Ayna the first Crow female since the gods cursed my people, I'm no longer hopeless.

By the time I make it to the bottom of Clio's vantage point, I've fully changed, my wings beating the night air into submission, and I climb, climb, climb higher until I land on the wreckage of stone Clio is leaning against. The heat of the shift is as familiar as the back of my hand, as is the vulnerability coming with this smaller, softer body, but my magic hums in my chest like a well of liquid silver, ready to propel me back into my fae form and find a target.

"This never ceases to be creepy," Clio says by way of greeting when I don't shift back. "Honestly, it's a special talent to freak out a centuries-old fairy with a parlor trick like that."

Shrugging, she pushes off the remains of the wall, stepping to the edge of the frazzled piece of floor of the top room in the west tower she's standing on. I only recognize it because of the carvings adorning the cracked, soot-stained stone.

"It's not a parlor trick if you can sneak up on your enemies like that." I shift back into my fae form, feathers retreating from my arms last, and plant my boots next to her by the edge.

We could throw each other over the frazzled corner of this ruin without concern. What with one of us able to turn into a creature bearing wings and the other one defying the laws of time and space with her disjointed mode of transportation. For some reason, neither of us makes an attempt though. We've formed a sort of truce.

I'm still staring at the stars above this godsforsaken burnt wasteland when Clio sighs through her nose. "What are you going to do about the bargain you made with Tori?"

Her question takes me by surprise so much I tear my gaze away from the skies. It's been a while since I made a bargain with Tori, and back then, it was about finding both our mates. *Find one, find both.* Not a bargain, really, but a promise. "The only deal I made with him is that I'll take my people and leave Eherea if he works with me to find Ayna and you."

The gaze Clio gives me tells me she already knows the finer details of it all. "You'll leave eventually." It's not a suggestion, and I am fully aware any objection of mine would be a breaking of my promise.

"Eventually." Suppressing a sigh of my own, I glance over my shoulder at Ayna's peaceful face. "I'll take my people and leave, eventually."

Clio's smile is the one reaction I don't expect. "Good. Because, my brother might be a stubborn ass, but I believe that working together is the only way to save Eherea. We have Erina's army coming for Askarea. Ephegos's insane thirst for power. But that's not all. Those damned Fire Fairies are coming for us left and right, and they're merely an envoy of this war."

Raising my brows at her, I rock back on my heels, folding my arms over my chest. "And you'd rather work with the son of the male who wanted to force you into marriage than kick him out of your realm at the next opportunity?"

"My *brother's* realm. And yes." She places a small, calloused hand on my shoulder, her grasp almost as strong as my cousin's, and tilts her head to the side. "Have you forgotten that you helped save Tori? My mate has grown rather

213

fond of your broody constitution, and I'd rather not be the one to break it to Tori that you're taking off early."

Inclining my head at her, I breathe in the fresh, cool air drifting from the skies, savoring the lack of stench it comes with. "I'd hate to disappoint your mate."

"Only because you know he'd tear your head off." A grin plays on her lips that's more feline than human. It's the first real grin she's given me, and it feels like I've won an uphill battle.

The moment doesn't demand for more words, so I refrain from searching for any. Tomorrow will be soon enough when we all head out to hunt down what's left of my court and then follow the same path we'd taken when we set out to find Clio and Ayna—and pay Jeseida a visit about those missing fairies.

TWENTY-FIVE

AYNA

The sun is rising when I come around, my limbs screaming at me with punishing soreness. It's not like I trained with a sword or did other physical workouts. What is causing my condition is the uncontrolled use of my magic. I remember the blast of power rushing from my veins like lightning. I also remember the wall of fire hitting me.

On instinct, I reach for my face where my skin should be raw.

My fingers find smooth skin and the absence of pain a burn mark would come with.

It takes me a moment to understand we're in the ruins of the Crow palace and the two graceful outlines on the half-shattered wall are Myron and Clio.

"About time you woke up," Royad's soothing voice greets me from a few feet away where the other Crows are gnawing on dried fruit and passing a waterskin around.

Herinor nods his agreement. "If I didn't already know you're a menace, I'd be convinced now."

With an eye-roll, Kaira elbows him, sitting down beside him with just enough distance that their bodies don't touch. "My sister is *not* a menace."

"But you are?"

Honestly, if Herinor is trying to collect extra points with Kaira, he's not doing well at all.

"What made you doubt before?" Sitting up, I stretch my arms over my head, ready to take a full breath when a black, feathery form flutters into my shoulder. I barely get in a gasp of air before the bird expands into Myron's familiar shape. His lips find my cheek, arms winding around me so tightly I cough, even as I lean into him, inhaling his scent greedily.

Turning my head, I brush my mouth against his, the warmth of his breath filling me with new strength, new life.

"Good, everyone's awake." Clio's voice nearly startles said life out of me once more as she sneaks up behind us.

Royad bursts out in laughter as I jump into Myron's lap, and the male winces as I land roughly on the sensitive pieces of his malehood.

When I glance over Myron's shoulder, determined to glower but incapable of doing so when all I really want to do is take hold of Myron's pants and check what damage I did, Clio is grinning sheepishly. "Once the Crow King's got his cock back in order, we can go find the rest of those feathery creeps."

I'm surprised neither of the males glares at her with death in their eyes. Even Myron grunts a pained but humorous sound.

"Off we go, Crow hunting," Kaira chimes in.

"No hunting," Herinor corrects, snatching her bow from where she's placed it on the ground beside her. "You like Crows, never forget that."

"Only the ones who deserve it."

Royad and Silas are still laughing when they get to their feet, lifting their packs onto their shoulders and sheathing their weapons. A few minutes later, we're on our way to comb the wasteland that is now the Seeing Forest for leftover Crows.

We find no one on the first day. The Flames have thoroughly burned everything to the ground, and there are no tracks we could interpret to figure out if Crows have recently passed through. By the end of the second day, we have searched the entire north-western part of the forest, finding no sign of life other than a few birds picking for scorched nuts. A day later, we arrive in the eastern regions of the forest. The Crows in our group search from up in the air, shifting back and forth to report, while Clio, Kaira, and I stay on the ground.

I could shift. Deep down in my bones, I know I could shift if I gave in to the tug whenever I watch the flock of birds take off to the skies, but there's a part of me that fears my own power, fears the lightness of that other body and where the winds could carry me if I dared to give in. I could easily lose myself and forget I have a kingdom to save. So, I find reasons why I need to stay with the females.

On the third day, we find a black feather on the ground. Myron lands just in time to watch me pluck it from the charred soil, his elegant bird form expanding into the broadness of his fae body, shoulders widening as layers of feathers retreat, giving way to his leathers.

"Could be a regular crow's," Herinor comments as he plants his boots next to Myron's in the ashes.

"Could be," Royad agrees. He's been quiet these past days, retreating more and more into himself as hope to find any remaining Crow Fairies in this joke of a forest dwindles.

"Or it could be one of ours," Myron points out, brushing an invisible feather on his forearm.

"Could be." Silas shrugs as if humoring the others, then turns to gaze into the distance where gray turns to green and tree skeletons turn to grassland. "We've found more bones than we can count in this godsforsaken forest. If you ask me, whoever was hiding here is either dead or has left for good."

"No one is asking you," Herinor snarls, but I can see the anger is superficial. The tight lines around his mouth tell a different story. One of loss.

Elbow braced against the stump of a tree, Silas grimaces. "Too bad I don't care. I would have long disappeared had I not been busy spitting blood at my captors for the better part of the past month."

"You wouldn't, and you know it." Kaira steps in front of the grumpy male, bracing her hands on her hips, the bow slung over her shoulder sliding down to her elbow. "You would follow Myron to the ends of this land and never even shed a tear about it. You know it. I know it."

Herinor is smothering a chuckle as he carefully pulls Kaira's bow back up to her shoulder. "Crows don't cry." He leans in so close Kaira shouts a startled curse—in her mind—and I stumble a step forward, ready for an attack.

"*Damn it, Kaira,*" I warn through our channel. "*Do that again and I might accidentally stab someone.*" The danger in my trembling hand is suggesting exactly that might happen.

Myron raises a brow at me as his gaze bounces back and forth between Kaira and Herinor and me. "Do I even want to know," he whispers.

Shaking my head, I sheathe my dagger, casting my gaze on the feather once more. "What if they all disappeared?"

"It's more likely they are dead," Royad gravely muses, head hung as if in respect for brothers lost in battle.

For a long moment, we all stand in silence. Even Clio doesn't comment, her sharp fairy tongue mute for once as she watches us absorb the fact that our search might be in vain.

Eventually, Myron clears his throat, voice hoarse as he tells us, "We'll search for the missing fairies first." What he doesn't need to add is the silent hope that maybe we'll come across a track that leads us to the Crows.

It's the fourth day when we get close to the Tavrasian border. There's been no sign of the Flames or the Crows. Perhaps it's a blessing in disguise that whatever's left of Myron's people hasn't shown up. Even death would be better than being captured by the Flames. No one has mentioned that option, probably out of fear it might be true.

Clio site-hops Kaira and me while the Crows fly the whole distance, gleaning for signs of fires or rogue features. It seems Recienne wasn't lying about the series of attacks. There are burn marks all over the borderlands, some fresh like from a few days ago, and some older, fresh ferns and blades of grass pushing through the layer of ash. Whenever we come across one of them, Clio's anger rises an inch higher until, by the time we make it near Jeseida's residence, the female is ready to slaughter the first creature looking at her the wrong way.

I've seen her protective of her mate before, but this is the wrath of a princess whose people have been wronged.

"The Flames have lived in this region since long before the Crows ever invaded Askarea," Kaira reminds me. "After the Crows took our home in the Seeing Forest, we had to find other niches of this realm to survive."

I remember the Flames have scattered throughout the lands, some even as far as the Southern Continent.

"What Jeseida built here"—she points at the estate whose roofs are peeking through the treetops—"is more than a shiny home. It's the beginning of a new generation of Flames. Those who will stop at nothing to claim what they believe is theirs."

"They can have the forest they burned down for all that I care," I murmur under my breath, scooting to the side to make room for Myron as he squeezes into our vantage point between a copse of firs and some hazel bushes. Herinor and Silas are keeping watch in their bird forms high up in the branches while Clio, Kaira, Myron, and Royad are talking strategy to scout if the fairies are really here.

"Thank the Guardians you don't have a say in who gets the Seeing Forest," Clio snarks, and I'm surprised she doesn't freeze me over with the look she gives me.

"She's working with Ephegos." Myron hides the hurt in his tone, but the betrayal of his friend still stings, I can tell. "That alone is reason to never let her get a foothold again. Once we've uprooted her," he adds with gritted teeth.

The anger runs deep. As deep as Clio's, even if for a different reason.

"I wonder where he keeps the other traitors," Royad throws in, ducking slightly to gain a better view on the estate. "They can't possibly all fit in there."

"How many did he take?" Clio takes a swig from the waterskin, wiping her mouth with the back of her hand. I can't imagine this female in finery and tiaras, no matter if she's a princess. Perhaps she's the best version of a princess; one who doesn't shy away from saving her people with her own hands.

I still don't know how I feel about King Recienne not bothering to make a trip to the locations of the attacks. Perhaps his sister has some insight. "Doesn't Recienne put on leathers and fight every once in a while?"

"I know he did in the Crow war," Myron notes, shifting his weight to glance at the princess.

Clio bites her lip, holding back words that obviously aren't meant for us. It shouldn't hurt that she's keeping secrets; after all, she's centuries older than me and couldn't possibly share all her stories in one human lifetime, but the bitter taste of being left out spreads on my tongue, and it takes more effort than it should not to push for an answer she doesn't want to give.

"He needs to look after his own priorities right now." It's all she says, and it's a weak excuse.

"His people should be his priority," Royad says with unusual bite.

"They are. That's why I'm here." And that's that. Clio's eyes are back on the estate where black birds are rising from the roof, taking off south.

Myron's arm wraps around me so fast I barely manage a breath before he's flattened me beneath the low branches of the closest fir. He's covering me with his body, arms braced on each side of my shoulders, ocean gaze locked on mine as we listen to the wingbeats in the distance. My heightened senses are alert and awake, taking in the danger of being spotted by what must have been Crow Fae in their bird form.

That's not the only thing I perceive, though. The scent of fresh moss, of evergreens and damp soil, and … Myron. His scent is so prominent in my nose that I almost lose my breath. Then there's the feel of him. Even with two layers of leather between us, I can feel his powerful build. I should be focusing on Silas and Royad's whisper, I know, but all I can see is Myron. His eyes holding the enigma of the ocean and filled with awareness as he scans my face, his lashes two frames of night silk, his strong, stubbled jaw. His mouth…

My lips are parting, ready to taste him, and were it not for Clio's jab in Myron's bicep—which he deems with a growl of warning—I'd forget why we're here on the ground with his hips settled against mine and the intent of a predator on me.

"Save it for when you're alone, stallion." Clio is already getting to her hands and knees, crawling through the thicket back to where prying eyes from the sky cannot reach.

I don't protest when Myron pushes up and slides off me, but I do bemoan the feel of him in an instant. I can't lose him again.

So, I'll happily fight to make sure neither Erina nor Ephegos nor the Flames get to separate us again.

And the first step is to earn Recienne's full support.

TWENTY-SIX

AYNA

The estate is quiet when we sneak up from the back where the hedge has grown high enough to shield even the tall Crow males. After hours of watching the coming and going of Flames, spying no longer seems like enough to find out whether the missing fairies are locked up somewhere in a dungeon. I hope Herinor's torture chamber isn't where they are holding them; the memory of my first encounter with the male is enough to make my hair stand on my neck and an onslaught of nausea to assault my stomach.

Instinctively, I reach for my shoulder where Herinor sliced my skin to send a message to Myron that I was alive and where to find me.

When I glance to the side, Herinor's eyes are on me, conflict muddying their otherwise light green. He inclines his head, and so do I. It's not like we've become real friends—the deal he made with Ephegos won't allow that—but we've gotten closer. I no longer fear him the way I did when I first fled Erina's palace, but I know I can't rely on him for help, even when he wants to help me.

It's fucked up that Ephegos managed to trap him like that. Fucked up and unfair.

"*How do you think I'm feeling about that?*" Kaira throws in, and I jerk up the shield I've been working on to keep my thoughts private—even from my sister.

"*Like you can't trust him?*" I suggest through our mental connection.

Her dark laugh resonates in my head. "*No, that comes with the territory of Crows in general. I hate that he could be turned against my sister at any moment.*"

"*He's already been turned against me,*" I remind her.

To my left, Clio and Myron are whispering with Royad while Herinor's making space for Kaira to better see through the gap in the wall of leaves.

"*He seems to like* you *a lot, though.*" I imagine winking at her, and the feeling seems to come across because she glares at me for a brief moment before returning her attention to the massive male at her side.

We stay in our hideout a few moments longer before Myron and Clio deem it *safe* for the Crows to shift and take a brief flight across the grounds, and when they turn into their feathery selves and take off, my heart doesn't stop racing the entire time they are gone. Long minutes pass, my imagination supplying me with all sorts of horror scenarios of what could have gone wrong. Only when I spot four black birds descending from the roof once more do I take a full breath again.

Royad is the first to land—I've learned to distinguish the four Crows in their bird forms—but he doesn't shift. Silas comes in next, hopping a few steps before he settles beneath the hedge right in front of my boot. Myron and Herinor are last, but only Myron shifts back into his fae form to explain what they've found.

"The hole in the roof is still there." He means the one where they broke through old tiles when hunting down my scent months ago. His retelling of what happened here still haunts my nightmares. How they'd been trapped, captured, and their magic taken from them.

Swallowing the rising nausea, I focus on Myron's report rather than on the ball of anxiety raging in my stomach.

"If we're quick, we might make it in through there. We can start searching on the top floor and make our way down."

Clio doesn't have anything to say other than, "I'll site-hop them to the roof."

The glance Myron gives me as I reach for Clio's out-stretched hand is both warning and encouragement. My tat-too tingles and heats as he shifts so fast he's nothing but a blur of feathers.

"If we measured the intervals correctly, we have about a half-hour window to do our search. Be thorough and don't waste time. If you come across Crows or Flames, make sure they don't raise an alarm. Do what you need to do." Her instructions are cold and precise like a seasoned general, but her eyes dart to Kaira as if in apology for giving the order to hurt, potentially kill, her people.

Dismissing the gesture with a shake of her head, the part-Flame takes Clio's other hand, and the world blurs before my eyes as Clio drags us through it on her magic.

We hit the roof half a breath later. A breath now lodged in my throat as I find myself at the edge of a massive crater gaping in the spread of age-worn tiles. Myron is standing on the opposite side, back in his fae form, Royad and Silas flanking him with tight expressions on their faces. This is madness. The chances we'll find the fairies here are slight, but where else are we going to start searching? If they're not here, someone will know where they are, and we'll get the information out of them.

My magic is drawing taut in my body, readying for a fight, but if I haven't learned full control over it while using it, I've made great progress at holding it in. It tosses like angry waves as I tell it to stay put. One of these days, I'll *need* training, or I'll keep stumbling through this war.

At least, I'm swift with my daggers and light on my feet, my new senses and strength granting me advantages in combat I didn't have as a human.

My ears tell me there's no one awaiting us below the open roof, so I don't hesitate to follow when Royad and

Myron hop down, landing on their feet silent as cats. When I leap after them, Myron catches me around the waist, setting me down lightly, eyes serious and full of anticipation of an ambush.

Clio has Kaira by the hand, site-hopping the part-Flame down onto the weather-worn wooden floor. It must have recently rained; the streaks of old blood covering the patterned wood have been washed out to near-invisibility.

We step further into the large space, making sure not to stumble over heaps of debris as we make room for Herinor and Silas, both of them drawing their weapons as they seem to float from where the jagged tiles end. Herinor points toward the narrow wooden door at the far end of the room, gesturing for us to follow as he makes to open it.

Nobody speaks, our silence—despite the shields Silas and Herinor have thrown up around us—imperative to slipping in and out of this place undetected. In the hallway, we split into groups: Royad heads out to the left together with Kaira, who knows this estate like the back of her hand. Silas and Clio head off to the other side, leaving Myron, Herinor, and me. We'd debated leaving Herinor behind, just in case we'd be caught and he might fall back into Ephegos's hands, but the mighty warrior declared that, if we were caught, he'd rather be at our side than sitting by in a treetop. But that's not all; Myron wants to keep an eye on the Crow now that we're entering enemy territory again.

We head down the staircase, listening hard for any sign of life along the hallway lined with carved doors. Faint voices sound from the end, near the window, but they are cheerful and frequently interrupted by the sound of something clacking over wood.

Herinor cups his hands together, shakes them, and mimics throwing something onto a surface. It takes me a moment to understand he's telling us they're rolling dice. One by one, Herinor opens the doors that don't betray their interior with sound, shaking his head each time Myron and I stand ready to attack. Besides a simple bed, an armoire, a chest of drawers, and a wooden stand serving to hold armor, they're all empty, the only sound remaining that from the room at the end of the hallway.

By the time we make it near that door, I can make out at least two distinct voices.

"Fifty coins," a female voice declares, followed by the clinking of metal. Imagining a pouch of silver poured onto a table, I take one measured breath after the other, forcing my nerves to stay strong. I have Myron and Herinor with me, but if the wrong creature lurks behind the door we stop in front of, it won't matter who fights at my side.

One hand in the air, sword in the other, Myron waits, listening.

"You lost half of your salary last time we played, Chali. You sure you're ready for what comes if you lose the rest?" A male voice chuckles, but his words are slightly slurred.

The bubbling of liquid followed by the slide of a glass along the table confirms they must be drinking.

"I'm ready, but I'm not convinced *you* are." Innuendo floats on the female's tone, making my cheeks blush even when I don't even know what they're playing, but I'm almost convinced she plans on paying her debts with her body.

Myron rolls his eyes, gesturing for us to take the next staircase down, and we follow his lead, Herinor's brows knitted and my stomach in knots. The daggers in my hands weigh nothing, my feet light and fast as I keep up with the two males.

A few weeks ago, I wouldn't have believed I could achieve near soundless paces, but I've spent my time wisely, practicing and honing my other fae abilities if I couldn't train my magic. I've been studying them—all of the Crows. Their stealthy movements, the way they roll their soles to avoid noise, the patterns of scanning their surroundings.

My body might be human, but it follows Crow instincts now. Power hums in my veins, and I could turn into smoke and feathers if I wasn't so damned scared.

"*Find anything?*" Kaira's voice in my head nearly startles me to death, my hand stupidly grasping for the handrail as we sneak down the stairs.

"*Nothing of use,*" I inform her, focusing already on the next set of doors ahead, this one wider and one of two on a short segment of hallway before it ends in a large, open sitting area. I might have liked the design of russet and cream had this not been an enemy home where I was held captive. "*You?*"

"*Nothing. Only empty sleeping quarters. Seems they're all out training.*"

"*Or burning down more of Askarea,*" I suggest, wondering how many people the Flames have killed.

"That for sure. It doesn't take a whole house of Flames to do that, though. Most of the rooms we've seen haven't been slept in for days. Some for weeks."

"How do you know?"

Kaira seems to hesitate. *"I've stayed in one like these most of my life. Simple soldier quarters in a fancy home."* There's a sting to her words that has nothing to do with our search for the fairies or with the fact that she's been at the bottom end of the food chain in her own people all her life. How I can tell, I'm not sure, but I don't pry.

"We're entering a sitting room," I narrate, sending over the image of the grand arrangement of uncomfortable-looking brocade chairs and brass-adorned table. Fresh flowers are sitting at the center of it, bending their colorful heads this way and that.

In front of me, Myron shakes his head, pointing back toward the hallway, and we circle around before all of us have fully entered the room.

"Nothing there," I report while Kaira sends me the image of an empty hallway from their side of the estate.

The third group must have found nothing either, or we'd have heard signs of battle. Why the silence is so reassuring, I don't even try to unpack. Perhaps I'm not ready to face the enemy, or I'm just glad my friends aren't in immediate danger.

Not that sneaking around the Flames' home isn't the highest degree of dangerous.

For long minutes, we check one room after the other for signs of missing fairies. Personally, I would have started with the place of assault and gone from there, but with everything burned to ashes, there are no tracks and traces of life where the Flames captured Recienne's soldiers. Clio herself has visited each and every scorched battlefield to confirm.

"*Anything?*" Kaira prompts as we make it to the second floor without coming across more Flames. It's like the house has been abandoned without us noticing. I could swear we saw at least twenty Flames come and go, and as many Crows; there should be more people in this place.

All we find is the empty main hall and reception room. And inside the next room—

My stomach folds in on itself as I recognize the heavily ornamented walls and ceiling, the russet brocade and cream filigree. And there, covered in impeccable sheets speaking of the innocence of a welcoming guest room, the bed I'd been sleeping in for long, long days stands against the opposite wall. Nothing speaks of the torment I've endured in here, but it doesn't matter that they've cleaned away every visible trace of me.

Myron's nostrils flare, grip tightening on his weapon as he scents the air. A low growl rumbles in his throat, and even Herinor has the good sense to stand aside as Myron prowls into the room, squinting as if struggling to keep his eyes open, and rams his blade right into the pillows resting at the head of the bed. With a powerful tug on the pommel of his sword, he slices through the length of the bed, covers, mattress, down to the wooden frame, until it splits apart with a marrow-freezing creak.

"*What was that?*" Kaira's voice barely breaks through the sound of Myron's anger breaking the bed where I'd once been stuck.

"Nothing." Determined to console him, I follow Myron into the room, sheathing one dagger as I reach for his hand.

He rips it away, rounding on me, breath ragged and eyes wild. I've never seen him like this. Even when he realized Ephegos had betrayed him, he hadn't been boiling with rage like he's boiling now.

"Didn't sound like nothing." The obvious alarm in Kaira's tone catches my attention. *"Do you need reinforcements?"*

She'd be there in a heartbeat if I said I needed her, but I shake my head at myself, at Myron, and at her. *"Just keep your eyes open in case the noise attracted any attention. We're safe for now."*

At least, that's what I hope when I reach for my dagger once more, gesturing for Myron to leave.

With a last, hateful glance at the room, he crosses the threshold, Herinor and me following suit. I don't dare look back over my shoulder for fear of what the ghosts of my past will show me if I allow my thoughts to wander there.

My tattoo is heating anyway, claiming my focus as we wander down a familiar set of stairs—the one the Flame guards dragged me down to visit Herinor's torture chamber.

The tension is palpable, rolling off both males the closer we get to the fateful door behind which Herinor first alerted Myron to my location by hurting me. I try not to think about it, but the pain has permanently settled into my memory, and I suck air through my teeth not to drift back into those moments of agony altogether.

One slow exhale. One inhale. Another steady exhale.

I can see the ostentatious entrance hall again, the set of stairs turning away from the main corridor to our right. Herinor leads us straight there, and my heart pounds like a traitorous drum.

I'm not afraid of you.

I haven't thought that sentence in a long time. But now, I need it, or I'll crack apart.

The corridor is lit by eternal torches left and right when Herinor guides us past the door to his torture chamber into a dark tunnel which I can't remember from last time. What I know immediately is that we're on our way to the dungeon. Within a few paces, iron bars come into view. I instinctively keep away from them, remembering the magic-draining substance painted on the bars at the palace in Meer.

Myron hasn't left my side since we exited my old bedroom, his muscles taut, features grim, and cold rage simmering beneath the surface that I wouldn't wish upon anyone—except for Ephegos and Erina, perhaps. They deserve it.

It's become unnerving that no one has come to investigate what caused the noise on the second floor, but who am I to complain? If we get in and out of this house without being detected or confronted, I'll be a happy person. If we get to bring a bunch of missing fairies along, I'll be ecstatic. It will ensure us the alliance with the Fairy King and potentially help us win a war.

I keep my mind away from the fact that Recienne will have to fight this war whether or not he works with us. Erina is determined, and Ephegos won't be satisfied without his share in the whole plan.

A shiver runs down my spine at the mere thought of fairies at the Tavrasian king's feet, their strength and powers gone.

We're halfway down the line of empty cells when I see them in them.

Tall, beautiful shapes, hanging from the ceiling like slaughtered deer. My breath catches as I smell the tang of iron and decay.

"They killed them all—" I can't help the words from slipping out while Myron and Herinor seem to have lost their voices.

Detaching from Myron's side, I rush ahead, sheathing one of my daggers so I'd have a hand free in case there is a way to unlock the cell. At first, it's mere outlines, long and heavy bodies, tied by their wrists to steel rings screwed into the stone ceiling, their bodies sagged and motionless. Blood covers their bare arms and faces—such beautiful faces distorted with grimaces of pain. Puddles of urine are drying up under their feet where their bladders loosened the moment life left them. The stench hits me as if the wind just turned to shove it in my face. But there's no wind down here. Only stale air carrying proof of the fairies' suffering.

"Guardians—" Covering my mouth and nose with my free hand, I catch my breath, trying to count the number of corpses.

"What the fuck happened here?" Herinor's tone could cut through solid rock, and he looks nothing like the seasoned, ruthless warrior I know him to be as he takes in the cruelty inflicted on the fairy captives.

TWENTY-SEVEN

AYNA

"This is madness."

Myron rushes past me, silver power cracking at his fingertips as he inspects the heavy cell door for weakness, then makes quick work of the hinges with a few powerful strikes of his blade. The steel sways on the threshold, moving painstakingly slowly as it collapses into the corridor. Myron steps out of the way just in time not to get hit on the shoulder by the tumbling obstacle, apparently too eager to free the fairies from their bindings. To give them dignity, even in death. That's the kind of male Myron of Winghaven is. He's inside the cell a heartbeat later, getting to work cutting down one limp fairy after the other and laying them down on the ground.

Herinor is right beside him, searching their bare and relatively clean arms for something I can't see from this angle, so I join them inside the cell, heart ricocheting as I cross the ancient threshold.

Trap, something inside of me warns.

"We need to get out of here." My words get lost in the shaking of my voice as I realize what Herinor has been inspecting.

Little puncture holes dot the fairies' arms, their size a perfect fit for the needles Ephegos used to inject his victims with the magic-nullifying drug. At least, all the parts of their skin that are whole. The rest of their bodies are charred and singed, blistered and bleeding. All, except for their features, as if the Flames want us to recognize whom they mangled.

"Something feels off," I try again, the sense of foreboding in my chest becoming an unforgiving pressure.

"Something *is* massively off," Herinor agrees, but he's gesturing at the corpses now littering the ground. There have to be at least twenty of them. "Someone used these poor bastards to experiment on them while they were tortured."

My stomach turns, and I vomit right in front of my feet. I've seen Ephegos and Erina do some sick torture, have experienced some of it myself, but this level of cruelty... How long did these fairies suffer before Eroth showed them mercy and took them behind his veil?

The nausea won't fade, but Myron and Herinor are doing the only thing we can: Showing the deceased this last kindness. So, instead of following the impulse to bolt, I join the two males' efforts and cut down the female closest to me. She sags into my arm, not stiff like the dead the others have laid down on the packed earth floor but like someone who passed out. Her dark, dirt-smeared skin is warm enough to suggest she might still be alive.

Hammering a melody of hope, my heart speeds inside my tight chest. If we can save one—just *one*—of these fairies, it will be a victory in itself.

"Can you hear me?" Supporting her lolling head, I lay the female down and crouch beside her. Her torn shirt and pants are soaked in blood, but she hasn't peed or shit herself, I can tell by her odor.

A groan is the only response I get, but it's a sign I was right. Her chest heaves fast breaths, and her eyelids flutter, but she's too far gone to wake up. Perhaps that's a mercy in itself.

"Over here—" In an instant, Myron and Herinor are at my side, both their free hands landing on patches of intact skin, and their power flowing into the female's system. It's not enough to heal her completely, but some of the oozing burn marks turn into welted scars, and the gash along her abdomen seals enough to hold in the trickle of blood running down her side.

"There might be more alive." I'm already on my feet again, dashing to the next fairy and the next, touching their faces to feel warmth or breath, searching for a pulse where the skin on their necks hasn't been burned away. Only four more are hanging, but I force myself to be thorough with each one, that flicker of hope ready to spark and take flight.

Each life saved is a victory for us. Each fairy taken from the claws of the Flames is a blow in their faces.

"*We're done on the ground floor,*" Kaira interrupts my focus. "*Where are you?*"

"*Don't come,*" I warn her. "*We found the fairies. Find the others, and meet us in the forest.*"

There's nothing they can do down here, and between Herinor, Myron, and me, we can handle carrying out one survivor.

One.

Because that's all there is.

The others are dead.

Sending Kaira a glimpse of the horror that is this dungeon, I let her know we'll be out in a minute, too. We'll sneak back up the stairs, leave through the roof, and find the others in our hideout in the forest.

"*Get out of there immediately.*" Kaira's warning comes a split second before I notice them from the corner of my eye.

Figures in brown leather, slender silver blades in their hands and the promise of death on their faces. We were so busy cutting down the dead that we didn't notice the Flames sneaking up on us on their damned silent feet.

"*Shit!*"

"You could say so." Herinor is the first to drop the fairy survivor and step to my side, but Myron is faster. He's blocking the path between me and whatever the Flames might throw our direction, sword glimmering in the low light of the torches. His hair is floating on a phantom wind which I know means his power is rallying beneath his skin.

240

A part of me understands that we've walked right into a trap, that the Flames knew we were coming and wanted us to make it all the way down here where they could smash our morals and attack in close quarters.

With a glance over my shoulder, I confirm there's no other exit. It's through the group of Flames blocking our path or not at all.

"Let us go, and we won't fry you with our magic," Myron barks, silver tendrils of power climbing up the blade of his sword.

Beside me, Herinor has become the calm before a storm while, inside my chest, the wild oceans of a hurricane are fighting to break free.

"We need to take the female to safety."

At my whisper, Herinor raises an eyebrow as if to ask if I've lost my mind.

"We need to bring her back to Aceleau," I insist.

Herinor rolls his eyes, but I know he will grab her when it's time to run. If not, I'll do it.

The first ball of fire hits like a clap of thunder, blasting off the shield Herinor and Myron have crafted around us, and I duck behind my dagger like it could protect me from the hot ash raining through the cracks in the male's magic. One moment the tunnel is bright like a bonfire; the next, all light flickers out, even the everlasting torches on the walls retreating into themselves as if guided by invisible hands.

My eyes fight to adjust to the absence of light so hard I almost miss the flare of silver right in front of me. All I can do is pull my dagger to my chest, pointy end outward, and meet whatever is coming my way with a blind stab.

A female hisses in a language I don't understand, making relief dripping across my skin alongside cold beads of sweat. Not Myron. I didn't accidentally stab Myron.

The Flames are upon us, and, judging by the clashing of metal, both Myron and Herinor are already engaged in battle.

"Shield!" Myron shouts, followed by a crack of power in the air. A silver sheen coats the nearby walls as Herinor throws up a stronger shield, and I could swear the ground is trembling.

Myron is a shadow cutting through flesh and bone as the Flames charge. Ten, maybe fifteen are coming for us; it's hard to tell with how dark the dungeon has turned behind the reach of Herinor's shield. All I know is they keep coming. One after the other, they crash against the male's power while Myron has fallen into a killing calm. Blood sprays left and right, but it's not just that of the Flames Myron and Herinor are cutting down. I'm contributing to the melee as well.

I've inched close enough to the edge of the shield to stab and slice at the coming Flames, drawing blood with each hit I land. My body is singing with strength, and in my veins, magic is swirling.

One by one, we're pushing the Flames back. From the end of the corridor, shouts to order speak of the disarray ruling the Flames' formation. They are losing this fight, and fast.

Fire flares against our shield once more, the impact hard enough to make Herinor stagger, but he holds his ground, one arm wound around the legs of the fairy female he's carrying over his shoulder, the other arm straining as he holds both the shield and his sword to take down whoever skips through.

Heat blasts my face, singeing the fine hairs in my nose and I pray that the Flames won't send another onslaught of fire right away. I've only recently been a living torch. No need to repeat that experience. The Flame closest to me grins, and I stab without delay. It's not my most elegant move, but it's effective: The Flame topples over as I pull my dagger from his chest and crouch down to slice behind his knees. He almost hits me when I hesitate for a moment before leaping out of the way.

We're making progress. Slow, but progress. Every step forward is a step toward freedom.

Reinforcements are within reach. It can't be long until the others show up. Kaira must have already informed them of the trap we walked into.

Stab, slash. Stab, slash. Herinor's shield flickers with each new ball of fire the Flames hurl at it, hissing and steaming at the contact, but it holds. It holds long enough for us to make it to the stairs leading up to the entrance hall.

"When we get out of there, run." Myron's voice is full of authority. It's not a suggestion but an order, and I'm ready to listen for once. "You, too, Herinor. Run."

Before either of us can object that he'd better run, too, Myron curses and shoves a Flame pushing through the shield

243

right back into the darkness and over the threshold to Eroth's Veil. "I'll be right behind you."

"Promise?" This single word is all I have breath for.

"Promise." Myron's response loosens the knot in my chest, sending the concern for my mate to the bottom of my thoughts. He promised. He won't stay behind.

"Where the fuck are the others?" Herinor is now fighting alongside us up the stairs, grunting under the strain of balancing the shield and carrying the unconscious female. "The moment I spot Clio, I'll shove that creature into her arms, and she can take her to her brother."

He sounds like a grump, but I hear the genuine concern for our rescue in his tone.

"They can't be far," Myron grits out, pressing his blade against a Flame's silver sword.

We've been fighting for minutes; the noise of our battle can't go unnoticed.

"*Kaira!*" I shout in my mind.

No response.

"*Kaira, where are you?*"

The entrance hall greets us with spacious russet and cream. About five more Flames are fighting, but they are strong and ready. They've been waiting for us, preparing to strike the moment we set foot into the room. Walls of fire hit from all sides, heat blasting apart Herinor's shield. Myron throws his arms around my shoulders, cradling my head against his chest as he shields me from the flames with his own body. I taste iron and salt as I bite my lip at the impact, but the momentary pain is nothing compared to the panic grabbing hold of me. Herinor's curse echoes through the hallways.

"Fuck the gods! Where are those boasting fairies when you need them?" He means Clio, but the female isn't there to save the day. Not this time. None of the others are.

The air stills as the Flames wait for their magic to recharge so they can smother us with another blow of power.

Myron nods at me as if expecting me to understand, then at Herinor.

He wants us to run while the Flames are dependent on their blades. The door is about fifteen feet ahead, and the Flames are standing well away from it. If we run, we can make it.

"I'm not leaving y—"

"Go, Ayna. I can hold them off on my own." Silver lightning crackles at Myron's fingertips, and an expression of collected menace graces his features.

It's that moment that I know he's right. He can blast those five Flames out of their boots if he wants to—he's just that powerful—but he's scared to hurt us with his still uncontrollable magic. So, he wants us out of the way before he brings this estate down for good.

"Now!"

Grabbing my daggers harder, I bolt, darting for the door. Herinor is right beside me, his shield wrapping around us like a shimmering target.

We get close to the doors. Closer. The Flames are coming for us, but we're faster.

At the last two paces before we would crash into the carved wood of the entrance, Herinor sends out a blast of his own power, dropping the shield to let the shot through.

The door splinters into a million pieces, but I don't stop. Hands are thrown over my head to shield my face and neck.

Myron's roar is an echo at the back of my mind as we stumble through the door, coughing and panting and featuring an array of scratches along the backs of our hands.

Behind us, silver light flashes, and I know Myron is fighting in earnest now.

"To the hedges." Herinor points with the tip of his sword, but he doesn't wait for me or make sure I get to safety first. The deal he struck with Ephegos is still in place, and if he as much as tries to help me, he'll suffer greatly. He can pretend he's aiding Myron instead for all that I care, as long as we make it to the tall hedges and off the premises.

The plan is better than reality will allow.

Around the corner, where the trees surrounding the estate form a small meadow, a group of at least forty Flames is gathered, silver swords at the ready and tendrils of fire flaring in their raised palms.

TWENTY-EIGHT

AYNA

"**F**uck—"

We skid to a halt, Herinor almost losing his grasp on the female bouncing over his shoulder as he throws up a fresh shield. "You could say so."

Kaira's corporeal voice hits me in the chest like a ball of fire, and every last bit of hope gutters as I find her at the front of the group in the tight hold of a Flame male who's pressing a sword to her throat. *Bastard.*

"What the fuck happened?" I send my question out before I allow myself to identify the leader of the group and let them intimidate me with a look. I don't search for the others either, just yet. For a heartbeat, I wait for information.

Herinor is a seasoned fighter. He knows how to figure out rank and order in a group of opponents like that way faster.

"*It was a trap.*" I can't turn away when Kaira whimpers into my mind. "*The fairies, the estate. It's all a trap.*"

For a long breath, I believe that Recienne set us up, that he used Clio to lead us into an ambush; then I spot the female behind the male who's restraining Kaira. Like liquid copper, her braid bleeds over the forearm of the Flame, locking her back to his chest. He's at least a head taller than her and at least as broad as Herinor.

"Welcome to the party, little Wolayna."

I know the voice. Have had nightmares about it. So polite and collected yet dripping hatred with every drawn-out vowel.

"Erina." I spot him next to Clio, right next to the two Flames grasping Silas by his shoulders and arms. His wrists are bound behind his back—to keep him from using his hatchet or his magic, I can't tell—and his head is hung, a curtain of dark hair blocking out the view of his features. He could be unconscious by the way his captors are struggling to keep upright.

"What a coincidence, dove." The expression on Erina's face tells me nothing about this is a coincidence.

He smooths out the front of his sepia uniform jacket, playing with one of the golden buttons at the top of the double row. With his polished boots, clean pants, beard groomed to perfection, and hair cropped short, he's a vision of control and deadliness. Not in the way the fae and fairies are. His power doesn't run in his veins. It's not in his build or his sword. Erina Latroy Jelnedyn is King of Tavras.

He commands an army ready to destroy Askarea and hunt Myron and me to the ends of this realm.

I try not to quake with fear as he gestures to the daggers in my bloodied hands. "It doesn't bode well for a king's wife to fight with a blade, Wolayna." His smirk is that of a man who has a group of bullies at his beck and call to do his dirty work. Only, those bullies are Fire Fairies, and they have two of my friends and my sister under their control. "In fact, a king's wife shouldn't *fight* at all."

"I'm not your *wife*," I spit at him, ready to remind him with words and blade that no part of me belongs to him.

"*Be careful, Ayna. Don't let him goad you.*"

Taking my sister's advice, I force down a slow breath. Sweat beads my forehead and neck, my arms tired from fighting and my legs shaking from strain and terror.

"*What does he want? Why is he here?*" The more information I get before reacting to Erina the better.

Beside me, Herinor is still frozen, sword at the ready as if he was going to strike. Around us, his shield tightens and thickens, a layer strong enough to hold off the fire of the Flames.

"*I don't know,*" Kaira admits. "*One moment, we were sneaking down to help you; the next, we were being dragged into the clearing. He was waiting here with the Flames.*"

That doesn't sound good. Erina was waiting for us. He knew we'd come for the fairies. Well, perhaps not *we* exactly, but he knew *someone* would come. Fairies, Crows. It doesn't seem to matter to him as long as he has more magic wielders on whom he can test his weapons. I'm surprised they haven't attacked us with the magic-subduing drug yet.

"*Did he take your powers away?*" It's the only question I should be asking.

Kaira rolls her head an inch in a silent no. "*Didn't have time yet.*"

With a quick scan of the Flames, I reassure myself there are no syringes in anyone's hands and find it easier to breathe when I don't spot any.

"Wife, fiancée… Does it really matter when you'll end up *mine* anyway?" Erina says when I don't say anything else. "You've caused quite a fuss, Wolayna." The reprimand in his tone makes my blood boil, makes me want to scream my hatred at him.

I'm not yours. I won't be yours. I don't even want to breathe the same air as you. I don't scream the words at him, though, keeping Kaira's warning in mind. Erina wants something, and the clearer I can keep my head, the better. If I manage to buy some time, Myron will be at our side, his power ready to blast Erina out of this world.

"*Not as long as we're standing at the center of the group,*" Kaira points out, and I realize only then that something is wrong.

"*Clio—*" My head whips to the female, meeting her gaze of solid jade.

If no one took her magic away, she should be able to site-hop out of there.

The princess of Askarea stares me down, clear warning in her eyes.

"*Where is Royad?*" Snapping my attention back to Kaira, I scan the clearing.

No sign of the Crow male. Not even a feather.

"He managed to get away before they got us."

Good, at least one of us is safe. And Myron…

I can't even begin to fight the terror of what will happen when he realizes we've been betrayed—again.

"Did Clio—"

"Shhhh. Focus." Kaira shoots me a sharp look just in time for me to hear Erina's next sentence.

"I have to admit, my court was in upheaval for a day or two when they figured out the Milevishja princess had disappeared."

"So, you sent your bloodhounds after me?"

Herinor's grumble of warning is too late. The words are out.

"My bloodhounds?" Erina laughs while the Flames all stand at attention, awaiting his order to fire those growing balls of flame at us. "Come on, Wolayna. I don't need bloodhounds. *You,* better than anyone, must know I'll always find you." He leans forward as if sharing a secret, and the hairs at the back of my neck stand erect at the thought that he just used the exact same words Myron once used. *I'll always find you.* "I found you on the ocean. I found you at Fort Perenis. I found you after your time at the Crow court was over. And I found you *here.*"

Beside me, Herinor stands so still I am not sure he's even breathing, his muscles taut and his features tight. I don't know what to do. Don't know if I should negotiate for the others' freedom or draw upon that restless well of magic in my veins.

"Shall we fight?" Asking Kaira's opinion is the only thing I can think of. *"Forty against five of us… The odds aren't in our favor."*

"*Plus Silas got a hit to his head,*" Kaira adds, "*I'm not certain he could fight if he wanted to.*"

Behind us, something crashes inside the estate, screams following with a blood-stilling shrillness that allows me to believe it's not Myron who's fighting for his life but the Flames who confronted us. As long as he's safe, I can play Erina's game.

"What do you want?" It's time to lay out the cards, learn why he's hunted us down. *If* he's even hunted *us* specifically.

Tilting his head, Erina glances from Clio to Silas, then back to me, stepping through the front row of Flames, careful not to touch them. "You didn't think you could escape my hand, did you?"

So, he *has* been looking for *me*.

"It's time to return to Meer and take your place at my side."

"Over my dead body." My voice trembles as pure rage wells up inside of me.

Eyes on the swaying treetops closest to the estate, Erina takes another step toward me. Fifteen paces lie between us. That's the same distance as Herinor and I had to cross to escape the Flames inside the entrance hall. We made it there.

Out here, we won't make it anywhere. Erina doesn't need to voice the threat to know Kaira, Clio, and Silas will pay if I refuse.

"Don't even think about it," Herinor growls. He's not supposed to help me, but it wouldn't prevent him from considering saving my family and friends. "Myron will kill me if you—"

"That's not your choice to make." I cut him off before he can make me feel guilty.

The shield he's still projecting swallows our words, but it doesn't keep out Erina's as he continues. "Your *dead* body won't be very useful for making a few heirs, dove." He is halfway between the Flames and Herinor's shield now, fingers not even close to the blade at his hip. At his feet, a gust of wind stirs dry leaves and blades of grass, carrying it toward the waiting Flames. They settle on the boots and leather armor of the soldiers while Erina's clothes remain impeccably clean like he has a shield of his own.

"What do you say, dove. Will you come willingly?" A glance over his shoulder is enough for the closest Flame to direct their fireball at Kaira's chest. My sister locks eyes with me, imperceptibly shaking her head.

"You're the rightful queen of Tavras. You won't yield."

Scraping his fingers over his beard, Erina turns back to me, a false smile on his lips. "I'm waiting, dove."

Dove. My stomach threatens to turn at the mere thought of what Erina has planned for my future, how he's using the people I love against me.

"Your friends here will make a great addition to my court if you come willingly. I'll allow them to live—without their magic, of course—and they shall resume their service as your servants. The two females had been delightful handmaidens if I recall correctly." He doesn't even look at them now, so sure of himself and his claim. "And the male can become a foot soldier in my army. We'll soon bolster their ranks with the likes of him."

"The *males*," I correct, "won't ever lift a finger to fight on your side."

That costs Erina a laugh. "Maybe not the one behind me, but that one—" He points at Herinor, who's still standing like he doesn't know if he should abandon me or stand by my side. "The male will cut off his own hand before he helps you. He'll kill himself before ensuring your freedom."

He's not wrong. Herinor will die if he tries to help me directly, and then there is little he can do once he's dead.

"I will not—"

"It's all right," I stop Herinor before he can attempt a lie. We both know lies are beyond his capabilities, and we both know where the deal with Ephegos leaves him.

From the corner of my eye, I notice Silas's hand twitch. His head is still lowered, but a new tension has entered his shoulders even as he's leaning on the Flame soldiers to hold him.

He's faking. And so is Clio. I don't know what they're waiting for, but they are ready to attack from where they stand.

"*Forty against five is madness,*" I say to Kaira, who must know what they're up to.

My sister shakes her head, resolve streaming through our bond.

"Last chance, Wolayna." Erina lifts a hand, and I hold my breath, steeling myself for the onslaught of fire that will surely come ... and blink with surprise when half of the Flames march off toward the estate.

No.

No!

Myron is there. He's fighting a few Flames on his own and will be here soon. He'll come for us, back up Herinor,

Silas, Clio, and Kaira. He'll draw his blade at my side, and together, we'll send Erina to an early grave—

The Flames are rounding Herinor and me, not heeding us a look, but I can sense the attention of the others as they keep aiming at us. One wrong movement and we're history.

"Don't worry, dove." Erina comes even closer. Either he doesn't have a sense of self-preservation, or he delights in walking a thin line at the edge of what's healthy for him.

A few more paces and he'll be within reach. If I leap, I could surprise him and cut open his throat.

The Flames have almost reached the corner; a few more steps and they'll be out of sight—and so will we. If I'm quick—

It happens so fast I can barely comprehend it.

Clio disappears from her captor's grasp, popping up behind the last row of Flames and snapping a soldier's neck. At the same moment, Silas grabs for the swords of the two Flames holding him up, nothing more than a flash of dark black hair and leathers. They aren't fast enough to prevent him from cutting into their sides just below their ribs, and they lose balance, cursing and toppling to the ground where they soak the grass crimson.

Chaos breaks loose as Kaira joins them, stealing a fireball from one of the Flames. She might not be able to create her own fire, but apparently, she can hijack that of another. With a jerk of her hand, she sends the fire sailing into the Flame next to her.

Arrows are flying from a nearby tree—Royad. Thank the Guardians, he didn't leave us to our fate.

As if on a signal, Herinor unfreezes, but he doesn't go for Erina's throat. It's me who darts for the Tavrasian king, dagger raised and aiming for the side of his neck.

Wide-eyed, Erina stares at me, frozen in shock or anticipation of death, I don't care. All I care about is that no one stops me as I drive my blade through skin, cartilage, tendons, and bone.

At least, that's what I expect when my blade slices into him, but there is no resistance. I don't collide with the Tavrasian King, don't land on top of him with a scream of victory on my tongue. No, I land face-first in the grass, tasting earth and blood as my lip splits open at the impact. Someone screams my name, and I want to answer, but the breath is knocked out of me yet again as a heavy weight lands on top of me, smashing me face-first into the grass.

I writhe beneath the knees pushing into my spin, bucking to throw off the attacker until I'm able to lift my head enough to spot brown gloves that belong to Flame armor instead of Erina's manicured fingers. "Ayna!" Clio's voice shrills across the clearing, but it's a cry for help rather than one of war.

Somewhere in the turmoil of flying fireballs and glinting swords, Clio needs my help.

Terror grasps me in a vise as I spot Silas at the edge of the battle, leathers ripped open on his thigh, revealing a gashing wound. He's unstable on his legs, but he keeps fighting with hatchet and magic, keeping the two Flames coming for him again and again at bay. I don't have time to look for Herinor and Kaira; the Flame on my back pushes his knee down on my neck so hard I think it might snap.

Magic. I need to use my magic. For my sword had been ripped from my grasp when Erina disappeared—or I simply flew through him like through a hallucination.

Streaks of silver collect behind my eyelids as I call to my power, but when I try to release a hazardous blow like the one that saved me in the Seeing Forest, a sharp sting in my neck makes me cry out with pain.

No.

No-no-no-no-no.

Not now. Not the drug.

It takes about fifteen heartbeats before the numbing sensation of the magic-sedating serum sets in.

No, *please, no.* I need to get to my feet, need to push the Flame off my back and fucking get up so I can fight. So I can protect my family.

On my shoulder, my tattoo tingles as if in question.

I need you, Myron. I send the thought out into the world even if he can't hear me. Maybe the connection of our mate mark will call to him the way it's always called to him.

And where the fuck is Erina? He can't simply have vanished into thin air?

My vision is swimming, but the polished boots stopping in front of me are all I need to see to know he's right there. That he never left.

Or he was never truly here.

The grass doesn't bend under his weight, and the dry leaves carried on a breeze don't touch him. They float straight through him just like my dagger did.

I'm hallucinating because this can't possibly be true.

As if reading my mind, Erina crouches down in front of me, tapping his fingers against his knee. "You really should have taken my offer, Wolayna. I would have taken you home and left things be. But you leave me no choice."

No choice. No choice. The words ring in my ears like a promise of doom as Erina nods over my head at the Flame holding me down.

"Since you won't comply otherwise, I'll need to eradicate all traces of the one thing that keeps standing between us."

"You mean you and your delusions of grandeur?" I spit at his feet. "You'll never rule Askarea, Erina. You'll never rule Eherea. You'll never find anyone who loves you. You'll die bitter and alone even if you force someone to marry you and give you heirs."

The ire in Erina's gaze tells me I've hit home.

"Burn him out of her." His order is brief, dismissive, as he pushes back to his feet and stalks a few steps away, observing from a distance.

I can see it now; the little flaws in the picture. He avoided touching anyone when he stood between the Flames, made sure to not even brush their shoulders or ends of their braids. He's not real, but not a figment of my imagination either.

"*A projection,*" Kaira whispers in my mind as if she's been following my entire thought process from afar.

A projection.

I don't have time to ponder the meaning when rough hands tear the right sleeve off my arm then rip open the back of my leathers.

"What do you mean, *burn him out?*" I barely finish the question in more than a whisper when a flash of orange light glows behind my shoulder.

Someone screams, a ripple going through the fight still raging behind the Tavrasian king, and the world seems to hold its breath.

Hands secure my wrists at my sides with iron strength as I thrash in anticipation of whatever new horror Erina has come up with, but I'm not prepared for this. I could never be prepared for *this*.

Fire erupts on my skin, eating into the flesh on my right shoulder as a torch is pressed into the inked bird connecting me to Myron.

I can't breathe-can't-breathe-can't-breathe. Pain like I've never experienced rakes through me, rushing down my arm, battering through my chest, wrecking my heart, my soul, my everything.

Everything that I am is connected to that bird ... and the male it stands for.

"*Myron*," I huff his name when all I want is to scream at the top of my lungs. But there's no air left.

I can feel the tattoo melt under the weight of the smoldering torch, can feel it dissolve into tears of black ink until they're spilling from my eyes.

Until I'm crying the sorrow of the world.

"*No—*"

No one hears my protest. No one feels me burning.

I'm alone.

And where a bright, glowing connection once represented my bond with my mate, absolute, solid darkness falls.

TWENTY-NINE

MYRON

Five tired Flames are no match for me on a good day, but five times that many?

I'm panting, my magic sluggish as I send one silver whip after the other to lash the Flames' fire out. At least, Ayna is out of the building, safe with Herinor—or as safe as she'll ever be with him. He might not lend her a hand to protect his own life, but he's doing about anything he can to make sure he aids me in my attempts at protecting her.

How I wish I could trust him to do whatever is necessary to keep her alive. He won't lay down his life without a second thought the way I'd do for my queen because, deep down, his heart is no longer his own.

I shove all thoughts aside, focusing on the reassuring sensation of Ayna's presence through our bond while I slice into one godsdamned Fire Fairy after the other. They are surprisingly fast and agile for how clumsily they're setting their feet. A few months ago I would have been terrified of even one Flame, but my full Crow strength and power has its advantages—and I don't only mean those in the bedroom. I'm faster than the Flames, more accurate with my aim. Also, I'm flammable, which makes me an excellent target for the Flames' magic.

Fireball after fireball rushes at me. The moment I bat one away with my sword or my magic, the next one is coming at me. It was way too easy to coordinate my efforts with only five Flames to fight—four after the initial minute when I ripped one Flame's throat out with a well-placed strike of my sword—but with the reinforcements joining them, I'm at my limit. One by one, they draw nearer, the entrance hall shrinking with dizzying speed. Not long and they'll have cornered me.

At least I was able to buy Ayna some time. Shaelak knows I owe her my life, my sanity, and then some. Perhaps this is my way of paying her back.

Wherever those reinforcements came from, they wouldn't have simply come for me had they spotted Ayna and Herinor outside. They did come in through the main door after all.

If I only knew where the others are. They should long have found us and backed us up.

The male closest to me sneers at me before sending a fireball at my chest. I duck, letting the heat bounce off as tiny a shield as I can master to save my strength. It won't matter how many Flames I've fought if some escape to go after my mate.

Hurling a stream of silver light at him, I sever the male's neck, watching his grin slip as his head slides off his shoulders.

"Not so funny now," I murmur, attention already on the next one.

They are shooting at me, drawing their circle ever tighter, but they aren't going for the kill the way I am. Something feels very off about that.

I can't detonate the entire building without burying myself alive, so I refrain from extreme measures—for now. If I manage to get to the door, I can lead the Flames into the forest where I can seek cover behind tree trunks. Even if they'll burn, I'd rather have a place to shelter me from their fire when they decide to hit full force. Herinor and the others can also join the fight more easily if they can sneak up on the enemy rather than having to step into a room devoid of hideouts.

I remember playing hide and seek with Royad at the palace in the Seeing Forest. My father never liked the game, said it was for cowards and Crows never hid from anything. Not even in a game.

My opinion differs from his, though. Battles are all about tactics, and places to hide mean time to think, to take a breath, and quickly heal a wound. It means the difference between life and death in a fight twenty-three against one.

That thought in mind, I lash out to the side with my power, leaving my back unprotected while I let my magic escape my shield. It's a necessary move to bring down the numbers stacked against me, and I pay for it with a hit in the spine. Pain explodes in my back, taking my breath for a heartbeat, making it difficult to lift my arm to block the next blow. That one is aimed at my neck, and if I fail to greet it with my blade, it will end with me headless and bleeding all over the pretty floor.

Shield up and sword moving, I twist out of reach, slicing into the Flame's arm, severing it, if I'm precise, but I don't have the time to notice in detail how the lower half of her sword arm plops to the floor. I'm already on the next opponent. This one seems to be dead set on striking me on my cheek like he is challenging me to a duel.

Honestly, I want to laugh in his face, want to flash my teeth the way I used to when stabbing my way through a battle, but something feels off in my shoulder.

It starts with an intense tingle, the sort I'm used to when Ayna experiences heightened emotions. That's not where it ends, though. My vision blurs as a trail of fire runs through the outline of the bird tattoo on my skin, searing pain stealing my breath, my thoughts, the last of the strength that I thought I had.

Knees buckling, I collapse to the blood-smeared floor right next to the stump of one of the Flames' necks I've severed.

"*Myron!*" Her scream is a song on the storms that have always tried to force us apart. It's a melody of anguish, gut-wrenching onslaught of terror. My entire world goes dark as my skin bursts into figurative flames. Not one hint of orange glow fills the entrance hall. Not one single fireball. The Flames have vanished from view in the starless cocoon wrapping around me. Yet, the excruciating pain won't yield.

"*AYNA!*"

She's hanging on by a loose thread, and my fingers are slippery with blood, too clumsy to spool her in.

They are trying to rip her away from me. Those *fucking bastards* are trying to take *my mate*.

There's no room for coherent thoughts as I turn into the monster I've resented for millennia. Talons grow from my fingertips, feathers from my arms, covering them from shoulder to wrist. My mouth and nose become the beak of a crow, and my eyes turn into pitch-black pits as the feathers take my neck, my hair, my face. The leathers are too tight, too hot, locking in the raw power of the creature breaking through the surface.

With a growl, I tear my leathers open, jacket falling off my chest, my wings springing free. I'm death and darkness. The storm in which Ayna is being tossed like a doll. I'm the anchor, and she's the boat, and whoever is trying to sever the chain holding us together will. Fucking. *Die.*

The roar ripping out of me puts the gods to shame.

I won't—I will *not*—not in a thousand lifetimes let anyone take her from me.

A flash of fire enters my darkness, and I remember I should be afraid, but the orange sphere is swallowed by night like water in ink. Everything inside of me pulls and twists. Everything is pointing in one direction.

So I follow. It's an order. A command pulling me straight through the folds of the world, and I obey. I'd obey that call anywhere.

From the edge of my consciousness, I sense words raining down on me, but they don't cut. Not one single blade slices into my skin as I fight my way across the entrance hall. Like a current of blackest night, my power bleeds across the floor, the walls, taking everything in my path. Flames cry out in panic as I rip their heads off with my power, my talons, my sword… I no longer hold a weapon in my hands. I *am* the weapon. And I embrace every last monstrous thought as I kill my way out of the estate. The ground shudders as I half walk, half fly out the door, leaving a trail of destruction behind me.

Even in my darkest hours of the curse, I never allowed for that beast to break loose, but today, I embrace it. Today, I become one with it as I spot my *mate* face-down on the ground. A Flame is kneeling on her back, pinning her like a rabid animal as she thrashes under the torch they are pushing into her flesh, right where our mate mark is inked into her skin.

Blind rage hits me, taking away the last of my humanity, and I fucking lose it. Silver spears fly across the clearing, taking down everyone and everything in my path. At the back of my mind, I remember there are people I care about out there, that I might hurt them if I don't watch out.

I can't bring myself to hesitate as my power lashes from my talons, rays of silver wrapped in smoke and death. There is no time to wonder if my magic can tell friends from foes; I will it to do so, and where it hits, Flames fall left and right like flies, like wheat stalks cut down with a razor-sharp blade.

But Ayna is slipping away from me. With every breath, there's a little less of her wrapped around my soul.

I cling to her for dear life. Because she *is* my life.

All I hear is her whimpering. Even when there is no Flame left in this godsforsaken clearing, she's still writhing in pain.

I don't allow myself to land from where I'm hovering just beneath the treetops and rush to her. Not just yet. There is one more thing I need to do before I take her in my arms and kiss her with all I am, all I have.

"Erina." My voice is a hiss, but the King of Tavras hears me anyway. Across the battlefield where he's watching with horror as I let my power ruin all life in the clearing.

Leaves tumble to the ground where I pass, telling the story of my touch with their wilting.

"You will pay for this."

The fear in Erina's eyes is real, but when I send a stream of unadulterated power to eviscerate him, it doesn't tear him apart as it rips through him.

It's then that I realize he's a projection. The fucker has found a way to be in two places at the same time—and his body is somewhere safe while he's smirking at me when I realize the limits of my power.

"Nice show, Myron." Erina smirks and tips his head as if admitting defeat in this round of what he thinks of as a game.

Then he's gone.

And I'm left to collect the pieces of the female who's saved me in all ways that matter. But she can't save me from this. Not when, where her mate mark was once telling the story of our joined fate, all that stares back at me is scorched, blackened flesh.

I beat my wings, dropping to my boots as all resolve crumbles, and my feathers melt away.

Ayna's staggering to her feet, defying pain, defying death, even now, when she's beaten, bleeding, barely keeping upright.

And her voice hits me like an arrow in the chest as she whispers, "I'm sorry."

THIRTY

AYNA

My legs are shaking as I push into an upright position, arm and shoulder bare where the Flames tore my leathers open. How I manage, I can't possibly tell. All I know is the moment Myron swept across the clearing like a cloud of feathers and death, my heart slowed and my breathing became deep, defying my battered, broken body. Then the Flames fell off me like bad fruit from a tree, and the darkness filling the air slid over me like ink in water, licking over the raw flesh of my shoulder as if it had a mind of its own. I don't want to think about what once graced my skin there. It's gone, *burned out of me* like

Erina said. And the whole world is trembling as I refuse to acknowledge what he did to me.

Around me, the battlefield is a sight of destruction, leafless trees framing the patch of grass littered with bodies. I can't bring myself to search for the others. All I see is *him*.

Like the wrath of the Guardians, Myron plummets from the sky, wrapped in clouds and thunder as he shifts on his descent. Feathers stream from his arms in a storm of shimmering black, whirling for a heartbeat before they puff into whisks of smoke. The earth shakes as his boots hit the blood-soaked ground a few paces from me, at the center of the small meadow, and his eyes… His beautiful eyes toss like the ocean east of Eherea where my peace is now buried. Veins of black pull back into the corners of his eyes, revealing the turquoise of his irises. Feathers retreat from his face, revealing the features of a vengeful god, beautiful and terrifying. And full of an anguish I know deep down will destroy him.

"Ayna—" With a few long strides, he closes the gap between us, arms falling around me like a pair of protective wings. On my right side, his hand lingers on the small of my back, careful not to touch the wound on my shoulder. I know now that he understands how they mutilated me. All his bird features are gone except for the black talons tipping his fingers and the last feathers disappearing from his arms. "I'm sorry."

I try not to focus on the mind-numbing pain in my own shoulder, right where the bird tattoo we shared was inked into my skin until a few moments ago. He probably felt my pain the moment the torch touched my skin. The fact that I can already sense his magic seeping into my body, attempting to knit it back together, proves he's aware of *what* exactly they did to me.

The pain doesn't ebb, and the wound doesn't close. In my shoulder, nothing is tingling; no tug is telling me he's reaching for me with more than his arms. "I'm all right." It's a lie, and we both know it, but if I admit that I'm not, I'll shatter. And so will he.

I don't move when he carefully takes my face between his palms, hot breath pouring over my mouth as he leans in to kiss me. "I'm not." He stops an inch from my lips, his scent evoking a cocoon of emotions that seem both too strong and too weak for what I'm used to feeling. "I won't be until I've sent them all to Hel's realm."

His features are blurring from the proximity or from the tears collecting in my eyes, his fingers trembling against my cheeks, but when his lips touch mine, I can't smell the stench of burned flesh; I can't feel the pain. For a moment, it's him and the softness of his lips, the tender sweep of his tongue as if he's pouring words into my mouth he can't fathom to speak.

I can't speak them either because, if I pause to acknowledge the hollow ache inside my chest, I know that it won't matter if the flesh on my shoulder heals. I've lost a part of my soul.

THIRTY-ONE

AYNA

It's been ten days since the attack.

Ten.

Long.

Days.

I've counted every heartbeat.

One million and seventeen beats.

Myron came to see me the first two days.

I sent him away.

Royad came on the third, pleading on his cousin's behalf to hear him out.

I sent him away, too.

On the fourth day, Clio and Kaira came together, telling

me the female we saved at the Flame estate survived. They told me how lucky we were that Jeseida wasn't there that day.

I shook my head at them before sending them away.

They came back on the sixth and the seventh day again.

I told them not to return.

On the eighth day, Myron poked in his head, a crease between his brows as he asked if he could stay with me for a while.

I didn't look him in the eye when he sat silently at the foot of my bed for hours.

Silas visited on the ninth day, his sarcastic grin wiped off his bronze features for once and his eyes black like the night.

He told me to pull myself together.

There is nothing to pull, so I continued gazing at the high ceiling.

The tenth day has been quiet. Darkness is falling over the gardens behind the fairy palace in Aceleau, my eyes adjusting with every vanishing ray of sun.

I haven't lost my fae senses even when I've lost myself.

I'm sick of the elegant wallpapers in this room, but I don't complain. My voice is inconsequential. It can't change what happened. Stacking my fingers on top of each other on the windowsill, I continue to stare at the twilight creatures crawling from the trees and bushes.

From my place by the window, I can see the tower on the edge of the palace and the balcony adjacent to King Recienne's throne room. Yesterday, the Fairy King was standing there with his sister and his general, locked in an animated discussion.

I didn't even try to listen in.

Absently, my hand reaches for my braid, tugging it over my left shoulder so it won't slide into the wound on my right that refuses to heal. The soft, cream dressing robe I wear hangs loosely over the bandages Recienne's healer changes every day.

After Clio got all of us off the battlefield, site-hopping one after the other to this palace, every fairy available tried to heal my wound. Myron was the first. For long minutes, he snapped and growled at everyone who would come near me. When he realized his own powers weren't enough, he fell into a brooding silence, stepping aside to let the others try.

To let the others *fail.*

"You look awfully cheerful."

I only mildly startle at the sound of Herinor's voice inside my room—the room that was meant for Myron and me, but he's sleeping elsewhere since I screamed at him until he left when he attempted to lie down beside me the night after the attack. What's the point of startling in a palace full of fairies who can site-hop in and out at their leisure?

Herinor doesn't take my silence as an invitation to leave, but I don't have it in me to speak either, so I keep watching the rabbits ducking under the bushes.

"You know I'm a horrible creature, Ayna." He lowers himself into the brocade chair a few feet to my side, stretching out his legs and crossing them at the ankles. "You've seen what I'm capable of."

From the corner of my eye, I can see his brows rise when I don't react.

"Do I need to spell it out again?" There is no anger in his tone, no aggression. Only endless calm.

Because he hasn't come to talk about the attack, I tolerate him, but I don't know if I want to hear any of the stories of his past, so I shrug with my good shoulder.

"All right. Since you're so eager to hear it." Herinor gets up, draws his chair up to mine, and sits right next to me, elbows braced on the windowsill as he studies me from the side.

"Back in Neredyn, long before Vala decided we were unworthy, I liked to go hunting."

He pauses, waiting for my reaction. When I show none, he continues.

"Deer was one of my favorites. Rabbit too." He gestures at the two brownish-gray rabbits searching shelter under low-hanging branches of a hazel bush like they can feel his gaze. "But do you want to know what I'd hunt on special occasions?" He doesn't wait for me to tell him I really don't want to know. "Human."

My stomach constricts, making my lungs suck in a startled breath after all.

Herinor grins at me from the side, but he doesn't continue to speak for so long that I wonder if he's pondering the merits of slaughtering a broken once-human. His gaze travels to my neck, then to my shoulder where my wound is covered but never ceases to throb. "I never ate human meat. That was for the lowly bastards who couldn't control their urges."

"And killing them isn't lowly?" The question is out before I can think. Herinor's grin widens when I turn to face him with a gasp.

"Who said I killed them?" The look in his eyes spells victory.

"What did you do to them then?" It's easy to be angry, to face Herinor and despise him for what he's saying. Much easier than hearing Myron's apologies, his self-blaming for what happened at the Flame estate.

I still can't think it. It's easier to remain numb.

"Most of them, I let go—only to hunt them down again the next time that felt like a special occasion. But some of them…" He stops himself as if what he's about to say might be too much. Apparently, he decides I can handle it since he leans in a bit further and whispers. "Some of them begged me to get a little taste of them between their legs."

My cheeks are hot, and my heart is stuttering in my chest. He didn't just say that.

Herinor merely shrugs, leaning back in his chair as if that was nothing. "Others begged me to let them have a drop of my blood." When I blankly stare at him, he explains, "It's not commonly known, but apparently, our blood is intoxicating to humans."

"I'm not human."

Herinor barks a laugh. "I'm not offering."

Ignoring his amusement, I turn back to the window. The sun has vanished entirely, leaving the purplish shapes of the night. My Crow senses allow me to track the two figures meandering the gardens, and my heart throbs.

Clothed in familiar black, Royad and Myron are conversing as they slowly follow the gravel path leading from the palace to the fountain at the center of the greenery. While Royad has tied back his hair, Myron's tresses are billowing in the wind. There's something wild about him that I haven't noticed before, and I tell myself it doesn't matter if I do now.

"Why are you here?" My tone is flat, but the bite is there anyway.

"Better." Herinor nods, acknowledging the change. "And because I'm the only one allowed to be mean to you without consequences."

He shoots me a grin that doesn't reach his eyes.

"Because you're Ephegos's tool?"

"Because you need someone to push you out of your wallowing, and I don't feel the least bit guilty about it."

"Even when you're helping me." I grit my teeth at him, a grimace resembling an animal about to attack.

"Doesn't feel like helping when it's basically torment." A dark laugh follows his words.

"So, you do enjoy tormenting people after all?"

"I've already told you I used to be the worst of Crows."

"But you're not anymore."

He doesn't correct me.

My eyes follow Myron's movements, the powerful strides even when he's walking at a casual speed, the strength resonating in each of his gestures even when his shoulders are hunched. Royad is reaching for his cousin's arm, squeezing, and Myron stops, lowering his head in defeat.

"You want to know what they're talking about?"

"I don't." I *do*, but I can't admit that. I can't, or I'll start crying and will never stop.

"They are talking about why you keep rejecting your mate."

Mate. The word hits me like a blow to the gut. On my shoulder, the wound is pulling with pain, and my head swims at the mention of what I lost.

What was *taken* from me.

I want to be angry, but I'm not strong enough, so I resign to defeat.

"I'm not rejecting him. They *burned* his mate mark out of me. I can't feel him. I can't fucking *feel* him anymore."

I didn't mean to say that out loud, but Herinor has a way of provoking a response out of me that not even Myron manages.

"So, you decide blocking him out entirely is the best way to deal with this?" The disapproval in his tone isn't the Herinor I know. It's a different version, one who cares about me.

"There is no way of dealing with losing a mate." No emotion makes it to the surface as my eyes keep following Myron and Royad on their gradual tour around the gardens. "Erina had them take my mate mark."

"I was there when it happened." Guilt wells in his voice, but he buries it like he'd bury any weakness. He can't be on my side in any of this; his life depends on it.

"At least, you weren't the one to hold the torch if you weren't the one to prevent it." My stomach is sour, my mouth, my heart. I'm a lemon squeezed out over salt that's to be spread over my own wounds.

Herinor's fingers come to gently rest on my forearm. "No one could have prevented it, Ayna. It was an ambush. Erina set up the attacks so the fairies would come looking. He was hoping we'd be with them so he could get his hands on you."

"When he had the information of us conspiring with Re-cienne tortured out of one of the fairy scouts, he knew it was only a matter of time until you'd show up."

"He's been tracking all our moves…" The fact hits me in the chest, forcing my focus away from the aching burn on my shoulder for once.

Herinor nods. "He really is. He's been working with the Flames through Ephegos. I know that because I was there when Ephegos gave the order to bring you to him that first time after the battle at the old Crow Palace."

"Flame Palace," I correct.

Herinor tilts his head. "Does it matter?"

I realize then how much information he's giving away, and a sense of unease fills me. "Aren't you helping me with all this knowledge? Ephegos surely wouldn't approve of you spilling secrets."

"They're not secrets if they're in the past and there's nothing to be gained from them." A big frown distorts Herinor's features, stretching the thin scars scattered over his face. He measures me for a long moment, fingers interlacing, pulling apart, playing with the hem of his black sleeve. In his light green eyes, doubt and worry fight a battle until he can't sit still anymore. "Talk to Silas. He's older than any of us."

He leaps to his feet so abruptly I barely catch the trickle of blood from the corner of his mouth, but I do catch it.

"Herinor—"

I call after him a few more times as he bolts for the door like he's running from Eroth himself, but he doesn't reappear once he crosses the threshold. And I remain with the screaming emptiness where my mating bond lived inside me only ten days ago.

THIRTY-TWO

AYNA

Clio isn't half as understanding as I remember her. When I ask if she's seen Silas the next morning, she rolls her eyes, demanding whether I've gotten over myself and stopped wallowing in self-pity. Then, she points toward the training grounds before she stomps away. It's a bit childish in my opinion, but who am I to judge? I've spent ten days behind closed doors, not speaking to anyone in a way that could be considered sociable.

Stuffing my hands into the pockets of my linen pants, I make my way to the training grounds, determined to get Herinor's words out of my head by confronting Silas about his age. Not that I know what I'm asking for, but the way

Herinor bled gives me curse-whiplash, and I really don't want the grumpy warrior to suffer. It's enough that I'm suffering.

And Myron. But I don't think that because his name alone is enough to make me want to cry.

In the arena, Silas is wielding his sword against an imaginary opponent, the calm of a cleric on his features and the steadiness of a tree in his legs.

"So, you made it out of solitary confinement," he mocks by way of greeting.

I sit on the lowest of three wooden logs stacked in the corner next to the rack of training swords, careful not to catch my toes on one of the gashes that must be etched there from testing the blades of sharp weapons. At my back, the stone benches rise high enough to block out the low-standing morning sun and, a few feet to my right, a gap wide enough for five men to walk shoulder to shoulder that serves as a side entrance. "Not really. But your friend mentioned I should talk to you."

Silas turns his head without stopping his flow. "Myron?"

His name tears through me like the hatchet on Silas's belt. "The friend I mean you've known for much longer than the King of Crows."

Silas chuckles. "There's only one bastard alive whom I call friend and who's lived longer than the King." He drops the tip of the sword to the dusty ground, bracing his hands on the pommel. Sweat drips down his temples and neck, making his hair stick to his skin. His chest is slick with perspiration where his shirt clefts open over his pectorals.

"You shouldn't be looking at me like that, my queen." He inclines his head. "Myron won't like it."

Caught, I shove my hand through my hair, fingers getting stuck in my braid, and awkwardly glance at the ground before his feet. "Like what?"

Silas chuckles. "Like you're ready to peel my shirt away."

"I'm not... I wasn't..."

He laughs as I blush bright pink.

"It's all right, Ayna. You're undergoing the stages of un-mating trauma."

There it is. Like a slap in the face, the words ring and ring and ring in my ears. "Un-mating trauma," I repeat. It sounds right but feels wrong.

"Erina tried to un-mate you, that fucker." He brings his sword over his shoulder, resting the flat of the blade right above his collarbone as if he's carrying a sack of grains.

"What do you mean, *tried?*" *Don't let the hope flare. Don't let it.* "He burned a fucking hole into my flesh. There's nothing left of the mate mark." And it won't fucking heal. I don't need to add that last part. Everyone who wields healing magic in Recienne's palace knows I'm walking around with a giant hole in my shoulder, and there's nothing anyone can do about it.

"He did a thorough job, I have to admit." Silas raises a brow. "I don't know who told him about un-mating, but I'm happy to decapitate them the next time I see them."

The murderous humor in Silas's words is both comfort and shock. "Un-mated. Is that what we are?" My hand wanders to the edge of my bandages, aching to feel Myron's mark on me. Aching for the tingling sensation that comes when I turn my focus on it. Then I remember it's no longer there.

"To a degree, yes you are."

My world tumbles.

"And in a way, no."

His dark eyes pierce into mine when I try to comprehend which of the two is true. With a quick leap, he's sitting beside me, ramming his sword into the log right beside my left foot. I cringe and nearly fall off the stack, but Silas stabilizes me with a casual hand. "No need to jump off the ledge, Queen of Crows. Even if you feel like you can't tell left from right at the moment, it takes more than an angry human king to sever a sacred bond such as the one between Myron and you."

The breath I take might be the first full one since the Flames shoved the torch into my flesh.

"So, we're still mated." I don't phrase it as a question for fear he'll answer with a decline.

"Technically, yes." Lower lip pulled between his teeth, Silas gazes at the cloudy sky.

"*Technically?*" My shoulder is hurting, but I'm ready to shove him off the logs if he doesn't speak. "What's that supposed to mean?"

"That it takes more to sever a gods-given bond than clearing away the mark of one partner."

A sigh sweeps from my lips—relief? Confusion? I'm not sure. It's something other than the numbness that's been dominating me for the past days. But the knowledge that there's still a bond between Myron and me doesn't feel as soothing as it should. "Then why can't I feel him?" I avert my eyes as if the

Crow King himself were sitting next to me. "I can't even look at him." The admission tears a hole in my heart. The most beautiful male in the world, and I can't bear the sight of him.

"They burned away your mate mark. Your body is in shock."

It feels more like I don't have a body at all.

"It will take a while before you go through the stages of un-mating, even when you're not technically un-mated." When I throw him a questioning glance, he specifies, "They used to do that on occasion, the ancient Crows, before the curse, when they were unhappy with a pair." Without warning, Silas reaches for the collar of his shirt and pulls the sticky fabric over his head.

"What are you—"

"Look." He lifts his right arm over his head, angling his body so I can see the inside of his bulging bicep.

It's a tiny scar, roughly the size of a Tavrasian silver coin, but it's clearly a burn mark.

"I was a young male. A hundred and ten perhaps. She was about three hundred years older. Her family didn't approve, so they came for us in the night and tied us to a post when we fought for our lives. We thought they'd come to kill us. That would have been more merciful than what they did." He gives a bitter laugh. "Turned out they only wanted the bond broken."

I don't breathe, terrified of whatever he'd share and terrified he'd stop if I interrupted him.

"It took me a solid seven years to start talking afterward. Dahlia never recovered." He lowers his head. "She went into the waters and never returned."

My heart is breaking, cracking wide open for the sarcastic warrior whose side I've fought at, whom I've feared and hated. Who's become a friend just like Clio and Tori.

"I'm sorry."

Silas lowers his arm, fingers locking around the handle of his hatchet so hard his knuckles turn white. "After ten years, I started noticing every female's tits and spent a solid decade fucking my way through Neredyn." His eyes wander to his bare chest then to me as if to remind me of the way I'd ogled his muscles earlier.

"I'm not going to—"

"Of course, you won't. Your body merely thinks you're no longer mated. It's fast-tracking through the un-mating process until you find the leftovers of your mating bond." The '*obviously*' is something he doesn't need to add. "They tried to separate more pairs than you can imagine in the old days, out of spite, for sport, politics, jealousy. Not all Crows were as valiant as Myron and Royad. Our people were uncivilized brutes, and the gods had a point to curse us."

I don't ask the crimes he committed. It's enough that I know about Herinor. For now, I'm just grateful that I still have a piece of Myron within me.

"What can I do? Will I start randomly climbing males?" Because I honestly don't want that. I want Myron. And I want to be able to look him in the eye and see that there is more than the emptiness devouring me from the inside.

That costs Silas a barked laugh. "If you do, I'd love to be there to see Myron tear the poor male's head off—and other body parts."

"Not helping."

Silas's face turns serious again, but his eyes are still dancing with humor at the thought of me rubbing myself against a male and Myron dismembering one for it. I don't care. If this is a known process, I need to understand what to expect and make sure I don't do all the things Silas said he did.

"It's the way of nature to make sure we carry on if our mate is taken forcefully. It puts us back on the market."

The pause that follows is heavy and loaded with unspoken truths of his past, all those things he's been locking in behind a fence of sarcasm and snide, grumbled comments. This male isn't the cold-hearted warrior I believed him to be; he's a victim and a survivor, and he's learned to hide his pain so well the world believes him to be a monster while he grins and lets them.

"Does it ever hurt any less?"

All humor is gone as he meets my gaze. "It never stops hurting. But that's me." His throat bobs. "You and Myron have a future ahead. You merely need time for the wounds to heal. And I mean that literally." Without warning, he pokes the edge of my bandages, pressing the fabric into the open injury. "Your mind is stronger than you believe. A bond is not only in flesh; it's in your mind as much as it is in your soul. All you need to do is face it."

"And by *it*, you mean *him*?" The thought alone makes my knees go weak.

"How did you guess." Silas gets to his feet, ready to march off, but I'm not done.

"Is there anything else I need to look out for? Any spontaneous enamoration syndrome or gut-wrenching pain I should expect?"

Turning on his heels, Silas raises his brows at me. "What happened with Dahlia and me was a tragedy. It happened more often than not that the un-mating failed, and when it did, the reunion was something even the most experienced of Crows only spoke about in hushed voices."

"What does that mean?" I follow him a few steps down the path leading from the arena, waiting for an answer I can work with.

"I don't know, Queen of Crows. You tell me when you figure it out."

I'm stumbling through the gardens, mulling Silas's words over in my mind, when Recienne pops up, blocking my path with his tall, broad form.

"Shouldn't you be resting?" Genuine concern tugs at his features, and he's offering an arm, obviously under the impression I'll collapse any moment. I sure feel like I'm on the verge of exhaustion. My shoulder is throbbing, my heart is aching, and ... there is this tingle in the pit of my stomach when I glance up at the Fairy King, meeting his golden eyes.

Beautiful eyes... And his mouth. Full and soft and—

A mental slap on my wrist reminds me that this is the process of un-mating. I'd probably find the statue of a horned and hoofed fairy attractive right now if put face to face with it if Silas is to be believed.

"Everything all right, Your Majesty?" Recienne gives a charming bow of his head, and when I don't respond, says, "Let me take you back to your room."

With a broad, masculine hand, he encloses mine, spiriting me back to solitary confinement.

Only, my room isn't solitary. Recienne bows at his waist, opening the door with a small smile. "Your King asked earlier if I'd seen you, and when I stumbled across you in the park, I thought I'd bring you back where you belong."

He doesn't mean the room, though; I can tell by the sparkle in his eyes.

From behind, Myron's gaze weighs like ounces of the glimmering stone this palace is made of, but he doesn't move, doesn't speak as I bid the Fairy King a good day and tear my eyes away from his pretty face.

When I finally turn around, Myron is leaning against the windowsill, hands braced left and right of his hips and spine stiff like he's expecting a physical blow. "Herinor said he talked to you."

I don't dare meet his eyes, but I do note the purple smudges beneath, speaking of sleepless nights and endless worries.

"He did."

Myron's cheeks are so pale I could swear he's a ghost. But a ghost doesn't flick his fingers to brush back my hair like with invisible fingers. I shudder under the touch, and Myron flinches.

291

"I'm sorry. I didn't mean to… I—" Searching for words isn't something I ever see the Crow King do, but he's at a loss now as my eyes find his at last, and pain and sorrow fill the ocean depths of his.

"Erina burned my mate mark." The anger in my voice surprises me more than anything.

Myron's sorrow turns to fury, and from the corner of his eyes, black veins creep toward the ocean blue of his irises. So fast I can barely tell it's there, he turns his head to the side.

His whole body is shaking with barely restrained power as he pushes away from the windowsill, swallowing once, twice. "He tried to take you from me, Ayna." He's fully facing me now, and I can see it in the way his gaze skims my form, up and down and up and down, that he's not suffering the same symptoms I'm going through. He isn't scared to look at me because he fears the emptiness yawning like a chasm in his chest. He's burning with ire and with all the feelings that have been squandered with the heat of the torch to my shoulder. He's burning for both of us.

"You said you'd be behind me."

His eyes shutter with lack of understanding.

"At the estate. You said you'd hold them off and be right behind us."

And you weren't.

The thought runs deep, slicing like a sharp blade.

Myron's anger gutters as fast as it flared. "I was going to be. We were tricked."

"I know." It's a whisper, but I take a step toward him when he leans back against the windowsill, the darkness in his eyes gone.

"Erina knew we'd be coming."

"And he was ready to break you in the only way he knew he could."

I don't breathe as Myron prowls closer, circling the furniture in his path in slow, deliberate steps. When he's five feet away from me, he reaches for the top of his shirt, undoing a button, then the next.

My breath is coming hard and fast, and I can't look as he tugs the shirt over his head, but I have to. His chest and abdomen are perfect, the V of his muscles disappearing behind the waistband of his pants drawing my eye. Trying not to think what this is, why he's taking off his shirt, why I can't seem to get a full breath down, I lean against the door for support. The wound on my shoulder throbs viciously, giving me no other option but to ignore it the best I can.

By the time Myron is standing two feet in front of me, my heart is beating out of my chest, my mouth dry, and I haven't blinked in forever. Heat rushes through my veins like a gushing river.

I'm looking anywhere but him, though. It hurts too much to remember what it used to feel like to see him like this—and what it has been reduced to.

It's not the same. *I'm* not the same. And I fucking hate Erina for it.

Instead of reaching for me, Myron turns around, exposing his right shoulder for me. "He took from both of us, Ayna."

293

Whatever I expected, I'm not prepared for the sight of smooth, pale skin stretching over his shoulder blade where the mate mark once lived.

"It's gone," I whisper.

Myron nods, black waves shifting so the point of his right ear peeks through them. He doesn't turn around as he tells me, "I talked to Silas, too. He said I should be prepared to live with a few days of jealousy."

Begging the floor to open and swallow me, I hum a non-committal sound. "He told you about the un-mating?"

"He told me that all I can do is continue to love you. That I'm powerless before the threads of fate that were untangled."

He stands so still I'm not sure he's breathing, muscles so tight I believe he might start trembling if he doesn't do something, say something.

"Are you afraid?" Because I am, and I want those emotions back—all of them. But whatever memory I recall, it is whisked away on a wave of pain that makes me bite back a moan.

So slowly I have time to look away if I choose to, he turns around, facing me fully, every mask stripped away. "I was never more terrified than the moment I realized what they were doing to you. And I'm afraid now when I see how differently you look at me. I'm scared I'll never experience a smile on your lips again or hear a word of affection from your tongue. I'm anxious every time I step into your presence that you'll reject me. When I sleep, it is with nightmares of you turning your back on me forever. And when I see the others talk with you, there's a voice in my mind telling me you might be glad to be rid of me."

I lower my head, but Myron catches me by the chin, gently holding me back until my eyes lock with his.

"They might burn me out of you, Ayna, but they can't burn you out of me. Ever. You're the fabric my world is woven from, the ocean my soul floats upon. You're the starless night and the brightest sun, and the dawn and the twilight and the storm that blends the two. No matter what they do, you'll always be there, inside my heart." He places his palm over his chest. "I don't need a mate mark to tell me I'm yours."

A tear slips from my eye. Myron catches it with his thumb, sweeping it from my cheek.

"And I'm ready to wait for all eternity for you to remember you're mine, too."

He doesn't look back as he lowers his hand and picks up his shirt, inclining his head at me as he walks out the door.

THIRTY-THREE

AYNA

"I'm not going to ask you what the fuck you did to him," Clio bites as she brings down her sword on mine.

Raising an eyebrow in question, I parry her strike, once again grateful for the extra speed and strength Vala and Shaelak gifted me when they decided to make me something more than human.

"I asked *him*, but *he* wouldn't tell me. Tori, perhaps, if he pried. But your mate is a pretty private person, so *my* mate has the decency not to push him." On light feet, she twirls away, lifting her sword as she leaps back a foot. "Technically, it would be *your* responsibility as his *mate*"—she makes a dramatic pause, summoning ice to her free hand before she comes at me again—"to make sure he's all right."

"Can you please stop saying the word?" It's hard enough to run into Myron at breakfast, lunch, and dinner, let alone every time I walk out of what should have been our shared bedroom into the living area connecting the suites of what's left of our little group. Pouly and Andraya are missing, and Clio and Tori have their own rooms in the palace, of course, but the rest of us returned to the same quarters Recienne assigned us in the first place.

"*Mate?*" She gives me a deadly grin right before hauling her magic at me. "What's wrong with the word *mate?*"

Crystals of snow and ice dance around me in a tornado ready to sweep me up and carry me away. Perhaps I should let it.

It's been another four days since the attack. Four days since Myron acknowledged he'd never stop waiting for me. He hasn't forced a conversation, merely greeted me with those eyes that promise the waves of the ocean. My heart opens into a ravine of despair every time our gaze meets, and my stomach empties into a pit.

"Nothing." I'm not sure Clio hears me over the thunder of her power, but she grimaces and pushes harder.

"Your *mate* asked me about your progress. I assume he meant with training, but I'm not entirely sure that's what he's really desperate to know." The expectant half-tilt of her head as she watches me stand idly at the center of her blizzard tells me she's waiting for me to demonstrate that *progress*.

With a sigh, I pull on the silver power I've been cultivating over the past days since Clio showed up on my threshold, ready in battle leathers and the words, "Time for wallowing is over."

From the settee in the corner of the common room, Silas shrugged at me and Herinor echoed the sentiment with a grim set of his features—basically his usual expression, but it seemed extra-dark that day.

Myron wasn't there, and I didn't ask where he'd gone.

She hasn't failed to pick me up for training at the exact same time every day since. A part of me is grateful for the push, for making me forget the wound on my shoulder that has gone numb even when it hasn't made any progress at healing, and for the time spent in company where no one asks how I'm doing, how the bond is progressing. If I can *feel* him again or if things are still ... awkward. That's the question I fear most. Especially from the males. It draws my eyes to their muscles, to their broad shoulders, their handsome features, makes me wonder what it would feel like to have their hands on me—

"Askarea to Ayna!" Clio shouts, sending a ball of snow right at my face that rushes down my throat so fast I nearly choke on it. "Stop fucking around and defend yourself."

"I'm not *fucking around*." Even though I wish I were. Gods... the guard Recienne insists on sending after me wherever I go is extra handsome today. Whether the Fairy King doesn't trust me or is simply concerned about what I'll do in my condition, I haven't bothered to find out.

"Perhaps the snow isn't enough to cool you down." Clio's part-amusement, part-annoyance should hurt. Instead, all it does is make me wish I'd never been born.

"I didn't do anything to him." With a blast of my Crow magic, I send Clio's ice storm hurtling across the arena, right into the stone wall closest to the palace.

The guard shifts at his post but doesn't glance my way, eyes on the grounds outside the arena and following his assignment.

"Who are we talking about?" Clio reels in the ice, her power leaving a trail of frost where it touches. "Myron or Garrison?" Her gaze follows mine, landing on the male's shoulders.

"Certainly not Garrison," I huff. "I didn't do anything to Myron either."

For a heartbeat, Clio eyes me like she's about to burst out with laughter. Then she seems to remember this is serious, and I'm not choosing to be attracted to anything on two legs that features a dick. "Perhaps *that*'s the problem."

"What do you mean?" I rally more of my power, readying to strike before she calls me out for not having practiced.

"Perhaps you *should* be doing *something* to him."

"Like what?"

Clio rolls her eyes, sending a snowball flying. I bat it away with a flick of my fingers. Crow magic seems to channel easier when I'm uncomfortable, humiliated, and generally awkward, but hey, I'll take whatever works. When Erina brings his armies to the border, I'll thank Clio for every annoying question and every moment of discomfort she's caused during these training lessons.

"Like throw him on his back and ride him like a stallion."

I choke on my breath. For the blink of an eye, I can see it: Myron's powerful body sprawled across the night-blue silk covering the bed meant for both of us, his muscles taut with coiled-up pleasure as I move on top of him. Heat shoots up my legs, straight to my core, but when I try to think of his face, of the black half-moons of his lashes when he closes his eyes, the deep moan parting his lips... My chest locks up, and the wound on my shoulder comes to life, cutting off any romantic thought I could have been capable of.

Perhaps I should be grateful I'm still feeling *something*— even when it's pain.

"You don't just *throw* a Crow male on his back. They're too strong." Kaira chimes in from the side.

I didn't notice her joining us, but now that she's here, my head automatically turns to scan the arena for Herinor.

"You've tried?" Clio teases, and Kaira—Guardians help her—blushes.

"In training?" Why she phrases it like a question, only the deities of the realms know.

Clio finally does explode with laughter, but she doesn't comment.

"Myron is with Herinor and Royad, by the way."

Of course, my sister would think I'm searching for Myron, not the hulk of a Crow who follows her around like a puppy.

Instead of reacting, I send another strike of silver power at Clio, savoring the release of pressure that has been building in my chest as it flows from my palms. She blocks it with her blade this time, dispersing my power like little stars that rain down along her shield.

"You don't care what he's doing?" Kaira prompts in my mind, the only one who has such deep insight into my mind when I occasionally forget my shield. *"Hasn't it been long enough? Silas said the un-mating phase should pass quicker for you, based on how long you refused to communicate with any-one. Ten days. He said, for him, it was ten* years." She chuckles as if Silas lusting after every skirt in the realm was something funny. *"It should pass fast."*

The next blow I land on Clio's shield tears a crack into it. The female staggers back with surprise.

"Well done, Ayna. You're learning more control by the day."

It's more like I'm *losing* more control by the day with every male taunting me with his mere presence. Every male but Myron. He's my *mate*, yet I can't fathom touching him. I can't even think of his lips on mine…

The taste of earth and moss and the salt of the winds above the sea coat my tongue, fill my lungs, a soft pair of lips grazing the side of my neck. Black strands of hair tickle my cheek, the sensitive skin along my collarbone and my sternum as he moves down inch by inch. Heat blows over my peaked nipple, sending a flare of fire through my core.

I'm liquid starlight floating on the ocean, no, fire. I'm fire. And my body is alive with desire.

"I'm not sitting front row in your daydreams, Ayna." Kaira's reprimand quenches the warmth between my legs, and I could swear the earth is taunting me with the tiny puffs of dust rising as I shift my feet in request for it to finally do its task and swallow me.

"I'm not daydreaming."

"Definitely not." Kaira shoots me a grin. *"And most definitely not about Myron."*

Groaning my frustration, I lift my dagger, coating it in silver power as I lift it over my head and attack.

Clio is ready. Of course, she is. That female is never flabbergasted by my shifting moods and seemingly random attacks. As if she has a sixth sense for what it means to be in a weird place with her mate.

Perhaps I should ask her sometime.

"If you've come to annoy me, you can turn around and leave right now." I don't even look at Kaira, channeling my anger and embarrassment into my magic instead.

Clio whoops her approval when I crack her shield wide open with the next blow.

"You've been secretly practicing, admit it." A laugh bubbles up her throat, spilling into the arena like wind chimes.

I hate the cheerfulness of her tone. Hate how I want to laugh with her.

I'm supposed to be mourning my mate.

I can barely think the word.

He's not lost for me. Not in the way of a true un-mating. He's still there, inside me. Yet, I can't sense the bond. I can't tug on our connection and summon a flicker of the emotions I'm used to.

It's overwhelming and the dryness of a desert both at once.

I still *have* a mate. Why am I going through the un-mating symptoms?

"I thought you'd never ask." Tori steps into the arena, a shadow in wicked blue and dark brown garments of the finest making. His auburn hair is tied back at the nape of his neck, and his eyes sparkle with the glimmer of the sun.

"Get the fuck out of my mind."

Kaira attempts a response of outrage, but Tori is faster.

"Not a chance, Ayna." He stalks to Clio, pressing a kiss to her temple, fingers delving into her hair in such a proprietary way I believe he's marking his territory so the guard won't take a wrong glance at Clio, but that's not it. Not at all. I can see the warning in his eyes when he finally lets go of his mate and approaches me with arms crossed over his chest. *He*'s reminding me he's not fair game, no matter what the un-mating process is doing with me.

"Silas warned me you might be asking exactly that question." He jerks his head at the stack of logs at the edge of the arena, where I sat with Silas the first day I left my room, and starts walking.

Kaira and Clio follow, leaving me with the choice to remain where I am and ogle the guard, or join them.

I do the latter, climbing onto the edge of the lowest log and sheathing my daggers.

"Did he have an answer, or was he merely being a smartass?"

That costs Tori a chuckle, Clio a frown, and Kaira a twist of her lips.

"He's suffered through true un-mating. Don't make fun of something you can't begin to fathom."

"*I*'m not fathoming this?" I glance around, pretending to be checking whether there's someone else he might be talking to. "If I remember correctly, I'm the one whose mate mark has been burned away and who's now going through exactly what Silas predicted.

The patience innate in Askarea's general must be Guardians-given because I can't begin to think the things I'd already have done had someone else acted the way I'm acting.

I can't help it, though. My body is a battlefield of a different kind, and if the mating bond is still there, my heart must have been ripped out.

"It takes time," Tori said, eyes sincere and full of compassion. "And you're not the only one suffering."

He leaves it at that, even when I want to demand if Myron is in pain, physically the way I am, or if he means heartbreak. I want to ask. Want to know every last detail, yet I can't bring myself to open my mouth.

"Talk to him," Tori merely says. "No one knows better the ways he's suffering than him."

That takes all anger, all annoyance, all distraught emotions right out of me, and I inflate. "What if he no longer wants me?"

The words scatter on a breeze like they've never been spoken, and I hope they'll never make it past the walls of this arena, but Tori lifts his gaze to the entrance where the guard has left his post, replaced by a figure in black leathers and the gravest face I've seen since I watched the inmates of Fort Perenis marched to the gallows.

Myron inclines his head at me. It's all he does, but it sends a storm through the wasteland that is my heart.

My hand lifts on its own accord in a small wave. It's more than I want to do and so much less than what he deserves.

"Maybe Silas doesn't have all the answers to your questions," Clio says as she locks her fingers with Tori, and to-

ANGELINA J. STEFFORT

gether, they stand from the logs. Kaira hops off the tree trunks, holding out her hand to Clio as if begging.

"Take me with you when you go, will you?"

Clio's fingers close around hers, and together, they site-hop away, leaving me alone with the one person I fear most.

THIRTY-FOUR

AYNA

For long heartbeats, Myron just stands there as if he doesn't own the silky voice I hear whenever I close my eyes.

"Have you ever wondered what happens if two fairies site-hop in different directions while holding hands?"

It's not what I'd expected, but I'll take it. At least, he isn't asking if I've made up my mind whether I still want him.

Because I do. I'll always want him. Just my body is confused, and I hate-hate-hate every last minute I'm hurting him.

The war in his eyes is killing me, so I decide not to watch. The ground in front of him is less dangerous.

"I suppose they'd end up separated?" I don't mean to say it that way, but the words are out, and the uncomfortable silence stretching between us tells me he gets the double meaning.

"Perhaps." His tone is light, the exact opposite of the painful knot forming in my stomach when I keep telling myself it would be so easy. That it's all right to feel empty and still yearn for him. It's all right to wonder if it's better this way… "I suppose it depends on how strong they are and who is stronger."

Stronger… Ha! I'm weak. Silas says it's the un-mating symptoms messing with me, but my flesh is weak every time a male steps into the room. I hate it.

It will get better soon. Kaira is convinced, Silas is convinced—probably everyone but me is convinced.

"If one is stronger than the other, I guess the stronger partner will dictate the direction they're going."

Myron stops so abruptly I wonder if he is going to say something else—if he *means* something else—but he continues eventually, "If both are equally strong…"

I don't give him time to make up his mind what might happen then. "They might never find the same path."

Because that's what happened to us. We were both strong. And now we ended up in separate places, the bond connecting us no longer durable enough to hold us together.

It's all in your fucking mind, I tell myself. *Give it a few days, and you'll be fine. You won't want to dry hump every other male, and you won't shy away from your bonded partner anymore. You love him. You want him. There is no other person for you in the universe.*

"Unless they decide they have a common destination."

Fire burns in my stomach, flaring high at the question he's posing. If *I'm* willing to meet him somewhere between where we used to be headed and where we're headed now.

It hurts as fuck that I don't have an answer.

"Is that something one can decide? What if it's not us choosing our destinations? What if our paths have long been written in the stars?"

"What if it doesn't matter because my love for you is stronger than the forces holding the stars in the skies?"

For a heartbeat, Myron stares at me, the weight of the universe in his gaze. I don't need to look up at him to know his expression, but I do. Our eyes collide, and a spark of him ignites inside of me, leaving me raw, bleeding. It hurts to see him aching. Hurts even more to know I'm the cause.

I'll be better tomorrow. I'll speak the words on the tip of my tongue tomorrow, that I will never stop loving him either, that the frayed bond between us will heal. That I *want* it to. That I'll cling to that hope until the day the gods decide I'm no longer worthy. "The gods made the stars, and the stars are eternal." *And we are the stars, you and I.*

Something shifts inside of me. It's minuscule and it results in a piercing ache in my shoulder, but it's there. I want to reach for Myron, touch his hand if only for a moment, and it's the first time I'm not paralyzed in his presence since the attack.

Before I can tell him, he rearranges his expression—so open one moment ago, so vulnerable—into all-business.

"I came here to let you know Recienne says the female we rescued is much better. He wants to talk to her today, and he offered for us to join him."

The horrors of that cell beneath the estate flash through my mind, but one thought shines bright like a beacon. She survived. We saved someone. Our sacrifice wasn't in vain.

When he doesn't say anything else, I realize he actually came here to pick me up, not to discuss what happened to us. A weight drops from my chest, and energy fills my limbs at the prospect of having something to do that isn't about me or him or about what our future might hold. This is about making a change in this war, and every last bit of information we can get might help us in the weeks to come. "You mean right now?"

I'm ready to leave, leaping to my feet so fast I almost stumble over the logs as I turn toward him. "Lead the way."

Recienne does look after his court.

When we enter Tata's—that's the female's name—room, it's like walking into a puff of clouds. Light blue kisses along the cream walls like a summer sky peeking through sun-pierced clouds. A rounded glass vase holding white flowers sits atop an azure silk tablecloth on a low bedside table. A pale blue plush rug spreads in front of a carved bed covered in white sheets. Buried beneath the covers lies Tata, her thick black hair curled in a bun atop her head and the sleeves of her nightgown drawn back to her elbows to expose the bandages the healer is about to change as we enter the room behind the King of Askarea.

Tata doesn't flinch or try to get up to kneel or bow. Instead, a warm smile spreads on her brown features, eyes sparkling when they meet her king's. Thick black hair frames her face where all traces of bruises and cuts have been cleared away by healing magic and enough rest. I wonder about those hidden injuries, though, the ones only time can heal, if she's braver than me to be able to smile like this after what she endured or simply better at concealing her brokenness.

"You look better, Tata." Recienne flicks his fingers, and a carved birchwood chair appears next to the bed. He doesn't sit down like I'd expected, though. With a smile, he motions for me to take a seat while he pulls two more chairs out of thin air, choosing the one closest to the bed for himself while he offers the other to Myron. The one closest to me. A shiver runs through my body as Myron's thigh brushes my shoulder when he squeezes past to sit down, the sensation so unexpected my eyes snap to the side, half wishing for his to be waiting for me, but he's smiling at the female, politely listening as Recienne introduces us as the people who freed her.

"It's a pleasure to meet you both." Tata's rich voice doesn't sound like that of a female who went through torture and nearly died in a stinking cell a couple of weeks ago. "King Recienne told me your rescue mission wasn't without cost though."

"We didn't suffer any losses," I quickly say, chest aching at the thought that we might have lost any of my friends that day yet were spared, but Tata's gaze lingers on my shoulder as if she can see through the light leathers I'm wearing.

"Not in the sense we count casualties on a battlefield," she agrees, but her gaze tells me she knows what happened. "I am grateful for your sacrifice. If you hadn't decided to come looking for us, I'd be dead like the rest of the scouts. You went into the belly of the beast to free us."

"We're grateful for the one life that was saved," Recienne says like he isn't the king who waged war on *my* people.

The fact that I am identifying as a Crow more by the day isn't lost on me, and I have no idea how to feel about it when my feelings for Myron are confused on a good day and an outright disaster on a bad one. I'm nowhere near fit to be their Queen—three Crows or thousands, they deserve someone who will stand by their king no matter what.

As if reading my thoughts, Myron's head snaps to the side, eyes finding mine, and days' worth of suffering pour from his ocean irises. My hands want to reach for him, console him, but he pulls up his mask so fast I can't take a full breath before he turns back to Tata, inclining his head.

"We are grateful for your bravery. Going out there full-knowingly that Erina's sentries has been scouting the area, especially with his magic-nullifying drug at hand, is something only a hero would do."

Tata grins at him, cheeks flushing a shade darker. "I'm not the only hero in this room then."

Why it bothers me that he's returning her smile is beyond me. Thank the Guardians, Recienne is here to keep me from making a comment and embarrassing myself.

"We didn't know for certain it was Erina's troops. Only that the Flames had been scouring the borderlands for something." He laces his fingers together, bracing his forearms on his knees as he studies the scar running down the side of Tata's neck climbing from the collar of her cream and light blue nightgown to her ear. That must have been a terrible cut if it leaves a scar on a fairy. Crows only keep scars from Crow claws, I've learned, but how scars work for Askarean fairies is something I've never thought to ask Clio or Tori.

Tata inclines her head. "We knew we were onto something when the scouts from the last mission didn't return." She smooths back her thick black braid with one hand, exposing more scars along her wrist and forearm. The horrors she must have endured...

Of course, she catches me staring and holds up her hand to let me assess her marred skin like it's a trophy to show off. "Bastards burned my wrists before they strung me up to settle a debate whether it will leave scars."

The tick in Recienne's jaw is the only sign of his anger on the behalf of one of his subjects, but his lips remain a polite smile. "Those low-lives got what they deserved." His pointed look is meant for both Myron and me, but it lingers on my face longer, a crease forming between his brows. "You said you had something you wanted to share with us?"

His words are clearly meant for Tata; still, the way his golden gaze bores into me makes my insides squirm. It's not the thrill of a male's attention, though, that puts my body on alert. It's the way that look is drilling deep into the layers of me I've so desperately been trying to bury.

Shifting in my chair, I listen for Tata's response, hoping it will release me from the Fairy King's scrutiny, but he continues, speaking directly to me, "Tata woke a week ago. She was in such deep trauma that her body shut down until the mind was ready to catch up with the healing process."

There's a deeper meaning to his words than I can understand, but it's resonating in a wild cacophony like a set of off-kilter bells.

"When I first woke up," Tata says, her tone tired, "I couldn't believe I was alive. I didn't even want to be alive with all my comrades gone." She glances between Myron and me. "It could have been any of them who survived, but it was me. Not the captain or one of the more experienced soldiers. Me, a female who stumbled into King Recienne's army like a youngling into an armory."

Recienne opens his mouth to say something, but Tata is already speaking again. "I'd never planned on surviving my service, yet here I am." Her laugh is rough, only humorous in parts, but those parts come straight from the heart. "It seems the Guardians have plans for me."

This female endured serious trauma and has picked herself up so fast, not a hint of bitterness on her features. I don't know what bothers me more, how well she's dealing with what life has dealt her or how poorly *I* am.

A soft knock sounds on the door, and Recienne waves his hand, granting access.

"Apologies…" Silas is halfway across the threshold when he realizes the room isn't empty. "I can come back later."

In his hands, he's holding a plate with one single piece of cake.

Not cake—fig-pie. I remember the scent from Myron's palace in the Seeing Forest.

"It's all right, Silas. Please come in." Recienne waves the male over, simultaneously summoning a fourth chair next to mine.

Silas's eyes wander between Tata, Recienne, and Myron before they settle on the chair, and he prowls over, unsheathing his hatchet and laying it over the foot-end of the bed before he sits down, small porcelain plate clutched in both hands like he has no clue where to put it or why he brought it to begin with.

"My favorite, Thanks." Tata holds out a hand toward him, and for a heartbeat, I believe she's reaching for him, but Silas pushes up a few inches, bending forward to hand her the dish.

Recienne's lips twitch, and my stomach sours. Myron sits quietly like he hasn't just witnessed one of his grumpiest warriors awkwardly hand a female a piece of cake.

Tata brings the plate up to her nose, inhaling deeply before she leans back against the stack of pillows, setting the plate on the bedside table, right next to the flowers. "For later," she murmurs, a small smile on her lips. "I was just going to tell them about the weapon," Tata says to Silas, who merely nods, face wiped clean of all emotions and the usual frown back in place.

"I'm glad you're feeling brave enough to share today." The words out of Silas's mouth take me by such surprise that I don't realize I'm exchanging a look with Myron until something in my stomach starts eating at me.

He averts his eyes first, training them back on Tata, and I follow his lead.

"Please tell us more about the weapon," Recienne prompts, his tone gentle, cautious in a way I hadn't believed the Fairy King capable of, but today seems to be full of surprises.

Loose black strands shift into Tata's face as she lowers her head, a deep breath lifting her chest. "Some days were worse than others in the Flames' dungeon, but the day we overheard the guards' conversation about the weapons delivery was the worst."

The air catches in my throat as I brace for details.

"They strung us up on the rings that day and didn't take us down again. It was the day the first of us died." She closes her eyes as that particular memory flickers behind her eyelids. "Some of us had been there for a while, captured during earlier attacks. But they were all alive, ready to fight our way out should the opportunity arise. After that day, no one believed we'd get out alive."

Like a dark cloud, images of the dungeon return, making it hard to inhale a steady breath. But I'm not the only one. Myron's fingers are digging into his thighs like he's holding on for dear life, his eyes narrowed as if squinting away the horrors of his own memories—not from our rescue mission but from his days in Erina's dungeon. His shoulders rise and fall with slow, controlled breaths. I might have not noticed it, had something inside my chest not alerted me to his discomfort. A flicker of a memory of that connection once brilliant and strong between us.

I don't reach for him the way I might have two weeks ago. This isn't his story, and I don't want to embarrass him by bringing attention to him. I'll ask him later.

It's a promise I make to myself, and I pretend it's as binding as any Crow's.

"I'm sorry," Recienne murmurs, his tone soothing and gentle. How many soldiers he has consoled like this in his long, long years, I can't begin to fathom. He's fought in both Crow wars, and so have his sister and his general. The history in this room is loaded and dangerous, but we're all working together now, there's no doubt about that.

"What did they say about the weapon?" Silas is the one to ask, but even his usually rough, sarcastic tone has smoothed into a quiet melody as he studies the female's hunched shoulders, the crease between her brows, the lines bracketing her mouth as she searches for words.

Eventually, she heaves a deep breath, lifting her chin and straightening her back in defiance against the horrors haunting her. "There's a delivery on its way. Erina and his Crow friend—the name of which I keep forgetting—"

"Ephegos," Silas supplies with a growl.

"Exactly, Ephegos," Tata repeats as I remind myself that Ephegos supposedly is now leading Erina's armies, and anything involving the traitor Crow and weapons can't be good news. "They have refined the magic-nullifying serum and sending it to the Plithian Plains where their army is gathering."

Fuck…

Even Recienne loses his composure for a brief moment as he takes in what seems to be news to everyone.

"They are sending them in wagons. Vials of liquid, apparently, to apply to blades and arrowheads. It's more potent than the version they used on you when they captured you." Her gaze slides to Silas. Whatever happened in those few days since she woke again, Silas must have spent a lot of time in this room, sharing stories, or she would have never heard about how they got captured by the Flames.

"Ephegos is getting ready to equip his own army with the weapon, too, and if that happens, there is no chance we'll defeat even a small group of Flames and Crows." Her gaze wanders from Recienne to Myron to me before it returns to Silas.

His own army. The Crows, not just Erina's legions.

"I knew that fucker would be trouble," Silas grumbles more to himself. "I knew, if we let him live, he'd eventually fuck up our lives."

"It's not like we had a real chance to unlike him," Myron points out with tone so dark I can feel the afternoon light fade from the room for a few breaths.

Silas shakes his head. "But I'd like to believe that we showed him mercy and could easily rectify that mistake. It makes me feel more in control."

His admission is a hit in the gut, as are the black veins creeping into Myron's eyes as he turns to the warrior, features hard as stone. "There will be no mercy next time we face him."

THIRTY-FIVE

AYNA

At the dinner table a few hours later, none of us is showing great appetite. Recienne has briefed Clio and Tori about Tata's news while Myron took it upon himself to inform Kaira, Herinor, and Royad. Silas already knows everything firsthand, so he helped fill everyone in while I went back to my room, not to wallow, this time, but to stare into the mirror for the better part of an hour while I tried to decide if I can make it through a conversation with Myron without hurting either of us.

Now that everyone is seated around the long oak table in Recienne's dining room, I still don't have an answer. So, I'm leaving my odds up to fate, chewing on my food while

Myron inserts his thoughts here and there into Tori's commentary of how to best proceed.

"There is no question we need to stop the weapons delivery," the general drives home his point. "Waiting and seeing will get us killed faster than we can spell our own names backward."

"That's a fairly long time," Clio notes, and I faintly remember their full names are obnoxiously extensive. No one laughs at her comment, not even Silas, who usually would let his dark humor get the best of him at any chance.

Tori is right. "If we allow the delivery to arrive, we'll lose our advantage," I throw in, pondering the merits of fighting with my new abilities compared to my mere human strength. The Crow senses and powers are an immense upgrade to my ability to survive. I can match Clio's and even Silas's strength because of them, even when I need to put in my all to defeat them in training. I was able to hold my own against the Flames—until they put me on my stomach and pushed a torch into my mate mark. Gritting my teeth, I allow the resentment and anger to flush through my veins, sitting out the wave of emotions as I wait for them to make way for the awkward emptiness that comes with the after-effects of what they tried to do to me.

No matter what they do, you'll always be there, inside my heart. I don't need a mate mark to tell me I'm yours. Myron's words echo through my mind. *And I'm ready to wait for all eternity for you to remember you're mine, too.*

From the corner of my eye, I glance at Myron as he chews on his food. The signs of exhaustion are more prominent, as if he exerted himself since we spoke this afternoon, and I notice the slight tremble in his hand as he spears a bite of fish and leads it to his mouth.

A part of me withers, seeing him like this, while the other part is ready to take his fingers in mine to steady them. The thought feels natural enough not to make me question what it means—if things are improving inside my messed up self. I don't want to do this to him. I don't want to do it to us, un-mating symptoms or no.

Closing my eyes, I reach deep into the darkness inside my chest to search for the fragile thread I know lies buried beneath pain and insecurity, and find a thin glimmer of light.

For three quiet breaths, I hold onto it, wondering how long it will take for the bond to grow thick and strong again. When I open my eyes, Myron's gaze is lingering on my face, hand steady mid-air, fork halfway to his mouth.

Someone clears their throat, and I'm back in the conversation that has been carrying on without us.

"We don't know nearly enough about the delivery, and Tata doesn't know where exactly the army is gathering, does she?" Herinor wants to know. He's been mainly listening, studying the dynamics at the table with a stony expression on his scarred face.

Next to me, Kaira is plucking on her slice of rye bread, nibbling on little pieces but not making much progress. My own plate is half full with steamed vegetables and a delicious type of fish I haven't eaten before, even after spending so many years on a ship.

"*Where does the fish come from?*" I try my luck, prompting Tori in my head. While I've been dealing with the un-mating troubles and wondering if things will ever go back to normal,

321

I've made it a daily routine to practice my mind-reading, projecting, and shielding skills.

The surprise makes me choke on a piece of said fish, though when Tori lifts his head as if I addressed him with my normal voice.

"*I've never eaten anything like it,*" I let him know with as much of a victorious grin as the situation would allow.

Tori subtly inclines his head. "*So, you've decided fish is a good topic to converse about in our minds? How about 'Why the fuck haven't you put your mate out of his misery'?*" His expression is blank as he adds, "*Thanks for practicing that shield, though. It's a relief not to hear you acknowledge the abs of every last male in this palace.*"

"*Hey, I haven't been—*" I stop right there. Because it's true.

I haven't been ogling anyone since the conversation with Myron in the arena. "*Perhaps Silas was right, and things are getting back to normal.*" I try to keep the relief out of my tone—and the hope.

"*We're at war. There's nothing normal about the situation, with or without your mating hiccups.*" The softness in his eyes tells me he doesn't mean to hurt me as he puts my problems into perspective, and he's right. Guardians, is he right.

"*I'm sorry.*"

"*For what?*" An auburn brow rises on his forehead as he plops a bite of fish into his mouth.

I try not to turn crimson as I admit, "*For checking out your abs...*"

He stops chewing, grins, continues chewing. "*You only checked out my ass, my dear. And that's all right. Everyone does it."* Winking at me, he takes Clio's hand, placing a kiss on the back of her palm, much to the protest of the female who's trying to get a bite of vegetable onto her fork.

"What was that for?" she demands, earning Tori's amused chuckle and a confused glance from the rest of the table.

Tori merely shakes his head. "So, the weapons... We don't know when they will be arriving, or where. We only know they are on their way."

"A gathering army can't be that hard to spot from the air," Herinor throws in. "If we can find them, we can intercept the wagons before they reach their destination."

Recienne nods his agreement. "Better than site-hopping through the realm for sure. More efficient. The four of you can easily cover the Plithian Plains in a day or two."

"Five," I correct.

All eyes turn to me as I gather my resolve. "I'm a Crow, too. I can shift and fly."

The blend of pride and fear in Myron's expression sends a tingle down my spine, and I can sense the numbness in my shoulder ease just enough to remember the wound is still there. There, but gradually shrinking.

The gleam in Myron's gaze as he studies me from his seat next to me tells me he felt it, too.

I'm not done, though. Yes, I'm ready to try my luck and shift again so I can help, but the Crows aren't the only valuable assets in this unavoidable mission.

"We need to deliver a message to Andraya and Pouly," I tell Clio.

Kaira understands first, dipping her chin as she nods her agreement.

"The rebels have a network of spies. If anyone can find out when exactly the transport is to happen, it's them."

Clio leaves the same night, a piece of paper clutched in one hand, a bundle of fruit cake in the other. "They might take the news better if I deliver them with sweets," she says with a shrug before disappearing into thin air.

"Just like she does with me." Tori shakes his head.

When I give him a questioning glance, he explains, "When she decided to fake her own death and go into hiding, she told me over chocolate cake."

I need to do a double-take. "What?" I knew the history of their relationship was difficult, but—"What did she do?"

Tori drops back into the armchair he was getting up from, obviously settling in for a night of storytelling. The others retired to their rooms, leaving the common room to Tori and me when we prepared the note for the rebels. Clio joined us shortly after we crafted the short letter, a heavy bundle in her hand, and informed us that the kitchen had planned fruit cake for dessert. None of us wanted any sweets after we decided we had work to do.

Now, Clio is on her way to Andraya and Pouly. Since Tori was the one who dropped them off he shared the location of the rebel's hideout with us so we know how to find them. The Crows are resting so they'll be fresh and ready to set out first thing tomorrow morning, and Kaira decided she might as well do the same since she's dead set on taking on my training lessons during Clio's absence.

That leaves Tori and me and the loaded silence.

"Clio and I were going to marry when she was announced the next *bride to the Crow King*." He grimaces. "Before you ask, that was during Carius the Cruel's time, not Myron's."

"I wasn't going to ask." It's the truth.

Tori smiles softly. "I know. I just want to spare you doubts. You have it difficult enough as it is."

The consideration and kindness from this male has surprised me many times, but it's this moment when I realize how deeply he understands the suffering Myron and I are going through.

"To escape her fate, Clio faked her own death and went into hiding for long, long decades. That was the time when she rejected me as a mate, even when we'd been ready to start our lives together."

My heart breaks for him, the pain in his eyes chiseling a spiderweb of fissures.

"She firmly believed it was better for me to find someone else since I could never be with her the way we'd planned. We didn't know how long she'd need to stay hidden, believed perhaps it would be forever. She thought she was saving me by setting me free when, in reality, she was breaking me. I'd have stayed hidden with her until the end of our days had she asked me to, had she said one single word." He lowers his head, shoulders hunching like the weight of centuries is pressing down on him. "All she ever said was that she wanted me to be free to live my life and be happy."

The look he gives me is enough to bring the toughest warrior to their knees, and I need to sit down in the chair across from him.

"She told me to find another female and start a new life so one of us could be happy." A tear drips from his lashes, staining the dark brown of his pants right at the top of his thigh. "I couldn't do it. I couldn't abandon her. So, I stayed with her in my heart, holding onto the bond she was hoping would one day dissolve if she convinced both of us enough that we didn't want it anymore. I clung to it with every fiber of my being; with every breath and every heart-beat, I held onto her. I'd never give up my mate. Never in a million lifetimes."

The words rush from him like a confession, like he's embarrassed to have disappointed her when she'd made up her mind. His shoulders shake in a quiet sob, and he takes a breath so deep I believe he might use up all the air left in the room.

"Don't let Myron slip away, Ayna. He's holding on to you the way I was holding on to Cliophera. If you don't find a way, you will be the end of him."

He means it with all his heart as he locks his wet eyes with mine. "Don't let anyone take away your chance at happiness."

Fighting for breath, I stare back at him, at the strong male crumbling at the mere memory of what they've gone through. But there is joy in the depths of his auburn irises. They had a happy ending.

"How did you win her back?"

Perhaps I shouldn't have asked, perhaps there is more pain he doesn't want to remember, but I need to know.

Tori closes his eyes, speaking to me in his mind, "*A human came along and turned Askarea upside down. The rest is history. Now, go get some sleep. Myron said he'd help you shift tomorrow so you can come on the scouting trip.*"

ANGELINA J. STEFFORT

THIRTY-SIX

AYNA

My room looks only half as pretty when I stare at it bleary-eyed from a fitful night's rest. Tori's words haven't left my mind, and I don't mean those about Myron helping me shift. I'm grateful the most powerful Crow alive will be there to guide me through my first deliberate attempt at shifting, no matter the mixed feelings meddling in my stomach.

Clio returned half an hour ago, startling me out of my bed as she popped up beside it with a message from Andraya and Pouly saying they'd be honored to help the true queen of Tavras in any way they can, and that they'll be putting their network to good use.

Good news at last. We all needed a heap of it.

She conjured simple fighting leathers from that place between worlds where she keeps summoning things from, and dropped them on top of the covers with the words, "Don't lose them during shifting. I'd hate to have to get you new ones." Then, she disappeared, leaving me to a nervous stomach and all sorts of worries over how I might end up naked during shifting the way I had the first time when Herinor had to get a blanket to cover me.

Struggling out of bed, I pick up the leathers then head into the adjacent bathing room to wash up and get ready.

I have about half an hour before everyone else will be awake, so I decide to go for a short walk through the gardens.

Yesterday's guard greets me at the door, tilting his head as he lets me pass before falling into step behind me.

"You don't need to follow me everywhere," I inform Garrison, shamefully remembering how appealing he appeared to me not even a day ago.

"The king ordered you escorted if you don't have one of your friends with you," the male says in his deep baritone, trotting along as I make my way down the stairwell of glimmering stone and into the hallway leading to the back door.

I've spent enough time in this palace to memorize the layout and find some shortcuts that might come in handy should I ever need to bolt.

"Why?" It's a question I should have asked a long time ago. "Does he not trust me?

After a brief pause, during which I'm certain Garrison is fishing for a proper response, he heaves a breath. "I remember a time when another human with magic first came to live here. He sent guards after her everywhere, too, to make sure she didn't run into trouble. It might be a habit. Or an instinct. I'm not one to judge what my king does."

"Thanks, Garrison." It's all I can think of to say. He *is* doing his duty after all, and I'm not his queen to order him around.

We're almost by the wide oak door when I spot a figure in the shadows where the corridor to the kitchens meets the main hall.

Hands flying to my daggers, I spin on the spot, ready to fight, and thank the Guardians for remembering to arm myself before leaving the room.

"Oh no, please—" A melodious, clear voice carries from the shadows, and I need to blink as a fairy my height steps out of the doorway she'd backed into, obviously hiding until she realizes I am ready to kill. "There's no need for those."

Garrison is in my path so fast all I can make out is a blur of leather and steel, blocking the sight of the female ahead. "Stand back," he hisses over his shoulder at me while I try to figure out who we ran into. Then he bows his head at the female. "Is there anything I can do for you, Your Majesty?"

Your Majesty…

"Thank you, Garrison. I was merely hungry." The female holds up a plate of pastries that make my mouth water. It's all I can see of her even when I try to glimpse around Garrison's broad frame. "Tell Recienne he can call off the search party." She bubbles a laugh, and I instantly like her.

"Your Majesty." I step to the side, inclining my head at the Fairy Queen everyone has referred to but nobody shared any details about.

She's beautiful, delicate features set in a heart-shaped face. She doesn't look older than me even when I know she's been alive for more than a hundred years. Raven black waves fall over her shoulders in wild tangles as if she hasn't bothered brushing them this morning. Eyes of liquid amber scan me from the distance, and her mouth quirks into a smile of delight.

"I've been wondering when I'd get to see you, Ayna of Tavras." The Fairy Queen inclines her head, placing a long-fingered hand on her stomach, and I nearly forget my manners when I spot the rounded belly she protectively cradles.

"You're pregnant." All right, I do forget my manners.

The female laughs, walking up to me and entirely ignoring Garrison as he tries to shift between us like a living shield. "Ayna isn't going to hurt me, Garrison."

Reluctantly, the male makes way for his queen to pass, and she stops within arm's reach, holding out her free hand.

I take it, wondering if she expects me to kiss it or shake it when she squeezes mine, a warm smile on her lips.

"I remember that's how human equals greet each other, or has that changed since I left the human realms?"

I'm so surprised that I barely stutter my agreement. "Human equals. Not a queen, though. Not really." At least not one wearing a crown.

The Fairy Queen places her hand back on her belly, grimacing like the baby just kicked her ribs. "He's never quiet, that little monster." She laughs again, the sound so unbelievably cheerful I can't find my voice. "Pastry?" She holds out the plate. "I haven't talked to a human in forever. Not that you're entirely human according to Recienne. He is wondering how your shift will work out today, by the way." She loops her arm around mine, guiding me back toward the kitchen, and I let her. Who am I to stop a pregnant human-turned-fairy from breakfast? If I get to have a piece of pastry in the process, all the better.

Garrison follows us with a step distance, attention on my daggers like he worries they might accidentally slice the Fairy Queen open.

The kitchen is smaller than I expected. Then, this is a magical palace, and who knows what sorts of powers are at work to keep things going? Preparing meals with magic most definitely doesn't require the same task force as a human kitchen does. Pots and pans are sitting in a corner, ready to be used; in an open oven, bread is baking, and a male with a crooked nose and two curled horns so big they cover the sides of his skull stops to bow at us mid-motion. A glance at me and he summons a plate from thin air, loading it with an assortment of pastries from the platter at the center of the working island at the heart of the space.

"I hope you'll enjoy them." His eyes twinkle as he lets the plate float toward me, waiting for me to pluck it from the air before he returns to his task with another bow.

"Thank you." It's all I can push out, too flabbergasted by the display of domestic magic.

The Fairy Queen leads me across the kitchen to an adjacent dining room that appears to be for the staff.

"Recienne and I sometimes come here when we want to get away from court duties." She picks up the caramel-scented croissant on top of her pile and bites into it with a moan. "Elliot makes the best pastries."

When she motions for me to follow her lead, I take a bite of the crooked thing the cook chose for me and almost groan with delight at the explosion of buttery sweetness in my mouth.

"I prefer to eat down here most days because Recienne and I chose not to announce to the world that we're expecting just yet. In times of war, it's always best to be careful with vulnerabilities. I'm sure you've already seen for yourself that my mate is a master at doing just that."

Those first conversations with the Fairy King come to mind, the mask of the unforgiving king he presented when we first came here. How he managed to keep his mate out of our conversations. Even Clio's evasiveness makes sense now. She didn't want to spill their secret. Not even to me.

"I understand." And I do. New life is precious in the human realms where children are part of a natural progression of the world while, here, they are rare treasures. I wouldn't want to leave anything to fate by potentially alerting my enemies to my pregnancy.

"How have you been dealing with the whole magic situation?" She looks me up and down over her plate, a conspiratorial expression on her features, and brushes her hair behind her ear. They are rounded like any human's.

"I'm still adjusting. Clio has been helping me a lot."

"She's the best to coax those new powers out." She takes another bite, considering me. "But your mate has certainly been there for you as well, given your magic is more similar to his than to ours.

"He is doing what he can." It sounds like a lame excuse, but it's the truth. Myron *has* been doing what he can. It's not his fault we were thrown into battle without time to prepare, and he is still ready to aid me with my shift or anything else I ask him for, I'm certain of that.

"Magic takes time. Even with a hundred years of using it, there's always something new." Her words should be an encouragement. Instead, my stomach drops at the prospect of always wondering if I'll accidentally blow up something or someone when I try to achieve a task by magic. The Fairy Queen laughs at my expression. "Don't worry. You'll get used to it." She finishes her pastry and gets to her feet, making Garrison snap to attention as she turns to the door. "Be careful on your mission today, Ayna. It will be nice to continue this conversation some other time."

I barely get to stand before she's out the door, plate of pastries in one hand and the other resting on her belly.

When I make my way back to the suite, the door to Myron's room is open. I stop in the common room, right between two silver brocade armchairs, listening for sounds informing me he's in there, but all I can hear is the soft snoring from Herinor's room and the grumpy morning humming from Kaira's mingled with that of running water.

"Myron?" With a few strides, I'm at the dark wooden threshold, trying to decide if the view of his empty room is a relief or disappointment.

A single bed stands against the sand-colored wall right of the door, between a desk and a narrow, empty bookcase, all made of the same dark wood as the door. The window across the room is open, crisp morning air carrying Myron's scent from the rumpled sheets to my nose. I inhale a deep breath, relishing the familiarity and the fact that there is no one to witness this moment where I allow myself to remember what Myron of Winghaven means to me.

"You can come in."

I nearly hit my head on the door frame as I jump at the deep rumble of his voice.

"I… I'm… I didn't… Sorry, I didn't know you were here." My heart is pounding in my chest like it's a creature of its own, and my head swims from the force of his scent as he shakes out his wet, dripping hair.

Myron is standing in the doorway to the bathing room I missed while being so focused on his *bed*, dressed in nothing but a beige towel slung around his hips and a look of pleasant surprise on his face.

"I mean it. This room is always open for you. You don't need to knock or ask permission." He tries to smooth his features over, but a hint of what he's really saying is shining through anyway. *Please stay.*

I collect myself, grabbing onto my daggers for support. "I was looking to see if you're ready. I want to try a few times without the others first so Silas won't tease me about it for the rest of my life if he finds me naked."

Myron looks at me like I just spoke a foreign language.

"Shifting. I mean shifting," I clarify.

Why is my pulse racing? This is my mate. I've seen him naked before. Why can't I form a clear thought at the sight of droplets of water running down the grooves of his abdomen, vanishing in the soft material of the towel covering his—

My lower lip cracks open where I'm biting into it, and I'm not proud to say I taste blood before the day has properly started.

Myron's eyes scan my face, cautious amusement dancing behind the collected expression he's pulled up. He runs his fingers through his hair, sending a fresh assault of water dripping down his chest, and I need to take a deep breath to clear my head. If only the air wasn't Myron-scented.

"I'll just put on some clothes."

I'm about to turn on my heels and walk out the door when he gestures to the bed. "I'd offer you a chair, but the one at the desk is broken."

He wants me to *stay*. Sheepishly, my eyes dart to said chair, confirming that one of the legs is missing, before continuing to the bed.

"Do you think it's…" I clear my throat as my voice fails me. "Do you think it's a good idea for me to be in here while you—"

"We've been mated for a while, Ayna. Our current … *situation* … doesn't change anything." He pauses, arm already reaching for the shirt hanging on the doorknob. "Not in that regard, at least. I have nothing to hide from you. Body or soul."

He grabs the shirt, sliding one arm into the black fabric, then the other, and then pulls it over his head. My fingers ache to peel away the wet strands of hair sticking to the side of his face. I sit on the bed, shoving my hands under my thighs.

In my shoulder, a stinging pain is informing me the numbness is lifting further, and I can't help but flinch, biting harder into my lip as the sensation spreads all the way to my neck.

Myron is in front of me so fast I nearly shy away. Nearly—but he places his hands on my thighs in a silent plea to stay where I am as he kneels in front of me, eyes alive like the ocean in a storm. "What is it?"

Had I been braver, I might have reached for his face and brushed those stubborn strands of hair away after all, but staring at him is all I can do. Taking in the warmth of his palms as they continue to rest on my thighs is all I can do.

The scent of wind and pine and the winds blowing along the coasts of Eherea fills the space between us, and Myron keeps waiting for my response.

I don't have one because the pain in my shoulder is already fading, tuned out by the nearness of the male who knows how to make me forget my own name.

The shimmer of light inside my chest is pulsing once, twice, throbbing against my ribs like a heartbeat of its own, and I remember to breathe.

"Nothing," I whisper, my left hand finding its path into his hair, fingers tangling with the drying waves. Myron's eyes close, nostrils flaring as he scents me, the tip of his nose grazing the inside of my forearm. His brows and lashes are dark as night, stark shadows painting the angles of his face, and the top buttons of his shirt are still open. It would be easy to slide my hand down his neck, under the fabric...

"I miss you, Ayna." His words aren't more than a breath, a sigh as my fingertips wander to the nape of his neck, but his hands remain firmly planted on my thighs, fingers curling into my flesh as if to hold themselves in place.

Leaning into my touch, he tilts back his head, lips parting with a low moan that shoots through my veins like a flare of fire. A drop of water is resting above the side of his lip, daring me to kiss it away. He doesn't flinch when I trace the outlines of his face with my index finger, leaving my other hand tangled at the back of his neck, doesn't move his hands even an inch. His breath stutters from his mouth in hot gusts, heart thumping so loud even I can hear it.

There are no questions, no expectations. All he does is relish what I'm willing to give, drinking in my touch, inhaling my scent.

I could watch forever the way his brows draw together the slightest bit when my finger glides along the edge of his jaw, the way his tongue flicks over his upper lip when I reach the crest of his chin, lingering there. I could stare at him all day, forgetting that we have a purpose or a mission.

Trust Royad to remind us as he stumbles in through the still-open door and stops with a cough.

I pull my hands back so fast I could swear I tear a few hairs from Myron's scalp.

He doesn't move.

"I thought a king knelt before no one," Royad says, leaning into the doorframe and tapping a finger on the wood.

Myron's eyes blink open like stars coming to life in the falling night, his gaze finding mine and lingering. "Before no one but my fate."

Fate, not *mate.* I'm sure I heard him right.

"I'm sorry to interrupt, but it's almost time to go." Royad sounds as awkward as I'm supposed to feel, but Myron's gaze has captured me, and I'm no longer part of this universe. I'm part of his.

"Then get the fuck out of here until it's actually time to leave." Myron's growl reverberates through the room, through my bones, like a command, and the heat shooting up my thighs is no longer just the one his skin emanates where his palms linger.

Royad disappears so fast I almost miss him grumbling, "Better not let Recienne wait." And he shuts the door behind him.

"We should really be going," Myron says, making no move to actually follow his own advice. "I don't care if we let Recienne wait a year and then some, but you need to manage shifting before I'll allow him to throw you into the skies."

Heat flares in his gaze as I fidget under his touch, his fingers sliding an inch up my thighs.

"If I don't stand up now, I won't leave this room before I've fucked you raw."

I whimper, my core melting at the mere thought of what he suggested. I'm ready to entertain the idea, daring him to try, when a rough knock followed by Herinor's grumpy voice stops me from doing something I might regret. "Time to go!"

Myron's gaze doesn't leave mine, but the desire living there a moment ago has been carefully tucked away when he slowly stands, one hand lingering just above my knee until the last possible moment while the other is keeping his towel from slipping. I don't dare lower my gaze when he drops it to reach for the pair of pants draped over the backrest of the chair and slips into them.

ANGELINA J. STEFFORT

THIRTY-SEVEN

AYNA

Tata is there when we arrive at the arena, her braid bobbing as she shakes her head at something Silas asks. I try not to notice Royad's smirk or Herinor's frown or the way Kaira seems to be eternally amused about whatever Herinor just grumbled to her.

At least, she's not paying attention to us. Everyone else sure is, and I can't help the feeling they all know exactly how close I was to ripping Myron's towel off myself and doing exactly as Clio suggested a few days ago. Somehow, I'm under the impression they can *smell* it on me.

"We haven't figured out shifting, so you all better get lost until we call you back." Myron plants himself at the heart of the arena, shooting Herinor a deadly glance that would have sent lesser males running.

To his credit, Herinor inclines his head at his king before gesturing for Kaira to walk ahead of him and following. Royad raises a brow at Myron as he walks out next, leaving Silas and Tata the only ones dwelling.

"You, too, Silas." Myron doesn't even look at him, gaze wandering to Tata instead and tone softening. "Apologies, Tata, but I need you to leave, too. I want this to be a safe place when my mate shifts."

Tata inclines her head, but a question lingers on her tongue—I can tell by the way her eyes bounce between Silas, Myron, and me.

"What is it, Tata?" I eventually ask.

Tata gives me an embarrassed look. "I've never seen a Crow shift. The older fairies keep telling stories about the fearsome monsters shifting into feathered coats, but I wasn't old enough to fight in the last Crow War."

A part of me believes that's good news. At least, she never knew the Crows for the creatures most fairies feared. At least, not in person.

"You're welcome to return and watch as we all shift later," Silas offers, but something inside of me pushes to tell her to stay.

"I've never shifted deliberately. I might not even be able to, but you're welcome to stay, Tata," I explain as we wait for a grumbling Silas to leave on his own.

Myron claps his hands, obviously not happy about the audience, but doesn't comment, accepting my wish. "You can sit over there," he tells her. "Don't disturb us, though. Crows in bird form rely on their instincts more than in our fae form. If you startle a new Crow and she takes flight, she might take off and never return."

I hope he's only saying that to frighten her because, chances are, if that's the worst case, exactly that will happen to me.

When Myron turns to face me, a smile graces his lips, and his gaze is warm and tender in a way that gives me a fuzzy feeling. "Don't fly away, little crow," he whispers as he holds out both his hands for me.

With a sense of nervous anticipation, I place mine in them, waiting for instructions.

"How did you shift the first time?"

His question takes me by surprise, and I'm not prepared for the images of horror flooding my head.

"I don't know. It happened when I begged the gods for a way to save you." It's a dim memory, Myron's blood coating the metal table in Erina's dungeon, the knife at my arm, the pain... So much pain.

"How did you change back?"

Herinor's firm but gentle hands wrapped around my little bird body, imagining my human form. Willing myself back into it...

"Think of the wind beneath your wings, Ayna. Think of freedom."

That's the opposite of what I experienced the last time I shifted. "Freedom is something I haven't known for a long time."

The words hurt. Perhaps even more so because they are true.

Myron squeezes my hands, strong fingers enveloping mine, and steps up so close we're chest to chest. "You're free, Ayna. No matter what bonds may hold you, you're always free to make a choice."

I feel it then, the question whether I'd prefer to sever our bond, to do as Clio tried with Tori. *Do you want me to let you go, Ayna?*

It's only when I tilt my head to meet his gaze that I realize he spoke those words out loud. And in his eyes, the world is holding his breath.

I don't have words to tell him, so I grasp his hands harder, holding onto him with all that I have, and a cautious smile spreads on his lips. "Then shift with me, Ayna. Fly with me. Be *free* with me."

I feel the tingle in my chest first, then my arms. My legs follow, falling away from me as they turn into small bird feet. Feet with wicked claws that could scratch out eyes and open arteries. My torso is light, small, and airy, as are my arms as I try to keep my hold on Myron. Feathers slip over feathers, our wings coming apart as we beat them to remain mid-air. Magic pulses in my veins, smaller and weaker than in my human form, but it fills me beak to claw.

He was right. Instincts rule my bird form. I need to move; remaining stagnant is dangerous even if I'm a predator. With a few efficient beats of my wings, I'm up in the air, high above the arena. Tata sits on the side of the angled structure at the foot of the stone benches, staring up at me with wide dark eyes. It amazes me that I can see such detail from so high up, but it doesn't surprise me. Those senses are part of me the way the wings are and the tiny heart pumping my blood in frantic beats.

This body is breakable but fast, vulnerable but light. I'm the eyes and the ears of the sky, and a few feet above me, another crow is circling, this one larger, feathers so black they swallow the light of the sun hiding behind clouds. He caws at me, the sound familiar yet foreign. A part of me wonders if I could understand him if I tried hard enough, but then I see something move on the ground. It's smaller than me, and fast.

I'm faster.

I'm death wrapped in feathers, and my claws rip into the mouse a heartbeat before it skitters through the gap between two rocks. Victory makes my blood gush through my veins in a frenzy, and I want to take my trophy to the skies, but I'm not fast enough to pull up as the wall approaches at neck-breaking speed, and I have to resort to bracing myself for the impact—*impacts*—when I first hit the stone enclosing the arena, then the ground, and roll to a halt.

Someone shouts my name, heavy footfalls shaking the packed earth I'm lying on. I'm shaking. My wings at first, then my legs, then my shoulders and my torso. My arms, my hands.

"Myron," I croak, still breathless from the crash.

He skids to a halt beside me, on his knees again as he scoops me up in his arms.

"I'm all right," I tell him.

He doesn't believe me until I wriggle out of his grasp, scrambling to my own two feet and cursing as I realize my clothes are gone.

"Damn it."

With two quick moves, Myron peels off his jacket and strips out of his shirt, offering it to me.

"Clio will kill me." I'm not half as embarrassed about Tata seeing me naked as I am about what Clio will say when she realizes she will need to get new leathers for me after all.

When I dare glance at him, Myron shoots me a wicked grin. "The good news is you shifted in and out of your bird form."

"What's the bad news?"

He raises both brows as if to ask whether that isn't obvious.

"That I'm naked?"

"I wouldn't count that as bad news," his grin widens. "At least, not for me."

Groaning my frustration, I tug the shirt over my head and roll my eyes. "So, what's the bad news?"

Myron turns his head, glancing at the entrance to the arena. "That I will need to start a new war, hurting the King of Askarea for having seen my mate naked.

He's obviously joking because Recienne doesn't summon his power to destroy him as he steps into the arena, clapping his hands. "That went faster than expected. And your wound is looking much better, Ayna. Did you notice?"

Myron grinds his teeth but doesn't draw his sword or wield his silver power.

"I'm happily mated, Myron. Hold your feathers." Recienne laughs at his own joke, but he can't fool me anymore after meeting his mate this morning and realizing he's just as much a protective shit as any other fairy male.

Folding my arms across my chest, I stand at Myron's side. Of course, Myron's gaze lingers on my shoulder, where not one tug or numb place remains. I don't want to look if it's all healed. Askarean fairies can lie after all and I'm not ready to be disappointed, but I cock my head, staring the golden-eyed male down with bravado. "You'll make for an interesting father."

Recienne stops dead, all masks slipping as he puts two and two together. "When did you meet her?"

"We had breakfast together this morning."

The confused expression on Myron's face would have been amusing had this not been a moment I realize that, with everything going on, I forgot to share this knowledge with him. Shame fills me from head to toe. We might not be exactly where we were two weeks ago, but I don't want to leave him in the dark. I don't want him to be taken by surprise in front of someone he has such a complicated history with. I don't want him to look weak.

On instinct, I grab Myron's hand, ignoring the sizzle running up my arm when his palm slides against mine.

"I forgot to tell you since you put other things on my mind when I returned from my little walk." Myron stiffens, but he doesn't say a word, thumb brushing over the back of my palm. "I ran into the Fairy Queen. She's with child."

For a long moment, the air is palpably thick with questions, with warnings and unspoken threats.

Myron swallows then smiles. A real smile. "Congratulations."

When I think Recienne is going to combust, he finally inclines his head. "Thank you, Myron. The Guardians have blessed Sanja and me with this pregnancy. It's a secret for no one to tell." He glances at Tata, who sits quietly where she was ordered, probably wishing she'd left with the others. "Not one word," he warns.

"Not one word, Your Majesty." Tata stands from the rock she is sitting on and lowers herself to one knee. "I swear."

Recienne seems satisfied since he turns back to us. "My secret lies in your feathery hands, Myron. I would ask a promise of you to never share this information with a soul, but I will make this moment the start of our true alliance instead. I trust you with this knowledge, fully aware that you could sell me out and make my mate and my unborn child a target in this war. Whoever threatens them, threatens me. Whoever takes her and uses her against me will own this kingdom. I will give up everything before I lose her. I will die before I see her harmed. And now you're carrying this responsibility with you." His eyes wander from Myron to me, gold hard and piercing. "And you, Ayna of Tavras. I trust you, too."

THIRTY-EIGHT

MYRON

Strong wingbeats sound from in front of me, but it's the more quiet, cautious ones beside me I listen for as I circle the dead land at the borders of the human territory. Ayna has been doing incredibly well, not once faltering despite the long distance we've been flying. It's the second day of our search. Silas and Royad have split off to head west and east while Herinor, Ayna, and I fly directly south, scouting the center of the Plithian Plains.

So far, it's been mainly horses and a shed here and there, but as time progresses, we spot more farm villages along the dusty roads.

After Clio spent a few minutes lamenting the leathers Ayna made disappear with her shift, she site-hopped us right to the Tavrasian border so we wouldn't need to fly the entire way from Aceleau. We've been searching ever since, making sure to stay on schedule to return at the pick-up spot on the third day so Clio can take us back.

In the meantime, Recienne and Tori are strategizing how to best prepare an army of creatures used to fighting with the aid of their magic without it. It's not a task I envy them. At least, Tata is there to speak to the soldiers as one of their own with first-hand experience.

I'm still in shock about Recienne's reaction to Ayna finding out about the Fairy Queen's pregnancy, and I'm even more surprised about how excited I am for the male I used to despise. Younglings are so rare among fairies, and Crow younglings haven't been around since I was a little one myself. I can't even fathom what it would be like to have one of my own.

A tear runs through my chest as I glance at Ayna in her proud bird form, gliding on the winds. She's made for this. Shaelak had mercy on me and gifted her this sort of magic so she no longer needs to miss the oceans. But will we be happy like Recienne and his queen? Will we live long enough to find out?

We've been scanning the territory for two days now, my chest constricting every time something moves on the ground below and relief filling me every time it wasn't the army we've been looking for.

The sun is setting slowly, creeping toward the edge of the world as I make out the silhouette of a dark mass that doesn't belong in the Plithian Plains slowly winding along the seam of a small forest. There they are, hiding in plain sight.

I huff a caw Herinor will instantly understand. He takes off slightly west, following my order while Ayna flutters closer to my side as if in a prompt to fill her in.

She doesn't notice them at first. Only when we make it a mile farther west does she realize the dark stripe on the horizon isn't merely the layers of a forest. Soldiers—hundreds of them if not thousands have gathered along the seam of trees by the farm village. They've put up tents and ignited fires.

The mere thought of those makes me wonder how many Fire Fairies have joined Erina's army. And how many Crows.

My gaze darts ahead to the treetops. A perfect spot to hide a flock of Crow sentries.

With a deep caw, I order Herinor back to my side.

We found them. Now we need to return to warn the others. Silas and Royad will return soon enough when they don't find anything. We'll wait for Clio to come get us and carry the information to the King of Askarea that an army large enough to take on his fairy legions is readying, and if they get the magic-nullifying weapon, there will be no winning this war.

When we land by the Askarean border hours later, Clio is already pacing beneath the trees, her copper braid a strip of fire in the near darkness. Royad is hopping from tree to tree in bird form, keeping a look out for Silas and us.

When he spots us, he descends, feathers disappearing into leathers as his form uncoils into his human shape.

I follow his lead, waiting for Ayna to be close enough to the ground before I shift and hold out my hand for her to land upon.

Her feathers fall over my fingers as she curls her claws around them, one black eye studying me curiously.

"Time to shift, little Crow," I whisper, ignoring Clio's rant that we really don't have time for fae-bird pillow talk.

A shudder runs through her body, claws slipping and wings elongating into arms as her whole body stretches until she's her beautiful, human self again. My other arm catches her under the knees so I can cradle her to my chest, shielding her naked form from view.

"Catch!" Herinor calls, tossing me a bundle of fabric, which I shake out and drape over Ayna's shoulders as I set her on her feet.

"Three leathers in two days," I tease, holding her gaze as she shrugs as if the way our bodies are pressed together, the rough leather of my chest protector, isn't scraping along her bare breasts. As if I can't smell her physical reaction to me.

Gods, I would kill for that scent.

"Clio looks positively murderous." With efficient movements, Ayna slides into the shirt from Herinor's extra supplies and buttons it up to her collarbones. "She nearly bit my head off when she had to summon new clothes for me yesterday. Next time, I'll just shift naked."

The thought does all sorts of things to the lower regions of my stomach, but I blow out a breath, clearing my head and reluctantly releasing her from my embrace.

"We found them," I say the moment Royad and Silas join us, their shifts quick and unspectacular, yet my heart will never fail to lift a fraction when I see all feathers vanish from their arms and their eyes clear to their normal colors.

Royad is at my side in an instant, Clio right behind him, the frown first directed at the lack of Ayna's clothing now hitting me.

"How many?" In her mind, she's already calculating the odds, I'm sure. I've never met a female fiercer and better equipped for battle than Princess Cliophera of Askarea, and the gods are kind enough to put us on the same side of a war for once.

"So far? About a thousand men." Hearing it out loud from Herinor is worse than seeing the black mass gathering in the plains. "They seem to have only started to arrive. Tavras is a large territory, so there could be ten times that within a few weeks."

"You think they are drafting all legions to the Plithian Plains?" Ayna rolls the sleeves of her shirt up until they no longer cover her hands. "And how many Flames are there to join them? How many Crows?"

I refuse to cringe at the mention of my own kind partnering with the enemy. They've made their choice.

"Kaira said five hundred Flames, maybe six hundred." Herinor has obviously used the time spent with the part-Flame wisely and collected information. "She says their strength is ranged weapons."

"And swordfight, of course," Clio adds.

Herinor nods. "With those Shaelak-damned silver pokers, yes." He glances to his hip as if expecting one of said swords hangs on his belt and shakes his head. "Their magic is dangerous since anything flammable continues to burn once it catches fire." Unlike our magic where the silver light can gut a person or blow up a structure, but it doesn't continue to sizzle once it's hit its target. He doesn't need to say that.

I can feel Ayna's gaze on the side of my face as she leans against the closest tree, questions pressing in on the narrow space between us, but I don't dare look to find out what they are. She saw the unadulterated power flowing out of me when they tried to un-mate her, and I don't know if I can deal with the fear in her eyes. So, I focus on Herinor. One thing at a time.

"We don't know how many of the traitor Crows fell in the battle in the Seeing Forest, but we can expect about a hundred to stand with Ephegos." I've done the calculations several times, and no matter how I twist and turn the numbers, they won't get any smaller.

Clio dips her chin. "Are they with the army in the plains?"

"That's something we couldn't verify without exposing ourselves." Clio is a smart fairy. She understands exactly how difficult it is to sneak up on an army in an open field, even in our bird form.

Tugging a buckle of her leathers in place, Clio glances west. "Now we need a map and some figurines, and then we'll wait for the rebels to send word."

Without another sound, she holds out her hands and spirits us away.

THIRTY-NINE

AYNA

The endless sparkling of the palace can get annoying when my vision is already exhausted from staring into the distance for hours with my Crow eyes. But when I close them to tune out the colorful blend, images of the undefined accumulation of darkness fills my head.

An army of over a thousand. Flames and Crows and humans. If they get the magic-sedating weapon, there is no telling how this will end.

The scent of white roses and sweet apples fills the dining room where Recienne is awaiting us with Tori and Kaira, poring over a sprawling map of Eherea, heads tucked together as if they are planning a conspiracy of their own.

"Where did you say the rebels are hiding?" Kaira prompts, drawing her finger along the trees illustrated in the northeast of Tavras.

"In a small village along the southern edge of the plains." Clio doesn't turn her attention away from where she's shifting figurines of fairies back and forth along the Askarean border.

Dead land burned by the Flames has been marked with an overlay of red color Tori magicked onto the map to highlight where we can fight without the risk of our surroundings going up in flames, but the goal is not to fight at all—for as long as we can avoid open battle, we'll do it. Lives lost on both sides is something to be prevented for as long as possible.

I lean back in my chair, pulling on the shirt Herinor provided and which I'm still wearing. I put on a pair of pants Clio offered when we arrived at the palace, but apart from that, I'm still the wind-torn creature who shifted in Myron's arms.

My mate sits next to me, his thigh close enough to brush mine if I move a few inches, but he doesn't push the contact. He's leaning back in his chair, observing Tori working on the map and how it changes with highlights and markers whenever someone throws in a new fact, an idea, or merely a concern. By the time this war is over, it will be a piece of art documenting the brutal efficiency of the fairy general's planning.

I gave my report on everything I spotted earlier, but I'm not leaving when the future of both realms hangs in the balance, no matter how exhausted I am.

Flying for two full days with no prior experience or practice was a bit optimistic. My body is a battlefield of sore muscles and aching bones, too limp to sit up straight in my chair, so I mimic Myron's posture, my eyes the only part of me moving. When all this is over, I'll take a long, hot bath.

"Any news from their side?" Royad prompts. After hours of sitting patiently, he's gotten to his feet, pacing the side of the room facing the gardens and glancing out into the darkness. "Can they tell which route the weapons will take?"

"If they aren't already on their way," Herinor throws in, face hard as stone. He hasn't smiled once since we spotted the army. A part of me wonders if he wishes he was there with the rest of the traitor Crows rather than waiting to face them on a battlefield.

"No news from Andraya and Pouly," Tori confirms. "I site-hopped into the village yesterday, and they didn't have an update."

"Meer is a good distance from the Plithian Plains. If they want to be inconspicuous, it might take them longer than usual to find out anything," I put into consideration. "Perhaps as long as it will take for Erina's army to gather."

"Which would decide the outcome of this war before we've even lifted a blade, no thanks." Silas leans his hips against the table, studying the array of streets and terrains on the map. "The rebels are a spy network passing on information through the realm for decades. They have established channels and trusted men on the inside. They'll be quick."

Royad stops his pacing, brow lifted so high the scar on his cheek is tugging the end of it down. "When did you turn into an optimist?"

Herinor clears his throat, pointing at the broadest road running north from Meer. "If I were Erina, I'd avoid the main roads. Even if it took me a few days longer, I'd sneak my ammunition through the backlands where no one bothers with what's on the wagon and where I could quickly hide it in the wilderness."

He's right. And he probably knows more about Erina's and Ephegos's strategies than any other person in this room.

"There are a thousand little paths leading through the plains," Clio complains. "Even if we know which one, they might just go cross country the moment they realize someone is tailing them."

Recienne nods, sitting down at the head of the table. He picks up an apple from the bowl holding down the corner of the map and bites into it with sharp, white teeth.

The room is silent except for his chewing while I count my own heartbeats. Royad continues to stare out the window, no longer pacing, back turned toward us. Kaira studies the map, and Herinor studies Kaira. Silas silently taps his finger against the edge of the table, stopping when Clio cuts him a glance, and Myron is the calm before the storm, sitting so quietly only the rising and falling of his chest informs me he's still breathing. It seems to have become his new go-to strategy for dealing with uncertain situations.

Recienne swallows, makes the apple core vanish with a flick of his fingers, and laces his fingers together at the edge of the table. "It seems there is nothing we can do for now but wait."

Why his words make me want to dive out of my skin is beyond me. Perhaps because I've never been a patient creature, but with the premise of Erina coming for us, I'm near ready to pick up the next best blade and hack my way across the lands to make him meet his end.

"What about Ephegos?" Myron's voice rumbles through the room, stopping everyone where they are.

Recienne cocks his head at him.

"We haven't seen or heard from him since Ayna fled the palace. He's practically disappeared from the map. What we know of is Erina. The Flames seem to be working with the Tavrasian king directly. Even the Crows, if their presence at the Flame estate is anything to go by."

Icy cold slides down my back. I hadn't thought of that. In all these weeks, I've been so focused on the immediate dangers that I'd not once questioned Ephegos's involvement in this war.

"Erina projected to the Flame estate, not Ephegos," Herinor points out as if that was evidence. "Projecting is not a skill known to be achieved by Crows."

"Or by Flames," Kaira throws in when all eyes turn to her.

"Fairies don't do it either. We site-hop if we have the ability. But Projection?" Clio muses, earning a long look from her brother.

Herinor clears his throat. "Erina has been experimenting with magical blood so much; I wouldn't be surprised if he has more tricks up his sleeves than we can imagine. However he did it, Erina was there as projection, not Ephegos. If Ephegos could do it, he wouldn't have let anyone take away the opportunity for causing you and Myron pain."

Stomach sinking, I try to remember the last time I saw the Crow traitor at Erina's palace. That was a few days before my escape, when he stopped injecting me with the drug himself, handing off the task to his guards.

I can't even tell when was the last time I saw him at court.

"He's planning something bigger."

All eyes land on me, so I force my sore body into submission and sit up, bracing my forearms on the table. The twinge of pain in my shoulders should be enough to bring human Ayna to her knees, but I'm Crow Ayna, and fae strength flares as I summon it, propping myself up against my own power.

"*He* wants to be King of Crows. He wants to establish a new Crow Kingdom. He said so himself. And he also believes he has a claim to the Flame throne. He doesn't care much for Erina's place in this war. The King of Tavras is a means to an end."

"End of what?" Kaira blinks at me, brown eyes big and round.

"The end of everything that is good in this realm."

"That fucker really *is* the worst of them all." I'm not surprised Silas agrees. He's the first to go for a good conspiracy theory, but Herinor's nod of approval is a bit disconcerting. We've been rolling this over in words and thoughts, looking at it from every angle, but the only way to stop him is to stop Erina, so it doesn't change anything.

We still need to destroy the magic-nullifying weapon. If it were that easy, we could have worked on an antidote, but Erina has a head start, and the cargo is on its way. We still need an army big enough to meet Erina's forces, magical or no. And we still need the rebels' help, or we'll never know where to strike to take Erina's most valuable asset.

Outside, dawn has broken, stealing the shadows of the night, and my exhaustion has turned into a numbness spreading from the muscles lining my spine all the way to the tips of my fingers.

I'm ready to collapse into bed, but the staircase is in my way when we slowly make our way out the door toward our rooms.

Clio, Tori, and Recienne site-hopped probably straight to their beds, and Kaira, Herinor, and Silas are leading our remaining group at a faster pace than I have in me.

"Do you need help?" Royad walks beside me as I approach the monster of wide steps leading to the residential levels of the palace.

I shake my head at him. "No help, just time."

He nods, a sympathetic smile on his lips, and shifts into his bird form, fluttering ahead as Myron's shadow falls over me from behind.

"I can offer both."

When I give him a confused glance, he gestures at the stairs. "Help or time." His eyes are darker than I'm used to, deep shadows circling beneath them. It's been a long day and night for all of us.

"You don't need to—"

"I never said I needed to. Just that I can offer both."

363

We're now standing at the foot of the stairs, facing the obstacle in my path.

"It can be a lot for a new Crow to fly for the first time, and you did so for two full days with only a few hours of rest in between."

I try not to remember the sensation of falling when I landed on his hand after we found the army. If he knew how close to plunging from the skies I'd been, he'd never take me on another mission again. My muscles cramp in response to the thought of flying, and I twitch to work against the sensation of someone twisting my limbs.

"I'll manage." Because I need to know I can handle this. Being a Crow, shifting, flying, the power, the strength. I need to know I can stand on my own even with the most powerful Crow alive next to me.

Myron doesn't offer me his hand. He doesn't walk away either. "Time it is, then." He simply waits, looking at the lowest stair with me as I gather my will and shape it into a rope to pull my legs forward.

One step. Just one step and my muscles are on fire.

I can do this. I'll fight in a war soon. I'll throw all I have at the enemy, and I can't let my legs be what fails me when the time comes.

Another step.

I groan as the back of my thighs take my weight, pushing myself forward.

Myron takes both stairs in one stride, but he remains at my side, patient, silent, no judgement in his eyes as they follow my every move.

By the time I make it up half the stairs, my calves are burning like fire, my left hand is shaking, and my neck is ready to snap.

"Just a few more," I tell myself.

Myron follows, still by my side but a step below the one I'm tackling now. "You know you did amazing today," he murmurs, breath at my ear, and I stumble forward, taking another step in the process. My hand finds the handrail, clutching it so hard my knuckles turn white.

"I'm proud of you, little Crow."

I take another step.

"You're the first female Crow in millennia, and you're fast like the wind."

Another step.

"Your wings shimmer like silver when we fly beneath the clouds."

My hand slides up the rail, pulling me another step higher.

"Two days of flying and you haven't complained about the aches and pains of unturned muscles."

I want to tell him that I have plenty to complain about, but I need my strength to make it up the stairs.

"I would sweep you into my arms and carry you straight to your bed, but you set your mind on doing this on your own, and what mate would I be if I didn't support you with all I have."

A heavy leg refuses to make it up the next step, but I will it into submission.

"I'll always do that." He waits as if for me to ask what he means, but I bite my lip, pushing myself higher. "I'll always cheer for your achievements, no matter how big or how small. I'll be there to watch you shine and grow."

My toes slide over the edge of the next step—only, there is no next step. I've made it to the top of the stairs, legs shaking and arms quivering. I can't let go of the handrail, so I lean against it, heaving a breath to loosen my tight chest.

The room is still a good fifty feet down the hallway, and my legs are killing me.

Myron steps up in front of me, smiling down at me like a blessing of the Guardians, but his eyes give away how much it costs him not to scrape me off the railing and throw me over his shoulder. "May I please carry you to your room, Ayna?"

No. I want to say *no*, but my knees buckle, and my hands slip from the carved wood I'm leaning against as I slide to my ass.

Myron is still waiting. "My arms can do wonders, transporting you from one place to another, Ayna. I assure you it's a luxury service you won't regret using." Humor dances in his eyes, a sight so exhilarating I can't help but sigh and nod my approval. "Don't tell the others."

"Of course not." So gently I barely notice he's touching me at all, Myron sweeps me up from the glimmering tiles, wrapping me in his arms, head resting against his shoulder, and marches down the hall.

FORTY

AYNA

The arena is slick with rain, rocks dripping and dust swirling in little puddles where the water collects on the uneven ground. I'm drenched to the bones, leathers sticking to my body like a very tight, very uncomfortable skin, but at least I'm still wearing them. A week of practicing shifting has worked wonders for Clio's mood with not having to replace my wardrobe every time I manage to return from my bird form to my human form. I've tried to get my water magic to return at full force yet haven't been able to summon anything remotely as spectacular as the armor the water from the lake at Myron's palace formed around my body.

The Crows have been taking turns working with me on my Crow powers. All but Herinor. It wasn't him refusing to help me, though; I decided to not put him through any more risk after seeing him bleed the day he hinted that Silas knows something about the un-mating situation. I absently rub my hand along the edge of my bicep where the burn wound is almost gone.

Today is Royad's turn. He's sitting on the highest wall encircling the arena, legs dangling and chest bare.

"Why is it that Crow males never wear proper shirts?" I shout up at him instead of attempting another shift. I've done three without losing a buckle on my jacket, and I don't want to push my luck. Clio is scary enough as it is; I don't need her to take my head for another set of leathers I make disappear. I don't even want to know if there's a secret stash of clothing tucked away in the in-between that will one day drop onto my head when I least expect it, or if they dissolved into dust and wind during shifts.

Royad holds out both hands to the side in a shrug. "Habit." Within a few heartbeats, he shrinks into a feathered bird and flutters to the lower levels of the arena where he shifts back. "I grew up without a shirt. I believe I only wore one at your wedding because Myron forced me to."

"You wore a shirt at my wedding?" I clearly have no recollection of that day or the horrors I endured when I believed Myron was going to eat me alive on our wedding night.

Royad shrugs again. "Does it matter? When given the choice, I'll always choose shirtless." He circles me, scrutinizing me from head to toe. "You know your stance is shit, right? You won't last a minute in hand to hand combat."

368

We're not here to train that, but I know enough about hand-to-hand from my time on the Wild Ray, have fought my fair share with fists when capturing and looting ships. So, I adjust my feet anyway, bracing for the impact a moment before it comes.

Royad's hand is at my shoulder so fast I lose balance before I can even hope to fortify my standing—good for a human opponent, but for a fae?

I land on my ass the way I seem to be doing every other day now, be it from exhaustion when climbing stairs or from harsh training in the arena with any of the Crows or fairies.

Royad chuckles, offering a hand to help me up at the same time.

I hop back to my feet without his help.

Again, his hand lands on my shoulder, same spot. And I land in the mud.

"What, by Eroth, was that for?" I spit out the rain and wipe a splatter of dirt off my cheek.

Royad grabs my hand and pulls me up without warning, setting me to my feet and kicking them slightly apart so I end up in a proper fighting stance. "You keep forgetting that your magic will not be worth a thing if you end up on the ground and can't find your footing. The Flames will burn you. The Crows will rip you apart with their claws. And the humans will inject you with their drug and drag you right back to Erina's chambers."

There's wisdom in his eyes, despite the mocking of his tone.

Turning on the spot, he puts three long strides between us. When he faces me again, his features are grim.

"I thought I was here to improve my shifting." That's what he said when he picked me up for training a long, wet hour ago.

Royad nods, water dripping over his ears from the bun tied at the back of his head. "That's where this training started, but we're far from done. Myron has been cautious with you because he doesn't want to break that fragile thing you're regrowing between the two of you. His main priority is to give you time to heal from what Erina did to you. He's so focused on not pushing you that he keeps forgetting it won't matter if the bond still exists when Erina gets his hands on you. He'll do it all over again just to spite you. To *break* you, Ayna." His brows knit together, his tan skin pale in the morning light. The ocean blue of his eyes is an exact copy of Myron's, but where Myron has been careful and deliberate with me, Royad is losing patience. Not with me but with his cousin. "He's destroying himself over you, Ayna. Day and night, he's waiting, listening, searching for a sign that you're ready. That he can shove you into the next stage of training, tell you the truths of what life will be like if we lose this war." He swallows, hands balling into fists as he approaches— one step, then another, exasperation and determination warring on his features. "I can't watch him break. I've seen it happen in the Seeing Forest. I've seen him give up hope. I'm not ready to see him break for good this time, so you better learn to defend yourself on every level that counts, or I'll hold you personally accountable for it when he shatters over the loss of you."

My body turns cold, center of gravity lowering as I bend my knees. Royad has been quiet the past weeks, a shadow aiding Myron, consulting Tori and Recienne, cheering up Kaira and helping me improve my already mastered skills. I've never seen him like this, but he's right.

I've been wasting so much time hesitating that I can't tell anymore how strong the bond between Myron and me has regrown. I haven't dared tug on it to see if he'll feel it—for fear he would and fear he wouldn't.

Royad pins me with a stare as if to drive home his point—or biding his time before his next attack. Instead of waiting for him to throw a punch, I launch into action, landing a blow on his shoulder that makes him do a double take.

"Your king's heart is as precious to me as it is to you, Royad. I love him. I want to protect him. I'm ready. To. Die. For him."

He stares at me, rubbing his shoulder, breath coming hard and fast, and I stare right back, rain mingling with tears as such violent anger grabs me that it's hard to keep a straight thought.

Erina took my mate mark. He hurt me, but even worse than that, he hurt Myron. He tortured my mate, locked him up in a cage and let him bleed. He took his powers, took his strength, his senses. He took everything from him. And at our last encounter, he tried to take me as well.

"Try me, Roy," I dare him. "I might be a queen, but I was an outlaw first. I learned to fight on the railing of a ship, held my own against pirates and soldiers alike. I'm not the fragile little bird you think I am."

"I never said you were fragile." The grin he gives me is wicked and victorious, and I know he rallied me on purpose to test my limits.

The next punch I throw is straight to his jaw. Royad ducks, blocking me and delivering a blow to my side that takes my breath. I don't pause to catch it, though. Already coming up, I spin and kick out with my leg. My heel connects with Royad's sternum, putting him on his back.

Mud splatters in a circle, and we both gasp for air as I hold out my hand, helping him back to his feet, studying his movements. He's tall and broad. Not as tall as Myron but equally fast, I'm sure. My Crow senses help me analyze every tell of his muscles, the way he slightly sways to his left leg before attacking.

With a hook of my knee, I catch him in the stomach as I twist from under his punching fist. Royad grabs me by the leathers as he falls, pulling me down with him, and his knee lands on my back. How he got on top of me is beyond me, but I'm back in the clearing by the Flame estate, guards shoving me down, forcing me to lie still as their torch took Myron's mark away.

"No—" I pant, chest tight, air eluding me. "Please. Not the mark. Not the—" I'm thrashing. Kicking and screaming like a wild cat when the weight mercifully slides off my back, hands gently rolling me over so I face my attacker.

"It's just me." Royad's blue eyes stare down at me, full of terror as he realizes it takes me a few moments to recognize him. "It's all right, Ayna. You're safe."

Royad doesn't attack again that morning.

CLAWS OF DEATH

We return to the palace, dripping wet and ready for the fried bacon and fresh toast the scent drafting from the kitchens is promising, but when we enter the dining room, the table has already been cleared, and the others are standing around a map rolled out instead of our breakfast, various expressions of worry marring their features.

"What happened?" Royad is by Myron's side first, bending over the spot his cousin is fixating with a troubled gaze, and I notice the crimson-topped pins sticking out of the paper in inch-wide intervals.

"The rebels sent word," Recienne responds. "We know what path the weapon will travel. We only need to get there in time to stop the delivery."

FORTY-ONE

AYNA

Using my water magic to draw the worst of the wetness from my leathers and Royad's and dumping it in an empty vase on the carved mahogany sideboard by the back wall, I join the others, eyeing the distance from the Askarean border to the final pin marking the most recent location and ready to leave at a moment's notice. I'm already in my armor; all I need is a weapon, and I'm ready to enter a battlefield.

"They've been following reports of the caravan passing through for a while, but it's only today that they were certain they know which direction they will travel." Tori catches us up. "They would have tried to stop it on their own, but there is a small army travelling with the delivery, and not all of them seem to be human. It would be too great a risk. They'd lose and expose themselves at the same time. We need their network to build an army from the inside of Tavras."

However Tori comes up with those strategies, I fully agree. We can't lose the rebels. They got me out of Erina's palace, and I will not send them to their certain death because of a delivery we can destroy on our own. "When do we leave?"

At my request, Royad throws me a concerned glance that is echoed by his cousin whose eyes wander back and forth between us, reading the silent communication.

"Pouly said it will take about two more days before the caravan is out of the settled regions. We don't want to attack around people and risk the destruction of their livelihoods." No one is more surprised than I am when Herinor states he wants to make sure to keep civilians safe.

Interestingly, Kaira doesn't bat an eyelid at his comment. "*Is he secretly a teddy bear? Because if he is and you're not telling me, I swear to the gods of his sacred Neredyn I'll rip his head off and dig out the stuffing.*"

Kaira gives a startled laugh, but in her mind, she shoots me a sharp warning. "*He's exactly the bloodthirsty grump you know him to be. Only his priorities of bloodshed have shifted.*"

There is so much to unpack in that statement I don't even want to begin.

"No civilians." Silas nods his agreement. "That will shorten our window of opportunity for the attack, though." He leans over the map, drawing a line with the tip of his knife, the film of color peeling away and rolling to the side as if to form a corridor for the steel. "If we attack here"—he pins his blade into the paper right above the symbols of a small farm village by the edge of a forest—"we might need to accept some collateral, but we'll have enough time to get it done, and we'll easily hide all traces of our carnage."

Myron puts down his hand on the table with a slap. "No. Carnage. No. Civilians." His growl is death and night, and Silas sinks back into his seat.

I'm hypnotized by the expression on Myron's beautiful face, the black veins creeping into the white of his eyes, but from the edge of my vision, I can make out a trickle of ink-black fog coiling around his fingers.

"No civilians." Silas lifts his hands in defense.

No one else dares to look at Myron, except for the King of Askarea, who nods his approval. "You make for a formidable ally," he says, brushing his hand over the map and eradicating all traces of Silas's suggestion. The knife slips from the sealing paper, color bleeding over the scar like it's never been gone in the first place.

"We'll wait the full two days and attack during the darkest hour of the night after the second day," Recienne decides, pointing at the spot where the Plithian Plains open and the number of settlements slows. "Human soldiers will be at a disadvantage. We could be in and out without slitting throats. All we need is to spill the magical weapon so it can no longer be used. From all that we know, it should be as easy as that, and once it's destroyed, we won't need to fear the attack of a full army any time soon. It will give us time to plan ahead and figure out a smarter way to defeat Erina than by slaughtering his army. Without the magic-nullifying serum, they are no match for us."

Clio and Tori nod, but the wary glance of the general tells me he fears it won't be that easy. The Guardians shall turn his fears into past concerns which never came to pass.

"Let's hope we'll manage without bloodshed," Royad agrees.

Across the table, Kaira is chewing on her lip, fingers digging into the edge of the table. I haven't seen her nervous like this. Not even when we were escaping the palace in Meer.

"You all right?" I prompt her, not switching to our mental channel because, if she has concerns, we all should hear them.

Kaira's eyes meet mine. "I don't know. After what happened at the Flame estate, I wouldn't put it past Erina that this is another trap."

She has a point.

"Erina needs the weapon with his army, and his army is clearly gathering. Unless he has legions collecting elsewhere that we haven't found." Herinor's tone is not gentle but not harsh either as he speaks to the part-Flame.

"He might have already sent shipments to the army. This might not be the only delivery," Kaira objects. "It's possible he has everything he needs in place and is merely waiting for us to walk into an ambush."

My chest tightens at the mere thought of another situation like at the estate.

"Then we'll be prepared for it," Myron says, his tone that of the king who won't show mercy if anyone dares harm us the way Erina and the Flames did at the estate.

The black veins have retreated from his eyes, and his fingers are no longer wrapped in shadows, but the resolve in his face tells me he's ready to do whatever it takes.

"Tata will be joining us," Clio announces, earning a sideways look from Silas that could murder. "She shared the details of the shipment with my brother and Tori while you were scouting the plains. "We know it's supposedly still liquid, and it's too heavy for humans to carry. The caravan the rebels reported fits the description Tata provided. Three carriages with four horses each. Guards ride with them, and foot soldiers march along. From what we know, they don't stop for the nights but exchange their horses every other day."

Memories of riding north in a carriage with Andraya and Pouly float into my mind. We didn't stop for rest either. "Whatever Erina has in mind, delivery or trap, he is under time pressure if he doesn't dare to stop."

Tori nods at my assessment, folding his arms across his chest as he slides his gaze back to the map as if he can see everything Clio just mentioned, as if the whole terrain is coming to life in his mind. I wouldn't be surprised if it did; that male *can* melt stone after all.

"The rebels' hideout is closer to the point where we'll attack than the border. We'll site-hop there then rest for a few hours to restore our energy before we find our vantage points," he explains, all business, and I can see why Recienne relies on him for strategy—the way his mind flits from point to point, connecting them and creating a full picture out of the bits and pieces we have been providing. "Use the time we have left to train and rest. We'll set out tomorrow at sunset."

Wordless, Recienne, Clio, and Tori disappear from the head of the table, leaving us to ourselves. The map is gone, replaced by a basket of bread, a large pan of scrambled eggs, and a bowl of fried bacon sits between a platter with sliced vegetables and a glass jar filled with some thick, red paste I have never seen in my life. Small plates are laid out in our usual spots, alongside silver cutlery. A steaming pot of tea and a carafe of water share the space at the center of the table.

I'm no longer hungry, but I walk over to my usual chair and sit down, reaching for the pan and serving myself.

Kaira eyes me like she's ready to throw up.

"If I want to be prepared for anything, I'll need my strength." Without another explanation, I start shoveling the eggs into my mouth, barely tasting the aroma of the chopped chives that magically pop up on top of my serving.

Myron is the first to follow my lead. Whether it's because he's hungry or he wants to support my endeavor, I don't know, but I appreciate his presence as he sits himself in the chair next to me and summons a slice of bacon to his plate with his magic.

Herinor and Silas sit across from us, in Clio's and Tori's places, pulling over their plates and heaping them with food. Even Royad joins, picking up a slice of toast and smearing it with the red paste that smells surprisingly like spring and winter all at once. I don't ask what it is. I'll be able to figure it out when we return if we succeed. And it won't matter if we walk into a trap.

We finish our meal in silence, each of us lost in our own thoughts. Not even Kaira disturbs my mind with a comment as scenarios of doom play before my inner eye.

"What do we do now?" the part-Flame eventually asks when none of us lifts our forks anymore and the teapot is empty.

At first, I believe no one is going to answer, and I take a deep breath to inform her I have no idea, but Clio storms in, shortsword at her hips swaying with her purposeful gait as she waves her hand at my sister and me, a knowing expression on her face.

She walks up to the head of the table, bracing her hands on the high backrest of Recienne's empty chair, and pins Kaira and me with a look.

"Now, my friends, we get you ready for battle."

We follow Clio down the hallway in a single file. She's provided us all with leathers and weapons before, but this time, she seems to have something different in mind. A stairwell wide enough for two leads down to a windowless corridor with a single, wide steel door at the end.

"We don't know what we'll be facing out there, so everyone better pick their own weapons." Clio pushes the door open, sparks of magic running along the outline of the threshold, and the magic locking it dissolves at her command and exposes a room lined with racks and shelves full of armor and weapons.

Silver spears sit next to black steel; curved and saw-edged blades cross along the walls. Wooden stands hold up pieces of leather embossed with emblems and shield crests I have never seen before. There are even assortments of helmets with horns attached and helmets with holes on the sides that make me wonder if those are meant for creatures with horns growing out of their skulls.

"Welcome to the armory." Clio's voice trembles with excitement like a little girl's. "My dear brother approves for you to take whatever you want."

"Whatever I want?" The disbelief in Herinor's tone is almost comical. His gaze isn't on the weapons, though, and thank the Guardians, Kaira is standing in front of him where she can't spot the way his eyes have landed on the back of her head.

"Any piece of armor or weaponry in this room that fits you and that you can carry into battle, yes," Clio specifies, but there's humor in her voice.

A part of me wants to tell Kaira to put Herinor out of his misery already, but I'm not one to give relationship advice considering where I've ended up on my own. Right now, I can't even tell my own mate how badly I want him.

Silas is already wandering through the rows of swords and hatchets, picking up various items and weighing them in his hands. A shimmer of enthusiasm I rarely find on the sarcastic male's expression has settled on his features while he quietly evaluates their worth for his fighting style.

"That's very gracious of the Fairy King, and I appreciate the gesture." Myron inclines his head at the princess of Askarea. His gaze slides over the display of armor on the side of the room until it lands on a set of black leathers decorated with silver ornamentations. It's definitely too small for him, and the wide hips of the pants suggest it's made for a female form. "This one looks fit for a queen," he notes, stepping to my side and sliding his fingers along my arm in a silent question.

"It does." Clio flicks her fingers, summoning the set and holding it out for me. "It's Sanja's, but she's already agreed that you could wear anything of hers as long as you've made sure Erina and Ephegos never set foot into this palace."

My throat tightens at both the trust and the responsibility the Fairy Queen instills in me with such a simple statement. "I'll wear it with pride."

It takes three long minutes behind a changing screen at the side of the room to get my body stuffed into the sheath of black leather, but once I'm in, silver vines climb along my body, flexible despite the hard steel they are made from. They seem to shift with every movement, protectively wrapping around my side when I lift my arm, crawling over my knees to the outside of my thighs when I bend my legs. They even slither over my throat when I tilt my head backward, making panic rise in my gut.

"They are spelled to protect their bearer," Clio explains, gently stroking along the living metal, and it retreats to the collar of the leathers, allowing me a deep breath. "The vines are made from steel infused with magic by one of the ancient mages that once walked Eherea. It's the last one of this making."

Air floods my lungs in a deep inhale. "It's beautiful." Because it is.

From the side, Myron is eyeing me with awe so profound it takes my breath all over again.

"Let's see what the others are choosing, shall we?" Whether Clio is oblivious to our moment or is deliberately saving me is irrelevant. I'm grateful when the female twirls around, stalking between Myron and me toward Royad, who's set his sight on a carved bow made of black wood.

"This bow was a gift from my mother to my father." Her shoulders hunch ever so slightly as she runs her finger along the curve of the bow.

Royad is about to put it back on the rack, probably not wanting to offend Clio by taking something of meaning to her, but the female stops him. "Take it. It hasn't been used in centuries. She'd want it to belong to a decent male for once."

While I'm struggling to unpack the meaning of her words, Royad seems to understand. "I'll take good care of it and return it after our mission."

Clio shakes her head, closing Royad's fingers around the bow. "Keep it."

"This one looks wicked." Silas, oblivious to or purposefully ignoring Clio and Royad, swings a double-bit hatchet with swirling engravings so close to Herinor's ear he cuts a few hairs off.

The warrior doesn't flinch. "Stop playing and pick something already," he grumbles.

Next to him, Kaira is sorting through a row of slender swords without enthusiasm, avoiding Herinor's gaze.

"Aren't you going to choose anything?" I ask him.

Herinor shakes his head. "If we come across Ephegos, I'd rather have the worst blade in the world in my hands so I won't stand a chance against Myron or you when the traitor orders me to kill you."

I don't know whether to laugh or cry at that admission, so I look away, watching Myron pull a long, broad blade from the rack closest to him. He slides a fingertip along the engraving an inch from the edge, listening as if he could hear the sword sing, and nods to himself.

When we leave the armory half an hour later, we're all clad in black armor and carrying new weapons. All but Herinor, who sticks with his decision to keep his old things. Kaira abandoned the sword and opted for daggers like me, and from Silas's belt, the double-bit hatchet is dangling, happily ready to cut throats. It's the most prepared I've felt in years and the least prepared I actually am.

It won't matter. Trap or real, Erina's delivery needs to be intercepted. We can't take chances with our fate.

As I glance up at Myron, who's walking by my side, I know what I need to do.

FORTY-TWO

AYNA

A sizzle so hot it makes me want to scream runs through my palm. From my skin, steam rises like miniature clouds.

"Damn it, Kaira!" Hopping from the chair, I nearly fall over my own feet as I hold up my hand in Clio's direction.

The female flicks a finger, crossing her outstretched legs at the ankles where she's sprawling on the couch of our common room. Thank her ice magic for working fast, and thank my Crow powers for healing minor wounds in a flash. My palm is cool and skin no longer angry red within a heartbeat.

"I'm so sorry. I thought I had it right this time." Kaira is sitting on the windowsill with her hands in her pockets and guilt on her features.

"Oh, you definitely had it," I inform her. "Worse than the last three times."

That earns me a chuckle from Clio.

The three of us have been spending the past two days working on Kaira's *spark of fire*, as she once called it. After her stealing a Flame's fireball at the estate, Clio has been pushing her to test her powers.

She hasn't lit a single piece of straw, nor a candle or twig. What she *has* done, however, is burn my palm. Three fucking times.

It all started with Clio's suggestion to reheat her tea, which she was floating in front of her after it cooled down over a training session. When Kaira managed to bring it up a few degrees, I had the stupid idea to pull on the flicker of water magic still remaining within me from Vala's gift and have her heat a drop of it so I can make a boiling projectile out of it.

She managed. Gods, she managed so fast I can't catch up and get the water to rise from my skin before it scalds my palm.

"Next time, try water that I'm not controlling," I tell her with a grumble that sounds too much like a grudge I'm not actually holding. I'm happy she's making progress; I just don't appreciate the pain. With a smile, I add, "I can always pick it up later."

Clio has been watching the whole thing, offering her ice magic to stop the burn on my skin and observing with amusement and interest.

With a sigh, Kaira dips her finger into the water glass next to her and lets one drop settle on the wood of the windowsill. For long moments, she stares at it, but it doesn't turn into steam the way it does in my hand.

Clio sits up, copper braid sliding over her shoulder as she tilts her head. "Try again."

Small lines of concentration form on Kaira's forehead before she gives up.

"That's interesting." The female stands from the couch, circles the table, and joins Kaira by the windowsill. When she touches the water drop, nothing happens.

"It's not even lukewarm." I don't mean it as an insult, but Kaira's shoulders drop with disappointment anyway. "Try again when Ayna is controlling the water."

With a grimace, I summon another drop, this time letting it hover in the air to escape another scalding.

Within a breath, steam replaces the drop.

"How is that possible?" Both Kaira and I ask at the same time.

Clio shakes her head. "I have no idea. I've never seen an ability like this." She studies Kaira for a long time then turns to me. "Every fairy is different and has unique talents. Tori can read minds and melt stone; I wield ice. Recienne has the strongest affinity for name control I've ever seen and then some." She notices us both looking at her with distress. "Oh, don't worry. Even if he likes to use the threat of name control against people he wants to intimidate, name control doesn't work on Crows or Flames. It's the creatures with little to no magic that need to be afraid of it, and you both have plenty of power." I remember the first day at the Fairy Palace, how Recienne had pointed out he knew all of our names like that was a threat, and I shudder. "Besides, in case you haven't realized, my brother wouldn't harm a fly if he didn't need to." She rolls on, dismissing objections lingering on our tongues. "It could be something about your blood connection that allows Kaira to siphon your power."

Siphon.

It hits me like a rock in the head. "Make an ice crystal, Clio."

Clio snaps her fingers, conjuring a snowflake out of thin air, and lets it hover above her palm. "Sure. Why?"

"Now melt it, Kaira." I nod my encouragement at my sister, and she hesitantly reaches out her palm the way she always does when attempting to use her power.

The snowflake implodes into a wisp of steam.

"Siphon." I beam at her. "You can use your fire, but not to create flames. Your power siphons magic that is already in use and transforms it into heat. It has nothing to do with us being siblings."

Kaira's jaw drops. Before Clio can start asking questions, I summon my Crow magic and let a thin ray of silver rise from my palm. "Siphon it," I order.

Kaira's mouth presses into a thin line the way it always does when she is holding back words, but she raises her hand, and the silver light dances above my fingers, fluttering and swirling with heat like an illusion in the desert.

"Fucking brilliant," is all Clio has to say.

The door to Herinor's bedroom creaks open, and the male stands on the threshold, studying the spectacle above my palm with surprise and pride. "Couldn't agree more."

The news of Kaira's secret power makes the rounds in our group faster than the feared wildfire the Flames are able to spread. For the first time since I met Kaira, she practically glows with confidence, even when she hasn't explored her skills enough to understand the boundaries or limits. We'd be helping her with it, each and every last one of the Crows, and even Tori or Recienne, but the time to leave for the rebels' hideout has come, and Clio, Tori, and Recienne are awaiting us in the throne room.

When we leave our chambers, dressed for battle and armed to the teeth, Myron walks close by my side, his hand brushing against mine every other step and his gaze focused on what lies ahead.

Buttery afternoon light filters in through the open balcony doors, the scent of fall in the air despite the green treetops in the gardens. The floor of black and white marble contrasts the glimmering pillars and the plain, carved stone throne stands out like a sore thumb in this space of pomp and glory.

Recienne is waiting with his sister and his general, dressed in armor for once like the rest of us. Next to them, Tata stands at attention, hand on her sword. Recienne inclines his head at us, taking a step forward.

"You're coming with us?" I ask by way of greeting, half impressed, half worried.

"Only to the rebels so we can transport all of you faster. I'll return to the palace right away." He glances back over his shoulder to the shadows where I spot a rounded female form. "I won't leave Sanja alone longer than necessary. You have my general and the female who successfully defied the late Crow King at your side. You don't need me."

But his pregnant mate needs him. Warmth spreads through my chest at the level of adoration in his tone when he speaks of her, the shimmer in his eyes when he looks at her. And the fact that he shares this secret with all of us—

It's hard to breathe.

"Take good care of yourself, Ayna," Sanja says from the shadows. "And make sure that, if you return with blood on my armor, it's that of our enemies."

I can see it then, a different version of this queen. One with a blade in her hands and the wrath of the Guardians in her eyes. She's as fierce as her mate, as protective and true.

"It will be my honor." I bow my head, not in deference but a sign of respect.

No one comments. Not on our dialogue or on Recienne's revelation—a secret we've been keeping as he requested and which he now chose to share with all of us.

Clio and Tori step up to us, offering their hands to Kaira, Herinor, Royad, and Silas. "Tata can site-hop on her own," Clio informs me when she notices my gaze drift to the female. "I've taken her before, so she knows the path."

Just as they all disappear, Recienne walks over to his mate, taking her face between his palms and kissing her fiercely before planting a kiss on her stomach. "I'll be back before you can miss me," he whispers, but Myron and I share a look that makes me wish I could speak all things that have been accumulating in my heart. I will before it is too late. It's a promise to myself.

Recienne lets go of Sanja with as much reluctance as I feel when turning my gaze away from Myron, and starts back to us, offering a hand to each of us. "Time to steal a magical weapon." A dark wind rushes through the room, winding around my wrist and dragging my palm into his. His fingers snap around mine, and he grins down at me as the world falls away.

The room is stuffy and dusty and entirely too small for the number of people squeezing into the tight space—clay walls lined with bookshelves to one side, three doors to the other, the front and back of the cabin features a row of three bunk beds each. The windows are small and high up, the roof high enough so not even the tall Crow males need to stoop. That's an advantage, even when it feels like we were shoved into a broom closet. A leather jacket pushes into my shoulder, and someone is standing on my foot.

So much for us all site-hopping together.

"Ayna!" Andraya's voice flies to my ears like a breath of fresh air. "Guardians above. I didn't believe them when they said you were coming."

I shove Tori off my boot and stumble out of the ball of people gathered at the center of the room to find Andraya standing in the door to the far left, a big smile on her brown face. She's wearing leather pants and a plain blue cotton blouse that reaches high up to her neck. Her grizzled braid is pinned to the top of her head leaving free the view of her human ears and the slender, golden earrings dangling there.

"Come here." She steps over the threshold, meeting me halfway in a tight embrace while the rest of the Crows and fairies untangle and form an awkward crooked circle around the room. "It's so good to see you alive and well."

"And you." I squeeze the lady back, satisfied when she doesn't show any signs of harm or pain. "Where is Pouly?"

Andraya pulls back, waving us along with her into the next room. We file into a kitchen roughly the same size as the bedroom with a long table at the center. "Sit down. Pouly will be here shortly. He's just making sure everything is prepared. We've been spending most of the past weeks here, manning this hideout while other rebels ran errands to gather information on the state of Erina's warfare and Tavras's armies." She walks to the basin in the corner, picking up the bucket before it on the floor with a groan. "That thing is heavy. I miss the running water from the palace. You wouldn't believe how fiercely Erina has been combing this realm for missing palace guards. Pouly couldn't leave the house for weeks. It's all dying down, though, now the king is shifting his troops."

Either she is oblivious to the eight Crows and fairies with pointed ears now sitting at her table, or she's ignoring them. It's only when Myron gets up to help her with the bucket that she acknowledges him. "Thank you, dear. It's always good to have young men around who don't shy away from hard work."

Royad snickers, and I can't help but stare at the boyish gesture. "He's about a millennium older than you, Lady Andraya," he informs the woman, who raises a brow at Myron, unimpressed. "Well, I'm glad you don't look the part."

She gestures for him to put the bucket down on the table before fetching glasses from a cupboard and placing them next to it and, with the ladle attached to the handle by a string, starts filling them up.

When I realize she's getting us something to drink, I snatch the ladle from her hand with an apologetic smile and set it back into the bucket, already drawing on my water magic to help her.

Andraya's eyes are as wide as saucers. "When did you learn how to do that?"

It's not exactly a secret I have magic, but we're no longer in the fairylands where magic is as common as the pointed ears my travel companions feature; plus, she's never seen me wield that sort of magic before. Only the silver explosion when we were fleeing with the carriage and Myron found us in the middle of the night.

"It's a useful little power," Kaira says with a smile, reminding Andraya she's still there. I'm pretty sure they already exchanged greetings before Recienne site-hopped Myron and me in and disappeared into a puff of dark wind again. "If you need anything frozen, Clio can help as well."

The Fairy Princess shoots her a warning look, but Kaira brushes it off. "If you need someone to annoy the crap out of your enemies, I can offer Herinor and Silas. They are a Guardians-given nightmare." She laughs at her own joke, earning an *are-you-serious* expression from Herinor and one of slight amusement from Silas, who sits across from Tata, forearms braced on the edge of the worn table, looking, like the rest of the Crows and Tori, too big for the furniture.

The warrior female, however, seems at ease in the human home. Who knows what conversations they already led the last time Clio sent her here?

Andraya glances between the two warriors Kaira gestured at, mild discomfort showing on her features even when Herinor is giving her a relatively harmless glance for his standards. "Is that so? I might borrow you to shut Pouly up every now and then."

She ushers Myron and me over, waiting for us to sit before she sits down at the edge of one of the long benches, right next to Kaira. "It's an honor to have all of you here." She means it, even when she isn't curtseying or bowing to the accumulation of royalty and high-ranking courtiers in this room, and no one calls her out for it. "When Clio visited last, she told me there would be a bigger delegation coming soon, but to see all of you again is just a delight."

Andraya was more cautious when she travelled with us in the fairylands, but this is her new home, and I can see how she doesn't fear any of us in here. We are allies in the truest of senses.

"We would have visited sooner, but there's been quite some drama going on in Askarea," Tori says with an unreadable expression on his face.

"So I've heard." Andraya's eyes catch on the scar on Tata's neck before meeting the general's. "The Fire Fairies seem to have fully aligned with Erina's plans."

"With those of the traitor Crow is more like it," Silas corrects, earning a nod from Royad and Clio. "Have you heard anything about Ephegos's whereabouts?"

Andraya considers the warrior for a long moment, wringing her hands in front of her as if his dark, piercing gaze makes her uncomfortable. "According to our spies, he hasn't left the palace in Meer where he keeps assisting Erina as his new general with his war strategies."

I can't suppress a shudder. It's better knowing where he is than wondering, but a part of me had hoped he'd disappeared for good. "And Erina? Is he in Meer?"

"Supposedly." Andraya faces me, but her eyes keep darting back to Silas as if he's the danger. He *can* be a disquieting presence, I admit, but he's been so much more digestible lately. "We withdrew the last of our spies from the palace a week ago. It's become too dangerous to keep a foothold there with everything going on. With Pouly's disappearance from Meer around the same time the rightful Queen of Tavras fled, people have started asking questions. Exposure would be the end of our movement, and we've worked so hard to get where we are today."

"Where is that?" Myron's tone is dry, not unfriendly, but not welcoming either as he seems to draw the answer from Andraya's mind by sheer will.

The lady holds her own, setting down both hands on the rough wood of the table. "We are a rogue army in a kingdom of tyrants. We have a queen we want to see on our throne and a cause to live for. We won't risk Queen Wolayna's rule, so we do what we must to be her eyes and ears in this kingdom. And when the time comes, we'll pick up our weapons and fight to save her kingdom."

Every last one of her words reverberates with conviction. Even Myron must feel it because he inclines his head at the woman, asking no further questions, but deep down in my soul, I wonder if I might disappoint them one day if I can't become the queen they are hoping for.

No one speaks until the door flies open, and in strides Pouly, dressed in leathers and a rabbit dangling from each of his hands. "I brought dinner." One look and he finds me at the overfull table. "Queen Ayna." He dips his chin before breaking into a broad smile that makes his mildly lined face look younger. He opens his arms wide, and I hop up to step into his embrace.

"Good to see you, Pouly."

He picks me up and spins me around, rabbits still dangling from his hands. "Good to see you, Queen Ayna."

From the corner of my eye, I notice Myron shift in his seat and Clio reach for her weapon. I roll my eyes at them and step out of the embrace the moment Pouly sets me down.

"You didn't believe I wouldn't come to pay my respects to our queen." He directs his words at Myron, the friendliness still fiercely in place. "We haven't been working to find her for generations only to fail her the first time she needs our help."

"And we appreciate your help," Kaira says before I can respond with the same words.

Beside her, Myron relaxes a bit, and Clio lifts her hand from her sword.

FORTY-THREE

AYNA

We sit around the dinner table an hour later. Silas offered to help skin and prepare the rabbits. Kaira, with my help, boiled the water for the stew, and Clio and Tori headed out to the back garden to grab the herbs Andraya promised they'd find behind the adjacent stables. The scent of rosemary and sage fills the air, reminding me of simpler times.

It's oddly comforting, how we have all settled into this human home so easily. Erina can't reach us here. Neither can Ephegos. The Flames are the last ones to suspect a thing about a secret organization supporting my claim to the throne of Tavras, so we could perhaps stay here and forget the world—were it not for the mission we are on.

I stir my second helping of stew, searching for carrots and potatoes in the mix, savoring the spot where my thigh touches Myron's, and my mind wanders to the oceans in the east beyond which his home lies.

"As requested, we've been tracking the caravan for the past few days. Our spies have been following it through the villages. So far, there haven't been any interruptions. No un-expected detours or long pauses," Pouly reports. "The cara-van passed this village a few hours ago and will be entering the plains soon."

"How many men are traveling with it?" Myron requests. He has been quiet, listening and observing, his presence steady by my side as we eat.

"About ten foot soldiers per wagon and four guards on horse when we last had eyes on them, but another rebel re-ported that he spotted more soldiers arriving from the west. It's possible they are bolstering their guards as they leave the settled area." Pouly takes a spoonful of stew, consider-ing. "That's at least forty-five foot soldiers and twelve cavalry. That isn't a problem for you, is it?"

The look of outrage Tori gives him is almost comical.

"Not if they're human soldiers," Myron responds before someone can say something that will ignite a discussion no-body needs right now. "Let's hope Erina didn't send along the traitor Crows or the Flames."

"I guess you'll need to wait until the attack to find out," Pouly says, chewing, and my stomach tightens squeamishly at the thought of going in so unprepared. "No one has reported on the shape of their ears. Apparently, they are wearing armor on their heads that hides that feature."

"Smart move." Should it be concerning that Tori sounds impressed?

Tata reaches for the wooden board with sliced bread, offering a piece to Myron and me before picking up one of her own. "Whatever we find, we'll handle it when we get there."

"If they have magic, the handling will take a little longer," Silas adds, but he doesn't disagree.

Tata rewards him with a clipped smile. "Your unholy Crow magic will certainly make sure it's not that much longer after all."

From the open window, humid evening air drafts inside, playing with loose strands of my hair and carrying the scent of hay and grains. The stables are visible across the yard of grass where two horses graze despite the late hour.

We sit and talk until the moon comes up and Andraya ushers us into the bedroom where the big males cram their bodies into too-short beds on the bottom of each bunk, and the females climb to the top beds. Andraya and Pouly shuffle off to take care of the dishes, but I'm not tired. A million thoughts run through my mind and a million emotions through my chest.

"How about a brief flight?" Myron whispers into my ear when he's done watching me fidget on the spot before the bed. Herinor is already snoring, and Tori and Clio are whispering something, the female's head dangling over the side of the bed as she watches him roll around without finding a comfortable position.

I nod at Myron, focusing on the feeling of wind carrying my wings, of freedom and wide waters.

My body shrinks, and my feathers slide out of my skin, replacing the leathers that belong to the Queen of Ask-area. I can't lose them when shifting back, but I don't think about that now. With a few hops on my bird feet, I'm back at the kitchen door, fluttering toward the window and out into the night.

Myron is right behind me, his powerful wings bringing him level with me fast, but he doesn't stay by my side, leading the way to the steep roof of the stables. There, he hops to the edge, already shifting back, and sits down on the old gray tiles. I land next to him, remaining in my bird form but close enough for him to touch. His warmth seeps into my feathers, making my little bird heart flutter. I want to shift back, but I'm worried what I'll say.

We haven't been alone much, and the few moments we have were loaded with the unspoken words and the ache for closeness I haven't been able to give in to.

"Look at that moon." Myron tips back his head, hair shifting to reveal his ears as he observes the almost perfect yellow circle above. "Isn't it beautiful?"

He doesn't wait for me to answer, not that I could give him more than a caw and a nudge with my beak.

"When I was a youngling, I'd sometimes sit on the top of the tower with Royad. We'd dream of a world where my father didn't think pain was the only way to learn how to be a leader. We'd dream of flying east, back to Neredyn. Sometimes we'd talk about the places we'd visit, the wild forests along the western coasts, the islands scattered along the coast before it which my people once called their home."

I stay still, afraid he'll stop talking, but he sighs, brushing back his hair and rubbing his hands up and down his face a few times like he can chase the memories away.

"I've been waking up every night since the Flame estate, wondering if I should knock on your door. Just to talk," he adds before I can wonder what he hoped to get out of a visit. "I've been meaning to talk to you about so many things." He pauses, lacing his fingers together and resting his hands in his lap. "But it all seems irrelevant in the face of a war we don't know we'll survive."

I don't know where he's headed with this, but I can't ask him either, so I nudge his elbow with my beak, hoping he'll get that I want him to tell me more.

"I've been thinking about my promise to Tori, that I'd take my people and leave when all this is over." Again, he pauses, and I can sense a question in the air. And again, I nudge him. "You're a Crow now, Ayna." He clears his throat, eyes lingering on the moon as if it holds all the answers in its swollen belly. "I don't know where we'll go or what we'll find there, but it's possible my promise to Tori won't be fulfilled unless you come with me."

Heat and cold rushes through my bird body, shaking it so violently I lose control and slip out of it, shifting into my human form. Thank the Guardians, my leathers are there, but I'm half sitting in Myron's lap. On instinct, his arms close around my waist, preventing me from slipping off the roof. His mouth is by my ear, hot breath familiar and exciting as it tickles my skin. "I don't need an answer right now. I just need to let you know there is a chance the magic of the deal will not be satisfied."

He means it. He's leaving it up to me if I want to join him wherever he goes.

"Then there's Tavras." He doesn't let go of me, sliding me fully onto his lap as he lies down against the tiles, bending a knee and bracing his foot on the edge of the roof to hold both our weights while my own legs dangle over the edge left and right of his thigh. My back is pressed against his chest, one of his hands resting idly on my stomach. It's comfortable. Safe. And for once, I don't think about what it used to feel like with him. I only feel how it is now.

"What about Tavras?" My eyes find the moon once more, wondering if we'll ever be like this again.

Myron's voice rumbles through my body as he answers. "You're queen of two realms. That of Crows and the very one we're in right now." His fingers find my hair, absently stroking down the side of my head. "You can't both leave with me and stay in Tavras unless I become King of Tavras."

It's not a question but a fact. "Technically, you're as much the King of Tavras as I'm the Queen of Crows. We're married, Myron."

"We are." Beneath my spine, his heart slams hard against his ribs. "Married and mated. What's mine is yours. You're not *technically* my queen; you *literally* are. In every sense of the word. You can rule our kingdom in my stead. I trust you with our people. With body, heart, and soul."

I can't breathe as his fingers splay on my stomach, the light touch turning proprietary. "I'm yours, Ayna."

But his hand says what his words don't. That *I'm his*.

The armor is suddenly too tight, the leather too thick. I want to feel his warmth skin to skin.

"Let's destroy Erina's weapon first. We can talk about everything else tomorrow."

It's the response of a coward, but I'm not ready to say I'll be his again if only he makes me.

"There are things that can't wait until tomorrow, Ayna." His lips are close to my ear once more, brushing the shell of it, and I shudder against him. "If things go wrong tonight, there will be no tomorrow where I can tell you I can't bear another day without you knowing that I feel you through our bond. It might not be as strong as it used to be, but it's there. I can feel your pain and your joy. And I can feel the heat flowing from you right now, Ayna." My skin tingles where his finger traces down the side of my neck, sweeping my hair aside to place a kiss to the sensitive skin right beneath my ear. My body reverberates with pleasure at that simple touch. "I need you, Ayna. All of you. If you're not ready, I can understand, but I need you to know that I'm ready to give you my all. And if this is the last night we have, I need you to take it."

His lips still below my ear, lingering, waiting for an answer I can't speak.

But I turn my head to the side, meeting his mouth with mine in a kiss that equals the storm brewing in my chest. A moan slips from his throat, deep and sensual, the sound running straight to my core. His tongue slides against my lower lip, followed by a nip of his teeth, and I open for him, inhaling his breath, his scent. Like honey over fire, his taste melts on my tongue, the brine of the ocean, sage and rosemary, but there's a sweetness to it that I've never noticed.

His hand traces the collar of my leathers where the steel vines form a hedge. Like on a silent command, they retreat at his touch, creeping back against my shoulders, and the buckles of my jacket come undone. Whether it's Myron's magic or that of the spelled leathers, I don't care. The cool night air kisses my skin through my undershirt, and my breasts are no longer trapped. Myron's fingers haven't moved from my collarbone, so I guide them down my chest to the sensitive flesh of my nipples. Myron sucks in a breath as his fingers graze the hard rosy buds. His hips roll against my backside, his thigh between my legs lifting me an inch so I feel his arousal pressing lightly against me.

"We'll fall off this roof," I mutter between kisses.

"Worth it." His breathless chuckle runs through me like sweet poison.

"I mean it, Myron. If we continue up here, we'll tumble over the edge and break our necks."

He pinches my nipple, eliciting a moan from me that he muffles with a kiss. "I'll blissfully tumble over any edge with you, Ayna. Preferably together. But tonight, all I need is for you to trust me. I promise I won't let you fall." He licks up the side of my neck, leaving a blazing trail of fire. "At least, not over the edge of the roof. I have a better one in mind."

The vines around my hips yield to his touch, clearing his path as his one hand moves from my stomach to the waistband, while the other continues to caress my breast. The small ache where he pinched me has turned into a sensitivity that makes me arch into him every time he brushes against it.

"Do you trust me, Ayna?"

I don't need to think about my responses. I trust him with my life. "Always."

His growl is guttural and predatory, but his fingers are gentle as they undo the laces of my pants and slide beneath the leathers. With a roll of his hips, he pushes me against his hand, fingertips sliding into the wetness between my thighs. I bite back another moan, bucking my hips to give him better access. Myron chuckles against my neck. "Even if I didn't have my fingers on you right now, I could smell how wet you are for me."

I don't object because I'm liquid, and I want him to slide deeper.

Myron uses his free hand to shove my pants a few inches down, as much as my spread thighs will allow. It's enough for his fingers to graze my center, and fuck. The. Guardians: pleasure explodes in my core, searing me like a godsdamned everlasting torch. My shoulder is tingling the slightest bit.

I haven't checked on the scar because my wound hasn't hurt in days, but this is the first time I've felt something more than pain or numbness.

Shimmying sideways, I skate my hand along his thigh, grabbing onto the hard muscle as he circles the bundle of nerves at the apex of my legs. He groans his approval, sliding deeper so his fingertips are at my entrance. I want him. So badly I don't think as I grab behind my hip where his cock is straining against his own leathers. Gods, I want that hard length inside of me.

"Patience, my queen." His voice is rough, breath a series of ragged gusts against my skin. "You will have your pleasure."

As he says it, he plunges two fingers into me, and my world splinters. A scream teeters on the verge of escape. I need him with a desperation I've never experienced in my life. Slowly, he pumps, his palm pushing against me with the most delicate pressure.

My fingers search for the strings of his pants, but they're tucked away, and I can't find the right angle. Myron's other hand is coasting my breasts, trailing up and down my stomach, and all the while, he's kissing me like this is indeed the last night we'll ever have.

"Promise me there'll be a tomorrow, Ayna, and I'll fuck you, then."

Between my legs, his hand moves faster, his braced leg making sure I don't slide off as I'm trembling around his fingers. My vision explodes in silver light like the stars decided to rearrange in the skies, and my pleasure spikes so hard I finally scream his name.

Myron doesn't cover my mouth with his, letting the proof of my climax sound into the night, but his shield wraps tighter around us, and I know the silver light was from the protective layer he's drawn around us. In the distance, an animal scurries across the ground. An owl hoots in the trees nearby. My hand slides from his hip right into his waiting one.

"I promise." Something stirs inside of me, like a string being pulled from a ball of yarn, and unspools, unspools, unspools, until it hits a mass of bright energy. It hooks itself into it, melting into the throbbing light. It's a flash of a vision, so brief I wonder if I really saw it, but when it's gone, the sense of the thread remains.

Myron kisses the corner of my mouth, a quiet sigh following like a ghost he didn't mean to let go.

"I'm yours, Ayna. I will always be yours. Mind, body, and soul."

ANGELINA J. STEFFORT

FORTY-FOUR

AYNA

The night truly is dark when we finally hover in the bushes near the crooked fork in the road we chose for our ambush. Clouds have chosen to clothe the moon in a layer of inky black, and the stars don't dare look for fear of what will happen if we fail.

They're not the only ones. Since Myron and I climbed off the roof in our human forms, I haven't been able to shake the feeling that we're walking right to our death.

Herinor and Royad are keeping watch from the trees above in their bird form. Kaira and Silas are on the other side of the road behind the set of rocks rounded by water and the harsh winds blowing over the plains throughout the season.

413

Myron, Tata, and I crouch in the bushes closest to the road. There isn't much space for the caravan to pass through; the guards and soldiers will have to walk in front and behind, which leaves us with the opportunity to attack from the side and the air at the same time without needing to fight our way to the actual wagons first. Tori and Royad sketched the plan, and after site-hopping us all in, we've scouted the location to confirm what we want to do is feasible.

Thank the Guardians, we don't need to improvise. Everything is exactly how Pouly described, and all we need to do is exercise patience. I've proven earlier tonight that patience isn't exactly my strong suit, I'm still carrying the proof of those moments on my body.

When Tori site-hopped us in, he sniffed once and gave me a knowing grin. Tata probably has the decency not to comment on my scent or the traces of it that still cling to Myron, no matter that we washed up by the rain barrel behind the stables.

Any moment now, the wagons will come into view. I can hear the clacking of wheels and the snorting of horses in the distance.

The air is so still I could have believed magic is holding the winds at bay had I not known none of us possess such abilities. My heart thumps in beat with Myron's. I can sense it like an ancient truth even though I'm not touching him. My hands are firmly on my daggers, drawn and ready to stab my way to the cargo if needed.

The fallen tree the males heaved onto the road nicely blocks the path north in a way that makes it look in the darkness from a distance like a carriage could pass, so the caravan won't turn around right away. Everything is in place.

Clack-clack-clack.

The wheels are close enough for me to feel them turning inside my body.

Clack-clack.

From the nearby trees, a caw sounds.

I hold my breath.

The outline of riders appears first, then the bulky corpus of a horse-drawn wagon. I don't see any foot soldiers.

Within a minute, they'll be here.

Sweat slips down my neck into my collar where the steel vines have reassembled like they haven't ever made way for Myron's hands. I grasp my daggers harder.

At the side of the rocks across, I spot Clio's copper braid as she scrambles an inch to the side to stay hidden when the caravan reaches the bend in the road. As they do, I see the foot soldiers.

Pouly had estimated forty-five, but I count fewer. Thirty or less.

With a breath of relief easing my chest, I coil to spring. The first rider reaches our ambush, raising his arm to stop the wagons behind. "We've got an obstacle here."

A second rider gallops up to him from behind the wagons. Both are wearing black and blue from toe to leather head piece. Humans then, from Erina's military.

"Looks like we can squeeze through." The man who rode up assesses the tree from above, waving forward one of the wagons. The foot soldiers have taken formation around the two others, spears at the ready. All of them wear the same uniform. It's not blue and black, though, but a dark gray that is neither Tavras, nor the brown of Flame leathers.

From the side, two birds rise, launching from the branches, diving for the canvas covering the first wagon. They shift as they plummet from the air, swords drawn and slicing into the dusty fabric.

The turmoil of Eroth's Veil breaks loose when the soldiers realize they are being attacked.

That's our signal, and I will my magic to comply when I send a streak of silver right for the wheels of the second wagon. Whatever soldiers are guarding this cage, it won't leave this place.

From the other side, flashes of silver hit the third wagon while Myron's power cracked the hind wheels of the first one. Horses rear up in panic, screaming and bolting. The axis of the first wagon breaks, and the horses tear free from their reins. One of the riders shouts commands, but half of the foot soldiers are already clashing with Silas and Clio, who leaped out of their hideout the moment the soldiers realized where the attack was coming from. Tori's sword is a slash of silver in the sparse light, and so is Tata's as she joins the melee. The soldiers fight like humans, their strength no match for ours. Kaira's arrows zoom past the rock from where she's still kneeling, taking down soldiers who attempt to flee.

But my eyes are on the first wagon.

From my hideout behind the bushes, I'm waiting for Royad and Herinor to emerge from beneath the canvas of the first wagon. Myron's taking down a rider coming in our direction to check where the silver light breaking his wagon came from.

"Where are they?" I'm ready to leap to my feet and bolt for the first wagon. Myron's hand clasps around my elbow.

"Not yet. Give them time to do their work." Because he trusts them while I… I don't trust Erina not to sit in the wagon himself with a pool of the magic-nullifying serum to drown the two Crows in.

My stomach clenches, but I sit tight.

Around my daggers, my hands are itching to slit throats. I'm not used to the bloodthirst, but I welcome it. If we fail at this, we'll fail at the war. These are mere human soldiers protecting the weapon. We can take them down. If Myron and I join the slaughter, it will be even faster.

I'm about to tell him that when something hits us in the back. Myron's shield wobbles but holds. Fast as lightning, we swirl around.

The sight of the soldiers in front of us makes my hands shake.

Rows of men in undefined gray armor, seven each, stand no less than thirty feet from us. In their hands, long, bone-white bows are pulled taut, silver-tipped arrows aiming directly at us.

"*Tori!*" I shout in my mind and can instantly feel his attention swing to me. "*We've got a problem here.*"

I send him an image of what we're facing and hiss a curse when I recognize the face at the head of the group. *Arebar.* A scar from the last fight is running down his cheek, but it's unmistakably him.

"Flames," I say to Myron, repeating the same word in my mind for Tori and Kaira.

Like on a silent command, the arrows flare to life, bright orange fire coating the tips and sizzling up the shafts.

They don't give a warning before they shoot.

Myron's weight nearly smothers me as he throws himself over me, rolling us into the bushes. His shield pulls in close to us, denser and visible as it glows against the onslaught of flying arrows.

"You all right?" We come to a halt, me on my back and Myron on top of me, a scratch on his cheek that makes me furious, even when it's just from a branch.

I nod, shoving at his chest so I can get up and face the Flames. They need to reload their bows, and I want to use those precious seconds to strike with my magic. Myron understands, leaping up and pulling me to my feet with him. Another arrow flies, and the bushes behind us burst into flames, making us stumble a step closer to the Fire Fairies so Myron's shield won't get eaten up by the heat.

Screams sound from the other side of the fire, and a part of me wants to go check on the others, but they are seven against a bunch of humans, while we... Well, we're facing an army of at least fifty. And they aren't here to negotiate.

My powers immediately react when I summon them, even when my pulse is racing and my palms are sweaty. I don't wait for Myron's signal as I send the streak of silver into the eerie glow of the Flames' formation. They have more arrows at the ready, but my magic hits their frontline so hard the three Flames at the center stumble into the row behind them, loosing their arrows into the clouds above.

Myron's attack follows suit, kicking deeper into the formation, and I hear necks snap where Flames tumble to the ground to never get up again.

A part of me fills with hope. We are strong together, my mate and me. We can do this.

Then, the Flames in the next row step over the corpses of their fallen, filling up the front lines, slender silver blades in one hand and fireballs in the other.

A volley of heat rushes at us, forcing us to sidestep the burning bush and expose our backs to the battle behind. Tori and Kaira are there, but they are still engaged in the battle around the wagons. It's a small comfort that, as long as they've got our backs, at least we don't need to worry about getting stabbed from behind.

So far, Myron's shield holds, but he can't attack with full force and keep the silver layer of protection around us flawless at the same time. The Flames take an organized step forward.

Arrows fly again, this time, over our heads, right into the action, and I think I hear Clio's curse. I don't dare turn around.

"Please tell me you're winning that fight," I beg Tori in my mind, whose presence has remained at my back despite Clio's outburst.

"We've got your back, Queen of Crows," he responds, and from the ground, small drops of liquid rock rise, zooming for the flames and knocking the arrows from their bows before they can send the next wave.

"The human soldiers fight well," Kaira notes, and I realize that we're all three hearing our silent conversation while the rest of the group is locked out.

Myron noticed the projectiles Tori created, though. He lowers his shield to let them pass before pulling it back up again, silver vines knitting tight around us.

It takes the Flames a moment to understand what's going on—a moment we use to deliver our next strike—but once they do, they shoulder their bows and charge, drawing their blades as they cover the ground between us so fast I barely have time to brace myself before they clash with Myron's shield. Fire cracks along the silver sphere, flames licking and lapping holes into the web of magical threads. Heat lashes at my face as single threads of fire spear through, but he draws the shield tighter, throwing his focus into keeping the danger sealed out.

No matter how strong, Myron can't hold them off forever, but I can stab at them with my daggers, so I do. One precise slice after the other, I pierce through the shield where it's already falling apart, bracing myself for the agony of seared palms as I meet both fire and steel. A wide-eyed Flame sees me coming, staggering back just far enough so only the tip of my dagger reaches her. With satisfaction, I watch it nick her throat, right on the column of her windpipe. Her scream ends in a gurgle, and she sinks to the ground, clutching her bloodied throat.

Another Flame is ready though, and her blade hits my forearm. It's a mild blow, sliding off my leathers as I'm already drawing my hand down and back, but I hiss anyway at the momentary throb of pain, swallowing down the urge to check on it. If I pause, they'll only close in on us faster, and the heat is already becoming unbearable with every inch Myron's shield contracts, holes allowing the fire to reach for us like glowing fingers of fire.

"*We need Clio's ice magic!*" I shout into the silent conversation. Tori is already on it. Then Kaira steps up to my side, slipping into the shield with ease the moment Myron notices her, like he can will his protective magic to differentiate between friend and foe.

Kaira sheaths her daggers, lifting her palms, and closes her eyes. I want to yell at her to watch out as a streak of fire enters the shield, effectively ripping it apart, and we stand defenseless except for our weapons. The blast of heat singes my skin where it licks over my fingers, and I can feel blisters rise on the back of my hand. Ignoring the burning ache, I summon my magic, preparing to strike, while Myron is already cutting down Flames with his sword, flickers of silver dancing around the blade and lashing at the opponents he misses.

The fire doesn't stop coming at us, though. Like a gushing river, it flows into Kaira's hands, dancing and coiling and weaving into a ball so big it could have been the moon Myron watched so intently on the roof an hour ago, and I want to shout a warning.

A smile graces her lips as she whips the fire back into the fighting Flames. *Siphoned,* I realize, and heave a breath as I watch the orange sphere zoom across the field.

Fire doesn't seem to burn them the same way it burns us, but they duck and scatter where Kaira's attack hits. It's enough for us to strike. This time, Tori's molten rock joins the attack, tearing through armor and flesh before it solidifies again in their bodies. I don't even want to know how that feels. The fire is still raging, though, and our progress is limited with the Flames hiding behind a wall of it.

"Where is Clio?" I call to Tori in my mind as he cuts into a brave Flame's arm when it steps out of the fire into his range. The soldier's scream curdles my blood, but I keep fighting. *"We need her ice magic to box in the fire."*

Tori nods right before leaping at the now armless soldier, taking off his head with an efficient swing of his sword. His shield pushes back enough of the heat so we can hold our ground, but just like Myron's, it won't last forever.

"She's a bit busy." He sends an image of the battle behind us at the same moment he says out loud, "The human soldiers aren't all human. Erina snuck a few Flames in there as well."

Fire explodes behind us, followed by screams and the whinnying of horses. Wood cracks, and scorched debris rains down on us. I throw my arms over my head just in time when a splinter of burning wood hits me, leaving blackened scratches on my armor and a bruise on my shoulder.

Water. I need *water*. If Clio can't help, maybe I can.

Reaching out with my senses, I pray that I won't be stabbed in the gut while I scan the ground for a droplet of wet.

There's no running water answering me, but the clouds above sing like a chorus of the Guardians.

Come to me, I command the water.

It doesn't move. It's too high up for me to draw it into droplets and make it rain onto the battlefield.

Clang! A flash of steel tears me from my thoughts, and I leap back in time to avoid a Flame pressing Kaira's sword into my nose where she blocked his strike.

My heart stops a beat at the certain death I've just escaped.

"Thank you," I mumble, stabbing beneath her arm and piercing through the weak spot of the Flame's armor under his lifted arm.

Myron shoots me a sideways glance, sword locked in battle. The clear warning resonates through the thread connecting us—not the mating bond, I realize, but the promise I made to him. *Promise me there'll be a tomorrow, Ayna, and I'll fuck you, then.*

Myron nods as if he feels it too. It's a binding promise. A fae promise. If I die, I'll have broken it.

Not that it matters, but what will the promise do to him if he can't hold up his end of it?

The Flames press forward, heat welling in waves as they switch rows whenever one of them tires or falls. It's a fucking nightmare we can't win.

At least, the bushes have reduced to ashes. That makes one less obstacle to watch out for, but now the two battles are melting into each other. I can see it as I turn to the side, standing back to back with Myron so we have the best chances to keep our promise: The wagons are burning, canvas an inferno, and wood disintegrating.

If we're lucky, we won't need to take care of the weapon at all. The fire might destroy it all on its own. The horses have long bolted, throwing off their riders, who are now fighting on the ground. They are wielding balls of fire and silver blades that identify them unmistakably as Flames, no matter what their armor looks like.

Too many of the human soldiers are still standing, their heads protected by the helmets hiding most of their hair and necks. It must be smothering, but at least the fire won't singe them where they're covered. Erina must have had this armor made for them, not to trick us but to bolster the chances of their survival.

With a deep breath, I summon my Crow power once more, swiping at the Flames who come too close with one dagger while I sheathe the other to have better aim with my magic. Silver light rips from my open palm, striking like lightning, but when it hits the Flames, they don't die. They stagger back, yes, but they don't tumble to the ground the way they're supposed to.

Guardians above—

It's not only my magic. Myron's isn't as effective on his targets either. And as I watch the Flames stand in their own fire, I understand there is something more at work than just their power.

FORTY-FIVE

MYRON

No idea how long we've been fighting those fire-loving bastards. I've lost track of time with the countless strikes of Crow magic I've delivered. My shield has long shattered, as has the fairy general's and the thin lining of protection Ayna summons without even realizing. Bruises are already developing beneath my scratched armor where I've taken minor hits, and I'm certain I've sacrificed an inch of my hair where the fire lashed through my shield earlier.

Kaira seems to be the only one who isn't afraid of the fire. With her siphoning ability, she can grab onto the Flames' power and wield it against them—in small portions, which do practically nothing to harm them, only to redirect their magical blows when they come too close for comfort.

It's useful, though. Both Ayna and I would have been singed more times than I can count, and it doesn't matter what we pit against them, they simply won't die. Unless we drive our blades into them, of course, but it's near impossible to get close enough to do so.

Silas, Tata, and Clio are still fighting what was supposed to be human soldiers. At least, they don't hurl fire at them every other breath. The cavalry seems to have been Flames, though. And where the fuck are Royad and Herinor? They haven't emerged from the wagon, and despite the fire that was there mere minutes ago, the canvas covering the cargo hasn't burned away like on the other two.

I swipe my sword at a Flame stepping into my range, gritting my teeth as I cut through leather and flesh.

Beside me, Ayna delivers a silver strike that rattles the marrow of my bones, but the Flames don't shy away like they're supposed to. They grin at her, using the moment she needs to collect herself to land a blow to her knee.

Ayna hisses like a real Crow Fae, countering with a slice to the Flame's throat. I don't watch him go down, already facing my own opponent.

Tori keeps melting rocks and sending them at the Flames, but there are too many, and what looked like a promising tactic isn't killing those bastards either. It's like their armor won't allow for any magic to go through.

"Use your blades!" Ayna shouts as if she is having the same epiphany at the same time. "Their armor is magic repellant!"

"Fuck!" Tori steals the response from my mouth, pulling a knife from his boot and throwing it right at a Flame's neck. The female goes down but crawls forward, blood spilling on the scorched ground. A trail of fire follows her like an armor of its own.

Ice crawls from Tori's boots up his legs and torso, covering his leathers in tiny crystals right as the female grabs for him, sending a blazing inferno of fire at him. The flames die before they can as much as singe a hair on his head, and the female's eyes widen with horror as Clio leaps from behind her mate, grabbing her neck and twisting it with a crack.

"That was close," Tori notes, sword already swinging at the next Flame who dares come too close. But it's not enough.

Even with Clio joining us, we're only seven, and our opponents are at least seven times that. It doesn't matter that Recienne hadn't joined us in this battle. His power wouldn't have made a difference. He's better off spending time with his mate and protecting their unborn child from danger when it occurs at the palace in Aceleau. But here—?

Without the advantage of our magic, we can't win.

That doesn't change that we'll fight to the death.

Smoke wafts through the air, taking my sight as I aim my next strike. My muscles burn from holding the shield for too long, and now my arms are sluggish when I strike with my sword. Faster than the average Flame, still, but my blows don't land as accurately as they should. More often than I care for, my blade misses the weak spots of my opponent's armor to the effect that I drive them back, but they keep coming at us.

Ayna is relentless, not a hint of fear on her features as she grabs for her second dagger and slices the cheek of a Flame. At least, Clio has realized she's doing more good alternately layering all of us with ice than trying to smother the fire in the enemy's hands. I welcome the cool trickle of power whenever it runs over my hands and my face, the unprotected parts of my body where the heat finds purchase.

Tata and Silas are nearby, fighting the foot soldiers in tandem, their hatchet and swords gleaming in the fire billowing from the wagons.

"Where are the others?" I shout at Silas, who's closest to the first wagon. I don't see through the inferno layered over the outline of it, but I know that's where the two Crows disappeared to. They might have long burned to cinders.

The thought fuels rage in my chest. Rage and the hollow sense of loss. These are the last members of my court. If they die, there won't be a Crow kingdom left.

I spin on one foot, kicking out with the other as a Flame charges at me. They go down with a grunt, fire winking out as they lose consciousness, and I don't hesitate to ram my sword into their back until it bites into the solid ground beneath.

One more down.

"Wagon!" Silas responds, but he knows as well as me the chances we'll find anyone alive are slight, even if we somehow manage to win this battle and put out the fires.

Every time we cut one Flame out of their ranks, they regroup, forming an unbreakable line all over again.

We need a fucking miracle.

FORTY-SIX

AYNA

W

e're not getting anywhere like this except to our own graves. When we were talking about a potential trap, we had thought of the type of soldiers they'd send or how they might not even be transporting that magic-nullifying serum. None of us had considered an army of magic-defying armor-wearing soldiers where it no longer matters what powers we wield. We still have them, but they are useless. It's almost worse than being injected with the serum.

Another explosion of fire hits behind me, making me duck, but there's no shelter. Flakes of ash swirl in the air, stirred off the path by the occasional arrow the Flames are still sending from their back rows. My breath comes hard as the ash tears past me.

Thank Shaelak for my Crow reflexes. I have maneuvered around them without a scratch, but Kaira's gasp informs me she took a blow.

"*You all right?*" I prompt in my mind, too focused to open my mouth to speak.

Kaira grits her teeth at the arrow protruding from her thigh, barely keeping on her legs. "*Fucking Fire Fairies,*" is the only response I get.

Clio is right beside her, but there's little she can do other than stand in front of Kaira to give her cover as she breaks off the shaft of the arrow so it won't catch when she moves. She's losing too much blood, though. If we can't heal her, she won't survive this battle.

There has to be something I can do.

The clouds shift, uncovering the moon, tinting everything in silver light. Even the bonfires that the wagons have become pale into subdued shades of orange and yellow.

The clouds—

I need the water from the clouds.

And there is a way I can get it.

"Give me cover," I shout at Myron, who blocks the Flame stepping into his space, slitting his throat and pushing him back into the next row and all without Clio's layer of ice. His hands must be covered with burns.

I try not to think about it. If I don't succeed, it won't matter. He won't feel the burns when he's dead.

Myron doesn't ask questions, merely dips his chin, stepping closer to my side and summing a thin, barely-there shield, but it's enough for me to sheathe my daggers and focus on the wind casing along the waters of the ocean, the freedom of being up in the air, the rush of flying—

My gaze locks with Myron's, and I can't reassure him that everything will be all right before feathers start sprouting from my shoulders. My legs are already shrinking and my eyes are turning into those of a bird. But I hold onto that human part of me for a heartbeat longer.

"I love you," is all I can say before the feathers take me and I turn fully into a crow.

Myron's shield wraps around me as my wings beat against the heat from the fires. One wrong move and I'll be too close to the flames, and my feathers will catch fire. I'll plunge from the sky and end up like Ephegos, scarred and wingless.

I push on, up and up, to where the clouds will give cover. Myron's shield falls away a few feet above his head, and I can feel his panic when he can no longer protect me, so I flutter on. Zig-zagging between balls of fire coming after me. The Flames have noticed my shift, and they know I'm an easy target. An arrow zooms past my left wing, forcing me to pull it in. As a result, I tumble through the air like a nutshell in the water. My left claw isn't anywhere near healed, even when I pushed my powers to take care of the wound I received earlier. It's a small cut, but it keeps me from using my claws to balance out the spin, so I lean into it, diving down a few feet before I manage to whip out my left wing.

Beating the air hard, I climb again, up, up toward the clouds. Just a few more feet and I'll find cover. I don't dare try to summon my water magic while I'm still an easy target; the Flames will shoot me down so fast I can't even think my mate's name.

A fireball lights the sky bright orange as it soars past me. My heart is fluttering so fast I no longer feel individual beats. If I push any harder, it might simply stop.

I push anyway.

Two more feet. One.

Cool mist coats my feathers as I dive into the clouds, washing away the panic, and cool air fills my lungs, easing the iron grasp the fear has on my chest.

With a few strong beats of my wings, I'm up high enough to see the stars while the clouds form a carpet of comfort beneath me. I could lie down in the moonlit cotton and forget the world, but there are people down below who need my help. People who I'd die for.

My bird mind isn't half as vast as my human one, but it holds enough capacity to remember Myron's face. To remember all of their faces. The scent of their blood on the battlefield.

Come on, I call my magic to my aid. *I need you.*

Like a million liquid diamonds, the clouds respond with a song. If only I could grasp them all at once and send them down in a splash. The fire would be quenched, and the Flames would lose one advantage.

Circling, I call the water to me.

The response is the same song, but it's mocking me, that I'm too weak to hold it all at once.

I'm small, not weak, I tell it, tugging on it again.

You chose Shaelak's power over mine. It's not the water but Vala's voice, soft but firm.

Please, no. I can't handle a quarrel between deities right now. I need to save *my family.*

I didn't choose, I think with exasperation. *I need you both. I can't save them without Shaelak's power, and I can't save them without yours.*

He is Chaos, I'm Order. We're two halves of one whole, Vala says so softly I barely hear her. *I granted you power to break my curse, and he granted you power as a reward for saving his creation. We can take it away.*

Please-no-please-no-please-no.

Her words register. *Chaos and Order? Like the Guardians?*

Like the children of Hel. Of Eroth. Of Zotarr. Whatever you want to call him.

My vision blurs as I realize two things: Vala and Shaelak are the Guardians. And we've been praying to the same gods all this time.

Be wise, my child, Vala says, her tone gentle, but there is darkness in it as she seems to speak right by my ear. *Order and Chaos have always been fighting for balance. If you use my power at the same time as his, I don't know what it will take for that balance to be restored.*

I want to beg her to help me anyway, but she didn't say she wouldn't allow me to use her power. All she did was warn me of the consequences.

The clouds beneath light up in all colors of a fire, and I know I'm running out of time. Screams and curses sound from below alongside the clanking of steel against steel. If I hesitate another moment, everything might have been in vain.

Whatever it is, I'll pay the price.

I don't wait for the Sister Guardian's response before I pull on my water magic so hard my little bird body threatens to tear wide open. I might not be strong enough to call all the water to me at once, but I'm strong enough to push it away.

With a mighty shove, I send the liquid diamonds careening to the ground, focusing on letting them gravitate toward each other until they form droplets, then drops, and splashes at last. The clouds clear, freeing my view of the ground where bodies lie scattered and flares of fire define the landscape. It's a scene from my nightmares that I will never stop seeing, not even if my plan works and I manage to put out the flames.

FORTY-SEVEN

MYRON

The fucking miracle comes in the shape of splattering rain.

One moment, we're close to burning, Clio's glacial magic exhausted and Kaira's siphoning abandoned with the gushing wound on her thigh taking all her focus. The next, hard, icy rain batters the fire without mercy. I throw my hand over my head, shielding my face as I glance up for a sign of Ayna.

I didn't realize what she had in mind when she told me to give her cover, but when she'd shifted, my heart stopped beating. And it started racing with fear. I swear it hasn't stopped throbbing near exhaustion since that arrow nearly got her in the wing.

Left and right, flames turn into steam as the fires wink out, the rain soaking the ground beating them into submission. The Flames curse, but they don't realize it's *my* Ayna who sent the wrath of the gods after them. If they did, they'd focus on the sky rather than relentlessly attacking the few of us still standing.

Tori is doing his best to meet every new opponent with a smirk on his face. I saw him like that in the Crow Wars where he stood against my own kind with brutal efficiency and unbreakable spirit. Now that I fight alongside him, I recognize the arrogance of the warrior for what it is: the last line of defense. As long as the enemies believe he has unlimited strength, that it's that easy for him to keep swinging that monstrous sword of his, they'll quake with fear.

Silas and Tata are fighting a Flame nearby, closer to the wagons, their sword and hatchet biting into the male's armor with ease now that the fire is dying down. Steam rising from the put-out fires takes my sight, but I'm no longer being cooked alive.

We're finally making progress.

The Flame in front of me goes down in a single blow. He doesn't even manage to lift his sword. I duck and swing as another Flame attacks from the side. This is far from over. More than thirty soldiers are still standing, but their fire no longer gives them an edge. Within minutes, the ground is slippery with water and blood as we slaughter our way across the field.

At the back of my head, a small voice keeps reminding me that Herinor and Royad are still missing. I don't want to accept it just yet, that they never stood a chance against the fire. The moment their wagon caught flames was a death sentence.

I should have been the one to attack from the air. Not the Crow who puts his life at risk, working against an oath he gave to Ephegos, and most certainly not my cousin. He's the better male—would have been the better king had there been a Crow kingdom to rule over.

Pushing down the emptiness rising with those thoughts, I face the next opponent.

A part of me wants to glance up and search for Ayna, but there is little I can do for her from down here. She's made her choice, and she succeeded. I only hope it didn't take too much out of her so she can still fly herself to safety. Far, far away from this place would be my vote, but Ayna knows how to take care of herself. She knows when to ask for help and when to fight her own battles. She'll survive this one. She *promised*.

I hold onto the thread that is the fae promise like my life depends on it. I won't let go of it, just like I didn't let go of the mating bond.

Sweat burns in my eyes, distracting me just enough for the Flame attacking from the side to get me in my shoulder. A shallow wound but it throbs like a fucker.

I faintly remember his face from the Flame estate when I tore everything to shreds in my monster form. How he survived with nothing more than a scar on his cheek is a story

I'd really like to hear—were it not for the battle raging in the background and the blade in my flesh.

"I didn't think I'd see you again so soon, Crow King," the male grins at me, pulling his blade out of my shoulder and shoving me back. I fucking stumble.

"Arebar!" Kaira shouts from the ground a few feet away. The male's head snaps to the side. I use the moment to stab him in the ribs, but Kaira is faster. She throws her dagger right at the male's neck, and it hits true, sending the male tumbling to his knees, and his eyes widen with recognition for a second as he realizes where the blow had come from. "See you behind Eroth's Veil."

With those words, she collapses, and I curse the gods as another Flame is coming for me. My shoulder screams with pain as I lift my sword. I breathe through it, ignoring the fact that the little part-Flame might have just saved my life and that I can do nothing to save hers.

Nothing but make this battle come to an end as fast as I can. We're two Crows and one part-Flame down. Three Crows, if I count Ayna's absence, but she's forced the clouds down upon us, so she did make a difference in this battle. The biggest of us all, perhaps. Thick drops of rain are still slapping my armor as I cut my way across the space, drawing closer to the first wagon with every soldier I put to the ground.

"Royad!" I kick the corpse of a fallen soldier out of my way, sword lifted in front of my chest and what I have left of my power channeled into a thin shield. I'd tried to wrap it around Kaira earlier, but I'd have needed to stand beside her to make it big enough for both of us, and it's more likely she'll get killed in my proximity than staying down with her wound and out of the way. Clio is close by to help her should a soldier try to end her suffering before the battle is over.

Silas and Tata have cleared most of the space around the wagons, drifting over to the other front where Tori and Clio are doing their best to keep the soldiers at bay. Slowly—so slowly my head has a million chances to tell me there is no point in looking for Royad and Herinor, I make my way closer.

The canvas is no longer burning; the clean cut Royad's sword sliced into the top runs all the way down the side. The two pieces of fabric don't come apart, though.

A Flame steps into my path, slender blade angled for my throat. I sidestep him, twisting under his arm and slicing upward into his ribs, and pluck his sword from his grasp as he falls over.

Wherever my mate went, she turned this battle around. The fighting is dying down, and a glance over my shoulder tells me we're winning. Only five more Flames are on their feet, and they are running into trouble when Tata and Silas join Tori and Clio's efforts.

"Herinor!" I dare focus on the wagon. Dare take the final step and touch the canvas.

I shouldn't have.

"Watch out!" Royad's shout reaches me a heartbeat before a splash of liquid hits me in the face, and I know the stench better than I know that of my own blood.

Fuck!

The serum. Someone poured the magic-sedating serum over me.

The canvas is torn aside, revealing a wooden platform with a bench the length of the wagon, and kneeling before it, heads down and blades at their throats, are Royad and Herinor. Fresh blood is dripping from Royad's nose over his soot-stained mouth and chin, and his lip is split. The guards standing behind them smirk at me as if they've already won, but it's the female that makes the hairs stand at the back of my neck.

Her fire-red hair is all too familiar, as are the mild lines on her face.

"Jeseida."

"I must say, I'm surprised you'd walk right into a trap after everything you've experienced. It *is* rather entertaining, though, to have you here yet again, magic gone and your friends in my power."

"I'm sorry," Royad grits out. The guard standing by the end of the bench steps forward and punches him in the side of his face. I flinch at a crack that means a bone must have snapped.

Royad doesn't even whimper. He's endured worse at the hand of my father. We both have, and we both have lived through it.

I'm here. We'll get you out.

"Tori!" I shout, fighting the beginning symptoms of magic loss. My head swims, my legs are weak, and nausea racks through me. "Tori, run!"

He'll know what to do. He'll grab Kaira and Silas, and together with Clio and Tata, they'll site-hop out of here.

When he and I talked in private before this mission, we swore to each other that we wouldn't abandon the battlefield unless all hope is lost. We've made it this far. We defeated an army immune to magic. Yet, hope is dwindling as the guard who punched Royad picks up a bow and arrow and aims at the fairy general.

Not again.

"Now. Tori." My voice is too weak, but Tori has already spotted the danger—and shakes his head at me.

He's too weak to site-hop.

So, I do the only thing I can think of. I gather what strength I have left and leap at the guard with the bow just in time to block the arrow. It doesn't gain enough speed to tear all the way through my body, but it's enough to pierce the flesh above my heart an inch. It's enough to make me stumble backward, catching my breath.

"I'm all right," I say to Royad, whose gaze finds me the moment I double over, bracing my hands on my knees. "It isn't deep."

"I can make it deeper," says the guard, stepping forward.

Jeseida holds up a hand. "We need him alive."

I want to ask what for, but my vision is blurring, and my legs are buckling. Instead of grabbing for the arrow, the guard catches me by my injured shoulder where my healing power has stopped working on sealing the wound. With a laugh, he pushes me to my knees next to Herinor, blade at my throat, and mutters into my ear. "If you think you'll ever make it off this battlefield alive, you think again."

I don't have time to process. Tori and Clio are standing ten feet from the wagon, Silas beside them. There's no sign of Kaira and Tata, and I pray to the gods that Ayna won't return either.

"What do you want?" The tip of Tori's sword is braced on the ground while, with his free hand, he's swirling droplets of molten rocks above his hand. Beside him, the ground at Clio's feet is frozen. Silas is the only one not displaying any sign of magic, but I recognize the tells of the pending shift in him. He's ready to take off and bolt if I tell him to. He's ready to stay and fight just the same. One word from me and he'll launch into action.

"Nothing much." Jeseida sounds like a girl despite her age. The Flame Matrone tosses her hair over her shoulder like a curtain of smoldering fire and steps to the edge of the platform. "King Erina of Tavras requests the return of his fiancée."

My blood is boiling with rage. "He can't have her."

Jeseida laughs a wind-chime laugh I'm used to from Clio when she's the deadliest. It drives a shiver up my back. "There is nothing you can do, Crow once-King. I have your friends at my mercy. I have you at my mercy. Wolayna will come forward to save you whether you want her to or not. After all, that's what mates do, isn't it?"

"No." It's my final word. I won't allow it. "I'll come willingly, but I will not be traded for her."

"I fear you don't have a choice, Myron." Jeseida leans down as if sharing a secret. "If she doesn't trade places with you, we'll take you back to Meer, and this time, Erina will make sure you don't fall unconscious during your little … talks." She pauses, letting the words sink in. "We have improved the serum, and the side effects are almost gone. You'll not have a minute of rest. And your mate will know you're suffering. That bond that hasn't broken? It will be the death of both of your sanity."

From the corner of my eye, I notice Tori twitch. It isn't much, but it's a tell. Whatever he's planned, it better be good. If Jeseida manages to get the serum on them, we're defenseless, and Ayna will have no choice but to give herself up.

I'll bury that arrow deep in my own heart before I let that happen.

Tori's eyes lift behind me to the sky above the platform, and I think I hear a pair of wings in the distance.

No. Fly away, little Crow.

The flutter vanishes, and I can breathe.

FORTY-EIGHT

AYNA

I saw Tata grab Kaira's arm and disappear into thin air. Thank the—I'm no longer sure what to call the deities once named the *Guardians*. Despite Vala's warning, I used my water magic. Nothing happened.

At least, not up here. Down on the ground, the rain smothered the fire, just as intended, and the Crows and fairies got the upper hand over the Flames. A small victory—and a temporary one.

Not two minutes after the battle was dying down, Jeseida got Myron into her power. Now, he's kneeling beside Herinor and Royad on the wagon, a guard behind each of them, a blade at their throats. Three more Flames stand by, plus Jeseida. How he got there, I didn't see. I had to circle back, or I'd have exposed myself, but the arrow protruding from his chest might have something to do with it. I can feel the uncomfortable sensation of something scratching at the edge of my heart through the bond, and the panic raging in my chest is nothing compared to what I felt when the arrow nearly got my wing.

I should have known the Flame Matrone would be here. When I saw her with Ephegos at Erina's court, I knew they were up to something but had no idea what. After learning everything about the development of the drug and how the Flames and traitor Crows worked together to test it, I know there is no way Jeseida will leave something this important unattended. She'll personally make sure it's delivered to the right place and the right people.

I can see from up here that this wasn't all a trap. The two burned-out wagons have the remains of glass vials sitting in stacks on the charred wood. That must have been enough to supply the army gathering in the northwest of the Plithian Plains to coat their armor, arrows, and blades with it. It was pure coincidence Royad and Herinor attacked the first wagon. They could have ended up in one of the other wagons and taken a bath in the magic-sedating substance instead. Perhaps this was the better fate.

Tori and Clio are standing with Silas, ready to step in but carefully waiting for an opening while Jeseida keeps talking.

I can't hear her from up here, but I'm sure whatever she's saying can't be good.

If only I could get a little closer and—

As I beat my wings to bring myself above the wagon, a tug at the base of my right wing rears me around, and I need to bank and circle back once more.

Whatever that was, it's not normal. Not once since I've first shifted have I felt anything similar to it.

"*Tori.*" I open my mind, calling for the fairy general. He stands closer and might be able to relay to me what's going on so my heart doesn't need to give out at the sight of Jeseida leaning over Myron. I want to rip her throat out.

"*Stay where you are, Ayna. Don't come down.*" His voice is soft in my mind, near inaudible, but I'm certain I heard him.

"*What's going on?*"

"*They got Myron, Herinor, and Royad with the drug. I can't talk right now. Just trust that I have a plan.*" Like a curtain falling into place, the connection is gone, and I'm on my own again.

I don't want to stay where I am, but Tori is the most experienced general I know. Plus, he's Myron's friend. He won't leave anything to fate.

So, I circle higher where the Flames won't spot me if they don't actively scan the skies. My heart is frantically beating as Jeseida straightens and Myron shakes his head, reaching for the arrow.

No!

If he pulls it out, he'll bleed to death. His healing magic won't work. But he knows that.

The panic I felt before turns into pure, unadulterated terror.

My instincts take over, and I'm flying toward him.

"*Stay the fuck away, Ayna,*" Tori warns, spotting me from the corner of his eye as he turns his head to the left. To where Tata reappears. But at her side, it's not Kaira carrying the expression of someone ready to tear the world to shreds but the Fairy King himself, clothed in battle black, a crown of silver and gold upon his head, and a single long-sword in his hand.

FORTY-NINE

MYRON

Recienne comes out of nowhere. I only see him because Tori's gaze darts to the side where Tata pops up with the Fairy King in tow. Someone curses behind me, and I pull back my hand from the arrow I was going to shove into my heart. Jeseida unsheathes her sword, an expression of horror on her face as she takes in the face of the male ruling the lands she wants to make her own, and readies it to drive into Royad's stomach.

"I wouldn't do that if I were you," Recienne warns.

It's the only warning she gets. The next moment, a dark wind rushes along the platform, plucking the blade from her hand and ramming it into the guard behind my cousin. The male doesn't even get a chance to scream as he goes down.

Royad uses the opportunity to spin on his knees. With two efficient kicks, he manages to shove my guard off me while Herinor doesn't move. The sword at his throat is already biting into his flesh, and one wrong breath will drive it so deep it could be his end.

Recienne stalks closer, site-hopping onto the wagon, and flicks his fingers.

The sword at Herinor's throat splinters, pieces crumbling over the male's neck. I want to get up and help, but someone bumps into my back, and I stumble forward. The arrow slides deeper. High above, a familiar caw echoes through the sky, the sound filling my veins with ice.

Turn around, Ayna!

Whether or not she feels what I want her to do is irrelevant when the taste of blood fills my mouth and every breath becomes hard labor.

In front of the wagon, Tori and Clio are fighting side by side, facing one Flame guard together.

A gust of wind flips me over, and someone slaps me in the face. "No sleeping," Recienne warns, but he's not standing close by. His power carried his voice to my ear. Didn't know he could do that. I'll tell him how this could be used for pranks if I survive this.

"I said, up with you." This time, Recienne is standing above me, his boot toeing my side as if to check if he'll need to carry me out of here. He lifts his sword arm to block an attack from the side, an elegant parry that I remember from our battles in the Seeing Forest. I'd hated it back then. I also remember that this is the type of movement that opens him for another attack.

"Watch out," I cough.

Recienne spins, but it's too late. It's not a blade that hits him but a splash of liquid that isn't the rain Ayna sent upon us that lands square in his face.

Recienne sputters as he stumbles back, knees wobbling, hands gripping his sword harder.

They got him with the serum, too. Had I believed a moment ago that we might stand a chance against the Flames, all illusions are gone now. Even with Tori's rocks firing at the Flames and Herinor and Silas fighting alongside Tata and Clio, we're all drained from either the battle or the drug. In my case, it's both.

Recienne knows it too. The odds have tilted against us within a breath, and if we don't get him to safety, Askarea won't have a king much longer.

"Take Clio and get out of here," he shouts at Tori, words slightly slurred as he fights the effects of the serum. They are too far away to take Recienne with them without risking getting showered with the serum as well. Tori—Gods bless him—realizes it too and doesn't hesitate to take Clio's hand and site-hop her away.

I don't know how far they'll make it, but out of sight and out of reach is enough.

Recienne swings his sword at a Flame coming for him, but his aim is off, and his power fails him. The blow slides off the Flame's shoulder piece, and Recienne stumbles into the enemy.

451

My vision goes dark, and the only comfort is that I'll die knowing Ayna still loves me. I couldn't have asked for anything more.

FIFTY

AYNA

I can't *think* at the sight of blood spilling from Myron's mouth. Whoever fired that arrow will die. I'll pick out their eyes with my beak and feast on them.

The Fairy King is standing over him, defending him, but he misses that the Matrone he disarmed is scrambling to her feet again.

My caw of warning comes too late when I spot Jeseida pull a small vial from the pocket of her armor. She uncorks it and tosses the contents into Recienne's face.

"*Get them out, Tori,*" I beg. He hears me, but his focus is on his king, who stumbles under the influence of the serum Jeseida dumped on him. The drug, I realize. His movements are sluggish, and it's a matter of moments before a blade will pierce him.

Herinor and Royad are both on their feet, but their strength is gone, their blows weak like those of human soldiers.

Tori is barely standing upright, but he's still wielding his sword and his magic. A general to the last moment. And Clio—

"Take Clio and get out of here," Recienne's shout reverberates in my mind.

I blink as Tori follows the order without hesitation, grabbing Clio by the arm and disappearing into thin air.

The Flame they'd been fighting stares into blank space for a moment, which Silas uses to take his opponent's head off with a swing of his hatchet.

Tata unceremoniously kicks the head out of her path as she steps around the Crow to face the next guard.

Only three more Flames are standing, plus the Matrone. Three of them and six of us—not counting Myron whose eyes have closed, blood trickling from the corner of his mouth.

I can still feel him but barely.

My chest aches where the arrow is perching into Myron's, my heart beats too fast, and my wings lose strength with every beat. If I don't make it down there in time, there will be nothing I can do to help.

Herinor stumbles next, landing on hands and knees mid-fight, and vomits onto the ground. Royad blocks the blow meant for him, driving the Flame back, but his strength is faltering, and he stumbles, nearly losing his footing in the mud. And that's when they start using their fire.

It winks out the moment it meets the soaked leathers, but the steam rising where it touches draws a scream from Royad's bleeding lips.

Thank Vala, Silas reaches him in time to hack into the Flame's shoulder. Royad embeds his sword in the opponent's chest, and we're down to two soldiers.

I trust Silas, Tata, and Royad to take them down. What I'm worried about is Jeseida turning to Recienne, who's shaking under the full dose of magic-nullifying serum. In her hands, she's holding a black dagger with wisps of fire dancing along the blade.

So close. I'm so close it will take only a few seconds to get to them.

Jeseida readies to strike.

I beat my wings harder.

Recienne spots the dagger just in time to block it, but he tries with his magic instead of his blade.

Jeseida grins as she pulls the dagger back, aiming.

One more beat.

The dagger sinks into Recienne's shoulder as my claws reach Jeseida first, digging deep into her eyes.

A scream tears from her throat, hands sliding off the hilt of her blade and flames dissipating into smoke and ash. Like a mad female, she bats at me with both hands, trying to grab me, but I'm small and agile. My feathers slip through her grasp as I wiggle and buck before I spread my wings and take flight.

The wail hatching from her mouth is almost pitiful, but I don't know pity. This female had my mate on his knees, and there will be no tomorrow for her.

I don't need to think as I dive for her throat: Easy like I've never done anything else in my life, I slip between her forearms where she's pressing her palms into the empty sockets in her skull. And when my claws rip into her skin, opening her artery, I don't balk at the feel of hot, thick blood soaking my feathers. I welcome it with the satisfaction of the monster I've become.

Only when a shout of warning hits me do I beat my wings and flutter high up into the air.

I don't know where the arrow comes from, but it pierces my wing just when I'm high enough that I can no longer shift without risking breaking all my bones.

A tortured caw escapes my beak, and I can feel Myron stir through the bond.

The world is a blur of moonlight and blood as I plummet from the skies.

FIFTY-ONE

HERINOR

"Ayna." My hands are shaking so hard I can barely know where they'll land if I reach out to touch her. "Fuck it, Ayna, don't be dead."

I shouldn't be saying that. I shouldn't even be kneeling here, in the puddle of mud and blood where the Crow Queen dropped from the sky, limp like a dead rodent.

The bargain I made with Ephegos clearly forbids helping Ayna, and this… This *is* helping Ayna. Sort of.

I could merely be making sure she's dead. But I'm not.

I'm not here because I wish to see her dead.

"Are you all right?" Royad wipes blood off his mouth. How he's managed to keep his bearings when the drug hit full force, I wish I knew. *I* withered like those tiny spring blossoms that used to grow in Winghaven before the curse.

How I hate this place. How I wish I could fly over my old homeland once more.

The decision is not mine, though. Despite my bargain with Ephegos, my loyalty lies with Myron. Where he goes, I go. Until Ephegos drags me back with chains and magic.

"All right might be a bit strong of a word." I shrug, but Royad doesn't buy it.

I was the closest when Ayna fell, and Shaelak fuck me, I wanted to catch her, but the bargain bound me in my spot. I would have needed to gnaw my legs off and drag myself over by my arms to help her. Even then, I wouldn't have survived the aftermath of binding magic.

Royad eyes me with that expression of pity he so often uses when he notices I'm fighting my stupid oath.

"I'll take care of her. You go get Tata. She and Silas are the only ones left with magic, and Silas is taking care of Myron and Recienne."

I push up from my knees, glancing toward the wagon where Recienne is sitting on the edge between bodies of Flame guards and Myron lying on the wooden boards. Silas kneels next to Myron, hand hovering on his chest where the arrow is still standing proud like it's paying rent and has the right.

"Our king is in bad shape." It's the understatement of the century.

Royad shrugs. "He was in worse shape when he *died*. He's tough. He'll get through this."

Royad's blind faith in his cousin has always astonished me, but this is next-level disturbing. When I turn to tell him, he's already leaning over Ayna's bird body. "You're wasting time. Get Tata, and then help Silas with the arrow. We need to get that thing out of him somehow."

Preferably somewhere with a healer at hand, I want to say, but he's right. I'm wasting time.

With a split heart, I leave Royad to tend to our queen and rush over to Tata, who's eyeing me like I'm a creature from Hel's realm itself. She doesn't look that way at Silas, but I'm happy to ignore that as long as Silas keeps ignoring the way I look at Kaira.

"Royad needs your help." I could be polite, but bile on my tongue and wobbling knees don't bring forward the best in me.

"With what?" She glances past my shoulder to watch Royad kneel in the dirt, talking to a mud-caked small form on the ground.

"Your healing skills, preferably. But basically anything that will save our queen." I don't look back, praying to the God of War to give me strength in this battle with my bargain I'm facing on a daily basis. Galloris isn't known to be kind, but he's known to steel one's will in the face of uncertainty. Like a soldier right before battle.

That's me. Every minute of my life since I walked out of Myron's palace and right into Ephegos's traitorous wings.

It's a miracle Myron took me back. Even more of a miracle he isn't keeping me on a leash. I'm a danger, and not just to him but to everyone he loves. Especially his mate.

Stifling a sigh, I stalk up to the wagon and climb over the corpse of an eyeless, blood-leaking Flame Matrone before I shove her off the wooden planks to watch her land in the mud with a splash.

"I didn't think we'd make it," the Fairy King says to me, a frown on his freakishly handsome face. He's the type of pretty that reminds me of elaborate ballrooms, embroidered dresses, string quartets, and glass slippers. *Male-pretty.*

Just like his general. But Tori at least has the balls to join a battle from the beginning, not sweep in at the last possible moment like a hero and nearly fuck up everything.

"Neither did I." It's not a lie. I'd made my peace when Recienne showed up to save the day. "Especially when you got yourself un-magicked."

The word doesn't exist, but I find it funny to point out his flaws. It's always been more fun to taunt power than to submit to it.

Much to my surprise, Recienne chuckles. "If I weren't so darn sick right now, I'd hurl you over the edge of the Plithian Plains."

"The plains don't have an edge," I inform him, then re-consider. "Well… perhaps by the coast."

Recienne raises a night-dark brow. "There are always the Cliffs of Ansoli in the north."

"Is that a promise?" A broad grin spreads on my face. One I know causes most fairies to squirm.

He meets it with a smirk of his own, flinching as the wound in his shoulder bothers him. "The only thing I can promise you right now is that I won't vomit all over you." He pauses, holding up a finger. "No, not even that."

He doubles over, clutching his stomach, and pukes over the edge of the wagon. Right between Jeseida's body and that of a Flame guard. Well deserved.

Shaking my head, I step past him, clasping Silas's shoulder as I squat next to him. "Is he still breathing?"

Myron's chest is evenly rising and falling, so it's easy to make a joke even when my tone remains rough and emotionless as usual.

"If that damn arrow hadn't seated itself so deep in his tissues, I would have pulled it out already."

The sight of my king, pale and motionless except for the slow breaths, is disturbing as the nightmares where Ephegos keeps forcing me to slit his throat. I don't know how many nights I've lost, keeping myself from sleeping so I won't be thrown right back into a torture chamber where I must hurt the only king who ever wanted the best for his people. I should have trusted him, should have had faith in him.

I guess it's a debt I'll never pay off.

"I can hold him down while you pull," I offer, but I already know it's not the way to go. This is an arrow made of bone. The tip is sharp steel dipped in the honey-like substance that is the distilled drug. I saw the guard coat the arrow in it before nocking and shooting. The fact that Myron blocked the arrow saved Tori's life. He was already drained and exhausted when Myron found us, but Tori wouldn't have made it through this battle with an arrow in his chest. That's more the fabric Crows are made of. Resilient.

Our power might not be as spectacular as the Askarean fairies, our shields not as strong and our site-hopping

461

abilities nonexistent. But we are tough and strong. We're all worth twenty fairies each. Myron demonstrated it when he ripped the Flame estate apart that cursed day when Erina tried to un-mate them.

A deep sigh runs through my chest, ending in a groan of frustration.

Without waiting for Silas's assessment, I grab the arrow and carefully break off the ends so the smooth shaft is the only thing left. "Roll him to the side."

Silas gives me a glance that informs me he's questioning my sanity. I don't care. We've dealt with worse injuries before the curse and survived them. We've dealt with even worse during the wars with the fairies. And we'll deal with this.

Silas gently rolls him to his side, bracing Myron's back against his knees.

I leap over to Myron's other side and take hold of the arrow. "I pull, you heal."

I don't ask Silas if he has enough in him to seal a deep arrow wound—he wouldn't be sitting here if he didn't—and slowly, with utmost care, I pull on the arrow, keeping the angle steady so I don't rip on the tissues. One inch, another. It's deeper than I thought, but we're almost there. Thank Shaelak, Myron's not awake. I hate it when they scream.

That thought lingers in my mind longer than it should. There was a time when I enjoyed a good scream of pain. Nowadays, it's only that of pleasure in the bedroom. I haven't heard that one in forever, though, so how can I be sure it still does the trick?

One more inch, and—*plop!*—the arrow comes free. Alongside a gush of blood.

"Your turn." I take over, reaching for Myron's shoulders and rolling him to his back once more. Now that the arrow is out, I no longer care about what angle he lies in. Silas can send his healing power into him from any angle while pulling out the arrow demands for the best possible one where the puller has the least likelihood of shaking.

I count my breaths—slow, steady breaths—until the wrinkles on Silas's forehead disappear and the sweat collecting on his brow no longer taunts me to wipe it away.

Myron blinks, and a mountain crumbles from my chest. "Fuck you, my king. You could have waited with the magic-nullifying drug crap until Royad and I were ready to see you kneel."

It sounds not even half as funny as I imagined, but Myron's lips tilt upward in a weak grin. It's the best sight in the world. Except for Kaira's smile, of course, but that's a whole different thing.

"Good to have you back, Myron." Silas says it much better. Then, he doesn't need to keep everyone at arm's length because of a horrible lapse in judgment leading to an unbreakable oath to a traitor. *Fuck me.*

Myron's gaze wanders to Silas then to Recienne, who got his puking under control. Now he can compare notes with his mate. If Askarean fairies are anything like Crows, the females will experience the most unfortunate of stomach situations at every other turn during pregnancy.

Also, I can't believe he left her alone at the palace.

I frown at the Fairy King over my shoulder.

"Is he all right?"

Of course, Myron wants to know if the male who used to make our lives the equivalent of the dark corners of Hel's realm is all right.

But I can consider that only for a heartbeat because his gaze searches the sky, and I know who he's looking for. "Where is Ayna?"

Silas's gaze skips to mine and mine to the uneven grounds behind the wagon. "She's with Royad."

FIFTY-TWO

MYRON

I'm running. How I'm running with the remains of an arrow wound in my chest, I don't know, but I'm on my feet, palm pressing against the hole between my ribs as I leap off the wagon and stumble in the direction Herinor pointed.

Royad is kneeling in the dirt, staring at something together with Tata whose back is blocking my Ayna from view.

"You'll tear that wound right open again, and I don't think I have any magic left to heal you all over again," Silas warns. It's the least sarcastic I've heard him in ages, and it scares the shit out of me.

I don't slow, though. The thin thread that is our bond is pulling me directly toward her. In my shoulder, a dull throb reminds me of the times when we were connected through the tattoo, when Herinor had used it to set me on the right track to find her. I haven't thanked him for that questionable kindness. Maybe, one day, if he ever follows up on his promise to kneel to Ayna and me, I'll speak those words of gratitude. But for now, I wave a dismissive hand over my shoulder at Silas.

A few squishy steps and I'm there, mud splattering my leathers as my knees hit the ground.

"Where is she?" I'm expecting to find my queen sprawled on the ground, but when Royad pulls back his hand, exposing a small, black, feathered body, my heart stills in my chest.

Mud covers her, beak to claws. Mud … and blood. I swallow the momentary relief at the sound of her heartbeat.

"What happened?" I'm not certain I want the answer when Royad opens his mouth and a long, deep sigh preempts his response.

"We're not exactly sure. One moment, she was clawing out Jeseida's eyes, and the next, she was up in the air. An arrow hit her in the wing. It went straight through, and Tata mended the damage, but she's not waking up."

She fell. The onslaught of panic should feel familiar by now, but I'd rather face the Flames all over again than fret for Ayna's life. Any number of bones could have snapped in a fall mid-flight. I don't want to even think about what damage an uncushioned impact on the hard ground could have done to her inner organs, her brain—

It's a delicate organism, that of a Crow. In both forms, we have the same vital organs, but the difference in size and our overall physique changes the way we react to injuries in either form.

"Why didn't she shift?" That's what a Crow would normally do, try to carry the weight on the wings until the last possible moment, then shift and run the final steps or roll to ease the impact.

Royad shakes his head, and Tata shrugs.

"She might have already blacked out from the arrow wound," Tata suggests. "It was *bad*." She shudders. And this is a seasoned warrior used to battle injuries of all sorts. "It's a Guardians-damned miracle her bones aligned that easily when I healed her."

Damn the Flames and their magic-nullifying serum. With my powers intact, I could easily sense if there's something wrong on a deeper level.

"She used a lot of power up there, summoning the clouds," Royad puts into consideration. "Perhaps she's exhausted."

I beg the Gods he's right.

"And if that's not it, we'll have the healers back at the palace take a look at her. They have more experience with fairies of all different sorts."

"We're not *'fairies of all different sorts,'*" Silas objects from behind her. Focused on Ayna's motionless bird form, I missed his approach. When Tata glances at him over her shoulder, a deep frown furrowing her brow, he adds, "We are *fae*."

"Who happen to turn into feathered birds that stalk the night. Lovely."

Exhaustion is evident in every last one of her words, and Silas surely didn't need to correct her about our heritage at this very moment, but he has a point. "We are more similar than you would think, Tata," I say gently, my eyes never leaving Ayna. "Our magic might be different, but we're from the same world."

"Where exactly is the corner of the world you came from?" No judgement clouds Tata's question, so I respond, hands reaching for Ayna yet hesitating when Tata holds up a finger to stop me. "I need to double-check her wing."

It's a test to be patient, but I manage. For Ayna. "East of Eherea, far across the oceans where no Ehereans have ever dared sail, lies a continent named Neredyn." My chest aches.

"Think of the Askarean forests but wilder and lusher. Think of the blossoms of spring and summer but with more color and stronger scents. Think of islands of beauty where the Gods used to walk before they made us. You might like it there." Trust Silas to be stepping in. He knows much more about Neredyn anyway. "One day, I will fly there again." He pauses, face grave like he doesn't truly believe it. "One day."

Carefully, Tata's hand covers Ayna's wing, fingers wrapping around the length of it and flexing it. With a nod, she turns to me. "All right, Crow King. You can take her now."

My hands are shaking as I reach for the miserable bundle of feathers in the mud and pick her up, fingers sliding around her form with ease.

She's so small—so freaking tiny in her bird form. One squish, and she'd be crushed beyond repair.

The thought makes me hold her out in front of me like she's made of glass. Her wing hangs limply over my blood-caked thumb while her head rests against my index finger.

This is perhaps the most completely I've ever held her … and it fucking breaks my heart to see her so fragile. My strong, beautiful Ayna. The female who can stand on her own legs, no matter what the winds blow her direction. Defeated.

The soft touch of Royad's comforting hand on my shoulder reminds me of his presence. "We need to get out of here, Myron."

He's right. We might have gotten away with our lives, but it's only a matter of time until someone will come looking for the remains of the battle when the Flames don't show up with the weapon.

"Is all of it destroyed?" I ask between my teeth, unable to tear my gaze away from the crow in my hands.

"The weapon?" Royad gestures at the burned-down wagons. "The big delivery is completely shattered. There's not a single drop of liquid left." He pauses, rummaging in his jacket and pulling out a small vial very much like the one Jeseida used to pour the serum over me, face victorious. "We saved this. One of the guards by the wagon had it clutched in his hand when I ran him through. I plucked it from his grasp. Maybe we can figure out an antidote."

He sounds less hopeful than he looks, but Royad has always been the cautious type.

"Maybe," I echo. My mind is on Ayna, though, on my failure that led to her sacrifice. "Come on." I turn north. "Let's go home."

Home, it turns out, is a loaded word for a Crow to use when speaking about the Fairy King's palace.

It's been an hour since the last Flame took a breath, the ground is still slick with their blood, and Recienne perpetually frowns at his own hands as he tries to send out his dark wind to test if his powers are returning—he'll vomit his guts up soon enough again when the effects of the drug fade.

Tata's black braid swings along her back as she stalks back and forth in front of her king, features unreadable as she muses about the inconvenience of not being able to site-hop after all the healing she's done and how, perhaps, letting a Crow die in order to keep enough of her strength to site-hop back to Aceleau and get help would have been the smarter choice.

"It better not be our queen," Silas warns with more bite than I'm used to, even from his generally sarcastic mouth. He means it. No matter how *soft* Silas has gotten over the past weeks, he's ready to return to being the ancient, slaughtering menace who used to serve in my father's guard. It's a miracle he sees me as a fit ruler with all the horrors he's used to from my father.

"Of course, not your queen. Do you think I want to incite a new war? No thanks." Tata turns on her heel and marches to the rocks from behind where the attack was launched. There, she plants her ass on the hard stone, gazing at the sky. "Wouldn't be a very fair war—five against an army of thousands." Before any of us can respond, she continues, "Can't you just shift and fly to get help?" Her gaze slides to Silas, whose features have changed into a grimace.

"I have exerted my strength healing *your* king, thank you very much." He spreads his arms in an *obviously* gesture, which Tata promptly responds to with a turn of her head to the Fairy King.

"Do something, Recienne." It's the first time I actually hear her call him by his name, but the familiarity was there the first time I saw them together. It no longer surprises me to see the Fairy King so familiar with his court. He's proven in every way that counts he isn't the bloodthirsty monster I believed him to be.

Absently, my finger glides over Ayna's back. "So, there is no way for us to get back to Aceleau other than *wait*?" It's ridiculous that a bunch of magical creatures should be stuck in the human lands, yet here we are. "Won't Tori and Clio come looking for us?" No one responds, but I already know the answer to that one: They were in such bad shape; they probably never made it all the way back to the palace. "Shall we send a search party?"

"I wish someone would send a search party for us," Tata groans, bracing her hands beside her hips and hanging her head. "We don't even have water rations on us."

"Beginner's mistake," Recienne chides and flicks his fingers, probably trying to summon a glass of water, a jar of water, or maybe even a whole pond of water, and curses when he remembers his powers are gone.

Thankfully, I've lived every minute of my life improvising during the curse, so I know how to pivot. "There's a forest a bit back east," I say with as much an upbeat tone as I can manage with my unconscious mate in my palms. "I'm sure we can find rainwater collected in leaves or between roots." Not in the mud beneath our feet—not without magic to filter it. "We'll walk until dawn; then we'll rest. Tomorrow either Silas can shift or Tata can site-hop. Whoever is first will get us help."

Nobody objects when I start walking with Ayna between my palms, Royad falling into step beside me and Silas and Herinor at my back. Tata and Recienne bring up the rear. The moon is our witness as we leave the battlefield behind, muscles sore, multiple cuts on various parts of our bodies, and stranded in the human lands.

"You'll need to do something about that wound of yours," my cousin says after a few minutes of me suppressing the cache at the center of my chest where the hole in my flesh is still bothering me. "No one will benefit from you falling over with your last breath in the middle of our escape."

Naturally, he's right. I've become all too used to him being right over too many centuries. But he isn't right about this.

"You'd be king," I say flatly, and Royad almost stumbles over his own feet.

"Not while your mate is alive to rule." He doesn't pause long enough for me to inform him my mate might not survive the night. "She'll bring you back from the dead just to kill you all over again for leaving her behind among these wrecked remains of a people."

My teeth cut into my lip as I bite back a response I know I'll regret. "Let's find cover first. Everything within sight has been burned to cinders. We need a place to actually hide until we recover enough to shift or site-hop. *Then* we can dwell on who might or might not make it through this hike. Because, once someone finds the melee we left behind, we won't get far." We'll be hunted down and brought back to Erina's dungeon. I don't need to add that, though. Royad can put two and two together.

"Why do you think they didn't use the serum on all of us right away?" It's a good question. One I'm grateful we need to ask, or we wouldn't have stood a chance from the beginning.

"And that magic-repellant armor…" Silas adds. "That was nasty. If Ayna hadn't figured it out, we might have continued wasting our power instead of simply cutting those fuckers down like twigs."

"It seems to be a new feature," Royad muses. Even when he wasn't there to witness the battle, he was right there with the source.

"Did Jeseida say anything?" I prompt, well aware they were probably fighting their own battle in that wagon. One of will if what I know of the Flame Matrone is anything to go by.

Behind me, Herinor grumbles something unintelligible while Royad cringes, and anger rises in my veins, pushing so hard I can almost sense a flicker of my power, but the serum is still blanketing all attempts of it to break through. If it weren't for that damn hole in my chest, I'd probably recover faster.

"You don't need to share if you—"

"Guardians be damned, they do," Recienne interrupts

473

me, less swagger in his tone than I'm used to. "If there is any information to be gained, I'd rather know now, *before* we face the Flames hunting us down, because they *will*. So, what happened inside the wagon?"

"He's right." To my surprise, it's Herinor offering up the information willingly, not my selfless cousin.

Tata must have given the Fairy King a recap of the fight, or he wouldn't even know Herinor and Royad were trapped there.

"They were practically waiting for us when we cut through the canvas of the wagon."

Beside me, Royad swallows.

"Jeseida and her guards had the serum at the ready and splashed us in the face." Herinor grimaces as if he can still taste the damn liquid. "They plucked our swords from our hands and knocked us out so fast we couldn't even react."

"That sucker of a drug," Silas comments, earning a nod from Royad.

Usually, our reflexes are fast enough to react to an attack, but the magic-sedating serum is its own brand of horror. It affects our organism so quickly we can barely keep up.

"They knew we were coming," Herinor continues, tone stony. "They were counting on all of us attacking from the air." He pauses. "At least the Crows. Jeseida expressed verbally and with fists just how disappointed she was so few of us had plunged into the wagon. She even had the other wagons set up in a way that we'd take a bath in the drug upon landing."

My entire body tightens at the thought of what would have happened had we not chosen to ambush them from all sides at once. Plus … she hurt them—

"If she wasn't already dead, I'd skin her alive. Slowly." It's all I have to say.

Silas growls his agreement, and surprisingly, even Recienne voices he'd gladly help.

"So, if they knew we were coming for them... Was it even a real transport?" A valid question Tata is asking.

"It was real. Very much so." The conviction in Herinor's tone is all the confirmation I need, but he continues. "Erina has been working with the Flames closely to further develop the serum so it's more efficient, its magic-dampening strikes even faster, and the side effects are minimized."

Jeseida mentioned that I'd be wide awake when Erina tortures me again and that I wouldn't have days off from the effect of the drug.

"They had to get it to the army, though, and this was the fastest route for them, so they used the transport as a test run for their newest development: the magic-repellant armor. An invention that allows to smother all magic coming from the outside but allows magic to pass from its bearer." Royad shudders but continues. "Jeseida had us watch the battle through a small gap in the canvas. She had us witness every time your powers failed to kill. To watch you deplete yourselves without even realizing what was going on." He shakes his head, clearing it. "The Flames will stop at nothing to get what they want. Not even watching their own go up in streaks of fire."

When I shoot him a questioning glance, he clarifies, "They had tested the armor before, but they didn't know how long it would last against Crow magic and if it would impact the ability to withstand their own fire."

Silas curses under his breath. "They would have let them burn." Not a question.

"Jeseida would have let the world burn to take revenge on us," Royad replies, and my stomach tightens at the guilt washing over me for all the things my father did to those people.

"Perhaps we would have deserved death at their hands." I hate the thought because, rationally, I know it wasn't me who took their palace and their home in the Seeing Forest. It was my father.

"Ephegos and his flock of traitors deserve it," Royad says before I can spiral into a hole I won't return from.

In my hands, Ayna's little body remains still, even when I need her to quench the rage welling up inside me. I need to look into her gray eyes and reassure myself that this storm the Flames conjured hasn't taken her.

The Gods must be mocking me because the air changes, and a cold wind whips the plains as we march toward the line of trees on the horizon. Water collects in the corner of my eye, and the hole in my chest aches as my legs grow weak, forcing me to lean on the arm Royad instantly throws around my waist to keep me upright.

"If I don't make it," I murmur to my cousin, fighting the pain and the weakness and losing, "see to it that Ayna gets a proper crown. One with feathers and diamonds shaped like teardrops. Tell her those are the tears I cried for her when I held her in my palms."

FIFTY-THREE

HERINOR

I fucking hate this continent. Down to the mosquitos in its forest. Even gravity seems to work differently from Neredyn. Perhaps it's having been locked in a cursed body for too long and still struggling after weeks to readjust to my usual self. Perhaps it's that the annoying and pretty Flameling isn't here to distract me from the fact that I hate it here so much.

Perhaps the past hours have something to do with it. Sharing Royad's fate in Jeseida's wagon was more than I ever hoped to get out of that ambush. I got magic-deprived, but we've endured worse than a few pushes to the stomach that made me vomit up my dinner. What bothers me is that Jeseida said Ephegos is looking forward to having me back in his service.

Her response, when I asked where he was, was another punch—in the mouth this time. A weak enough one not to even make my teeth clang while they didn't spare Royad any pain. By the time Myron found us, his cousin was already battered and bloody, almost like they handled me different-ly—to keep up appearances nobody cares for.

I'm no longer Ephegos's whore—even if he could fuck me over with one single command.

The surprise on Jeseida's face when she found me work-ing with Myron was priceless. Almost as good as Ephegos's when I managed to carry Myron out of the dungeon without bleeding out myself. It took a lot of effort to convince myself I was getting him away from Ephegos's reach to keep him alive for extended suffering. Had I seen it as anything else in that moment, I might not have made it more than three steps away from Ephegos that cursed day in Erina's dungeon.

We've found cover in a patch of bushes at the seam of the forest, nothing spectacular, where we could linger more than a few hours. It should be enough for Silas and Tata to either have restored enough power to transform and site-hop or to heal Myron's wound. He's still bleeding from that puncture hole even when he won't admit he's barely standing.

"Sit and rest," Recienne orders, unceremoniously slouch-ing against the nearest tree. "I'll keep watch."

I don't want to know what that *watch* will look like with his magic gone and his words still not fully straight. Under different circumstances, this would be comical, but my hide is on the line as much as his, so I drag myself to his side and plant my feet next to his ass. "I'll keep you company so you don't vomit at a potential attacker instead of throwing a blade at them." With more bravado than I feel, I draw my sword and swing it next to his head. Tata almost throws a tantrum at the sight of steel so close to her king's neck. Thank the gods for Silas and his ever-calming presence. As if.

But he's pulled himself together greatly around the muscular female. Not exactly my type. I like my females with more spunk. But to each their own.

Royad makes sure the Crow King lies down on a dry spot, ready to take Ayna from his hands and watch over her while Myron sleeps, but a growl rips from the male's throat that sends a shiver down even a brave warrior's spine like mine. Whatever Erina tried with that un-mating attempt, it wildly backfired. Myron is more protective than ever, and Ayna... She was a force to be reckoned with before. Now she's angry. All I've ever seen since the moment I talked to her after the attack was a female ready to lash out. Tonight, she brought down the wrath of the gods upon our enemies. I'll never look at her the same way again. When before I was worried she might not survive without help—mine or otherwise—I'm cured from the belief that Wolayna Milevishja, Queen of Crows and Queen of Tavras, needs the aid of anyone. Except to carry her off the battlefield, and Myron is doing a damn good job at playing the hero.

Ignoring Tata, Royad, and everyone else who might have an opinion on anything, I ram my blade into the soil at my feet and announce to Recienne that I'm not planning to slit his throat anytime soon.

He surprises me with a laugh. "Me neither, Herinor. I enjoy watching you squirm under the little Flame's stare way too much."

Ignoring his comment, I lean against the tree trunk and scan the surroundings.

It's a long few hours until sunrise. Silas and Tata fall asleep almost as fast as Myron, who's cradling Ayna to his chest, her bird body covered by his open leather jacket. Royad is keeping watch as was to be expected. These are the human lands, and it's more likely a random hunter will stumble upon us than a fairy, so magic-free creatures do the job just fine.

Recienne falls asleep halfway through our watch, not as accustomed to the side effects of the drug as the rest of us. When he cracks an eye at first light, his hair is disheveled, he's drooling on his sleeve, and his crown has slipped off his head. Not so kingly now.

I nudge him in the ribs with the toes of my boot, and he grumbles his mate's name.

"Sorry, I'm not a pregnant female around the age of one hundred and twenty, even though I look just as good in a dress."

Silas chuckles from where he's scrambling to his feet. At least, he's awake and in good spirits. I can't say the same thing for Myron. He hasn't woken from his slumber, and the crimson spot soaking the ground next to his chest makes me wish I had my powers back. I'd find a reason to justify my actions in front of the bargain with Ephegos.

"Quiet night," Royad prompts when he notices me staring.

"Thank Galloris." Dragging my sword from the soil, I sheathe it and leave the Fairy King to his own morning retching.

I'm halfway across the makeshift camp when a pair of boots slams into the ground right in front of me, and a massive form takes up my vision. My pulse spikes, my muscles coil as instinct takes over.

So fast I can't even think, my blade is back in my hand, pointing at the fairy general's throat. He's a bit wide-eyed and marginally winded, but he's here. His gaze sweeps the space, chest heaving as he notices Recienne sitting against the tree, waving and grimacing.

"Put that fucking toothpick away, Herinor. You'll hurt yourself." Astorian shoves my sword aside with two fingers of his gloved hand. He looks like he's seen better days, but he's here. "Where is he?"

He doesn't stop for an explanation or scold me for not being able to tell friend from foe as he launches across the space, scooping Recienne from the ground and disappearing so fast I can't even blink.

We all stare into the empty spot where he was standing a moment ago, even Tata, who's probably used to Tori's ways more than any of us.

"What the fuck was that?" Silas phrases it pretty well.

Of course, the fairy general gets his king to safety first. Everything else can wait. I would do the exact same thing.

About a heartbeat later, Clio pops up between the trees, Tori right behind her. Their battle wounds are gone, and the blood and soot has been cleared from their armor, but their wary eyes tell me they've been as anxious for this night to be over as we've been.

Clio's gaze skips from Tata to Silas to me to Royad to Myron, relief relating her features with every face she recognizes as alive. When she doesn't find Ayna, it flicks back to Royad. "Where is she?"

Her voice is shaking like she doesn't want to hear the answer.

Royad gestures at Myron's slow-rising chest. "She's still unconscious."

Almost stumbling over her own feet, Clio rushes to Myron's side, leaning over the Crow King. "And still in her bird form."

"She hasn't been able to shift back for some reason," Royad explains, "but I can tell you details when we're back at the palace. We need to get out of here. Someone will miss the Flames at some point, and if they find us without our powers, we're fucked."

Clio nods her agreement while Tori kneels down beside Myron to roll him into his arms. "I'll take the king first. We'll send others to pick you all up."

Clio takes Tata's hand and site-hops her away, leaving Royad, Silas, and me to ourselves.

"I guess that tells us where we stand," Silas muses with a frown.

Before Royad or I can respond, two fairy soldiers pop up, inclining their heads to us and magicking us away.

FIFTY-FOUR

AYNA

I'm in a boat. The little thing is swaying gently on the waves *of the sea, and a warm wind blows over me like a soft caress. It's the safest I've felt in years. From a distance, Ludelle's laugh travels across the deck. He's joking with his men, planning the next loot. Someone said there'd be royal ships passing through soon, right in the south of Tavras where the coast turns inward and the Quiet Sea becomes the Gulf of Tears. It's been forever since we last visited the mainland. Usually, we stop at the uncharted islands far off the coast where Ludelle likes to leave his treasures to pick up later when we need them. Or to pick up never because we always acquire new treasures. Someone someday will be very rich when they stumble upon his stash.*

Down at the bottom of all gold and jewel-filled chests lies a small, steel box with an item Ludelle promised me. I don't know what it is. A necklace perhaps. A bracelet. But the way he looks at me from the head of the boat tells me it might be smaller, round, and solid. It might fit on my left middle finger. If pirates married, I'd marry him.

His teeth gleam in the bright sun like a string of pearls, eyes sparkling with mischief as he catches me staring, and my stomach flips with joy, warmth trickling through my veins like honey.

With a slow hand, he smooths back his hair. It's longer than I remember, and his shirt is red.

Ludelle prefers white or black.

It takes me a moment to spot the thin line across his throat dripping crimson.

In a flash, everything comes back to me: the Wild Ray, the soldiers taking us to Fort Perenis, my mangled hand. Being held down on the ground with a knee pressed into my spine as they slit the crew's throats. The light leaving Ludelle's eyes.

A scream hatches from my lips as I tear my eyes open...

I'm not on a boat. The brine I thought I smelled is not from the ocean. It's the scent of forests and salt and freedom that I recognize in an instant. As I recognize the hands scooping me up, fingertips brushing along my side so carefully I'm not sure he's even touching me. I'm so tiny in his hands, all except my wings fit between his palms. My wings...

I want to spread them, but they barely twitch.

"Hello, my little Crow." Myron leans down, his words a gentle wind that tastes of mint and memories. I can make out the details of his flawless mouth and the dark stubble on his chin. His eyes, clear blue and alert, track every movement despite the obvious signs of exhaustion surrounding them in smudges of dark purple.

Hello, I want to say, but a harsh caw leaves my mouth, and I register I'm not in my human form.

The tip of Myron's finger brushes the place where my neck meets my wing. "You had quite the injury there." Shuddering into his touch, I lift my wing an inch to see if it's working. It twitches but doesn't fully spread. "Herinor says he saw you plunge from the sky."

Dark memories swirl before me. The battle. Flame after Flame after Flame coming for us. Myron fighting at my side. Blood and pain.

My heart pounds in my chest, hammering against my ribs, ready to escape. All the Crows were still alive and fighting when I last saw them. And the Fairy King—

Jeseida—blood on my feathers and the satisfying scream as I ripped her throat out with my claws of death.

On instinct, I try to stand, but Myron's hand isn't stable ground to push myself upright against, and my wings don't properly do their job when I use them to balance myself, which lands me right back on my belly, head resting between Myron's thumb and index finger, and a miserable caw on my beak.

"You'll be all right," Myron murmurs. "The healers said it will take time for you to fully regain control over your body. You fell out of the skies." With ocean eyes, he scans me, beak to tail feather. "Half of your bones were shattered, and your mind shut down for two solid weeks."

Two weeks. A sound of outrage escapes me, but it has nothing to do with the exasperation of having missed *two weeks*. It's not knowing everything that happened since. It's the uncertainty of who survived the battle after I blacked out and who died.

Are they all alive and well? I want to ask, but my damned bird body isn't made for human conversation, and every last word turns into a creaky caw.

"I know," Myron muses, reading meaning into the sound. "It's a long time. Your bones are back to normal, though—as far as fairy healers can tell with crow bones," he amends, leaning back in the tall armchair and placing me right over his heart, one hand protectively covering my form. "We'll know for certain everything is all right once you shift." His brows raise as if considering I should try right now; then he shakes his head. "They said it would be too risky to shift before making sure you're in full control of your senses. Can you nod if you understand me?"

I can hear you. I understand you. I can count the buttons on your fucking tunic if you'd like me to.

I nearly screech at him. Then I remember none of it is his fault, and deep sorrow spreads in my chest.

In my bird form, I won't be able to speak a word. The only possibility is to shift so I can ask him about the scratch running along the side of his chin and the shadows under his eyes. I risked everything to make sure he's all right—that all of them are. And I need to hold him in my arms and tell him that nothing has changed. I'll always be his mate, and I'll always love him.

A dip of my head is all I manage, but it's enough to paint a smile on Myron's features. Such beautiful, sad features.

With a huff, I nudge his hand, indicating for him to move his fingers so I can scoot out of his grip and try to stand on my own again.

That, he understands. Whether it's a universal gesture of Crows in their bird forms to let others know they want to be set down or intuition, I wish I knew, but eventually, Myron sets me on the armrest of his chair, watching my claws dig into the forest green velvet. One hand lingers on the side, ready to catch me should I lose balance and fall off the chair.

"There you go." He studies my clumsy movements as I struggle to keep upright. "Maybe you should give it a day or two."

I don't have a day or two. There's a war going on, and I need to fight at my peoples' side—Crows or Tavras, it no longer matters. If Erina keeps pushing, the soldiers won't be the only ones to die in this war. We might have been able to plan this past attack to avoid civilian casualties, but we won't be able to choose each and every battlefield. Eventually, Erina's greed for power will cost civilian lives, and that's something I'm not ready for.

With a tug on my power, I search for the sensation that always brings me back into my human form, for the warmth and the feeling of soil beneath my bare feet and rain on my skin.

Deep inside of me, the well of magic remains silent.

"You saved us out there, you know? If you hadn't summoned the rain, we would have lost that battle. But at what cost?" The near reverence in his tone strikes me like a hit to the gut.

Order and Chaos have always been fighting for balance. If you use my power at the same time as his, I don't know what it will take for that balance to be restored.

Vala's words drift back into my mind like a dark cloud.

Whatever it is, I'll pay the price, I told her. Now I'm dreading what that might be.

The first onslaught of panic evaporates when I search for the mating bond and find a thin thread connecting me to Myron. As if he's feeling me reach for it, Myron's lips curl into a wry smile.

"Clio has been pestering me about when she can ask you what, by Shaelak, you were thinking, dropping from the skies like that," Myron says with the tired amusement of someone who's been worrying day and night for two full weeks—or for a full millennium. "She'll be glad to hear you're awake."

He doesn't realize what a gift that simple line is, knowing Clio is well enough to snark like that.

Again, I push my magic—nothing happens.

Perhaps the healers are right and I should wait a few more days before I attempt to shift, but I'm restless. I want to look Myron in the eye and tell him I'm sorry. That it hurt to leave him behind on the battlefield and watch him get hurt from above like the coward I am. That I'm sorry for not waking up sooner.

Sorry, for not having told him sooner how much I love him.

Not a flicker of my power comes to life.

"Kaira checked in earlier with a bowl of soup," Myron rambles on. He never rambles, but my silence seems to warrant his monologue. "At first, I thought it was for me, but she plopped into a chair and spent the lunch hour staring me down with that guilt-inducing look of hers. You probably know what I mean." His chuckle is not as genuine as he tries to make it sound. "If you don't, you better not get on her bad side." He sighs. "She blames me for what happened to you."

I can't shift. *I can't shift.* My wings spread a few inches, and I flutter from the armrest to the dark hardwood floor. Myron's hands twitch to catch me, but the moment he sees I'm not falling, he draws them back.

From down here, his black leather boots are the first thing I see. Half of his torso is hidden by the chair, but his face is prominent as if there was no distance between us. With still blue eyes, he watches me, a crease forming between his brows while he quietly reaches for a small bowl on the low table between the arrangement of three armchairs and sets it down in front of me. "In case you're thirsty." Hesitating, he slides out of his chair and kneels beside me. He's so big. I can't remember ever feeling that dwarfed by a creature, even when in my bird form, and the distance between us becomes a chasm aching in my chest.

The words I want to tell him don't matter when I can't find my magic as I reach for it once more and a soft female laugh echoes in my mind.

Panic rises in my chest; I know that voice.

Ignoring the deep brown ceramic in front of me, I hop aside, fluttering wildly as I try to stretch my wings. Myron's gaze follows me cautiously around the room as I duck under the table, climb the side of a chair, and launch myself into a glide back toward the floor. Every beat of my wings aches, but the sensation of unease inside my body drives me to keep moving.

"It's all right, Ayna." Myron's voice is calm, but I see it for the facade it is. His heart is racing almost as fast as mine, the pulse in his neck thumping wildly with every time I hit my wing on the furniture and slither across the floor.

It's not all right.

I don't give up that easily. My Crow powers might not respond to me, but if I can't shift, perhaps I can draw water from the bowl Myron prepared for me.

I nearly stumble into it as I flutter past Myron's shoulder, ignoring the hand he holds out for me to land on.

Come to me, I command the water.

It doesn't move. Doesn't even taunt me with a lap against the slanted side of the bowl.

Come to me, please. The pain is spiking as the laugh sounds again, clearer this time.

Vala. I don't mean to think her name, but it's unmistakably the Goddess of Water whose voice fills my head.

I'm here, my child. Like a feather, her invisible touch brushes my neck, eliciting a shudder.

"What's wrong, Ayna?" I'm faintly aware of Myron's extended hand as he tries to pick me up, but I hop out of reach before his fingertips touch my feathers.

My caw is throaty and off-kilter. I need to shift. Need to tell him what I learned about our gods being the same. About

Vala and Shaelak being the Guardians of Eherea. Need to tell him Vala said there would be a price if I used her powers while using those of her brother at the same time—and that I was willing to pay that price.

My whole body is trembling as I cling to the idea of my human form, pushing hard and harder to make it happen.

You will exert yourself if you keep doing that, Vala says with that benevolent tone I want to shove up her ass.

I ignore her, forcing a part of me—any part—to turn human. A slight shift in my vision is all I get as a result, and Myron stares at me as I keep staring at him.

"Your eyes," he whispers as if he can't believe it.

What? What's wrong with my eyes? I bend over the water bowl, but the surface ripples as if Vala herself doesn't want me to see.

"They're gray. The exact shade of your human eyes." He scrutinizes me with such intensity I might break. "Are you shifting?"

The hope in his voice almost destroys me. Especially when Vala whispers into my ear, *Try as you may, Ayna. You cannot shift back. I warned you there would be consequences.*

MORE BOOKS IN
THE ALCUNAIRE

THE WINGS OF INK SERIES
Fall of the Wild Ray: A Wings of Ink Prequel
Wings of Ink
Heart of Night
Claws of Death

THE QUARTER MAGE SERIES
The Quarter Mage
The Hour Mage
The Never Mage
The Ever Mage

THE SHATTERED KINGDOM SERIES
Shattered Kingdom
Wicked Crown
Shadow Rule
Lost Towers
Secret Court
Dark Refuge
Reborn Throne
Fatespun

CAN'T GET ENOUGH OF ANGELINA'S WORLDS?

SCAN THIS CODE TO FIND MORE BOOKS BY ANGELINA J. STEFFORT:

ABOUT THE AUTHOR

"Chocolate fanatic, milk-foam enthusiast and huge friend of the southern sting-ray. Writing is an unexpected career-path for me."

Angelina J. Steffort is a bestselling, award-winning Austrian novelist, best known for her Wings of Ink series and her Shattered Kingdom series. With over twenty YA and adult fantasy and paranormal romance books under her belt, Angelina is far from done with inventing and exploring new worlds. That might have something to do with her passion for following the narrative of new characters and getting surprised by the twists they spin on her stories. Angelina has multiple educational backgrounds including engineering, business, music, and acting.

Currently, Angelina lives in Vienna, Austria, with her husband and her son.

Find Angelina on social media as @ajsteffort.

Scan this code to subscribe to Angelina's newsletter:

PRONUNCIATION GUIDE
Character Names

Adrian Katrijanov: A-dree-an KAH-tree-yah-nov

Andraya: An-DRAY-uh

Arebar: Ah-ree-bahr

Astorian Remanier Alves DeLoor: Us-TOH-ree-an Reh-mah-nyay AHl-ves Deh-Loor

Cliophera Clarette Tarie Amaryll Saphalea de Pauvre (Clio): Clee-oh-phee-rah Clah-rett Tah-rie Ah-mah-ryll Sah-PHAH-lee-ah deh POH-vreh (Clee-oh)

Ephegos: Eh-phee-gus

Erina Latroy Jelnedyn: EH-ree-nah LA-troy Yel-neh-dyn

Harian Aleji: Ha-ree-an Ah-jey-djee

Herinor: HEH-ree-nor

Jeseida: Dje-say-dah

Julj: Yoolsh

Kaira: Kay-ruh

Myron: My-ron

Royad: Roy-ad

Recienne Oilvier Gustine Univer Emestradassus de Pauvre: Reh-Syen Ol-liv-yeh Gü-Stin Oo-Nee-Vehr Eh-Mehs-trah-Dahs-sus deh POH-vreh

Pouly: Poh-lee

Odja: Oh-dya

Sariell: Sah-ree-ell

Sejen: See-jen

Wolayna (Ayna) Milevishja: Woh-LI-nah (I-nah) Mee-leh-veesh-jah

WORLD

Aceleau: Ah-Seh-Loh

Ansoli: Un-soh-lee

Askarea: Us-KAH-reh-ah

Brolli: Brol-ly

Cezux: Dje-Zush

Cliffs of Ansoli: Cliffs of Un-soh-lee

Dunai: Doo-NAY

Eherea: Ee-HEE-ree-ah

Eroth: Eh-roth

Fort Perenis: Fort Peh-reh-niss

Horn of Eroth: Horn of Eh-roth

Jezuin: Jeh-Zoo-in ("J" as in "jelly")

Ledrynx: Led-rynx

Leeneae: Lee-nee-ae

Meer: Meer

Plithian Plains: Pli-thee-un Plains

Ret Relah: Reht Reh-luh

Shaelak: SHAE-lak

Tavras: TUH-vrahs

Vala: Vah-la

Made in United States
Cleveland, OH
09 March 2025

14992904R00298